Yearning For Her

A STANDALONE NOVEL

TIFFANY ROBERTS

Blurb

A wicked incubus. A curvy, delectable human female. One night of passion that changes everything.

Willow Crowley's world comes crashing down when she discovers her boyfriend has been seeing another woman. The dream she'd held of a life with him is shattered in an instant, leaving her alone with nothing except heartache.

She vows to never open herself to that hurt again...

Until a seductive, otherworldly stranger with white hair, piercings, and icy blue eyes promises her a single night of pleasure. No strings attached.

But that night isn't enough for him. He wants more, more than she's ready to give. How can she trust him not to break her heart when he isn't even human?

Kian has lived promiscuously for four hundred years, feeding on the desire of the humans he and the fae considered prey. But when he locks eyes with a purple-haired female, something inside him shifts irrevocably.

No one else can sate his hunger.

He wants her.
Needs her.
Yearns for her.

Yet she refuses to submit to the carnal delights he promises. She wants more. She wants...love.
Can he mend her broken heart? Can he love a mortal woman?

Created with Vellum

To you, because you're beautiful.

One

Eli was going to propose.

Willow thrummed with excitement, which built with every step as she walked along Central Boulevard with Eli. Since he'd texted her this morning to let her know he'd made dinner reservations for them, she'd hardly been able to contain her giddiness, and no amount of begging had convinced him to reveal anything about where he was taking her. All he'd said was that it was a surprise, and that she should dress up fancy tonight.

He never took her anywhere fancy.

It's finally going to happen. He's going to propose tonight.

They were going to get married, and Willow would claim the happily ever after she had always dreamed of.

She grinned and looked up at her boyfriend of three years. His short brown hair was slicked back, his square jaw was cleanly shaven, and he was wearing a dark, perfectly tailored suit. Eli usually wore business casual attire for work, but Willow couldn't recall the last time she'd seen him quite like this.

Hell, she couldn't recall him having ever worn a suit for her before tonight.

He looked handsome.

And he's going to be my husband.

She squeezed his hand.

Eli shifted his brown eyes toward her and chuckled. "We're almost there, Willow. Calm down."

"How can you expect me to calm down when I've been waiting for this *all* day? You know how I am with surprises. It's torture!"

He smirked. "Well, I really hope you'll love this surprise." Eli faced forward again, and said in a softer tone, "I already do."

Giving her hand a tug, he led her around a group of people gathered in the middle of the sidewalk. The boulevard was always busy, but with this being a Friday night, it was packed. The entire area had been transformed by developers over the last few years, and nowhere else in the city of Memoree existed such a concentration of high-end stores, clubs, restaurants, and venues.

It wasn't hard to see why this area was popular beyond the businesses here. The golden glow of the streetlamps, the lights from the storefronts, and the conversations, music, and sound from all directions came together to form a welcoming, alive ambiance. Concrete pavers along the sidewalks, old-fashioned light posts, and the many trees and planters lining either side of the street elicited a sense of some bygone era. Just behind Central Boulevard, numerous footpaths and bridges allowed pedestrians to stroll along the river that ran through the heart of the city.

People had likely been lured out by the weather too. The air was pleasantly warm, which was never a guarantee here in western Washington, even on spring nights like this.

The petticoat beneath Willow's dress brushed her bare knees. Each touch only heightened her anticipation. She never dressed up like this, and it had been a long time since she'd gone anywhere nice, especially not on such a busy night. She'd normally be in her pajamas, cuddled under a blanket on the sofa, watching a horror movie or reading a romance book with her three cats curled up beside her.

Despite her eagerness to get to dinner, she couldn't help but let her eyes wander. Most of the boutiques nearby were places where she could've easily spent half her month's earnings on a handful of items. As nice as they were to look at, she just couldn't bring herself to spend money like that. Whether she was shopping for something for herself or for her business, she'd always had luck at the thrift stores she frequented, where she could find items with far more personality and uniqueness for much cheaper.

Those neat rows of shops were soon broken by a large brick building. The thumping bass of the music from inside vibrated the concrete under Willow's feet. Velvet ropes sectioned off the sidewalk in front of the establishment, containing a line of people that stretched around the corner.

The club's brickwork and blacked out windows created an industrial aesthetic on the ground floor, but the second story windows were filled with lights that pulsed and changed color to the beat of the music. The big sign over the entrance read *Reverb* in flowing red neon script.

When was the last time Willow had gone dancing? She and her long-time friend, Jamie, used to go occasionally when they'd worked together, but that had been...four years ago? Five? She wasn't sure why they'd stopped.

Probably because life got so busy for both of us.

Willow looked up at Eli. "We should go dancing sometime."

"Hmm?" He turned his head toward the club, and his lip curled. "It's loud and crowded. Why would you want to deal with that?"

She smiled and nudged him with her arm. "Because dancing is fun."

3

"If you like people sweating on you and spilling their drinks on your clothes, maybe." Eli shook his head. "Not my thing, Will."

Something inside her deflated, and she dropped her gaze to the sidewalk. He'd brushed aside something she wanted to do, and that hurt, but it was more than that.

Will. The way he always shortened her name grated on her, and she tried so, so hard not to let it get to her, especially not tonight. She'd asked him not to call her that so many times, but...

He just forgets, Willow. Let it go. He means it as...an endearment.

But that thought didn't sit well with her. It felt like she was making excuses for Eli when she hadn't asked much of him. It was such a small request.

Before she could explore those thoughts further, something called her eyes back up. They fell upon a man standing at the entrance of the alleyway on the far side of the nightclub, a man who somehow seemed entirely out of place and exactly like he belonged there.

A man who was looking right at her.

He stood at least half a foot taller than Eli, and his black coat, which hung to his shins, only accentuated his height. The red button-down shirt beneath the coat was only liberally buttoned, revealing his sculpted chest. A necklace with a silver dagger rested at his collarbone, directing the eye lower...but Willow's gaze rose.

Locks of long, white hair lay over his shoulder, swept aside to reveal the shaved side of his head and an ear with several silver piercings. He was sharp featured, with an angular jawline, a straight nose, and dark, arched eyebrows. His lips were full, sculpted, sensual, the bottom one adorned with two silver hoops near the corners of his mouth—a snake bite piercing. Black eyeliner enhanced the intensity of his ice blue eyes.

Those compelling eyes locked with Willow's and rounded.

Her skin prickled with awareness, her heart skipped a beat, and heat sparked low in her belly, blazing outward to flood her.

Willow's stride faltered, and were it not for Eli holding her hand, she might've fallen. Thankfully, nearly tripping over her own feet broke the spell the stranger had cast upon her, and she wrenched her gaze away from him.

"You all right?" Eli asked, placing his free hand on her shoulder to steady her.

The heat that had filled her coalesced in her cheeks, and she felt like her face turned so red that even her concealer wouldn't be able to hide it. She'd been a photographer for seven years. She looked at people all day, found ways to capture both their outer and inner beauty in still images, but never had she absorbed so much of a person in a single glance as she had with that tall, pale man.

"Yeah, I'm fine," Willow said as she looked up at Eli. "My, uh, heel came down wrong."

Eli's gaze ran down her body to her high heels. "I'd tell you to wear something more comfortable, but they do look pretty sexy."

Willow chuckled. "I'll leave them on for you tonight if you'd like."

"Mmm, I'd very much like that. But don't get me started now." He tipped his head in the direction they were heading. "We have a reservation. Let's go."

She made it a point to not look at the stranger as they passed him, but somehow, she felt his eyes on her. His attention was a siren song coaxing Willow to turn her head and behold him once more.

Really, Willow? Getting turned on by a complete stranger while you're walking to dinner with your soon-to-be fiancé?

Stop it. I have nothing to feel guilty about. It was just a look. I can't help my body's reaction, but I can control my actions. Feeling attraction toward someone is natural.

So why had that single fleeting look filled her with more yearning than she'd ever felt with Eli?

Her guilt resurfaced, and she shoved it aside.

Physical attraction. It was a spark of lust and nothing more. Besides, I'll never see him again after tonight.

Eli came to a stop, breaking Willow away from her tumultuous thoughts, and released her hand. Confused, she watched as he reached into his pocket to retrieve his phone.

"We're here," he said distractedly as he tapped something out on his phone. He glanced at her and smiled. "Wait here and give me a minute to make sure everything's all set."

Looking past Eli, Willow gaped. "Eden? Oh my God, you got us reservations at *Eden*?"

The intricate stonework on the restaurant's front was broken by three tall archways. The windows in the lower half of each arch were tinted dark, but the upper portions were adorned with clear glass and intricate, polished brass that allowed the intimate orange glow from within to spill out onto the sidewalk. The big entry doors were fashioned like gates—the gates of paradise, if local food critics were to be believed.

"Yeah. I just found out about it a couple weeks ago. Ma— My, uh, buddy at work said everyone should experience it at least once. Supposed to be the nicest restaurant in town."

A slight frown played upon Willow's lips. "I mentioned this place to you months ago."

His brow furrowed. "Did you?"

"You don't remember? One of my clients came here with her partner. They said it was amazing, and that the atmosphere was wonderfully romantic."

Eli shook his head. His attention had returned to his phone, which had flashed with a message notification. "I don't remember that, Will. I only heard about this place recently. But hey, guess it works out, right?"

Guess he also forgot that I suggested we try this place when I told him about it.

She couldn't prevent the pang of hurt in her heart, but it faded quickly. They were here now. The rest didn't matter. In the end, he'd still chosen to take her here, and that was all that was important, right? Eli worked a demanding job, and he had so many things to keep track of. She couldn't expect him to remember every little conversation they'd had.

She smiled again. "Yeah, you're right. This place looks incredible, and we're not even inside yet."

"I told you it was going to be a special night." Eli tucked his phone away. "I'll be right back."

"Okay."

After he entered the restaurant, Willow stepped aside and turned toward the window. All the dark glass allowed her to see was her own reflection.

Biting her lip, she ran her fingers through her long hair, pulling the loose curls over her shoulders as she looked herself over. She'd taken great care with her makeup, outlining her eyes in black eyeliner with the best wings she could manage, but her efforts felt inadequate now. When Eli had told her to dress up, she never could've guessed just how fancy a place he was taking her to.

She smoothed her hands down the satin and lace skirt of her dress and smiled.

The dress had caught her eye as she was passing a plus-size clothing shop a few weeks ago. She had no idea how long she'd stood outside, staring at the vintage-inspired dress with its cinched waist, flaring skirt, lacy bodice, and short, off-the-shoulder sleeves. It was beautiful, elegant. It was also her favorite color, purple, and perfectly complemented the lighter lavender shade of her hair.

She'd itched to own it, and that itch had quickly become

7

impossible to ignore. So, she'd splurged on it, paying more than she should've been comfortable with.

All she'd needed was the right occasion upon which to wear it. Now that she was standing here, it felt like fate that she'd happened to see it, that she'd decided to buy it for herself.

The perfect dress for what is going to be the perfect night.

Slipping her hand into her dress pocket, Willow pulled out her phone. She had two missed texts, both from Jamie. Willow unlocked her phone to read them.

Well?

Willow don't leave me hanging! Did he ask?!!!

Willow grinned and quickly sent a reply. *We just got to the restaurant. It's Eden, Jamie! Eden!*

She could picture Jamie curled over her phone, eyes glued to the screen as she'd awaited Willow's message, because Jamie's response came almost instantly.

HOLY SHIT! He's gonna propose!

"They're ready for us, Will," Eli said.

Willow turned toward him, and her smile widened. He stood at the front entrance, holding the door open.

This is it, she thought as she approached him, slipping her phone back into her pocket. *This is the next step in spending our lives together.*

They entered the restaurant, and were greeted by the maître d', who introduced them to their hostess. As they were shown to their table, Willow followed in a daze, unable to keep herself from looking around in awe.

The warm, gentle lighting made the plants, flowers, and metalwork on display come together beautifully, and the large, burbling fountain at the center of the restaurant only added to the relaxing atmosphere. The fountain was a combination of sculpture, natural stone, and flora, with a small apple tree—complete with golden apples—perched atop it.

Their table was toward the back of the restaurant, tucked away in cozy nook with walls of ivy on either side. An open bottle of champagne stood atop it, accompanied by three tall glasses filled with the bubbly, golden nectar.

Brow furrowing, Willow took a seat, staring at the extra place setting as Eli sat across from her.

"Enjoy Eden," the hostess said with a shallow bow before leaving them.

"Eli, is someone joining us?" Willow asked.

"Hey," he said, calling her attention to him. He reached across the table, settling his hand over her wrist. "Tonight's about us, right?"

Warmth bloomed in her chest. "It is."

"And we're not going to let anything ruin what we have, right?"

Willow shook her head. "Nothing."

"What we have is special, Will. And we're only going to keep building on it." Releasing her wrist, he plucked up his champagne glass and raised it. "To us."

Willow smiled and picked up her own glass, clinking it against his. "To us."

She brought the glass to her lips and drank, nearly moaning as notes of cherry, orange, and peach swept across her tongue. The bubbles tickled, but the drink was smooth and velvety as it slid down her throat. She couldn't stop herself from nearly draining the entire glass.

Eli laughed. "I take it you like it?"

Willow blushed, covering her mouth with her fingers as she set the champagne down. "Sorry. I've just never had anything so good."

He picked up the bottle and refilled her glass. "Enjoy it. Drink as much as you want."

"Eli, are you trying to get me drunk?"

"Of course not. But I do like it when you're tipsy." He leaned over the table, bringing his face closer as a devilish light sparked in his eyes. "You're extra...loveable."

"Ha. Extra horny you mean. Just be honest."

He laughed, sat back in his chair, and raised his glass in salute. "You said it, not me."

Grinning, Willow lifted her champagne in response. "To being horny then."

She drank half the glass before she set it aside with the intention of not touching it again until their meals arrived. She knew all too well that the sweet stuff often snuck up on her, and she'd already had enough to make her feel warm.

A muffled buzz sounded from Eli's pocket. He pulled out his phone, read something on the screen, and smiled.

Willow tilted her head. "Who's that?"

Eli tucked the phone away, stretched his arms across the table, and took her hands in his. His eyes met hers.

Willow's heart leapt.

This is it! Oh God, he's going to propose!

"You know I care for you, right Will?"

"Of course I do." She gave his hands a squeeze, trying to remain calm.

"I've been giving it a lot of thought lately, and, well... I think it's time we took our relationship to the next level."

Willow nodded enthusiastically. "Mmhmm. I agree."

Just breathe, Willow. Breathe. Let him ask!

Eli tilted his chin down and smiled. "Willow, I think you should—"

"Yes!"

"—meet Marissa."

Time stopped. Paradise crumbled around Willow, and in the swirling chaos that replaced it, she had no idea what was happening, couldn't make sense of anything. The air fled her lungs, giving voice to a single word. "What?"

He slipped one of his hands free, raised it, and beckoned to someone beyond Willow. "I want you to meet Marissa. My other girlfriend."

She was vaguely aware of movement as someone sat down on the vacant chair at their table. Slowly, Willow dragged her gaze to the newcomer.

The woman was beautiful, with olive skin, black hair, and hazel eyes. She wore a skin-tight silver dress that sparkled like diamonds under the restaurant's lights.

Marissa's red painted lips curled into a wide smile. "Hi, Willow. I'm so excited to finally meet you. Eli's told me so much about you!"

My other girlfriend.

Willow's heart hammered against her chest, which felt far too tight. Eli had a...a girlfriend. *Another* girlfriend.

No. No, no, no, no. This can't be happening. This is not happening. This... This isn't right.

Willow pulled free of Eli's grasp and dropped her hands onto her lap. "Eli... What's going on?"

Marissa frowned and looked at Eli.

He flicked his gaze from Marissa to Willow and folded his hands on the table. "Will, you know how much I love you. That hasn't changed. But when I met Marissa six months ago, we just clicked. I realized that love doesn't have to be exclusive. That it can grow to include others. Marissa is a wonderful person. She's been dying to meet you so you two could get to know each other, and then we could all finally be together."

Willow glared at him, the fog of her confusion and hurt parting to make way for rising anger. "So you brought me here... to ask me to join a threesome?"

"Don't say it that way. That makes it sound cheap, and this is so much more than a one-time thing. It's...an opening of our relationship. This would be another partner, for both of us."

"She didn't know?" Marissa asked.

Eli frowned. "I wanted it to be a surprise."

"You *know* that's not how this works, Eli."

"Look, I know her, okay?" He cast Willow a pleading look, as though she'd offer him support. "I knew that if I told her before we were all ready, she would've just stewed on it, and the longer she had to think about it, the more likely she was to chicken out."

Marissa scowled. "Chicken out? Polyamory is about trust and communication, neither of which you've demonstrated—to either of us. It's something people choose to do, not something you manipulate them into."

"And I just wanted Willow to give it a fair shot. She wouldn't have understood if I'd just talked to her." He leaned toward Marissa, softening his expression. "But being here, meeting you... how could anyone say no?"

Willow couldn't believe what she was hearing. Rage coursed through her veins, burning hotter with every word that came out of Eli's mouth. "Wouldn't have understood? Eli, you're cheating on me!"

He raised his hands placatingly and glanced around. "Will, please keep your voice down. Don't cause a scene."

She jabbed a finger at him. "Do *not* tell me to keep my voice down."

"I wouldn't have to tell you if the whole restaurant couldn't hear you right now." Eli sighed and ran his fingers through his hair. "I'm not cheating on you. My heart is fully committed to you. I love you. But it's committed to Marissa too. She's polyamorous, Will, and so am I."

He loved Willow? Why would anyone do this to someone they loved? Why would he disrespect her, dismiss her feelings, ignore her wishes, and keep secrets from her if he loved her? If Eli really was polyamorous, why would he hide it for so long?

Because he never truly loved me. He loves what I can give him, loves that I do anything he needs. Loves that he gets to be in charge.

That thought made her stomach churn. How could she have been so stupid? How could she have been so blind after all this time?

Because I desperately wanted someone to love me for once. To see me as enough.

"Don't pretend, Eli," Marissa snapped. "You are cheating. I don't know why I didn't realize sooner. I should've known something wasn't right when you kept refusing to let me meet Willow, when you kept saying she was interested but needed time. I should've smelled your bullshit from a mile away."

Willow should've smelled it too. She'd really believed he was going to propose tonight, but he'd never even seriously discussed moving in together. Every time she'd brought it up, he'd been either evasive or noncommittal, giving halfhearted excuses about commute times or convenience, or saying he wouldn't want to leave his apartment and she wouldn't want to leave her house. Then he'd always change the subject.

How had she convinced herself that they were about to jump into marriage when they hadn't even hit the milestone of sharing a home after three years together?

Marissa turned on her chair to face Willow, placing a gentle hand on her shoulder. "I am so, so sorry for this. It's my fault for taking him at his word, and it's not the way any of this is supposed to work. For what it's worth, everything he's told me about you makes you out to be a wonderful person. You deserve so much better than this."

Willow searched Marissa's gaze, recognizing the same anger and hurt in it that simmered within herself. "Thank you."

She didn't blame the woman. Eli had played them both.

Marissa dropped her hand and stood. "If you haven't already guessed, Eli, we're done."

"Marissa!" Eli called as the woman slipped past Willow and walked away.

Willow snatched up her champagne and gulped it down, not even tasting it this time.

Eli groaned and sat back in his chair, scrubbing a hand over his face. "This didn't go the way I hoped."

She glared at him and refilled her glass. "Ya think?"

"Please, Will, let's just have a nice dinner and talk. We'll work it out. You and Marissa will come around to this."

"There is nothing to work out." Willow rose to her feet and thrust her glass forward. Champagne splashed over Eli's face.

Eli sputtered, scooting his chair back loudly as he spread his arms. Champagne dripped down his face and hair. "Willow! What the fuck?"

A hush fell over the restaurant, but Willow didn't care. She'd cause as much of as scene as she damn well pleased. "You're a self-centered, manipulative asshole, and we're through."

She spun and strode away, shoulders back and head held high, ignoring the hushed whispers, the judgmental stares, the pitying looks, and the burn behind her eyes as she held in her tears.

At least until she stepped out of the restaurant.

Two

All Willow's fury came crashing down, leaving her only with shame, resentment, and worst of all, heartache. She'd begun the evening with such high hopes, with such boundless excitement, and it had all been shattered in a matter of minutes.

She didn't want to cry. Eli didn't deserve her tears. He didn't deserve a single damned thing more from her, especially not after all he'd taken, but here she was, walking along the busy boulevard with tears welling in her eyes.

Willow sniffled and wiped beneath her eyes with the back of her hand, keeping her head bowed so her hair hid her face. She didn't want anyone to see her like this. Didn't want anyone to see her falling apart.

She didn't have the words to describe the storm of emotions ravaging her, but her heart hurt.

She turned the corner and continued forward, putting as much distance between herself and Eden as possible. Her hurried steps brought her onto a footbridge spanning the river. Once she reached the middle, where the arched bridge was at its highest, she stopped, folded her arms atop the railing, and looked down. Dark water flowed below, flickering with reflections from nearby street-lights and buildings. The night breeze swept around her, fluttering her skirt and hair, and making the tears on her cheeks cold as ice.

Willow drew in a deep, shuddering breath.

"Stupid, selfish prick," she muttered.

Those words only brought more tears. She couldn't resummon her anger, couldn't use it to shield herself. Willow drew her lips in and bit down on them to contain the sob threatening to escape her.

Before Eli, she'd been struggling through the hellscape that was the dating world. She'd had a few disastrous dates during which she'd been told that she hadn't looked so fat in her profile pictures. She'd had one where the man had berated their waiter for bringing the wrong drink before turning to Willow, slipping on a smile, and continuing their conversation as though nothing had happened.

She'd encountered so many men who'd had no qualms about putting a woman down and making her feel ashamed of herself, her appearance, her preferences. So many men who'd talked down to her or treated her like she was dumb. And many of those men had considered themselves *nice* guys.

Still, there'd been relationships that survived the first date. Some had fallen apart within two or three weeks. A few had lasted for several months and had become, at least to Willow, somewhat serious. But her boyfriends' true colors always emerged eventually.

The last date she'd gone on, months before she'd met Eli, had nearly broken her. At the man's suggestion, she'd agreed to split the bill beforehand. She had no problem with that. It was totally reasonable, especially on a first date. But the man had given her the strangest, most judgmental look after she'd ordered a prime rib for herself. When she asked about it, he'd claimed nothing was wrong—in a snippy tone that suggested *everything* was wrong. She'd pressed him, and he'd ultimately launched into a rant about how unappealing it would be to watch her eat a dripping steak, how unladylike it was of her, how she should've ordered something daintier, something more feminine.

Something less fattening.

The date had ended before their food arrived.

She'd nearly given up hope then. At the tender age of twenty-three, she'd nearly decided her romantic life was over, that it was never meant to be. She'd been so, so tired. So hurt. But that pain had driven her to find herself, to learn to love herself, to embrace her body and her personality. Her whole life had begun to change as she altered her mindset.

That was when she'd found Eli. He'd seemed so different than all the others. Good-looking, charming, always saying the right things. He'd never once made her feel bad because of her weight. They'd had fun together. And sometimes, he'd been so kind, so thoughtful. She'd fallen for him.

She knew now that he'd only seemed so great because her past experiences had set the bar very, very low. She'd convinced herself that all the little things that felt wrong were normal, that it was just her.

But the signs had been there. The red flags. She could recognize some now, despite the rawness of her pain.

Those moments of thoughtfulness from him had been few and far between, and they'd only been memorable because of the long stretches of nothingness between them.

She'd spent so much time and energy being available for Eli whenever he needed her, keeping him happy, helping him relax after stressful workdays. When had he ever done the same for her? All their plans had always revolved around him, and any scheduling conflicts had always been resolved by Willow canceling whatever she'd had going on.

Willow had even stopped volunteering at the soup kitchen and animal shelter because she'd had to arrange her life around Eli's availability. She'd loved those places, had loved helping people and animals. Throughout their relationship, she'd been dealing with the stress and exhaustion of running her own business and trying to build a clientele, yet she'd given every spare moment to him.

He never went out with Willow and Jamie, but he'd expected her to be fine hanging out with his friends. He'd gladly had sex with Willow in her bed, but rarely spent the night, and anytime she slept at his house she always felt like she was in his way the next morning as he hurried through his routine—until he inevitably hurried her out the door.

Eli had always picked the movies and shows they'd watched together. He'd chosen the restaurants and bars when they went out, he'd chosen the food when they'd ordered in. And her suggestions had always been ignored or brushed off with excuses.

God, how had she never realized how many excuses he'd spouted to justify his dismissal of her ideas, her interests, her wants and needs?

She'd just been wishing for that happily ever after for so long, and Eli was the first truly long-term boyfriend she'd had, the first guy who hadn't treated her like garbage...

But he did *treat me like garbage. He was just the only one who remained subtle about it. The only one who always knew all the things to say to distract me from what was really going on.*

And as though everything else hadn't been bad enough, he'd done *this*. He'd cheated on her and tried to hide behind a claim of polyamory. Another excuse, another false justification for his behavior, another dismissal of Willow's feelings.

Because I'm just not capable of understanding, right?

If an open relationship was truly important to Eli, he

18

would've talked to her about it. He would've discussed it with her. That was what adults did, wasn't it? That was what partners did.

He was just...a pig.

Eli isn't worth my heart, anyway. He isn't worth any of this.

Telling herself that didn't stop it from hurting.

Her chest felt constricted, her stomach uneasy, and her head light and fuzzy. Lifting a hand, she pressed her fingers to her forehead and closed her eyes.

"I'm done," she whispered, lowering her hand. "I am swearing off dating, swearing off relationships, swearing off...assholes." Willow's lip trembled as more tears fell. "I'm done having my heart broken."

"Rough night?" someone asked from behind her, his deep voice sending a tingle along her spine.

Willow's eyes snapped open, and her fingers curled, nails digging into her arms. "I-I'm fine."

Oh please, just go away.

The scene in the restaurant had been embarrassing enough. She didn't need a random stranger to see her like this. She didn't want pity.

Heavy footsteps drew nearer to her, and a large, dark shape entered her peripheral vision, barely discernable through her hair. The stranger hummed. "Water's lovely with all the lights, isn't it? Looks like stars dancing across the surface."

His smooth, low voice had a faint lilt, just enough to fill it— and her—with unexpected warmth.

Willow turned her face farther away from him and wiped the moisture from her cheeks. "It does."

"I think I know what's wrong. You sat down in that restaurant, opened the menu, and made the mistake of looking at the prices. That's why you came rushing out, isn't it? Who wants to pay a hundred dollars for a half inch square of fish with some parsley sprinkled around it?"

A small laugh escaped her. "Yeah, it's ridiculously overpriced, isn't it?" Her brow creased, and her cheeks warmed as a mortifying thought occurred to her. "You saw me in Eden?"

He chuckled. The sound was even more enticing than his voice. "I saw you go in with your man. Then I saw you come out alone. Figured it was either the prices or..."

"He's not my man. Not...not anymore."

She peered aside to see the stranger lean his arms on the railing, but she was still only able to make out his dark coat. A breeze swept over them, carrying his scent directly to her nose—sandalwood, jasmine, and hint of something darker, something divine. Her eyelids nearly fluttered shut as she drew in that fragrance.

She'd never met a man who smelled so sensual.

"I see," he said, a slight rumble entering his voice. "That's his loss then."

Willow sniffled and wiped her cheeks again. "I'm okay though. Really. Thank you for checking on me, but you...you don't have to stand here with me."

"I'm not ready to walk away from you."

The provocative seriousness in his tone finally drew her full attention to him. Her breath caught, and her eyes widened when they locked with his.

Oh God, it's him.

"Hi," he practically purred, lips curling into a sultry smile. Light glinted on his lip piercings, but it was nothing compared to the almost preternatural glow of his blue eyes. "Lovely to see you again."

Her skin pebbled, and a shiver ran through her body that had nothing to do with the breeze. She stood upright, gripping the railing so hard her knuckles turned white. She'd been taught it was rude to stare, yet there was nowhere else to look but at him.

There was nowhere else she wanted to look.

He straightened to his full height and turned toward her. Her eyes fell to his open shirt, which granted her quite a view of his sculpted chest.

The stranger reached toward her and brushed the back of a finger down her cheek, leaving warm tingles in its wake. "Breathe, Violet."

Willow released a slow, shaky breath.

He stroked her other cheek. "That's a good girl."

Heat pooled between her thighs.

Oh God.

She never would've imagined being called a good girl could be sexy, but hearing it from this man? In that voice?

That finger didn't retreat when it reached her chin. Instead, he trailed the tip of his nail—his long, black, pointed nail—under her jaw, down her throat, and slowly, so slowly, along her collarbone. The warmth of his touch spread through her like wildfire, burning straight to her core.

Willow, you just broke up with your boyfriend. This is because of the champagne.

So what if it is? What does it matter?

He's a complete stranger!

A stranger who'd seen her going into Eden, who'd followed her when she'd left. A tall, strong, dangerous looking man with eyes she could lose herself in forever, with fingers that sparked electricity on her skin, with a scent that had suffused her and teased at all her favorite things. Just these little touches produced so much more sensation than Eli had ever made her feel.

But this man was still a stranger.

It took everything in Willow to make herself step backward, to cut off that physical contact and put a little distance between them. The path he'd traced over her skin went cold. She glanced past him and brought her hands up to her middle, wringing her fingers. "Why did you follow me?"

"You looked distressed." He slipped his hands into his pockets and leaned his hip against the railing. "I'm not going to hurt you, Violet. No need to be afraid."

Willow tilted her head and stared at him blankly. "That's what they all say before they kidnap you, cut you into little pieces, and hide the evidence at the bottom of the river."

He arched a brow and glanced down at the water. "Is that what happened? He promised not to hurt you, then cut up your heart and threw it away?"

Tears again stung her eyes, and she fought hard to keep them from falling. She faced the river and returned her hands to the railing. "You could say that."

He shifted to stand beside her, curling his hand next to hers. Silver rings of varying size and design adorned his fingers. One was set with a ruby gemstone, and the full knuckle ring on his middle finger was shaped like a claw.

"Sounds like a piece of shit," he said.

Willow let out a humorless laugh. "Yeah, that's Eli." She rubbed the toe of her shoe against the curbing. "And I stupidly thought that piece of shit was going to propose tonight."

"Contemplated revenge yet?"

"No. I just... I don't want anything more to do with him. I already gave him three years of my life, I don't want to give him anything more." Willow cast him a sidelong glance. "Why do you care? You could be doing anything right now, so why stand here listening to some stranger's relationship problems?"

The man snickered, and his hand inched closer to hers, rings lightly scraping the railing. "I keep my plans malleable. When an opportunity arises, I take it. And tonight, I'm going to help you forget him."

Willow looked up at him. "What do you mean?"

He turned his head, and those entrancing eyes captured hers. His lips curled into a slow, sinful smile. "I'm offering you the best night of your life, Violet. Pleasure beyond your wildest dreams. What better way to put him behind you?"

Her eyes widened. "You... Are you telling me you want to have sex with me?"

"No, I'm telling you I'm going to have sex with you." The glint in his gaze was almost irresistible. "You can't pretend it's not what you want."

Tingles spread over her skin, and a fresh swell of unbidden heat suffused her, blazing in her core. The image his words provoked—his long, wicked fingers trailing over her, those sensuous lips tasting her bare skin, and his strong, lean body nestled between her thighs—made her pussy clench and her breasts ache.

Yes, I want it.

Damn it, Willow, snap out of it!

"I don't even know your name," she said.

"Kian. Feel free to cry it out as often as you'd like. Yours?"

Blushing, she replied, "Willow."

"Willow." His deep, lilting voice caressed her name, flowing through her like a melody not heard but felt, resonating in her heart. "Tonight, you're *my* Willow."

She glanced around. There were a few people walking on the bridge, but no one paid her or Kian any mind. She'd never been propositioned like this before, and she never would've dreamed of accepting.

It wasn't like Willow didn't enjoy sex. She loved it, reveled in it. But sex meant something to her. It was an intimate connection between two people, a sharing of something deep and significant. It was as close as two people could possibly become physically, mentally, and spiritually.

So why was she tempted by this stranger?

Kian lifted his hand from the railing and turned his body toward her. His finger hooked under her chin, and the tip of his pointed nail rasped along the underside of her jaw. "Let me help you forget him, if only for tonight. I'll leave room for nothing but pleasure." He bent forward until their noses were nearly touching. "Let me take away the pain."

Willow searched his eyes. This close, she could see glitter-like specks of color in them, sparkling blues and silver. They were so beautiful, so mesmerizing...

Let me take away the pain.

She pressed her lips together against the rush of hurt that threatened to resurface—Eli's lies, his secrets, his betrayal.

Let me take away the pain.

Willow didn't want to think about Eli, didn't want to think about what had happened or what he had done. She didn't want to think about how her hopes for a shared future had been dashed so abruptly. She didn't want to feel this way anymore.

She just wanted to...forget. If only for tonight.

Then give in, Willow. A night of pleasure, no strings attached. A night for...yourself.

Willow drew in a shaky breath. Reaching up, she closed her fingers around Kian's wrist and nodded. "Yes."

Three

A maelstrom of emotions swarmed through Willow as she stepped through the door of the hotel room—anxiety, fear, uncertainty, curiosity, anticipation, desire. She couldn't pin down which was most prominent.

Maybe that was a good thing? That confused jumble was... well, it was kind of exciting, wasn't it? This was unlike anything she'd ever done, unlike anything she ever thought she'd do. But here she was, in a rented room, intending to have sex with a man she didn't know.

Willow's gaze landed on the single king size bed in the center of the room, over which fell the soft, golden orange light of the lamp on the nightstand.

I'm about to have sex with a complete stranger.

Oh my God, what am I doing?

The door closed behind her, and she started, spinning to face Kian.

His eyes narrowed, sliding down to her feet and then back up, so, so slowly, until he met her gaze. The corner of his mouth was raised in that devilish smirk that should've been alarming considering the situation—she was alone in a hotel room with a stranger. A tall, gorgeous man who had gone from 'rough night?' to 'I'm fucking you tonight' in a matter of moments.

Willow tore her attention away from him, turning it to the white walls, to the dark wooden dresser and the flatscreen television atop it, to the desk and chairs in the corner. To anything but him. She clutched the fabric of her skirt. "So, what am I... How do we..."

"Take off your clothes," Kian commanded.

She snapped her wide eyes back to him. "What?"

Kian was looking down at his hands. His long fingers moved with deliberate, tantalizing slowness, removing his rings one by one and dropping them into his coat pocket. "Take off your clothes." As he slipped his coat off his broad shoulders, he glanced up at her. His smirk tilted just a little more to one side. "I can do it for you, if you'd prefer."

"N-No. I can do it." Willow looked down and shifted her feet, about to give Kian her back, when words Eli had spoken earlier crawled up from her memory.

...the longer she had to think about it, the more likely she was to chicken out.

No. She wasn't going to run from this. She *wanted* this.

Shoving her thoughts of Eli deep into the subconscious abyss where they belonged, Willow summoned all the courage she could muster and reached for the zipper at her back. She drew it down. Cool air touched her bare skin as the dress gaped open. She slipped her arms out of the sleeves and pushed the dress past her hips. The fabric whispered along her legs and fell to pool at her feet, leaving her in her purple strapless bra, panties, the lacy black bands around her thighs, and her high heels.

Leaving her vulnerable.

Willow didn't care what other people thought about her. She loved her body, and she wasn't ashamed of her soft belly, stretch marks, thick thighs, and large breasts. But with a man like Kian staring at her... This was different. So, so different. He was so attractive it was practically otherworldly. How could she compare to the standards of someone like him?

He picked you, Willow. Out of all the people there, he chose you. He must have seen something he liked. Something he wanted.

Kicking the dress away, Willow looked up at Kian. Her heart stuttered.

He'd already set his coat aside and removed his shirt. She didn't know where to look first—his elegant neck, his wide shoulders, his hairless chest and abs. It was all so alluring. But what ultimately captured her attention were the silver bar piercings in his nipples. She squeezed her thighs together against the sudden ache permeating her core.

Where else was he pierced?

Her gaze dipped across the lean, defined muscles of his abdomen and followed the shallow grooves of the Adonis belt that disappeared into his jeans.

"Do you like what you see, Violet?" Kian asked, his husky voice coaxing her eyes to his. He stalked toward her, and though he didn't move fast, his long legs devoured the distance between him and Willow just as surely as his penetrating eyes devoured her.

Kian curled a finger beneath her chin and angled her face up, studying her. A low hum rumbled in his chest. His finger trailed under her jaw and to the side of her neck as he stepped around her, sweeping her hair back to bare one shoulder. His touch was fire, but its heat made her shiver.

"I can feel your desire," he whispered in her ear. Warmth radiated from his body.

Willow's skin tingled with the promise of pleasure as he circled to stand behind her. She was desperate to feel those hands all over her body.

He traced the tip of a pointed nail down her spine, catching the clasps of her bra. "All your yearning, Willow, it sings to me." The first clasp gave way to his clever fingers. "There's no reason to resist any more." The second clasp followed, then the third.

He lingered on the last, and Willow's heart sped. She felt him lean over her, though only his hair touched her, brushing her bare shoulder. His breath tickled her ear as he rasped, "Are you ready to give in to me?"

Willow turned her face toward him, her lips drawing so close to his, and met his gaze. "Yes."

"Then you're mine." He unclasped her bra, letting it fall to join her dress.

Before Willow could react, his long arms banded around her, and he cupped her breasts in his palms. She gasped, hands flying up to grasp his forearms as he drew her against his hard body. His cock, still restrained by his jeans, pressed against the small of her back.

"Perfect," he rumbled as he kneaded the tender flesh of her breasts. His fingers worked with dexterity beyond comprehension, twisting and teasing her nipples, eliciting sensations like she'd never dreamed possible. Every stroke felt like he was pulling on a tether connected directly to her clit.

She arched against him. Her breath quickened, and her body grew hot and restless. Slick gathered between her thighs. She rubbed them together and captured her bottom lip between her teeth, muffling a moan as she tipped her head back against Kian's shoulder.

His tongue flicked over the sensitive spot beneath her ear just as he pinched her nipples harder, coaxing another moan from her.

He chuckled. "So responsive, Willow. What other lovely sounds will you make for me when I stroke your pretty cunt?"

Kian smoothed a hand down her belly. His palm left fire in its wake. Willow would never have believed that anyone's touch

28

could be so powerful, so affecting, but she couldn't deny this. And she wanted more.

Without her even voicing that thought, he complied. His hand continued down, sliding under the waistband of her panties and over her pubic hair before his fingers delved between the folds of her pussy. Willow's breath hitched at the first brush against her clit.

"You're fucking dripping," Kian growled. He slipped his finger inside her, sinking it deep, and her sex clenched around it. "So hot and tight. So perfect." While his other hand continued caressing her breast, he pumped his finger in and out of her. His strokes began slowly, torturously so, but with each he built speed and intensity.

Willow undulated her hips, her breath ragged as he ground the heel of his palm on her clit. Pleasure unfurled within her, pouring liquid fire into her veins, growing and growing with every beat of her heart. And his hands responded perfectly, moving ever faster, ever firmer, keeping her just on the edge.

"Kian," she moaned.

"Do you feel how greedy your body is for this?" he asked, his breath warm against her temple. "Feel how hungry your cunt is for me?" He added a second finger, thrust them hard and deep inside her, and held them there, possessively cupping her with his hand.

Willow nearly wept with need. Her clit throbbed, and her pussy clenched, aching for more. She wriggled against him, rubbing his rigid cock against her back.

Kian groaned, chest rumbling. "I can only imagine what you'll feel like around my cock."

Willow turned her face toward him. Those icy blue eyes, ablaze with so much heat, met hers. Her gaze dropped to his mouth. Without a thought, she reached up, grasped his hair, and dragged him closer, touching her lips to his.

Kian stilled, and his grip on her tightened. Then his mouth molded to hers. His lips caressed and teased, soon joined by his tongue, which demanded entry. And Willow opened to him. Another rolling, sensuous sound vibrated from his chest. His tongue coaxed hers into a languid dance the likes of which she'd never experienced. That quickly, he seized control of the kiss, deepening it.

The things he did with his mouth and tongue might've made that kiss alone enough to bring her to climax—if his fingers hadn't already slipped from her depths to circle her clit.

Willow gasped against his mouth. She clenched his hair as she rocked her hips helplessly, every slick stroke of his fingers adding a new layer to her pleasure, a new intensity that made her skin thrum and her knees tremble.

"Kian," she whimpered, brows drawn low, thighs quivering and weak.

"Let go. Cum sweetly for me, Willow." As he spoke her name, he increased the pressure on her clit. It was a small change, a subtle change, but he might as well have shifted the ground beneath her feet for the earthquake it triggered within her.

Willow squeezed her eyes shut, and her body went taut. Kian recaptured her lips with his, swallowing her broken, silent cry. Sparks flashed behind her eyelids as ecstasy crashed through her. And Kian did not relent. He played her with his fingers, coaxing melodious notes from her very soul, conducting a symphony of sensation that utterly consumed her. She came again and again, her essence soon soaking her underwear and dripping down her thighs.

When her legs gave out, Kian wrapped an arm around her middle to support her and stilled his hand.

Panting, Willow clung to him with her face buried against his chest, her body quivering, and her pussy pulsing with the after-shocks. "That... That was..."

"Only the beginning," he said.

She lifted her head to look up at him. "What?"

Grinning, he withdrew his fingers from her sex and raised them. They were coated with her slick. "We're not done yet." He ran his tongue over his fingers before taking them into his mouth.

Her eyes flared.

Kian hummed as he slid his fingers free, sucking them clean. "You taste even better than you smell, Violet." He skimmed his nail along her jaw. "And I plan to have my tongue in that sweet cunt next."

Willow's mouth went dry. No one had ever talked to her like Kian did. No one had ever said things like...like *that*. It was so filthy, and yet so freaking arousing.

"Now"—Kian grasped her panties with his other hand— "take these off and get on the bed."

"Okay," she whispered.

He ran his thumb over her bottom lip. "Good girl."

Her belly fluttered at the praise.

Willow straightened and stepped away from Kian when he released her. Her legs were still unsteady, but she managed to turn and walk the few steps it took to reach the bed. She slipped off her heels, hooked her underwear with her thumbs, and pushed them down her legs. When she felt how wet she was, she blushed anew. She never thought she could orgasm so hard from fingers alone. That she'd...

Oh God, he'd made her squirt.

Eli never—

Stop. Do not think of him, Willow.

No, she wouldn't let anything ruin this moment, this night, for her.

She crawled onto the bed and turned to sit with knees bent and legs closed.

Kian toed off his boots and stepped closer to the bed, dipping a hand into his pocket. He withdrew a wrapped condom, which he tossed onto the comforter beside Willow, and then moved those wicked fingers to his belt. Willow's eyes fell to the prominent bulge at his crotch. Despite all the pleasure he'd already given her, that hollowness in her core was only greater now—her want for more, for him, had only grown.

Willow watched raptly as he unbuckled his belt, unbuttoned his jeans, and lowered the zipper. Once his pants were open, he shoved them, along with his boxers, down.

He stood, and her eyes widened. His cock was long, thick, and hard, and there, at the tip, it was pierced with a silver captive bead ring.

She curled her fingers into the bedding as he wrapped a hand around his shaft and hissed.

"Keep looking at it like that, Violet." He pumped his hand, and a bead of cum gathered on the end of his cock.

Willow's pussy clenched, and that emptiness within her expanded. She caught her bottom lip between her teeth. She had a sudden urge to taste him, to run her tongue along his shaft, to tease its head, slit, and piercing. To take him into her mouth. But the need at her core was far stronger.

She wanted him inside her.

"I see that hunger. I can fucking feel it," he said, releasing his cock. Bracing a knee on the edge of the bed, he bent forward, planted a hand on the comforter, and settled his other palm on her thigh. "But mine is far greater."

His fingertips brushed the lace of her thigh band and smiled. "I like these, Willow."

The material wasn't nearly enough to shield her from the thrilling heat of his touch.

He eased closer. Kian's long, pale hair hung over one shoulder, and his features looked absolutely predatory as he curled his fingers around her thighs and forced her legs apart, baring her sex. He groaned and spread her legs farther.

Kian lowered his head. For an instant, there was only the caress of his warm breath on her most sensitive flesh, making her shiver. Then his tongue lapped at her from bottom to top. When its tip brushed over her clit, she was hit with such a rush of sensation that her arms gave out. She fell onto her back and moaned.

But that first touch wasn't even a fraction of what he had in store for her. Using lips and tongue, using his breath itself, Kian lavished Willow with ecstasy. She writhed, her body's movements entirely out of her control. He clamped his arms around her legs and pinned her in place. When he growled against her, the sound pulsed straight to her core, and she clutched at the bedding as her hips bucked and desperate cries escaped her throat.

He pushed her thighs wider and pressed his mouth over her pussy. His lips closed around her clit, and he sucked.

Everything within Willow went taut. One of her hands darted to his head, grasping a fistful of his hair, and her back arched off the bed as another powerful climax wracked her. She sucked in a breath that couldn't possibly fill her lungs as liquid heat rushed out of her. And Kian drank it all greedily.

He relented long enough for her to collapse, panting, before he shook off her hold and lifted his face, shoving himself up. He reached aside, plucked up the condom, and brought it to his mouth. His other hand had already grasped his cock as he tore the packet open with his teeth, letting out a snarl that sent another shiver through Willow.

With a careless flick, Kian tossed the wrapper aside. He rolled the condom over his shaft.

His gaze met and held Willow's as he moved his body over her, arms caging her in, hips nestling between her thighs. His hair fell forward, tickling her shoulder. Willow flattened her palms on his abdomen and smoothed them up, relishing the feel of his heated skin, of his firm muscles. Her thumbs grazed his pierced nipples.

Chest rumbling, Kian bared his teeth and flexed his hips, pressing the blunted head of his cock to her entrance. Her heart quickened.

"Tonight, you're mine." He thrust forward, driving himself inside her to the hilt.

Willow's head tilted back as pleasure arced through her. Her lips parted in a gasp and her fingers curled, nails digging into his chest, but her gaze did not leave his. Kian's eyes burned, somehow dark and forbidding and yet bright and alluring at once. They were the kind of eyes that could consume her. The kind of eyes she was tempted to helplessly, happily throw herself into.

His expression softened, becoming faintly thoughtful. "Ah, my little Violet, how you shine." He lifted a hand and brushed the back of a finger down her cheek. "You are so beautiful."

Those words wrapped around Willow's heart and squeezed.

She felt closer to Kian in that moment than she had to anyone in all her life, and all she knew about him was his name.

This is supposed to be a one-night stand. It's not supposed to mean anything.

Tonight was about pleasure, not connection. She couldn't allow herself to get emotionally attached.

But she couldn't stop herself from reaching up to affectionately trace his brow.

His pupils dilated, and his breath caught.

"*Fuck,*" Kian snarled. Capturing her jaw in hand, he slanted his mouth over hers, drew his hips back, and slammed his cock into her again, making her whimper. He ravished her mouth as thoroughly as he did her body, his demanding lips setting her aflame with desire.

Eyes closing in sheer bliss, Willow moaned and cupped his jaw, returning his kiss with equal fervor. His taste was sublime, intoxicating, maddening. She teased his piercings with her tongue before biting his lip. He hissed, and his hand left her jaw to slap down on the mattress beside her as his thrusts grew more powerful.

Pleasured coiled in her belly. He stretched her, filled her, and her sex contracted around him, greedily drawing his cock in. She could feel all of him, even the drag of his piercing along her inner walls.

She wrapped her legs around his hips and pressed her heels into the backs of his thighs, meeting each and every thrust.

But she needed more. *Craved* more.

Dropping her hands from his face, she pressed her palms to his chest and pushed him to the side, forcing him out of her. His eyes widened in surprise, but he didn't resist as he fell onto his back. His cock stood straight, glistening with her essence.

She rolled, throwing her leg over him. Kian's hands were already around her hips, drawing her atop him, the pricks of his sharp nails adding an unexpected thrill to her pleasure. Curling her fingers around the base of his cock, she lowered herself onto him, gasping when he thrust upward. In this position, she took so much more of him.

Willow leaned over Kian, bracing her arms on either side of his head, and undulated her hips. Now he met her every movement, matching her rhythm perfectly. Each stroke drove him deeper than the last and struck a chord in her that sent electric pulses through every nerve in her body.

"Fuck, Willow," he rasped, his fingers digging into her hips. "Everything. Give. Me. Everything."

His lips grazed her nipple before he took it into his mouth. With tongue and teeth, he teased that sensitive flesh, sucking, nipping, licking, worshipping.

Willow closed her eyes, giving herself over to the sensation. Her movements became more urgent, more frenzied, and she felt everything, especially him, so much more intensely than before. Her heart pounded, and her breaths came short and fast.

With a final bite on her breast, Kian released her nipple. "Let me hear you."

Each shove of his cock into her was punctuated by a moan from Willow and a grunt from him. Kian's heat, his solidness, his sounds and touch, comprised her whole universe. There was only him, only the things he made her feel. No guilt, no sadness, no pain. Only the excitement, the fulfillment, of being someone's everything for a little while, of being completely, undeniably wanted.

And she yielded to it all.

She yielded to him.

Willow cried out in sweet agony as rapture blazed through her. The pleasure was pure, all-encompassing, inescapable.

"Kian," she rasped, body locking up as tremors racked her. He tensed in the same instant, inhaling harshly, and his rhythm faltered. She opened her eyes and looked down at him.

His lips were parted, his brow drawn, and his eyes... They seemed to glow an ethereal blue, and she stared into their depths. Willow could feel him—not just his body, but his hunger, his pleasure, his everything. It felt as though part of herself were flowing into Kian, and she was receiving some part of him in return, which nestled, warm and firm, in her chest.

Her climax tore her apart. She threw her head back, eyes snapping shut again, as Kian drove into her with a burst of speed and desperation that only prolonged the pleasure sweeping through her. He growled out his release. She felt a surge of heat bloom within her despite the condom, and her fingers and toes curled into the bedding.

Willow's arms gave out. She collapsed atop him, her cries muffled against his neck as her sex convulsed and her body quaked. One of his hands rose to cradle the back of her head, while the other shifted to her ass, clutching Willow against him as he ground into her. She rode out her orgasm in his embrace, their hearts pounding in unison.

When his hips finally stilled and the intensity of her pleasure faded, Willow experienced the oddest sensation, a contradictory mix of heaviness and lightness, like she couldn't move and yet was completely disconnected from her body, free to float away.

Kian's hand lazily glided up and down her back as his breathing steadied. "I was supposed to give *you* the best night of your life," he murmured, voice thick and gravelly. "Knew you were passionate when I first saw you, Willow, but that fire in you... Fuck."

She opened her eyes and inhaled. The air was heavy with his spicy, carnal fragrance, now mingled the scent of sex.

If only someone saw me as worth keeping.

Four

Willow didn't move, and Kian seemed to be in no hurry for her to get off. He simply held her, stroking her back, with his cock buried deep inside her. She closed her eyes and pressed her nose against his neck. For a moment, she took comfort in his embrace and let herself pretend that this was real, that she truly mattered to the person holding her.

Kian's hand went still, his fingers loosened in her hair, and his body relaxed beneath her.

Willow opened her eyes and slowly lifted her head. His hand fell away from her hair to lie limp upon the bed. She blinked, dumbfounded as she stared down at Kian. His face was turned toward her, eyes closed, features gentle in repose.

He fell asleep?

Her brow furrowed. What was she supposed to do? He...he wasn't supposed to fall asleep! They were supposed to have sex and part ways, that was all.

Well, seems you fucked him into a coma, Willow.

She pressed her lips together to hold in her laughter.

This wasn't supposed to be funny. She needed to leave. But as she gazed down at him, she found it difficult to pull away. He was so...beautiful. In his sleep, he didn't exude that air of confidence that bordered on arrogance. It was like his mask had fallen away. Her fingers itched to trace his features.

What they'd shared had been magical. There was no other word to describe it. It had transcended anything she'd ever experienced, and it had felt so right. *He* felt so right. The way he'd looked at her, touched her, moved inside her... The way her body even now molded to his, her softness against his hardness.

How could something intended as a one-night stand feel so...powerful?

But that was all this was and all it could be. A single night of sex, nothing more. She couldn't allow herself to get tangled up with him. He'd offered sex so freely to Willow, a total stranger, without hesitation. He wasn't someone she should get mixed up with.

Hadn't she already learned her lesson? Her luck with men was terrible. Her relationship with Eli had been the longest by far, but it had still ended the same way as all the others—with her feeling used, disrespected, and hurt.

Tears stung her eyes as she studied Kian's face. Willow had a feeling that if she let herself, she could fall in love with him far too easily.

And he would break my heart.

She needed to leave.

Reaching behind her, Willow took hold of Kian's arm and laid it upon the bed. He didn't stir. She watched him while she lifted her hips, biting her lip as his surprisingly still hard cock slipped out of her, and nearly moaned at the drag of his piercing along her inner walls. God, how could that still feel so good?

He did not wake.

She lifted her leg and climbed off him, moving with such care that she barely allowed herself to breathe until her feet were on the floor. Her legs trembled. The air was cold against her bare skin, and though her pussy still thrummed with the aftermath of what they'd shared, that hollow ache had already returned. Willow pressed a hand to her belly.

Something warm rushed out of her and ran down her inner thighs.

With a frown, she looked down, parted her legs, and wiped at the substance with her finger. It was thick and white, with a faint blue iridescence.

Oh, no. No.

Her gaze darted to Kian's cock.

All that remained of the condom was the ring around the base of his shaft and a torn flap of latex.

Cringing, Willow clenched her fist and whispered, "Fuck."

Fuck, fuck, fuck, fuck!

How could this night get any worse? She was on birth control, so she wasn't too worried about the chances of getting pregnant, but Kian seemed to be in the habit of picking up random strangers to have sex with. What if he carried some type of STD?

Snatching up her clothes, Willow hurried to the bathroom and closed the door as quietly as she could. She flicked on the light, laid her dress and undergarments on the counter, and sat on the toilet with her face buried in her hands as she peed.

Stupid, stupid, stupid. Why did I agree to this? Why didn't I just go home?

Because you were that desperate to feel loved, even if it was just an illusion. Because you just wanted to feel like you mattered for once.

Shame filled her, but she quickly pushed it away. She wouldn't regret what she'd shared with Kian. The condom breaking had been an accident. She'd...she'd just go to the clinic tomorrow and get tested to be safe.

Willow sniffled and plucked a tissue from the box on the counter to wipe her eyes.

After she cleaned herself on the toilet, she washed her hands and face at the sink before straightening to look at herself in the mirror. Her hair was in disarray, her cheeks were flushed, and her lips were swollen and red. Her nipples were dark from the attention they'd received, and there was even a faint bite mark on her breast. She looked like a woman who had been thoroughly fucked.

But at least her eyeliner wings were intact.

Thank God for waterproof makeup.

Willow rolled her eyes. As if that was important.

She took a deep breath, released it slowly, and got dressed. Her panties were cold and damp from her arousal, but there was nothing to be done about that now. She turned off the light and opened the door to peek out.

Kian was exactly as she'd left him.

Willow padded to the bed and retrieved her shoes before making her way toward the exit. The latch clicked, and she froze. When she heard nothing from Kian, she fled into the hall, closing the door quietly behind her.

Leaning her back against it, she squeezed her eyes shut. All she needed was a moment. A moment for her to compose herself, for her heart to slow, for that inner heat to cool. But her legs continued trembling, and an insistent throb pulsed in her core.

Fuck.

Shaking her head, Willow opened her eyes, pushed away from the door, and bent forward to slip on her high heels. As she made her way down the silent hallway, something from deep within urged her to return to Kian. It felt like she was tethered to him, like that line was growing tauter with every step, but she did not stop.

She needed to get away.

41

Willow fished her phone out of her pocket. She scowled when she saw the missed calls, voice mails, and texts from Eli. Anger swept in to block out her other confused emotions. Without checking any of the messages, she blocked his number and scheduled a car service to pick her up. She would have called Jamie, but it was late, and Willow really didn't feel like talking to anyone, not even her best friend. At least, not yet.

By the time Willow stepped out of the hotel, her anger had faded, leaving behind only the hurt and betrayal. She knew the truth—she deserved better, and what had happened was Eli's doing. She wasn't going to fall into that downward spiral of wondering what she could've done differently, of how she could've prevented him from straying. She'd done nothing wrong.

Perhaps the saddest thing about the whole situation was that she couldn't be sure whether she'd really loved Eli...or if she'd just loved the idea of the life she had imagined them sharing.

More and more, it seemed like the healthy, happy relationship she'd always wanted was nothing but a foolish fantasy. After all, it wasn't like her parents had been a shining example of a good marriage. Willow hadn't even known what a good relationship looked like—only that the Crowleys had been far, far off the mark.

The driver that picked her up was thankfully quiet, leaving the music on the stereo to fill the silence. The city streets passed in a blur. Willow had no real sense of where she was, but she didn't care. She could feel herself getting closer to home, and home was the only place that had any chance of providing her with solace. The only place that could act as her sanctuary.

Because it was hers, and hers alone.

Glad Eli dragged his feet whenever I mentioned moving in together.

She tipped the driver generously when they reached her house. He bid her a good night, and she only barely held back a bitter laugh before following the path to her front door. The weight of the world crept just behind her, threatening to crush her, but she hadn't let life hold her down yet. She wasn't about to give up because of one bad night.

Because of her ex-asshole.

Willow let herself in, slammed the door in life's face, and locked the deadbolt. Letting out a heavy sigh, she switched on the lights, removed her shoes, and let them drop to the floor.

Three distinct meows greeted her as Bebe, Remy, and Loki came running over to rub against her legs.

Willow smiled and knelt, scratching behind their ears and running her hands along their backs. "At least I know you guys love me unconditionally. You hungry?"

They looked up at her and meowed some more.

She snorted. "Of course. The way to a cat's heart is through their stomach." Willow chuckled. "Come on."

Rising, she made her way into the kitchen, where she filled the cats' dishes. She stood and listened to the little crunches as they ate. Weariness weighed upon her, but her mind kept returning to that hotel room. She could still feel Kian's hands and mouth on her body, could still feel his cock as it moved in and out of her sex. Could still smell him on her skin. And it only made her yearn for more.

I need to forget him.

Willow left her content kitties and walked to the bathroom connected to her bedroom. Setting her phone on the counter, she turned on the shower and undressed. In the mirror, she glimpsed the bruises forming on her hips—bruises where Kian had clutched her. She lifted a hand to touch them, but forced it away, hurrying into the shower.

Once she was under the hot water, she scrubbed her body, wishing she could wash away the memories of Eli and the pain he had inflicted. A sob escaped her. Shoulders quaking, she rested her forehead on the wall and pressed a hand over her heart as water sluiced down her body. Tears spilled from her eyes.

"I don't want to feel this way anymore. I'm so tired of being hurt."

Tomorrow, she would gather all Eli's things, including any gifts he'd given her, and throw them in the trash. She was done with him. She was done with dating, done with the lies, the deceit, the manipulation, the suffering.

She never wanted her heart to hurt again.

Five

Darkness did not exist behind Kian's eyelids. His consciousness was enveloped in a warm red glow, pulsing soothingly with the slow, steady rhythm of his heart. The afterglow, he'd always called it. The sweet period after feeding that was usually the closest he could come to true pleasure himself.

But it was different this time.

He was adrift in a sea of heat, his body languid, his mind at ease, untethered from reality. That warmth suffused him. It had become him. No body, no soul, just pure, undiluted pleasure. He didn't want to move, didn't have to move. He was wholly satisfied.

Willow...

Her name resonated through his spirit. It left its mark on every bit of him, emblazoned itself on his being. This bliss, this satiation, it was because of her. How had she accomplished what no one else had in all Kian's existence?

The moment he'd seen her in front of Reverb, he'd wanted

her. Something about Willow had called to him. He'd even considered breaking one of his rules and pursuing her despite her clear involvement with the man she'd been walking alongside. Kian had nearly dropped to his knees to thank the Fates when Willow had emerged from the restaurant not fifteen minutes later, alone and vulnerable.

Never under sunlight or starlight had there existed a mortal so beautiful to his eyes, so tempting to his hunger.

A low, distant groan echoed through the warmth cocooning his consciousness. It took him a moment to realize that it had come from his own throat. His body was still there, however far away it felt, and it was still his. But the willpower required to make it move...

Why waste the precious energy he'd been gifted?

To have more.

Yes, that was reason enough.

Not once in four hundred years had he been anything but hungry. Feeding had always abated his hunger, but he'd never once known what it was like to be replete. Not until tonight. And even experiencing it now wouldn't stop him from seeking more. More of Willow, more of her delectable, potent pleasure.

Kian followed a few simple rules when he hunted—never pursue prey with existing romantic partnerships, never feed from the same source twice, never let mortals know his true nature.

But by light and dark, he'd never had anything like Willow. He'd made exceptions for his first rule, hadn't he? He'd fucked couples who had desired a third sexual partner. He'd fed from both at once.

So why not break his second rule? Why not feed from Willow again? After what they'd shared, after experiencing the masterpiece wrought by the joining of their bodies and souls, he doubted she'd resist.

He willed his awareness of his body to return, but his muscles were sluggish and uncooperative. He felt like a lion that had gorged itself on meat. When his hands finally complied with his outlandish request to seek the luscious female he'd taken to bed, they encountered naught but the rumpled comforter to either side of him.

Kian stretched his arms, expanding his search, yet all he found was more bedding.

Only then did he notice the stifling silence of the room. All the sounds that gradually came to his ears were from outside—the *whooshes* of cars passing on the road; the sad, muted wailing of faraway emergency sirens; the muffled voices from a TV turned much too loud somewhere down the hall.

No satisfied sighs. No hums of contentment. No soft, even breathing.

Another groan escaped him, this one from deeper down, on the verge of becoming a growl. The tranquility of his red haze wavered, and shadowy striations broke the glow.

His eyelids fluttered, battling him for having had the audacity to demand they open. With a growl, Kian shed his lingering grogginess and shoved himself into a sitting position. His hair fell over his shoulder and brushed his chest. The sensation was an empty mockery of how it had felt to have Willow's hair sweep across his skin while she rode him, while she moved that enticing body of hers, while she sought greater and greater pleasure.

The orangey glow of the bedside lamp bathed the hotel room. The curtains were closed, the television was off, and the bathroom door stood open, revealing the dark, empty room beyond. Kian's clothes remained on the floor where he'd discarded them, but Willow's were gone.

She was gone.

The clock on the nightstand read four-eighteen A.M.

He bent his knees, rested his arms upon them, and covered his face, massaging his eyes. He'd slept for hours, oblivious to everything around him.

And she was gone.

That didn't make sense. It couldn't be right.

Filling his lungs with air, he stilled. Her sweet fragrance, reminiscent of violets—along with the scent they'd created together—lingered, but it was faint. Too faint. How long had she been gone?

"A night of firsts," he muttered.

He'd never needed sleep, and on the rare occasions during which he'd intentionally slumbered, it had always been briefly and lightly, and only to walk through his memories. Yet what need had Kian to wander such reveries when true pleasure could only be found here in the present?

Still, after fucking Willow... It hadn't been a choice. He'd fallen asleep as quickly and deeply as though she'd invoked his true name and commanded it of him.

But she was mortal, and he'd granted her no such power over him. He never would. Whatever had happened had been a result of the sustenance she'd provided. An aftereffect of her intoxicating, ambrosial pleasure.

This role reversal was unprecedented. He was always the one who snuck out in the dead of night while his latest human dreamt of the pleasure he'd lavished upon them. The mortals he'd fed from had always craved more, and some had become unpleasantly clingy. Hence rule two, which existed to prevent such attachments from growing. Human lives were fleeting and inconsequential. Their only value to Kian lay in the sustenance they could provide.

In their lust.

He couldn't recall a single mortal who'd left him like this. Who'd crept away in the middle of the night without a word, who'd shrugged off his charm so wholly. And he'd certainly never fallen asleep after the act, had certainly never been so wholly unaware of his surroundings that he wouldn't have noticed a female sliding herself off his cock and walking away.

What made Willow different? What was the strange tightness in his chest that had been created by her absence?

Kian swept his hair back and shoved himself off the bed. There was no point in exploring such thoughts. After centuries of life, new experiences were infrequent. Best to view the night as a welcome break in his routine, a fortuitous occurrence that had shattered the monotony of all the years he'd spent hunting and feeding.

Willow...

His cock throbbed at the memory of being sheathed in her heat. He tipped his head back and clasped a hand around his shaft only to pause.

The condom was still there—or the remnants of it, anyway. Dropping his gaze, he slid off the stretchy ring and held it up, staring at the torn latex dangling from his fingers. It must have broken while he was still inside her without either of them noticing.

It was only for her peace of mind, anyway.

He couldn't reproduce with mortals unless he willed it, and there were no diseases that could be transmitted between his kind and humans. But he didn't discard it right away. Instead, he lifted it higher, until it was in front of his face, and inhaled.

His eyelids fell shut as the scent of her essence filled his nose. His shaft hardened so swiftly and fully that it pained him, wrenching a groan from his throat. He clamped a fist around his cock again and squeezed, hoping to alleviate the pressure, to dam the sudden flood of want that swelled within him.

A wild urge sparked in his mind.

Find her. Make her mine.

She is mine.

This craving, this yearning, he'd never felt it before. It was at once the same as his usual hunger and yet entirely different. So much deeper and stronger, so much more compelling. He'd always needed to feed, had always been driven to hunt, but it had never been about his pleasure. It had been a matter of survival.

But he was full now. Full...and yet he craved Willow.

He bared his teeth and tightened his grip.

How would he even find her? He purposely learned as little as he could about the mortals he fed from. All he needed were their desires—and he sensed those naturally. He had no reason to get to know humans or bond with them. All they were meant to share was a moment of passion, of pleasure, before he vanished.

He knew only that her relationship had fallen apart earlier, and that her first name was Willow. She'd not lied about either; he'd felt the power when she'd given him her name, had recognized it as part of her true name. But a mortal's true name did not hold power over them like a fae's did, and a first name was hardly enough to find her in a city of hundreds of thousands. Why go through the trouble?

Kian didn't need her. She was just another mortal. Another vessel of pleasure from which he'd drunk. There'd been countless others before her, and there would be countless more after. For now, he'd hold onto what she'd given him, but he'd forget her soon enough.

Just like he forgot all of them. Their faces and names bled together in his memory, weaving a tapestry of conquests worth recalling only because of the precious energy he'd taken from them, because their lifeforce had briefly sustained him.

Soon enough, Willow's name would be another forgotten name. Her face, another forgotten face.

Still, if he ever saw her again... Perhaps he wouldn't say no to another fuck. How could he give up a second chance at this? This fullness, this contentment, this *fire*?

Releasing his cock, he tossed the condom into the trash and

stretched his limbs. He allowed his glamour to fall, spreading his wings behind him and rolling his shoulders and neck, savoring the feel of power flowing through his body. He felt more himself than he had in ages.

Thank you, Willow.

The tips of his wings brushed the ceiling before he let them dissipate, drawing their magical essence back into himself. He paused to snatch up his clothing before striding to the bathroom and starting the shower.

Willow remained at the forefront of his mind as he stood beneath the steaming water, and his cock responded accordingly. In his mind's eye, he saw her delicious body, watched her move, watched her passion bloom. And he felt whispers of her touch everywhere on his skin.

Heat flared in his soul, spreading outward to permeate him, and he embraced it. Why fight? Why not enjoy a last bit of pleasure before the memory of her faded?

Kian took hold of himself and pumped his fist along his shaft. Ripples of pleasure arced through him, and he let out a shuddering breath. He envisioned her bright green eyes, so expressive, so full of that deep, sensual light. He envisioned her rounded hips, and his hands caressing her giving flesh. He envisioned her pink cunt, so wet and eager for him.

His fist moved faster and faster, and his breaths grew short and harsh. It was nothing like the real thing, nothing like her, nowhere close, but he couldn't stop himself. Even if she wasn't here, he'd take what he could from her.

Kian's knees wobbled, and his hips bucked as his seed burst out. He slapped a hand on the wall to steady himself. Streams of cum spurted out to swirl around the drain before being swept away, and she flashed in his mind with each—her face, her perfume, her heat, her everything.

He huffed, spraying water from his lips, and stood motionless as the throbbing in his cock eased. For the first time in his long life, he was stricken with a new desire.

It was foolish, pointless, but ultimately harmless.

He didn't want to forget Willow.

At least not so soon.

Six

High-pitched screams blared from the surround sound speakers as the masked killer brought the knife down upon the woman again and again, but Willow was only vaguely aware of what was happening on the screen. Truthfully, she'd spaced out most of the movie, and wouldn't have been able to say with any confidence what had happened in it for the last half hour.

Which royally sucked, because she loved horror movies.

She ran her hand over Remy's fur. The gray tabby was curled up in her lap, only slightly more oblivious to the screams than Willow.

It was just... It'd already been a week since Willow's breakup with Eli. In that time, she'd thrown away everything of his she'd been able to find—every piece of clothing he'd forgotten at her place, every gift, every picture. It had been cathartic.

Eli had stopped by her house two days after the breakup to try to explain himself, telling her how much he loved her and wanted to keep her. She'd shoved him out the door and slammed it in his face. Thankfully, he'd left without another word.

Willow had broken down and cried afterward. All Eli had proved was that he'd never really cared about her feelings, wants, or dreams. That she had just been a convenient booty call.

But despite all that, Eli hadn't often occupied her thoughts over the week.

Her mind had been on Kian.

Just like it was now.

She'd replayed their time together over and over in her head during the days and had dreamed about it at night.

Though she'd been uncharacteristically rash in agreeing to have sex with him, she had no regrets. That night with Kian had been magical. To have felt so adored, worshipped, and loved, even for that brief while, had been worth it.

If only those feelings had been real.

Willow touched her fingers to her mouth, recalling the feel of Kian's lips, their heat, their firmness, and the fleeting hints of cold from the metal of his piercings. Recalling his taste. God, how could a man's kiss taste so good?

"Okay, what kind of look is that?" Jamie asked, startling Willow out of her thoughts. "Because you sure as hell should not be making that kind of dreamy-eyed face while that poor woman is getting her guts ripped out."

Cheeks warming, Willow looked at her friend and tucked the blanket more snugly around herself. The action disturbed Remy enough that he jumped off the couch and stretched before plopping down next to Bebe on the floor.

Jamie sat on the opposite end of the couch, wrapped in her own blanket with Loki on her lap. She wore black and green plaid pajamas with her long, curly red hair woven into two braids that lay over her shoulders. Willow's own hair was drawn up into a messy bun, but instead of a two-piece PJ set, she was wearing her pink cat onesie.

Because you were never too old to wear a onesie, damn it.

It was a Friday night. Jamie had Saturday off, and though Willow had a booking tomorrow, her client wouldn't arrive until the afternoon. So, Jamie had offered to have a sleepover to help get Willow's mind off her shitty ex-boyfriend.

Except Willow hadn't yet mentioned that she wasn't thinking about Eli...

Jamie grinned. "Unless you're picturing Eli getting his guts ripped out, because if that's the case..."

Shaking her head, Willow laughed. "No. No, I...wasn't imagining that."

"Too bad." Jamie shifted to better face Willow. Loki didn't budge, even when Jamie settled her hands in her lap. "Okay, so if you're not dreaming about revenge, what's up?"

Willow bit the inside of her cheek. She hadn't told Jamie about Kian yet. She'd wanted to keep Kian and her night with him to herself, at least for a little while. "I have something to tell you. The night that I broke up with Eli, after I left Eden...I met someone."

Jamie's eyebrows rose. "You met someone?"

"I saw him before I went into the restaurant with Eli, and... I don't know, Jamie, I just felt something when our eyes met. I know it seems crazy, and it sounds even more ridiculous as I'm saying it out loud now, but it was like something just....just clicked into place. Like I knew him. Like I've always known him. And I felt..."

"What did you feel?"

Willow pressed a hand to her chest. Her heart thumped against her palm as her face heated. "Turned on."

Jamie laughed. "Wow. So lust at first sight, huh?"

That was what Willow had thought. Now, she wasn't so sure, especially after their night together. It'd felt like so much more than that. But it didn't matter what they'd shared, because one night was all it would ever be—a single night of passion, a memory that Willow would never forget.

Willow tucked loose wisps of her hair behind her ear. "I felt so horrible about it. I was walking with Eli, literally holding his hand, yet there I was, getting aroused by a complete stranger."

"There's nothing wrong with finding someone attractive." Jamie nudged Willow's foot with her own. "I take it this guy was hot?"

Willow grinned. "Really, really hot. He was tall and had long white hair. He also had piercings in his ears and lips, and black painted nails. Long, pointed nails." And those otherworldly blue eyes...

"Like...a vampire?"

Willow laughed. "No, he wasn't a vampire. But he was definitely gothic."

"So when you say you *met* him...?"

"It was after I left the restaurant. I was standing on the bridge by myself, ugly crying for all the world to see, when Kian approached me."

"Kian, huh?" Jamie snickered. "Even his name is hot."

Willow drew in a deep breath. She just needed to say it, to get it out. The words escaped her in a rush. "We had sex."

Jamie's eyes widened as she stared at Willow. "You...you what?"

"Please don't judge me." Willow dropped her gaze to her lap and wrung her hands. "I was hurt and feeling so alone, and he... He offered me a night of pleasure. He didn't dress it up as anything more than that, didn't promise anything other than to make me feel good, didn't force anything on me. I just wanted it, Jamie. I wanted it so badly. I wanted *him*. So I took him up on his offer. And it was...more than words could describe."

"First," Jamie said, bringing Willow's attention back to her, "I would never judge you for having sex with whoever you want. But

I will say this—what the hell, Willow? You went off with a stranger you just met? You could have been kidnapped. You could have been killed!"

Willow grimaced. "The thought crossed my mind. I even asked him."

Jamie rolled her eyes and threw her hands up. "Yeah, because he totally would have told you the truth if he planned to do that."

"I know, I know. It wasn't the smartest moment of my life. But...I don't regret it."

"Danger and reckless choices aside..." Jamie playfully nudged Willow's foot again, grinning. "You go girl!"

Loki started and leapt down from Jamie's lap with a feline huff. He cast her a glare as he sauntered over to the other cats, and then slowly lay on the floor with his backside toward Jamie.

"Sorry, your majesty," Jamie said.

The cat very pointedly did not look at her again.

She shook her head. "Anyway, Willow, when are you going to see this guy again?"

Willow smiled, albeit a little sadly. "I'm not. It was a one-night stand."

Jamie snorted. "You had the best sex of your life, and you're just gonna let that man walk away?" She grabbed one of the couch pillows and tossed it at Willow.

Willow caught the pillow before it could strike her in the face. "Kian wasn't interested in anything more. Also"—she threw the pillow back at Jamie, who batted it aside—"it's only been a week since I broke up with my long-term boyfriend."

"So?"

"I'm not ready for another relationship, Jamie." Willow looked down and picked at her blanket as her eyes filled with tears. "As shitty as Eli was, he still hurt me. After having one failed relationship after another... I'm emotionally exhausted. I just... I just wish there was a guy out there who wouldn't betray me. Who loved me for me."

"Hey, hey. Don't cry." Jamie crawled across the sofa and put her arms around Willow. "It's okay. There's someone out there for you. You just haven't met them yet. But you will when the time is right, and they will cherish you like you deserve to be cherished." She tightened her embrace, and Willow returned the hug.

"Thanks, Jamie."

And yet as Willow leaned against her friend, she couldn't silence the thought nagging at the back of her mind. It was irrational, silly, exactly the kind of thought that should've made her doubt her own sanity.

What if Kian *had* been the one for her, and their chance for something more had been given up for that single night of passion and pleasure?

"After all you've been through, Willow, look at you," Jamie said. "You're not just surviving, you're thriving, right? This is your chance to take your life back after the shit Eli did."

Smiling, Willow drew back and wiped her eyes. "You're right. I have you, I have these furballs, and I have my studio."

"And who needs a man when you have a vibrator?"

Willow gave Jamie a shove but couldn't stop herself from laughing.

She decided that maybe it was best not to mention that Kian had been better than any vibrator she'd ever owned.

Seven

L ust thickened the air in the nightclub. Kian felt as though he could reach out and touch it, and he nearly tasted it upon his tongue. It cast everything in a faint red haze that blended with the club's moody blue lighting to fill his vision with shades of purple.

Perhaps this place had been a poor choice. The last color he needed to see everywhere he looked was purple...

No. He'd come here because it was a rich, reliable hunting ground. A place where he was all but guaranteed sustenance. When humans gathered like this and gave themselves over to music, drinks, and drugs, he often didn't even need to use his charm to get what he wanted from them. Seduction became a simple as a knowing look and an inviting smile. This should have been effortless.

From the vantage of his elevated booth, he scanned the crowd, seeking the right target. He couldn't afford to be picky tonight, couldn't afford to expend energy on a prolonged seduction. He needed to feed, and he needed to do so soon. Very soon.

For six days after fucking Willow, he'd been satiated. On the seventh day, he'd felt a vague sense of hollowness, a nagging ache. Over the next week, that ache had expanded at an alarming rate. More alarming still was that he'd been unable to draw energy from anyone to assuage that hunger. The pain was becoming unbearable, the hunger impossible to ignore. This void within him would eventually grow too vast.

And when it inevitably collapsed upon itself, it would destroy Kian in the process.

He was fucking starving.

How the fuck was an immortal being *starving*?

His eyes settled upon a dark-haired woman in a short, tight purple dress.

Her.

That dress couldn't compare to the one Willow had worn two weeks ago. Nothing would look as good on anyone as that dress had looked on her.

Not a purple dress, he growled in his mind. *It's red. Just the fucking lighting.*

This woman was not Willow. She was tall and thin, whereas Willow was abundant with curves. They were nothing alike.

Even through the cloud of desire swirling around the woman, he detected a hint of desperation in her, a touch of loneliness that she'd undoubtedly come here to combat. That was exactly what he needed for a quick feeding.

He fixed his gaze on the woman and sent out a wave of power. It made the lusty haze ripple around him, briefly heightening his awareness of it. Then the magic reached her, and he coiled it around her desires, sinking it deep into her need for companionship, into her hunger for sex.

The woman's eyes widened and snapped to Kian.

He forced that practiced smirk onto his lips. A desirous spark lit in the woman's eyes, and she smoothed her hands down her sides.

Kian crooked a finger, beckoning her, sending out a little more of his magic with the gesture.

She walked toward him. With her every step, he felt her desire realigning, redirecting toward him. Kian was exactly what she wanted, and she'd already hit that heady moment during which her raw, impulsive desire for him had superseded everything else. He was the only thing she could see for now. All her other dreams, her other wants, would sleep for a time.

"Like what you see?" he asked as she drew close.

The woman raked her gaze over him, wet her lips with her tongue, and nodded. He turned his body toward her without rising, fighting back the images threatening to overtake his mind —images of Willow and their too brief time together, which always came with the reminder that no one else could compare.

He didn't need anyone to compare to her, he just needed to fucking feed!

Stopping immediately in front of him, the woman reached forward. One of her hands grasped the lapel of his coat and tugged it aside. She pressed the other over his chest, which was partially exposed by his unbuttoned shirt.

"Wow," she breathed.

"Even better without clothes." Kian reached down and unfasted another button on his shirt, drawing her attention lower.

The heat of her want bathed Kian as she slid her hand under his shirt and down his abdomen. He already smelled her arousal, which held a hint of bitterness. It was...unappealing. Just as unappealing as the scents of every man and woman he'd tried to feed from in the last week.

Get the fuck over it and do what needs to be done, Kian!

"You don't waste any time, do you?" she asked.

"Why wait?" he replied, lacing his words with more charm as he slipped an arm around her waist.

The woman's eyes darkened further. The tips of her fingers

grazed the flesh just above the waist of his pants. He felt the warmth of her skin, its softness, felt the trembling need in her touch. He even felt her racing pulse. But he didn't feel excited.

Her desire alone, being so potent, should've been enough. His cock should've been so hard that it hurt. He should've been ready to take her right here, right now. But his body refused to cooperate. Refused to do its damned job.

Willow's touch had brought Kian's skin to life. Her passion had filled him with fire unlike he'd ever experienced, had—

She needs to get out of my fucking head!

The woman's smile tilted playfully. "A man who knows what he wants?"

"Who knows what he wants and takes it."

You're drowning yourself in a sea of lies, Kian.

Growling, he tugged the woman close. She let out a cry that was far more thrilled than surprised and shifted her legs up, straddling his lap. Her gaze dropped to his lips.

"God, you're gorgeous." Delving her hands into his hair, she smashed her mouth against Kian's. Her dress rode up her thighs as she ground her pelvis against him.

His insides twisted, and an unpleasant chill swept over his skin.

Pleasure, the very thing he sought, pulsed from the woman. But it was soured. It stroked his skin and scraped against his lifeforce, taunting him, intensifying his discomfort. His muscles tensed. Was this what mortals called *nausea?*

Mistaking his reaction as Kian enjoying himself, the woman intensified her movements. She didn't seem to notice how onesided the kiss was.

Or that his cock was unresponsive.

He turned all his willpower toward her pleasure. Even if he wasn't necessarily causing it, he could still feed. There was always a bit of residual pleasure for him to consume when mortals were enjoying themselves, though it wasn't potent enough to serve as real sustenance. Carnal pleasure was the strongest—just like this woman was creating for herself.

But all his concentration was not enough. He could not take in the energy this woman emitted. His magic could not grasp it, could not absorb it.

She was dry humping herself to climax. That should've been a feast for him. But he received nothing. Nothing but this strange, worrying feeling of...of illness. Of wrongness. He forced himself to move, to reciprocate. That excited the female further—and kindled secondhand desire in nearby onlookers—yet it did not change Kian's situation.

He couldn't absorb that much-needed sustenance. And though the woman's pleasure was laced with unpleasant notes, he would've gladly taken all of it just to dull his hunger.

The same thing had happened yesterday, and the day before, and the day before that. Every time he'd tried to feed in the two weeks since he'd fucked the purple-haired woman he'd met on Central Boulevard, he'd failed.

What had Willow done to him?

Frustration crackled through his muscles in a painful electric current, worsened by the sour chill of his repulsion. This never happened to him. He'd fed off humans of all sorts during his time, had always been attracted to them because it was their desire that appealed to him. He had no preference when it came to appearance or gender, seeking only potential—the potential for pleasure. This woman was attractive, passionate, and eager to feel good.

And he wanted absolutely nothing more to do with her. He couldn't bear another moment of this.

With a snarl, Kian tore his mouth away from the woman's and stood, shoving her off his lap. His hip bumped the table, rattling the glasses atop it. She fell to the floor with a startled gasp.

He'd dismissed countless sexual partners through the years,

but not before they'd been satisfied. Not before he'd taken what he needed from them. It had all changed after his night with Willow. Before her, he'd never felt this sickness when attempting to feed. Before her, his skin had never crawled at the thought of someone touching him.

His hair hung in his face. He swept it back with a quick, harsh gesture, turned, and stalked away. The woman called to him, but Kian ignored her.

The desire and lust radiating from the crowd as he hurried toward the door was intolerable. It was like a chorus of demons torturing him with their hellish song, dangling food just out of his reach as he starved to death.

His gut churned and clenched. Bitter fire roiled within him, possessing an acidic sting. The combination of the cold void and the scorching flames was too much to handle.

All the grace and ease with which he normally moved amongst mortals vanished. He pushed and shouldered people aside, battling for every inch of progress, and offered no apologies. They were meant to be his prey, each and every one of them, but now they'd become only sources of torment.

"Hey." A human stepped in front of Kian, planting a hand on his chest. He was about as tall as Kian, but carried at least fifty pounds more muscle, most of which seemed to be concentrated in his arms, shoulders, and chest. His black shirt had a single word printed on it. *Security.*

"Out of my way," Kian growled, pushing forward.

The bouncer shook his head and braced his feet, halting Kian's advance. "You the one that threw a woman onto the floor? We need to have a chat."

"Not in the fucking mood."

"I wasn't asking." The man grasped Kian's coat.

Kian curled his hands into fists and gritted his teeth. He wasn't an aggressive being by nature, but being provoked, especially now... These humans didn't know what strength was. They didn't understand just how outclassed they were.

He clamped his hand on the bouncer's wrist. "Neither was I."

A tingle raced up Kian's spine. The sensation blossomed at the base of his skull, triggering every sense these mortals didn't possess.

Magic. Powerful magic. And it was close.

How had he missed it before now?

His brow furrowed, and his eyes darted from side to side, searching for the source of that power—another fae.

Another incubus.

A hand settled on the big human's shoulder. One of its long, strong fingers was adorned with a thick gold ring.

"Just a misunderstanding, I'm sure," said the newcomer, his voice deep, silky, laced with charm.

Kian's muscles tensed; he recognized that voice, and though the magic wasn't directed at him, he felt its potency. Even were he not in his weakened state, he doubted he could ever match it.

The human relaxed, eyebrows rising as he tilted his head. "Yeah. It was."

"Good," the newcomer said. "I'm sure you have other matters to attend."

Nodding, the bouncer released his hold. As soon as Kian let go of his wrist, the man dropped his hand, turned, and wandered away.

The newcomer filled the vacated space. He was tall, with short, tousled black hair and the shadow of a beard complimenting his chiseled features. Angled eyebrows rested over his intense gray eyes.

He wore a gray modern suit, the same shade as his eyes, with a black button down beneath, but no tie. As he stood there and studied Kian, he seemed the epitome of effortless elegance and style. He reached forward with both hands and took gentle hold of Kian's coat, straightening it.

"Barrow," Kian grated, unease keeping his body taut.

"Barrow?" The fae laughed, eyes gleaming with dangerous mirth. "Haven't used that name in a long time, Pale One. Lately it's Lachlan, though you're always welcome to call me your prince. What are you going by these days?"

There was no compulsion here. Lachlan hadn't turned his charm toward Kian, but magic radiated from him like heat from a furnace.

"Kian."

Lachlan grinned, displaying straight, white teeth that were predatory despite appearing so human. "You're not looking so good at the moment are you, Kian?"

A growl nearly escaped Kian's throat. "Bit of a dry spell lately."

Those sharp gray eyes, still holding their amusement, looked past Kian, sweeping over the crowd. "Oh? How unfortunate. This city has proven bountiful for me."

Grasping the sides of his coat, Kian stepped back, breaking Lachlan's loose hold. "I'll leave you to it, then."

He stepped past the other fae, only to be stopped by Lachlan's hand against his chest.

The dark-haired incubus leaned close. His scent, a blend of oiled leather, spice, and musk, washed over Kian. "By right, Pale One, I could claim you. By right, I could demand your loyalty, your obedience. And by might, I could *take* it."

Kian held himself still, battling the violent urges lingering within him, battling his discomfort, battling the seed of fear that had taken root in his gut. Fae of all sorts were resistant to the charm of incubi and succubae, but not immune. And Lachlan's charm was the most potent Kian had ever encountered.

He'd resisted it before. How long would he last now? How

quickly would Kian's willpower crumble under the weight of that magic, especially while he was so drained?

"When I brought you to the Americas all those years ago, it was not so you could run free like a wild beast," Lachlan continued. "You were meant to be at my side, to stand with this realm's new king. To serve as my right hand."

"I prefer our current arrangement, in which you fuck off and let me be," Kian said.

Lachlan's fingers flexed, claws pricking Kian's chest. "Such disrespect. Being in the mortal realm does not excuse you from honoring your betters, Pale One. It does not protect you from the consequences of your insults."

Kian turned his face toward Lachlan's. "Forgive me, Hollow Prince. I'm just a bit moody when I'm hungry."

The other fae scowled, and crimson heat sparked in his eyes. The magic pulsing from him quaked, rocking Kian to his core.

Kian clenched his jaw. His heart thumped, and his insides twisted. He could still taste the female from earlier, and her smell lingered in his nose, layered beneath Lachlan's powerful scent. The humans in the club continued dancing, drinking, and talking, pumping their desire into the air.

All that sustenance surrounding him and yet completely out of reach. All Lachlan's magic bearing down on him, reminding him of his current weakness.

"I've so many other uses for that clever tongue of yours," Lachlan said, voice husky and eyes darkening as they dropped to Kian's mouth. "I'm not unsympathetic to your plight, Pale One, despite your disrespect. I have quite a collection, and I'm willing to share. Any type of mortal you could imagine, all obedient. They'll do anything I command. All you must do is ask it of me."

Amongst the fae, nothing was offered freely, nothing was given without a price. There was no help, only trade. And the more desperate one was, the more lopsided the exchange tended to be.

Lachlan, who styled himself king of the mortal realm, had asked a great deal of Kian in the past. How much more could he possibly want now?

Everything. He wants everything.

Pleasure had always been Kian's food of choice. Invigorating and sweet, and so, so easy to draw from mortals in little bursts. But not all his kind preferred pleasure. Some feasted upon darker things. Some gorged themselves by inflicting suffering.

Kian smiled. "Afraid I'll have to pass, Lachlan. Our tastes simply aren't compatible, and I'm sure the mortals in your collection have already been soured by the fear you wrench from them."

"Yes, I recall your objections." Lachlan's eyes searched Kian's. "Yet look at us now, Pale One. Who stands strong as an oak, and who dangles, weak as a leaf dying on the branch? What good have your foolish morals done you?"

"As much good as your ambitions have done you, Hollow Prince. Tell me, how fares your kingdom?"

A shadow fell over Lachlan's features, turning the mirth lingering in his eyes into something far more sinister. "Sometimes I wonder, Pale One, if you desire my wrath. If you crave my retribution. Seek me out when you are ready to learn the error of your ways." He patted Kian's chest with a gentleness that bristled with threat. "Until then, remember the accord. Watch for my mark, for those mortals who bear it are mine and mine alone. I look forward to our inevitable lessons."

Kian quirked a brow. "Do you mean to teach me how to live in delusion, Lachlan?"

Lachlan eased back, sweeping his gaze over Kian from top to bottom, and smirked. "No. You've always demonstrated a particular talent for that." He slapped Kian on the shoulder. "Happy hunting, Kian. I'm certain your luck will improve eventually."

Then Lachlan withdrew, slipping into the crowd. The power Kian sensed from him didn't diminish. Why would it have? Lachlan was undoubtedly making use of his charm, gathering mortals to himself like moths to a flame.

Kian's ragged breaths clawed in and out of his lungs, and the knot inside him grew tighter and heavier. What the fuck was wrong with him? How distracted was he that he'd missed the approach of a fae like Lachlan, who was strong enough—and arrogant enough—to flaunt his power? It was especially troubling to have not immediately recognized the unique signature of that magic, which he'd grown all too familiar with over the long years he'd spent in the mortal realm. He should've sensed Lachlan from a fucking mile away.

Lachlan claimed that royal blood flowed in his veins, that he was the bastard offspring of a fae prince and a succubus. No one knew the truth, though given the raw strength of Lachlan's magic, Kian was inclined to believe the story.

Now that Lachlan had moved on, everything else came back to Kian—the pounding music, the lust and abandon of the mortal revelers, the stench of alcohol, sweat, and a hundred different perfumes and colognes.

Kian needed to leave. Now.

He hurried to the exit and burst through the door.

The cool night air did nothing to alleviate his discomfort. He drew up the collar of his coat and set off along the street. The relentless bass beat from the nightclub followed him for much too long, unwilling to let him forget so soon.

His feet carried him away from the club, away from his latest failure, through increasingly dark, deserted areas. He crossed poorly lit parking lots, followed lonely side streets, and cut through narrow alleys. But part of him knew he would never get far enough, knew he couldn't escape the truth. Running would not change the situation.

Pain rippled through him, emanating from his personal void. Kian curled his hands into fists and sped his pace. His claws bit into his palms, but the physical hurt did nothing to dull the anguish permeating his lifeforce.

Kian was accustomed to feeding daily. When necessary, he'd been able to endure two or three days between feedings before that emptiness compelled him to hunt again. That was how it had been for four hundred years.

Yet the energy he'd received from Willow had sustained him for six days. Six days of satisfaction, of fullness, six days of freedom from that perpetual hunger. He'd not once had the desire to feed during that time, and he hadn't even tried.

Alarms should've been blaring in his mind by the fourth morning. He should've known something was amiss. Though he'd sensed nothing strange from Willow, the essence he'd drawn from her had been so potent that he'd begun to question whether she was human at all.

He'd tried many, many times to feed in the eight days since his hunger had returned, but he'd been unable to draw anything from the mortals he'd seduced. He hadn't even been able to have sex. His body had repeatedly refused to cooperate.

The only time his cock stirred was when he found himself reminiscing about Willow. When he imagined her face, her eyes, her hair, when he imagined her body. When he recalled the way she felt, both outside and inside, in body and in spirit. When he remembered the way her desire and pleasure had pierced straight to his core and lodged there...

He pressed a hand over his crotch, grating out a curse as his cock stiffened. Just the fucking thought of her was enough to get him going. But the moment he touched another person—or the moment they touched him—it was gone.

Sex was his purpose, and the pleasure he provided generated his sustenance. He'd never call it selfless, as it never was, but he only took what was rightfully his. He only benefited from the fruits of his own labor. Though the actions of incubi like Lachlan had inspired the human legends about soul-sucking monsters who would drain the life out of their victims, Kian had never taken enough to harm anyone. His prey suffered no ill effects.

Save those caused by the best fuck of their lives vanishing during the night and never reappearing.

"That what this is?" he growled, kicking a piece of trash to the curb before angling his head back. Despite the interference from the city lights, he could see the stars, countless twinkling points scattered across a backdrop of deep blue, violet, and indigo. "Divine fucking retribution? Time for me to know what it feels like?"

And worse, there was another incubus in the city, prowling the same hunting grounds as Kian.

Not just any incubus.

An older, stronger fae, who'd long sought Kian's submission. A fae who had sensed Kian's weakness.

Lachlan, like the fae royals from whom he claimed descent, exploited any vulnerability he could find in those around him, mortal and immortal alike. He'd taken advantage of young Kian's naivety centuries ago, when Kian had only just crossed into this realm. He would absolutely seek to use Kian's current state as a tool for control and manipulation if given the chance. Lachlan was the sort who always got what he wanted eventually, driven by his own sense of entitlement and superiority.

If Lachlan had pressed—if he'd used the fullness of his power —he very likely could've forced Kian's surrender any time he liked. It would've been a struggle, undoubtedly, but Kian had felt enough of that magic to understand that it was as vast and deep as an ocean.

Yet for all his haughtiness, Lachlan had never gone that far. He wanted Kian, that much was clear, but it seemed he wanted

Kian to submit of his own free will. Whether it was a matter of pride or a desire for a challenge made no difference. The longer Kian had refused, the longer he had resisted, the more determined Lachlan had become.

Decades apart had not been enough to cure him of his fixation on Kian.

For what were decades to timeless beings?

It was a precarious position for Kian to be placed in, but still not the most pressing of his problems.

Nothing else would matter if he couldn't feed.

All the people I've fucked, and now fate is fucking me.

Teeth bared, he shook his head. "No. No, I will not suffer because of what I am. Predator and prey, that's my relationship to humanity. And they should be damned ecstatic that I'm not one of the ones that actually fucking eats them!"

Talking to yourself now, are you? That hunger sure is taking its toll...

You know what you want. Know what you need.

Of course he knew. He needed to feed. Immortals weren't supposed to starve to death. They weren't supposed to experience this slow but undeniable breakdown, weren't supposed to face the possibility that their time was limited. Immortal was supposed to mean *for fucking ever.*

Stop playing the fool, Kian. You know *what you need.*

Lowering his gaze, he thrust his hands into his pockets and kept walking with his jaw clenched. "Not going to happen."

Gods, how he wished it was simply a matter of willpower. How he wished his struggle was merely against the idea of being tied down, of being dependent upon a human. The truth was much harder to accept.

He needed Willow. And he couldn't have her because he couldn't find her. He didn't know her last name, her profession, didn't know where she lived. He had no idea what she did in her free time. All he knew was that she was fucking gorgeous and that she'd flipped his promise around on him.

She had been the best sex of *his* life.

Four hundred years of fucking, and she'd blown it all away in a single night.

When his thoughts wandered, it was Willow who dominated them. When he slept—which was happening with disturbing frequency as his hunger intensified—he dreamed of her. Not even slumber provided him any respite. Her face was the first thing in his mind when he woke, and it was the last thing there before he succumbed to hunger induced exhaustion.

She'd cursed him. Somehow, that little mortal with the purple hair and alluring curves had placed a powerful curse on him, and now he could think of nothing but her. Now he could enjoy nothing but her.

Was there inhuman blood in her ancestry, or was she simply more than she appeared?

No. I would've sensed something. Would've tasted something.

But if she was only human, what did that say of him? Kian, who'd seduced and fed off mortals for most of his existence, had fallen under the spell of a woman who, despite her broken heart, despite her sorrow and pain, despite her loneliness and longing, had ultimately shrugged off his influence. She'd been the one to walk away. She'd been the one to leave *him* wanting.

He halted his steps and drew in a deep breath. Part of him longed for the sting of icy winter air, for the withering summer heat of the desert, for any extreme to suppress his feelings. Yet he knew at heart that no such distraction would work.

Kian lifted his head and glanced around. His heart stuttered when he realized where he was, when he understood where instinct had carried him during his aimless escape from the nightclub.

This was the bridge where he'd first spoken to Willow. He'd

walked dozens of blocks to return to the place where all his troubles had begun.

Hands trembling, he stepped to the railing and leaned on it, looking down. The reflections on the river's surface weren't nearly so vibrant tonight, weren't nearly so breathtaking, and he knew it was because of her absence. She'd granted the sight its beauty.

No, that wasn't quite right. She'd been the source of all beauty that night.

"This is where you agreed to be mine for one night," he rasped, squeezing the railing hard enough for his claws to scrape the metal. Kian closed his eyes, bared his clenched teeth, and let out a long, harsh breath. He almost swore he could smell her on the breeze, but no. That was his imagination, joining in with the rest of the universe to ensure he was suitably tormented.

Her laughter rose from his memory, ghostly and distant. Not mocking or malicious, not mean-spirited. It was simple. Delightful. As clear and pure an expression of amusement as there had ever been or could ever be.

Kian would hear it again with his own ears. He would taste her lips, her tongue, her flesh, would drink from her essence both of body and soul. He would hold her as they moved in unison, and he would ensure her pleasure was so immense that her mind would shatter. And he would feast upon that pleasure. He would gorge himself upon it. There was no choice in the matter.

Feed from Willow...or die this prolonged, agonizing death.

No more rest, no more sleep, no more futile attempts at seduction and feeding. Everything in him, all the strength and magic he had left, would be turned toward finding her.

Kian opened his eyes. "Sorry, Violet. One night wasn't enough. You're still mine."

Eight

~~~

The midday sun blazed down on Kian. It wasn't particularly hot, but gods was it bright. Even with the hood of his overcoat up and his eyes slitted, the light was barely tolerable. Each step annihilated a little more of his fading strength, but he kept walking at a steady pace, forcing his pained eyes to scan his surroundings. Every storefront, every restaurant, every car, the face of every pedestrian, none of it could be allowed to escape his notice.

Chance had brought him to Willow once. He'd given it every fucking opportunity to do so again over the last six days.

He'd been alive for more than four centuries. How was it possible for six days to have felt like a lifetime? How could his perception of time have been so drastically warped?

How could it be so fucking hard to find a single human?

Humans bustled along Memoree's streets, coming and going from various eateries. Lunch time, they called it. He'd enjoyed a midday feeding every now and then, though nighttime hunts had always been the most bountiful.

He'd spent his days scouring Central Boulevard, starting at

Eden and working his way outward. He'd been desperate enough to ask after Willow on several occasions, but such inquiries had produced no useful information. Most of the people he'd questioned had reacted to him with a strange blend of confusion and attraction. He'd chosen to ignore the third most common feeling they'd emitted—pity.

Kian didn't want their fucking pity. He just wanted to feed.

Just wanted Willow.

He glanced aside as he passed the polished windows of an office building. The reflection that greeted him was only moderately familiar. His cheeks were sunken, his eyes dim, and his skin had taken on an unsettling gray undertone even through his glamour. Though his body was hidden by his clothing, he knew what it looked like beneath. He'd always been lean, but he was thinner than ever now.

Four hundred years of inhuman vitality and beauty had nearly withered away in a mere three weeks.

He turned his face forward and kept walking. Willpower alone drove him onward. He wasn't even sure how he was maintaining a corporeal form. His core, his magic, was so depleted that it was a wonder he hadn't crumbled to dust. And as he'd weakened, his hunger had grown. It was impossibly vast now, impossibly dark and imposing. It was agony.

Kian had been a creature of desire, pleasure, lust. Now he'd become a thing of spite. He would not let the Fates win this cruel game. He would not succumb to this.

How could it be so difficult to find a woman with purple hair? A woman whose face was so ingrained in his mind that he saw it every time he closed his eyes, whose essence was so embedded in his soul that the memory of her haunted him at every turn.

He filled his lungs with air that reeked of garbage, sunwarmed concrete, and exhaust fumes.

If only he could've drawn something, anything, from anyone else, he would've had more energy to dedicate to finding Willow. But even the simple little pleasures humans constantly experienced had done nothing for him. Before, they would've been like snowflakes upon his tongue, not enough to quench his thirst but enough to dull it.

They were no better than ash to him now.

No. I will find her. I will have her. She is mine, and she will lift this spell, break this curse...

And then what? What could possibly come after that?

The answer that drifted up from the depths of his soul was quiet, soft, and startling.

I will keep her.

A harsh breath escaped his lips. Head spinning, he braced a hand on the low wall sectioning off the outdoor eating space of the restaurant he'd been passing. That thought couldn't have been his own. That wasn't how he worked, wasn't how he survived.

Pleasure always faded over time. It was as fleeting as the lives of the mortals who experienced it.

Humans were also finite. Even if a single feeding did them no harm, they only had so much to offer before there was nothing left—and in the modern world, a great many of them were pushing themselves to that point without any help from Kian's kind.

The notion of a single human acting as the sole source of sustenance for an incubus was laughable. It was the pinnacle of ridiculousness.

And yet...

One night with Willow had sustained him for six days. Not just sustained him, but *sated* him. He didn't know what was different about her, didn't know why she'd had that effect, but he knew he needed her. The why didn't matter right now.

All that mattered was that he find her. Soon.

Kian closed his eyes and steadied his breathing. The city's sounds wrapped around him—driving cars, honking horns, conversations from the nearby diners, the jarring cacophony of heavy equipment at a construction site. So much noise, so many people. Mortal cities had changed to an unbelievable degree during his lifetime, but their cores remained unaltered—people. People amassed in these places, so Kian had always relied upon cities to survive, to thrive.

But if he were able to feed himself from a single mortal...

Desire flowed all around him, so much of it from so many people that it formed an ocean, its waters rippling gently beneath clear skies but churning under the surface. All that potential, and nothing he could do with it. All that energy and no way to siphon it.

His heart skipped a beat as something familiar brushed against his senses. The breath caught in his lungs, and he held it there, expanding his awareness, searching out the thread that had teased him.

Just a whisper, nothing more, but so familiar, so strong, so alluring. He straightened, tightening his hold on the wall as he sharpened his focus, as he sifted through the desire of dozens of insignificant mortals to find that one strand he sought.

Laughter carried to him from amongst the nearby tables, and Kian's heart burst into motion. It poured fire into his veins, flooded him with delicious heat, opened a well of strength hidden deep inside him. In that instant, he felt more solid, more real, more powerful than he had in weeks.

He felt more hopeful than he had in weeks.

That laugh, light, high, and unassuming, unburdened by self-consciousness, that true, heartfelt laughter, belonged to Willow. It was a sound he'd longed to hear for what felt like an eternity, and it washed over him like balm for his flagging soul.

His eyes flashed open. Somehow, he only turned his head

toward the source of that heavenly sound, though his whole body itched with the urge to vault the low wall and charge toward it headlong.

Willow was sitting at one of the patio tables across from another female, her green eyes bright, her pink lips curved into a wide smile—a smile which she bestowed upon the waiter as he returned her card with a receipt.

Kian gritted his teeth, swallowing a wave of fury. After all this time, the first laughter he'd heard from her was not for him, the first smile he'd seen on her face was not for him. Her happiness was not for him.

Unacceptable.

The waiter left, and Willow and her companion stood, pushing in their chairs.

Kian's gaze indulged in Willow. She wore a white ruffled, off-the-shoulder blouse and light blue jeans that clung to her curves. His fingers twitched at the memory of how her hips had felt in his hands. Her hair was twisted up in a clip atop her head, with loose strands framing her face.

Willow stowed a tablet computer in her tote bag, slipped her arms through the straps, and made her way toward the patio exit with the woman from her table. "It was so lovely to meet you, Amanda."

"Thank you for this, Willow. I can't tell you how much you've eased my nerves." Amanda smiled, stepping through the arched gate and onto the sidewalk. "I kept telling myself there was no way I'd ever get pictures like this done, but after seeing all the pictures in your portfolio... They're so beautiful. I can't tell you how excited I am for tomorrow."

Their conversation was meaningless to Kian, not that he could bring himself to focus on their words. No, his eyes fixed upon Willow's lips, and he recalled how they'd felt against his. His hunger roared. Need coursed through his body, overtaking every fiber of his being. It rumbled in his bones, thrummed in his muscles, sizzled in his veins.

His cock pressed painfully against his pants, instantly hard and desperate for freedom. For her.

Kian wanted her every smile, every laugh, chuckle, and giggle. He wanted her pleasured moans, her warmth, her softness, her passion, her everything.

The rules he'd adopted to help him survive in the ever-changing world of humans fell to pieces. There was only Willow, could only be Willow. He shoved away from the wall and strode toward her, each step quicker than the last, powered by need, by lust—his own lust.

He'd hungered too deeply and for too long. He would feed *now*.

"I want you to be comfortable, and for this to be an amazing experience," Willow said, falling into place beside Amanda as they turned away from Kian to walk along the street. "I want to show you just how sexy and courageous you really are."

The breeze picked up, flowing toward Kian. The air was still rife with city odors, but they were overpowered by a different scent, one which he greedily drew into his lungs.

Violets, vanilla, and a hint of warm summer breeze. Willow's fragrance. Its fullness, its sweetness and allure, assaulted his hyper-aware senses, wrapped around them and squeezed them into submission. He quickened his steps, rapidly closing the distance.

"I've never felt sexy," Amanda said, head down. "It's so hard when everyone around you judges you for how you look."

Willow adjusted the tote strap on her shoulder. "I know. I've been there. I know what it feels like to look in the mirror and not be happy with what you see, to stand there picking at every flaw. But I finally gave everyone a big eff you and worked on loving myself. I took the leap myself four years ago and scheduled a boudoir session. I broke down in tears when I saw my pictures. I couldn't believe that was me, that I could be that sexy vixen staring at the camera so confidently, so seductively. Ever since..." She looked at Amanda and smiled. "I want to help others feel the way I did."

"Thank you, Willow."

"Of cour—"

Kian's hand darted out and caught Willow's wrist. He tugged her back, and she spun toward him with a startled sound, stumbling directly into his chest. Grasping a fistful of her clipped hair at the back of her head, he angled her face toward him.

Her eyes widened in recognition an instant before he claimed her mouth with his.

Lightning crackled across his lips. A conduit opened directly to his soul, and saccharine energy blasted through it, flooding him with a power he'd not tasted in weeks. His other arm banded around her, crushing her body against him. He took advantage of her surprise, his tongue delving into the velvet depths of her mouth, his lips devouring hers.

She wedged her hands between their bodies as though to push him away only to hesitate. Her fingers curled, bunching his shirt in her hold, and she pulled him deeper into the kiss. Her lashes fell shut.

Delirious pleasure flowed into Kian. He groaned, and his eyes also closed. His heart was thunder rolling in his chest, and his aching cock throbbed, trapped between their bodies, tortured by pressure, by heat, by his need for more.

One kiss. This one kiss gave him more energy than he'd gained from entire nights of sex, more than ever should have been possible from something so mundane. And gods, her taste! Her mouth was so damned sweet, and it only made him crave the flavor of her cunt even—

A hard shove against his chest broke their kiss. The imme-

81

diacy of the pleasure he was siphoning dwindled, but the magical connection wasn't yet severed.

He opened his eyes to look down at her with red-tinted vision just as a sharp crack of pain exploded across his face. His head snapped to the side, and Willow tore out of his grasp, leaving him swaying.

"What the hell, Kian?" Willow demanded.

Kian blinked and touched a hand over his cheek, which pulsed with a lingering burn. Not only had she pulled away from him during a kiss—a kiss she had clearly enjoyed—but she'd hit him. No one had ever withdrawn in the middle of any such act with him, much less stricken him. His innate charm should've kept her blinded by passion without any effort, even in his weakened state.

"You slapped me." He returned his gaze to her.

Her lips were kiss-swollen, spots of pink stood out on her cheeks, and her chest was heaving. She looked so fucking delicious.

Worth it.

Nine

W illow stared at Kian. His blue eyes were fixed upon her, so bright they practically glowed. Shock, confusion, and desire swirled within her, keeping her heart aflutter and her breath short. Her palm stung, and her lips tingled with the aftermath of their kiss, which had been brutal, punishing, *hungry*. And she'd succumbed to it—to him. The whole world had fallen away the moment his mouth connected with hers.

It had been like they were in that hotel room all over again.

Thank God she'd come to her senses before she'd started rubbing all over him.

What was Kian doing here? Why had he grabbed and kissed her as though he had every right to do so?

As he straightened, Willow's gaze flicked over his features. She'd glimpsed him for only an instant before his kiss had consumed her, but she swore he'd looked...unwell. Dark circles had surrounded his eyes, his cheeks had been hollow, and his skin had been ashen. He still didn't look quite like she remembered, but this was a far cry from what she thought she'd seen a moment ago.

Amanda stepped closer and settled a comforting hand on Willow's arm. "Are you okay?"

Giving herself a mental shake, Willow looked at Amanda and forced a smile. "Yeah, I'm fine."

"You're sure?" Amanda held Willow's gaze before shooting a worried glance at Kian.

He lowered his arm and opened his mouth, shifting his jaw from side to side. The faint pink outline of a hand was visible on his cheek. "I'm the one who nearly had his head knocked off."

"You deserved it," Willow said, leveling a finger at him. She turned to Amanda. "Sorry. Yes, I'm totally fine. He's...an old friend. He just surprised me is all."

"That makes two of us," he muttered.

Amanda nodded. "Okay." But her attention remained on Kian, and something ignited in her eyes as they roamed over him.

Willow cleared her throat. "I...uh, I know you have to get back to work, so I'll see you tomorrow then?"

The woman didn't respond. It was as though she were spellbound by Kian.

"Amanda?"

Amanda started and looked toward Willow. "Huh? Oh! Yes. Tomorrow."

Willow smiled. "Great!"

They bid each other goodbye. As Amanda walked away, she cast another lingering glance at Kian over her shoulder until she stumbled. Cheeks flushing, she faced forward and hurried around the corner.

"She's gone." Kian moved closer to Willow and reached for her. "Now we can pick up where we left off, Violet."

Willow batted his hand away and retreated, shooting him a glare. "I repeat—what the hell, Kian?"

His brow furrowed. He glanced at his hand like it was an alien appendage he'd only just discovered. "I don't understand, Willow."

"What is there to not understand?" She leaned toward him and lowered her voice. "You *assaulted* me."

Kian's features hardened, and fire sparked in his eyes. "I gave you what you wanted. And you can't tell me you didn't enjoy it."

I did. But that is totally beside the point.

"I didn't ask for anything," Willow said. "I didn't even know you were there. You don't just walk up to strangers and kiss them."

"You don't have to ask." He eased closer, voice becoming husky. "And we're not strangers."

Willow put up a hand, palm out, to halt his advance. "We are."

He frowned at her hand before placing his atop it and gently guiding it down. "I've been closer to you than anyone, Willow. I've tasted your sweetness on my tongue. I've filled you, felt you come undone around my cock, and listened to you scream my name in pleasure."

Warmth flooded her, staining her cheeks, and her sex clenched. For three weeks, not a day had gone by during which she hadn't thought of Kian and that night...and all the pleasure he'd wrung from her. "What are you doing here, Kian?"

"Looking for you." He skimmed his fingers up her forearm, sending a thrill across her skin. "The Fates finally chose to smile upon me again."

She took a step back and rubbed her arm, but she couldn't erase the effects of his touch. "Why were you looking for me?"

He slipped his hands into the pockets of his long coat and let out a slow breath. "Wanted to see you again. You vanished before I woke, Willow."

"If...if this is about the condom breaking, it's fine. I'm on birth control and I'm clean."

"I could've told you that."

Willow blinked at him. "Are you for real? You think that your word would've been enough to convince me? And how did you know that *I* was clean?"

"Call it..." Keeping his hands in his pockets, he spread his arms to the sides. "Instinct."

Willow shook her head and pressed her fingers to her temples. "What do you want, Kian?"

"You."

She froze. "What?"

"I want you. To touch you again. To feel you, to see the pleasure on your face. You left me with nothing but this...need."

"It was supposed to be one night," she said, lowering her arms. "That was all."

Kian tilted his face down, and his eyes held hers as he brushed wisps of hair off her cheek. "What if I want more?"

Willow's heart quickened with excitement and fear.

In the time since her night with Kian, it had been easy to get over Eli. Not because she hadn't loved her ex, but because that love had been so one-sided...and it had never been as deep as she'd told herself it was.

Kian had given freely, had read the cues of her body, had anticipated her wants. When she'd taken control, he'd gone along with it. No hesitation or complaints. For all the enjoyment he'd clearly had, he'd made it about her above all else. To have felt so much from a stranger in such a short while, to have felt beautiful, powerful, seen, desired, and loved—even if it was only physical— had really put her relationship with Eli into perspective.

She deserved better than Eli. She didn't have to settle for someone who didn't love her the way she loved them.

That didn't mean she wasn't hurt. But she'd soon realized

that Eli wasn't worth her pain, wasn't worth her tears and heartache.

Everything she'd felt for Eli had been based on an imagined future she'd held in her heart. A future she'd clung to so tightly that she'd blinded herself to what was truly important. Willow and Eli had sex, but not passion. It had never been about them; it had been about him. It had been about what he enjoyed, what he wanted, what pleasure he could take from her.

She'd never fallen into bed at night, swooning over the day they'd shared. She'd never lain awake in the dark, unable to sleep because he was dominating her thoughts.

Not like she had with Kian.

Eli had represented companionship and security, but neither had been real. In a line of subpar boyfriends, he'd simply seemed the most reliable. It was okay that he'd never looked at her like she was the only thing in his world. She'd convinced herself it was enough just to be *in* his world.

Kian had looked at her like he'd tear apart the universe until the two of them were the only ones left in it.

But she had a feeling that Kian would break her. What she felt for him was too raw, too powerful. If she allowed herself to so much as hope for more with him, she'd only be welcoming pain like she'd never known. She'd be welcoming true heartbreak.

Willow shook her head. "No."

Kian chuckled and quirked a brow. "Sorry, Violet. I can't accept that."

"Kian, that night was...beyond words."

"I can make every night like that," he purred.

Her pussy clenched at that rumble in his chest, and she squeezed her thighs together, hoping to alleviate the sudden ache.

It didn't help one bit.

She glanced at the nearby pedestrians and lowered her voice.

"I...will admit we have a connection—a physical connection. But I'm not looking for a relationship."

His lips spread into a slow smirk that made her knees weak. "If you're not looking for a romantic relationship, we can just stick to fucking."

Oh, fuck me.

Really, Willow?

That wasn't what I meant!

You did though. You just don't want to admit it.

"No, Kian." She lifted the strap of her tote from the crook of her elbow, where it had been dangling, and slipped it over her shoulder. "Sex is not something I can do casually. It means something to me. I get too emotionally invested, and I'm not ready for that right now. One night was all that was, and all it will be."

Kian's heart raced nearly as swiftly as his thoughts. His pulse had quickened plenty of times in the heat of passionate sex, but never for something like this. Never in...panic.

He'd never panicked. Not in all his life. What reason would he have had for it? He was immortal. A being elevated over humankind—faster, stronger, attuned to the magic suffusing everything, of which most mortals were totally unaware. His senses were keener, and he had benefited from hundreds of years to learn, to adapt, to become the best version of himself. His charm could reach into mortal minds, amplify their desires, seduce them. It could turn them into willing prey.

And none of that was making any difference now.

None of it was working on Willow.

The energy he'd received from their kiss wasn't going to last long, and it would be meaningless if he couldn't get more. He would not allow this to end.

Kian glanced from side to side. There were people all over,

eyes all over, and he couldn't afford any suspicion. But there was an alleyway nearby—just the sort of spot that would work.

He grasped Willow's wrist and tapped into that tiny reserve of newfound energy, empowering and altering his glamour. Normally, such a thing would've been trivial to him. Now it strained all the magic he had left.

But it would ensure no one else saw Kian or Willow, at least for a little while, and that was what he needed now.

He strode toward the alley, tugging her along behind him.

She stumbled but swiftly righted herself and attempted to pull her arm free. "What are you doing? Kian, let go!"

Kian didn't stop, didn't slow, didn't ease his hold. He dragged her into the alleyway, shoved her against the wall, and pinned her there with his body, pressing one of his knees between her thighs. Willow stared up at him with wide eyes. Before she could recover, his mouth fell upon her bared neck.

She gasped, and her bag fell to the ground.

All his remaining power went into his charm, focused on Willow and Willow alone. He cupped her breasts, squeezing and kneading, pinching her hardened nipples through her blouse as his lips caressed her neck and shoulder. He felt her lust and arousal, felt her heat, and he siphoned it greedily, desperately. She just needed to give in to it, to succumb to him.

Her hands settled on his shoulders.

Yes, Willow. Draw me closer. Beg me for more.

"Stop!" She shoved him hard, causing one of his fangs to scrape her skin as his head was forced away. "Damn it, Kian, get off me!"

Before he could respond, she grasped a fistful of hair and yanked. Hard.

"Fuck!" Kian snarled as pain shot across his scalp.

He lifted his head and drew back, breaking Willow's grip on his hair, but he didn't release his hold on her. Everything within him was still and silent as he stared down at Willow, this delectable, spirited little human over whom he had no power.

But she had power over him.

She braced her hands on his shoulders, locking her elbows to prevent him from moving closer, and glared at him. "What is *wrong* with you?"

"I need you," he rasped.

"What?"

"I need you, Willow."

"You said that. But this sure as hell isn't the way to go about it!"

Footsteps echoed behind them. A male wearing shorts and a tank top jogged into the alley.

"Hey!" Willow called. "Hey, I need help!"

The man continued past without so much as a glance at Willow and Kian.

Willow struggled against Kian. "Wait!"

Kian gritted his teeth and released her breasts, sliding his hands down to her hips to still her. Part of him—a very large, very loud part—demanded he not say what he was about to say. "He can't hear you."

"Kian, let go of me." She pushed harder against his shoulders and tried to buck her hips, but it was to no avail. He kept her firmly in place. She took in a deep breath and yelled, "Help!"

"No one can hear you," Kian growled. "Nor can they see you. All you're going to do is hurt my ears."

She turned those big green eyes back to him, chest rising and falling with her rapid breaths. "What are you talking about?"

What the fuck am I doing?

It was perhaps the simplest rule, but also the most important —mortals could not know the truth. How hard would it be for Kian and his kind to feed if humans were aware that they were prey?

But fuck, he craved her. He needed her. Something inside him desired her with an intensity he knew he'd never shake, burned for her with a flame that would never extinguish.

She was his.

His mate. His soul knew it with a certainty that his mind could not dispute, though it defied all logic and reason.

"You are glamoured, Willow. Invisible to mortal senses."

Her brow creased. "What? Kian, I...I don't know what's going on, or why you're doing this..."

"I already told you why I'm doing this. I *need* you. I wasn't speaking figuratively."

"If you need help, we'll get you help. Together. But this... Kian, you're scaring me."

"I'm not human, Willow." He let out a slow, harsh breath, and willed his personal glamour away.

Ten

Willow gasped, eyes flaring. Her heart skipped a beat, a chill spread over her skin, and everything around her went quiet.

Not real.

What she was seeing couldn't be real. It wasn't possible.

Kian stood before her, but it was a different version of him. An *inhuman* version.

His skin had paled to a light, cool gray, and his features had sharpened, making the curl of his full, sensual lips even more alluring—even more wicked. Two pairs of horns rose from near his temples, with the inner set longer than the others. All four tapered into fine points, as did his ears, which had become long and elfin.

But it was his eyes that held her spellbound. Their enticing blue was even more pronounced, more ethereal, and had spread to encompass his eyes fully. His irises were mere suggestions, where the color lightened just enough to be noticeable. No white sclerae, no black pupils. Just that piercing blue, which glittered with opalescent flecks and emitted its own glow.

He was breathtakingly beautiful.

And his scent. Oh God, his scent. Sandalwood, jasmine, and a spicy musk that was the embodiment of lust. It was stronger than before, and it enveloped her, invaded her senses, dragged her deeper under his spell.

"What are you?" she breathed.

"Fae," he replied. Even his voice was different—deeper, more layered, impossibly sultrier. "I'm an incubus."

An incubus? A freaking *sex* demon? No, this couldn't be happening. She had to be dreaming, had to be hallucinating.

Willow covered her eyes with her hands. "This is crazy." She parted her fingers to peek at Kian. "No, no, no. You still look like that."

"You're not seeing things, Violet. This is real." His fingers, tipped not with long, painted nails but black claws, brushed her hands aside, caught her chin, and tilted her face up toward his. "This is me."

"Are you going to kill me?" she asked in a quiet voice, her heart racing. "Suck my soul out through my—" Willow's cheeks blazed, and she tried to squeeze her thighs together, but they were blocked by his knee.

"I'm a fae, Willow, not a fucking demon," he said.

"But you said you're an incubus. Isn't that a...a *fucking* demon?"

"No. Unsurprisingly, humans are wrong about that. And you should be glad. Demons are usually real pieces of shit."

Fae and demons. They were real. Really, really real. And there was one standing in front of her, touching her.

And she'd had sex with him.

Holy shit.

Willow flattened her palms against his chest. His heart thumped beneath them. "W-what do you want?"

A low, satisfied hum rumbled out of him. "You, Willow. I want you. I need you."

"I don't understand. Why me?"

The corners of his mouth ticked down. "That taste of you has turned all else to ash upon my tongue. I haven't been able to feed since that night, Willow. Haven't been able to think of anyone but you."

He shifted his knee, pressing it to her sex, and ground it against her clit. A bolt of pleasure zipped through her. Willow whimpered and clutched the fabric of his shirt in both hands.

Kian's eyes brightened, his head tipped back, and he groaned. "Fuck, you're delicious."

Her breath quickened as a delightful shiver ran through her. Willow bit her lip to stifle a moan, and her eyelids nearly drifted shut as he continued that torturous grind against her clit. Heat slickened her core.

Stop. This needs to stop.

She dropped a hand between their bodies, pushed down on his leg, and stood on her toes, lifting off his knee. "So you want sex."

His thumb slid up to trail just under her mouth in a touch so delicate, so fiery, that it was nearly Willow's undoing. "I want your pleasure. I want you to writhe in ecstasy, to scream my name, to claw at my skin. I want you to come undone. And then I want to do it again, and again, and again, because you have made me yearn like never before."

Oh, fuck, fuck, fuck.

It would've been so easy to say yes. To succumb to the passion, the lust, the fantasy he personified. Because amazing was too mild a word for what they'd shared that night, weeks ago. It had been...indescribable.

And he needed Willow. No one had ever been so desperate to

have her, no one had ever pursued her like this. It was thrilling, if a little frightening.

But Willow knew that sex would never be enough. It never was. She knew she'd long for more. She *did* long for more, so much more. She wanted love.

That Kian was an incubus made this whole situation a thousand times worse. How many other people had he slept with? How vast was his hunger, his lust? How long before Willow simply wasn't enough? She couldn't throw herself into this knowing that he'd abandon her as soon as he was bored, knowing that his very nature was likely to lead him astray.

She was not willing to expose herself to that hurt.

Willow shook her head. "I can't."

"Violet," he purred, "we both know you can."

"No, Kian."

He brushed the backs of his claws along her jaw before cupping her cheek. "What must I do, Willow? What must I do to have you again?"

Willow turned her face away from him. Tears filled her eyes, blurring her vision. "I don't want meaningless sex."

Kian withdrew his leg from between hers, lowering it, and stroked her cheekbone with his thumb. "Rapture isn't meaningless. And what's wrong with being selfish, Willow? What's wrong with taking pleasure for yourself and not worrying about anyone else for a little while?"

"Because it's hollow. Lust sparks bright and hot, and then it fizzles out. In the end...you're left alone. Left with nothing." A tear escaped her eye, trickling down her cheek. "I want love. The kind of love that doesn't die. That keeps burning, on and on, and is so much bigger and brighter than any flame. The kind of love that only happens when two souls *see* each other and know they can't exist without one another."

Kian's frown deepened as he wiped away her tear. "Ah, little mortal. I've never been drawn to people. Only their desire, their lust, their pleasure. I've only ever been driven to fuck and feed." He guided her face back toward him, making her meet his gaze. "It's different with you. I felt it the moment I saw you. I don't know what you've awoken inside me, Willow, but I want you. I crave your pleasure, crave your lust, but gods, those desires are completely eclipsed by how strongly I crave *you*."

She didn't push him away when he moved closer, when he again pinned her against the wall with his body. There was something so right about it. Something so right about him. The way his fingers felt on her skin, the heat he emitted, his scent, his eyes...

"Give me a chance," he whispered before brushing his lips over her forehead. "Show me. Teach me about mortal love. Teach me how to love you."

Willow's heart leapt, and her pulse pounded. He couldn't be serious. He was an...an incubus! And he wanted her to teach him how to love? To...love her?

She pushed against his chest, coaxing him to ease back so she could look up at him. "Stop. You're just saying this to seduce me. You're trying to make me lower my guard, to butter me up so that I'll have sex with you."

His voice was husky as he said, "Make no mistake, Willow. I will have you again. It's inevitable. But I'm not trying to manipulate you." His features softened, and he flattened a hand over her racing heart. "This feeling is new to me. I can't pretend to understand it. All I ask is that you let me prove to you that it is real."

"How?"

"What is it you humans do? Date?" He chuckled. "I shall date you."

The way he'd said *date* almost made it seem like the word was foreign to him, though that notion was belied by the utter confidence with which he'd made his declaration. Willow couldn't hold back a laugh.

The ghost of a smile crept onto his face, and his eyes grew more vibrant. "I do enjoy that sound, Willow."

Willow sobered. "My laugh?"

"Yes. It's almost as enjoyable as your cries of pleasure."

A flush spread over her cheeks.

"Now"—Kian grinned, braced his hands on the wall to either side of her, and lowered his face until their lips were a breath apart—"shall we seal our accord with a kiss?"

"Hold on." She ducked beneath his arm to escape his advance, snatched her bag off the ground, and retreated a step. "I didn't agree to anything."

He dropped his arms and turned toward her, his mouth taking on a wicked slant. "You can't hide your desire from me, Willow. You want this as much as I do."

Her skin heated further. "Can you...can you sense all my emotions?"

"Yes, but none more clearly than your longing."

That was such an unfair advantage.

Why an incubus wanted to date Willow was beyond her understanding, but the greater mystery was why she wanted it so, so much. Why she was about to agree when it would put her heart at such great risk? And she still knew so little about him despite this revelation. How old was he? Surely, Kian was far older than he appeared. Would he remain eternally youthful while she grew old?

And yet... She felt something with him. There was that spark of lust, of course, more intense than any she'd ever experienced, but it went beyond that. From the moment she'd first looked into his eyes, there'd been an undeniable, indefinable connection between them. An attraction that had nothing to do with appearances or desire.

Something within this man—this supernatural being—called to her heart, and something in her soul called right back to him.

He has you bewitched, Willow. He's an incubus!

All the more reason for her to hightail it out of there.

Willow turned, giving him her back, and walked toward the street. "Nope. Not happening."

Kian's laughter followed her. "We'll see, Violet. No one can resist their desire forever."

Eleven

~◦~

Willow leaned over the bathroom counter, raised her eyeshadow brush, and paused. She stared at herself in the mirror.

Reality seemed oddly...thin today.

Her encounter with Kian yesterday had tumbled through her mind over and over throughout the evening and well into the night. He was the first thing she'd thought about when she woke up this morning. And no matter how many times she told herself that what she'd seen had been a dream, that it couldn't have been real, she couldn't convince herself.

Kian was an incubus.

"No. It's unbelievable. There is just...no way."

She'd spent a portion of her evening yanking books from her shelves and flipping through pages, seeking any information she could find about the fae. At one point, as she'd cross-legged on her living room floor with a couple dozen paranormal romance paperbacks scattered around her, she'd stopped and stared at the scene she'd created.

It was ridiculous enough that she was now meant to believe

supernatural beings were real, hidden everywhere in plain sight. But that her instinct had been to crack open some steamy novels to research the fae had added a layer of absurdity to the situation that left her laughing at herself.

Remy and Bebe, who'd been perched on the couch, had stared at her blankly, as though uncertain of what to make of her in that moment.

Loki, however, had offered no opinion. Her laughter hadn't roused him from his comfortable slumber, which he'd fallen into while stretched out atop several of her books. She was sure she'd still find little pieces of orange fur sticking to the pages were she to look now.

Then she'd imagined Jamie walking in on her, imagined the look that would've been on her best friend's face, and Willow had only laughed harder.

Most ludicrous of all was that she'd kept up her search for a little longer afterward, because what else was she to have done?

Unsurprisingly, humans are wrong about that.

Kian's words had implied that the legends and myths humans had shared for ages were inaccurate. If those old stories were wrong, that didn't make them any more reliable than the fiction they'd inspired, right?

In the end, Willow hadn't been sure if she'd been searching for answers or trying to show herself that it was all foolish. If she accepted that faeries and demons existed, what else did she have to believe in? Vampires, werewolves, boogeymen? Where did it end?

It was all fantasy. Creatures conjured up while people sat around fires on dark, cold nights. Stories meant to explain misunderstood natural phenomena, meant to teach lessons, meant to entertain. None of it was real.

But Kian wasn't human. She'd seen him with her own eyes— the real him. And every inhuman part of Kian only made him more gorgeous and irresistible.

She let out a huff and applied the final touches to her eyeshadow. "I'm losing my damned mind."

A loud meow called her attention down. She smiled at Loki as he rubbed against her leg. He was the most vocal of her cats, and also the most affectionate.

After putting away her makeup, she crouched and slipped her arms around him. Loki immediately turned into her embrace, and Willow stood, cradling him to her chest. His body rumbled with his loud purring. She turned off the bathroom light and stepped into her bedroom. Setting Loki on the bed, she dressed in the jeans and dark blue halter neck blouse she'd set out.

Just as she lifted her hair free of her shirt, the doorbell rang. She glanced at Loki, who only blinked at her, his tail lazily flicking.

Smiling, she scooped him back up. "Love you too. Shall we go see who it is? Amanda isn't supposed to be here for a couple more hours. Maybe it's a package?"

As she reached for the doorknob, Loki stiffened and growled. "What's wrong?"

He wriggled in her hold, and she hurriedly set him down before he scratched her. Back arched, fur standing on end, and ears flattened, Loki stared at the door and growled again.

Unease filled Willow. He'd never acted like this before.

"I know you're there, Willow," Kian said from the other side of the door, startling her. "The cat will be fine."

Willow's brow furrowed. Her ears must've been playing tricks on her.

She hadn't really heard his voice.

Had she?

No. No way.

And yet her lips parted, letting out her response unbidden. "Kian?"

"Are you going to make me stand out here all morning?" he asked.

She unlocked and opened the door. Surely enough, Kian was standing on her porch. His white hair was swept to one side as usual, baring the shaved part of his head and his pierced ear, which no longer tapered to a point. There were no horns jutting from his temples, and his eyes, though still a penetrating, icy blue, looked normal. His pale skin held no trace of that inhuman gray undertone.

He wore a black corset vest that accentuated his lean, athletic build, and the sleeves of his crimson dress shirt were rolled up to reveal his toned forearms. Why was that so damn sexy? A pair of snug black pants over leather boots rounded out the look. She barely noticed the paper bag in his hand.

He grinned. Was it her imagination, or did his canines look longer and sharper than a human's?

"Are you fucking me with your eyes, Willow?"

Her whole body flushed. "No."

Kian's chuckle rumbled from his chest, dark and velvety. "Your desire says otherwise."

God, that is so not fair. I can't even lie to him!

Willow crossed her arms beneath her breasts. His gaze dipped and remained focused there.

"My eyes are up here," Willow said.

"So they are. But how could I possibly keep mine from wandering when there is so stunning a view to take in?"

She rolled her eyes. "What are you doing here, Kian?" Then it occurred to her. "Wait, *how* are you here? I never gave you my address."

His grin took on a mischievous slant. "I didn't want to waste your time with something so trivial, so I just followed you home yesterday."

Willow gaped at him. "You're stalking me?"

He dismissively waved a hand. "I just wanted to ensure you made it home safe."

Loki hissed. It was followed by loud growls from Remy and Bebe, who now stood with their backs arched at Willow's feet.

"Ah, your cats. I thought I'd picked up their scent on you." Kian stepped forward and placed a hand on Willow's shoulder, gently guiding her aside as he entered her home. His exotic scent teased her nose.

But she could only stare on in shock.

The cats retreated from him warily, hackles raised and ears back.

Kian crouched in front of them and placed the paper bag on the floor. Slowly, he extended both arms, holding his hands to the agitated felines.

One by one, the cats eased toward him, whiskers twitching as they sniffed his fingers.

"Fae have a...complicated relationship with these animals," Kian said, voice low. "You could say they have a paw beyond the Veil, and their eyes can perceive things many fae would prefer to keep hidden."

The felines eased away from him. Though they'd stopped growling, they maintained their tense, cautious body language and didn't take their eyes off the fae in front of them.

"What are their names?" Kian asked.

Willow looked over the cats, who'd been her truest companions over the last few years—apart from Jamie, anyway. They were also her babies. Maybe they were just reacting to what Kian was, but she would've liked to think they were also trying to protect her. "The black one is Bebe. Remy is the gray tabby, and the orange one is Loki."

"Bebe, Remy, and Loki. I will do no harm here. Let my words be our pact."

As she quietly closed the front door, Willow asked, "Are you talking to them or me?"

"Them, obviously. You already know I mean you no harm, or you wouldn't have invited me inside."

"I... What? I didn't invite you. You let yourself in."

Loki was the first to settle, sitting down in place. Remy and Bebe followed suit. All three continued watching Kian, their tails moving with restless little flicks, but they seemed more wary now than agitated.

Kian picked up the paper bag, rose, and turned to face Willow. His heated gaze settled upon her. She felt it as though it were a physical touch.

"Gods, you are beautiful," he said, devouring her with those eyes.

No one had ever looked at her as intensely as Kian did. At times, it was disconcerting, because she didn't know how to react to such attention. But she couldn't deny how desirable, how beautiful, he made her feel. She couldn't deny the spark igniting in her core.

Despite her uncertainties, she couldn't deny she really, really liked when he looked at her that way.

"And I suppose you didn't invite me in," he continued, "but I'm here now. Peace has been made, and I can present my offering."

"Your offering?"

He held up the bag. "I brought you breakfast."

"You did?" Willow took the paper bag. It was warm, and as she opened it, the aroma of fresh coffee wafted up to her. She laughed when she peered inside to find a blueberry muffin sitting atop a lidded paper cup.

He arched a brow. "Is something about your breakfast amusing, Willow?"

Smiling, she looked up at him. "No. It's just that, after what you revealed, it's so hard to imagine you standing in line at a coffee shop and ordering food like a normal person."

"Ah. If it helps, know that waiting in line is always optional for me." He turned away from her and moved deeper into her home, studying his surroundings. "I've never had an issue obtaining what I want exactly when I want it." He glanced back at her over his shoulder, and his eyes were glowing. "At least until recently."

Willow dropped her attention to the bag, seeking refuge from the fire in his gaze. Maybe he did have some supernatural effect on her?

"Well, we can't always get what we want." She removed the muffin, taking a nibble from its side as she walked into the kitchen.

Kian's arm hooked around her waist, and her eyes widened as he spun her around to face him. Cupping the back of her head with his other hand, he dipped Willow back and leaned over her, his face drawing close to hers, his lips a hair's breadth away from her mouth. His dark, seductive scent washed over her. There was no ignoring it; she wanted only to breathe it in deeper.

"Oh, but I will, Violet," he whispered, "and so can you. Just say the word and I shall make it so."

A thrilling tingle spread through her, making her core clench. His face was so close. The slightest upward tilt of her chin would've been enough to bring their lips together. Then she'd taste him again, then she could lose herself in him...

Think with your head, Willow, not your suddenly overactive libido.

Clutching the bag to her chest, Willow lifted the muffin up between their faces. "Thank you for breakfast."

Kian laughed and straightened, drawing Willow upright. When he stepped back and released her, she didn't know whether to be grateful or upset. Either way, she released a heavy, relieved exhalation.

She knew there was no hiding her emotions from him, knew he could sense her desire. But did he know how wet she was? Did he know that her nipples had hardened to aching points? That his voice made her skin tingle? Or that she wished he hadn't stopped, wished he had swatted the muffin aside, pressed that sensual mouth to hers, ripped off her clothes, and made love to her right then and there?

If he knew, he said nothing, and instead stepped around Willow to precede her into the kitchen, where he resumed his casual perusal of her home.

She set her muffin on the table and removed the coffee from its holder in the bag, removing the little sticker from the opening on the lid. "Did you already eat?"

He cast her a knowing glance as he opened one of the distressed, seafoam green cabinets. "I'll have my breakfast after you finish yours."

"Oh." She wrapped her hands around the coffee and lifted it, only to pause when heat that had nothing to do with the warm cup between her palms suffused her. "Ohhhh."

She quickly took a drink to distract herself from her thoughts, neglecting to check the coffee's temperature in her rush. Willow hummed. Thankfully, it wasn't hot enough to burn her. It was actually...perfect. Creamy and sweet, exactly how she liked it.

Kian cocked his head at the eclectic collection of plates and bowls stacked within the cabinet. "Hmm..."

He opened another cabinet to reveal a similarly mismatched gathering of cups and mugs. No two pieces were from the same set, nor were any quite the same size or color.

How many times had Eli said her things looked cheap and tasteless? How many times had Eli asked why she insisted on buying other people's trash? There'd always been just enough lightness in his voice for her to brush the comments aside as jokes, but after hearing the same things so many times, she should've known. She should've listened to her gut, should've realized that he hadn't really been joking with her. He'd been judging her.

Willow shifted her weight on her feet self-consciously. "I like to treasure hunt in secondhand stores."

"I see." Kian shut the cabinets and opened a drawer, making its contents rattle and clank. "Ah, but these are a matching set." He plucked out a spoon and held it up. The stainless-steel utensil's color shifted as he turned it in his hand, a rainbow shimmering across it that favored pinks, purples, and blues.

"I...know it's tacky, but when I saw them, I couldn't resist. They're just pretty."

Letting out a sigh, Kian replaced the spoon and pushed the drawer closed. He turned toward her, leaning back against the counter. "I like them."

"You do?"

"Yes. Because they make you happy. And they are rather pretty, aren't they?"

Willow's heart did a little flip. She smiled and sipped her coffee as he continued his exploration of her kitchen. "So, what do you do when you're not...you know?"

"Having Sex?"

She inwardly cringed, desperately trying not to contemplate just how many people he must've had sex with. It was his nature, and it had happened before they'd ever met. She had no right to feel this way. It wasn't as though she hadn't had her own sexual partners. But she couldn't stop a twinge of jealousy, a pang of hurt, from tightening her chest.

Because she couldn't be sure if this was a game to him. She couldn't be sure if she was just a temporary diversion, a break from the monotony of his routine.

All the more reason not to let your heart get too attached, Willow.

"Yes," she replied.

"Well, I used to spend a significant amount of time looking for humans to have sex with," he said with a shrug as he moseyed into the living room. "But that has long been...stale. It's about feeding...and nothing more."

Willow followed him. Her cats, alert but curious, kept him within their sight.

"I wander," he continued. "Explore. Watch places and people. I listen to music, and when the mood takes me, play some myself. I also paint."

"So you're an artist and musician?"

"I'm just a bored immortal who happens to come in contact with very powerful human emotions on a regular basis." Kian walked to the bookcase, which held all her romance novels—and a certain photo album that poked out farther than everything else. Of course, because fate seemed to enjoy a good laugh at Willow's expense, he reached for the album immediately.

Willow's eyes rounded, and she rushed forward to grab it. "Wait!"

He snatched the photo album off the shelf before she could stop him, raising it out of her reach. A playful light danced in his eyes. "What secrets are you trying to hide, Violet?"

She stood on her toes and stretched her arm up, but the album was too high. "I-It's private."

"Ah, that just makes it all the more tempting." Kian turned away from her and lowered the album.

She tried to reach around him, but he strode forward, putting significant distance between them, and opened the cover. Face flaming, Willow abandoned the brief chase.

He came to an abrupt halt with the open album resting on his palm and stared at the first photo. She knew exactly what he'd seen.

A black and white image of a dark haired woman in black lingerie, her hair loose, leaning against a windowsill and staring out through the glass. The light played upon her skin, making it glow.

It was a picture of Willow.

Kian turned the page to reveal more photos of her in varying seductive, empowering poses, some in black and white, many more in color. "Oh Willow, Willow, Willow..." He turned the page again and again, browsing pictures of her in different lingerie —and some in which she wore nothing but a well-placed hand. "You sought to hide these from me?"

"They're not the kind of thing that you just show strangers."

It wasn't that she was ashamed of them. She loved every single photo in that album. Having them taken had been a turning point on her journey toward self-love.

She'd never shared them with any of the men she'd dated, not even Eli—though she might have considered it, had he ever asked about the photo album on her bookshelf. But Eli's interest in the contents of her bookcase had only gone as far as him making the occasional dismissive comment about her preferred reading material.

She was happy he'd never noticed it. She'd had the photos taken for herself, not anyone else. Jamie and the photographer were the only other people who had seen them.

With Kian see them now, she felt vulnerable.

Kian turned to face her, eyes smoldering. "I think we're well past the point of being strangers, aren't we?"

"I still don't know you, Kian. Having sex with you doesn't make you any less of a stranger. And knowing you're a...a fae, makes you all the more mysterious to me."

"Mystery creates excitement." He gently brushed the backs of his fingers along the photo on display. "Hence the appeal of lingerie. So much revealed, yet still so much left to the imagination. Still so much to wonder about. And even after having you, Willow, I know I've discovered only a sliver of your body's secrets."

He turned another page and caught his pierced lip with a fang. "Gods, this is enough to drive me mad."

Willow realized quite suddenly that he wasn't kidding. His snug pants left little to the imagination—especially when it came to his hard cock, which was pinned along his thigh. A hollow ache formed in her core as she recalled the feel of that thick shaft inside her. She squeezed her thighs together. Had it really been three weeks since their night together? It felt like much, much longer.

Kian chuckled and slyly glanced at her. "I can't wait for you to wear something like this for me, Violet."

"You're so sure that's going to happen?"

"Oh, I am." He stepped closer, locking his eyes with hers. "I'm also sure that you want it to happen."

Fully aware that her body's reaction was giving her away— and that he could feel her desire regardless—Willow took another drink of her coffee. There was no point in trying to deny the truth.

Without breaking eye contact, Kian snapped open the album's metal rings and removed a photo, protective sleeve and all.

Her brow creased. "What are you doing?"

The rings snapped closed with a piercing finality. "Taking a keepsake. Let's call it...artistic inspiration." Shutting the photo album, he returned it to the bookcase. Then he removed the photo from its sleeve, turned it around, and slid it back in with the image facing the thin cardboard backing. "For my eyes only."

Willow stared at the sleeve containing the picture, cheeks ablaze, fingers itching to snatch it away.

But she didn't. She knew there'd be no use fighting him or demanding he return it. When dealing with a paranormal entity, it was probably best to choose one's battles.

"What are your plans for the day, my Willow?" he asked nonchalantly, as though this whole thing hadn't affected him at all.

"I have a couple clients coming for private photo sessions later."

"So you're a photographer, then?"

She nodded. "I, uh..." Willow gestured to the photo album. "I specialize in boudoir."

His smile took on that roguish slant. "Did you take those yourself?"

Why did he have to look so sinfully beautiful? "No, those were taken a few years ago by someone else." She pressed her lips together and tapped a finger against her cup, uncertain of why she was about to ask him her next question, but it slipped out anyway. "Would you...like to see my studio?"

"Very much."

"You would?" she said with more than a little bit of surprise. "I mean, okay. Um, follow me."

Willow led Kian back into the kitchen, where she set the coffee on the table beside the muffin. She continued into the laundry room, opened the back door, and let Kian step outside before her. As she closed the door, she found herself nudging the cats back inside with her foot.

She frowned. Normally, they never tried to make a break for it, but they were still so fixated upon Kian...

The cool morning air made her skin pebble beneath her blouse. Her yard was decent sized, with an array of plants and flowers in small garden beds, tiered pots, and hanging planters dangling from the patio overhang.

But most of the yard was dominated by the workshop she'd

converted into a studio, its exterior painted dark gray with white trim and shutters to match the house.

Willow briefly met Kian's gaze, offering him a smile, before nervously following the stone path to the building's entrance. She opened the door, stepped inside, and waited for Kian.

He swept through, head turning from side to side as he took in her studio. She tried to see it through his eyes, tried to find all the things of which he might disapprove, the things he might find tacky or ugly. All the clothing she'd seen him wear looked high-quality, tailored perfectly for his frame. Even if he leaned heavily goth in his style, his tastes seemed rather...sophisticated.

All the more wonder that he's interested in me...

The vinyl flooring was designed to look like dark, distressed wood, pairing well with the faux brick faces on three of the walls. A large window allowed sunlight to stream inside for a natural glow that would reach its peak right about the time Amanda was due to arrive. The queen bed was positioned in one corner, its white, shabby chic pillows and blanket already neatly arranged. A free-standing, clawfoot tub stood in the opposite corner near the window, and beside that, a tall, vintage mirror with a thick decorative border.

Old chests filled with various costume pieces and props sat closer to the entrance, along with a folding privacy screen, her computer desk, and most of her equipment. Various backdrops and rugs stood neatly beside the door, each a quick, easy means of changing the room's ambience. The lights and reflective umbrellas were already in place for today's shoot.

Apart from some of her equipment, almost everything in the studio had been bought secondhand. Thrift stores had been her biggest source, though yard sales and even a few small antique shops had proven fruitful for some of the more vintage items.

Kian's boots thudded on the floor as he walked deeper inside, his fingers brushing over surfaces as his eyes roamed. He made a thoughtful hum and offered her a quick, heated glance when he reached the bed, but he said nothing before resuming his unhurried exploration.

Willow exhaled. Why was she so nervous? What he thought didn't matter to her. She was proud of this place, proud of what she'd built. Eli's opinion hadn't changed that—he'd only referred to the studio as her she-shed—and Kian's opinion, for good or ill, wouldn't change it either. She'd learned to hang the brick panels, lay the floor planks, run the extra wiring, and change out the doors. She had remodeled every inch of this space herself. It was hers.

But Kian... He simply fit. Somehow, despite the softness of the décor, his elegance and the surreal, timeless air he projected matched this space perfectly.

Willow picked up her camera from the desk and turned it on. "Can I...take a picture of you?"

Kian paused, slipped his hands into his pockets, and turned toward her. He ran his tongue over his teeth, again drawing her attention to his canines. "As an immortal being, it's best for me to avoid appearing in photographs. It prevents a lot of unwelcome questions when people find a decades-old image and notice the stark resemblance."

"This would be just for me." Arching a brow, she stepped closer to him and smiled. "And it only seems fair, considering you swiped a picture of me. Consider it a trade."

"A trade." He let out a huff through his nostrils and narrowed his eyes. "It's always a trade with fae, isn't it?"

"I wouldn't know. You're the first I've met."

"Oh, I doubt that. I'm just the first you've known about." Lifting a hand, he swept his hair back. The pale strands shimmered like spun silver in the light coming through the window. "A photograph for a photograph, then. You're the artist, Violet. Direct me."

Excitement buzzed through Willow. She hadn't known if he would agree, but now that he had, she had no shortage of ideas she wished to explore with him. So many poses, so many angles, and all with this natural light bathing his pale skin...

But no. One photograph. That was the deal.

She worried her lip as she looked over the room until, finally, a flash of inspiration struck her. "The mirror. Stand in front of it with your body angled toward the window."

Kian sauntered over to the place she'd indicated. Willow followed behind him, looping her camera strap around her neck and tugging her hair free. Once she was beside him, she reached up and, after a brief hesitation, adjusted his hair so part of it hung on the side of his face with the rest over his shoulder. Then she dropped her hands to his shirt to undo a couple more buttons and spread his collar wider.

When she glanced up at his face, he was staring at her, and his lips were curled in a smirk that almost made her weak in the knees.

"You can keep going if you'd like," he said.

"I'm sure you would like me to." She returned his smile. "I don't suppose I could convince you to...drop your glamour?"

"Are you going to accept that you're mine and give in?"

"Nope."

"Then you have my answer, as well."

She chuckled, raised the camera, and stepped back. She stopped when she was satisfied with the way he was framed in the viewfinder. "Look at me through the mirror and keep your body angled toward the window, but pose however you like."

His smirk lingered as he turned his face toward the mirror. He met her gaze through the reflection, and she watched as he transformed.

Kian didn't drop his glamour, but his smirk faded, and the playfulness that had danced in his eyes shifted into smoldering, desirous heat. He braced a hand along the top of the mirror's frame and leaned toward it, fingers bent to make his pointed nails look even more like the claws they truly were. When he grasped the edge of the mirror lower down with his other hand, his posture became like that of a beast about to pounce.

His eyes bore into hers, and she couldn't tell if their glow was due to reflected light or his magic. The hunger on his face, the yearning, the invitation...

Willow's breath quickened as heat flooded her pussy. This was exactly how Kian had looked when he'd spread her legs, dropped his mouth between her thighs, and devoured her.

And his expression said that was exactly what he wanted to do with her now.

This was how she wanted to capture him, to forever memorialize him.

She clicked the shutter button.

"All done," she said, voice breathier than she'd intended, as she lowered the camera.

Wordlessly, he turned toward her and advanced. Whether she wanted to retreat or not was irrelevant. Willow was frozen in place, and she knew, deep down, there was nowhere else she wanted to be in that moment. His lustful eyes pierced her, fanning the flames he'd ignited in her soul.

He wrapped his arm around her waist and tugged her body against his. A surge of anticipation forced the breath out of her lungs. Seizing the nape of her neck with his other hand, Kian tilted her head back, leaned down, and sealed his lips over hers.

Willow curled her fingers against his chest. His lips caressed hers with a warmth and tenderness he'd not yet shown, though she could not deny the underlying passion and fire. While their lips were connected, her skin tingled, her heart hammered, and every nerve in her body lit up. Her eyelids slid shut.

His lips stroked, his tongue teased, and his fangs nipped.

TIFFANY ROBERTS

Willow's belly tightened. Desire surged through her, and the ache in her core grew heavier. His heat and scent surrounded her, intoxicating and decadent, and she longed to lose herself in it. To lose herself in this.

Somehow, she understood what was happening. He was feeding from her right now. But it felt good. So, so good. Even when taking from her, he gave so damn much in return.

And that quickly, he snatched it all away. Kian lifted his head, breaking the kiss and prompting Willow, momentarily bewildered by his sudden withdrawal, to open her eyes.

Shifting his hand to her jaw, he trailed the pad of his thumb along her lower lip, and then ran his tongue across his own. "Thank you for breakfast, Willow."

He righted her, released his hold, and stepped back, leaving her unsteady, cold, and bereft. "I know you have a busy day, so I won't take up any more of your time." Kian strode toward the door only to pause on the threshold and glance at her over his shoulder. "I'll pick you up for dinner at eight."

Her thoughts were clouded in the haze of lust Kian had cast over her, and Willow blinked at him until her mind caught up and processed his words. "Wait, what?"

"Dinner. Eight o'clock. What you're wearing will be perfect."

"We're not going on a date, Kian!"

But he only turned his head away, offered an unconcerned wave, and left.

Willow growled. "Wicked, rotten fae playing dirty."

They were *not* going out together.

Twelve

Kian didn't know what the fuck he was doing.

How could a centuries-old immortal being not know how to do something as simple as wooing a mortal?

Because I know how to fuck humans, not how to...to win their love.

"Dinner," he grumbled, unlocking his phone. "It's just dinner. How hard could that be?"

He'd seen humans eating together all the time. Sharing meals was one of their favorite things to do as a species. Breakfast, brunch, lunch, dinner, after-dinner drinks, dessert, midnight snacks, drunken drive-thru trips—mortal lives revolved around food. What was there to mess up here?

Everything.

He had no idea what foods Willow liked and only the vaguest notion of what sort of atmosphere she'd appreciate. She'd been so excited on her way to Eden that night, but he couldn't be sure that it'd had anything to do with her destination.

Growling, he cast aside his thoughts of that night, of that

place. She'd been hurt deeply, and the time since had not been enough to heal her wounds. He could sense them from her constantly. The pain she carried was muted, personal, and deep, an ache that wouldn't go away. A sorrow that tinged everything else.

And yet her taste was still infinitely sweeter than that of anyone from whom he'd ever fed.

Though she'd declared they weren't dating, that was exactly what tonight would be. A date.

But what was appropriate for a first date? He was an incubus. His specialty had always been fucking and leaving. All this... courtship was beneath him. No one had ever resisted him like Willow had. She was different from all the rest, and he somehow knew he'd never find her like again even across a thousand human lifetimes.

Opening up a search window, he tapped out his query.

Dinner for mortals

His thumb hesitated over the little magnifying glass icon. Dinner for mortals...

No, no. That isn't right.

Like a cunning fae eager to trick victims into foolish bargains or play magical pranks, the internet could be misleading. There was misinformation everywhere, while important tidbits of truth hid behind obscure pathways. One needed to be careful. One needed to be specific.

Kian tapped the backspace button and amended his search.

Dinner with mortals.

Yes, that was better. He wanted a communal experience, didn't he? He wasn't simply going to set some food before his female and watch her eat. That wasn't how they did things. Though the idea of eating mortal food remained as unappealing to him as ever, it would probably benefit him to keep up pretenses while they were in public.

But he paused again before pressing the icon. "Dinner with mortals, Kian? That's not how they fucking think of themselves, is it?"

With a huff, he tapped the backspace button several more times.

Dinner with people

"Now you're thinking like a human." Grinning, he pressed the magnifying glass and perused the results. His brow furrowed. "Recipes for large groups? Sixty-plus easy dinners? Family recipes? What the fuck?"

He held the button that activated the phone's voice recognition. Once the tone sounded, he said, "I wanted ideas for where to take a mortal to dinner, not instructions on how to cook for a family of five, damn it."

"I'm sorry," the phone said in its unnatural, feminine voice. "I'm not sure what you're searching for."

"And humanity is afraid the computers will overtake them one day?" Kian muttered. "How are fae not masters over this realm?"

The phone made its chiming sound. "This is what I found for 'mastering old elms.' Is this what you're looking for?"

A list of links appeared on the screen, most of which were related to the care of elm trees.

"I can't decide whether technology like you is the result of human incompetence or demonic ingenuity." Turning off the voice recognition, he returned to the search window and typed furiously.

What do mortals like?

What to feed ~~mortals~~ humans?

How to ~~woo~~ ~~court~~ ~~seduce~~ impress ~~mortals~~ humans

His eyes flicked to the clock at the top of the phone's screen. He was running out of time. With the vastness of eternity stretched out before him, how could he possibly be running out of time?

Dates ~~for~~ with ~~mortals~~ people

He selected a link labeled 'Ten fun first date ideas!' and scrolled through it quickly. Listed between the intrusive and overwhelming advertisements—another demonic innovation if ever there was one—were activities like miniature golf, go kart racing, painting and wine nights, and, oh so helpfully, dinner.

Hand trembling, he drew his arm back and only barely stopped himself from throwing the phone across the room. His heart was thumping, and an uncomfortable heat skittered just beneath his skin.

Nervous. He was nervous.

How the fuck was he nervous?

Because he had to leave now to get to Willow's by eight, but he hadn't figured out where to take her. Because he existed in the mortal realm, but he'd never truly been part of it, had never truly been part of their lives.

And never had his relations with anyone, whether human or fae, meant as much as this did. Never had he wanted so much. Never had he *needed* so much.

Somehow, he knew it was more than hunger. It was more than that need for sustenance.

He forced himself to place his phone in his back pocket, stopped at the mirror to check his clothes, and snatched his keys from the tray on the counter. He paused at the doors of the private elevator, glancing around his residence.

The dim lighting and sleek, smart furnishings should've made his penthouse apartment the height of taste and luxury, but it lacked something. It lacked...heart. And it had never felt so cold, so sterile. Why had that changed so suddenly? This was his sanctuary, the one place across all realms where he could be at ease, where he could be himself. And yet for all his money, for all his years of life, what was there to show for it here?

This place didn't have even a fraction of the character present in Willow's house. The only room with any life was his art room, and yet something had always compelled him to keep it closed, separated from everything else.

Why? Who would ever see it? He never invited guests into his home, never brought his prey here. The only people who'd ever come into Kian's apartment had been contractors and technicians he'd hired to perform work that had been beyond his capability, and they'd never had reason to go into the art room.

This apartment hasn't changed. I have.

The thought hit him like a splash of icy water. It really was that simple—the apartment was no different than before, but his perception was. After seeing Willow's home, after noting all the ways she'd imprinted herself upon it, the way it reflected her so perfectly, how could he ever look at this place the same?

What would this apartment look like with a mortal's touch? A mortal's tastes? A mortal's...life?

Kian cast all those thoughts aside, pressed the call button, and entered the elevator as soon as the doors opened. He jabbed the garage button on the control panel until the doors slid shut and the elevator began its descent.

He'd gone centuries without such thoughts. Why was he having them now? This entire thing...

It was a phase. A needed break from routine. That was what he wanted to tell himself, anyway. But neither desire nor denial could alter the truth.

Willow was Kian's mate.

And he would have to charm her the mortal way. No magic, no power.

The elevator halted, and the doors opened. He stalked to his car, climbed in, and started the engine. Loud rock music blared from the stereo. Kian let it envelop him and blast away his worries.

He'd never failed to gain the attention of any mortal he'd set his eye on before. Willow would not escape his desire, and she would not escape her own. Tonight, she would become his again. He'd sink his cock into her hot, welcoming cunt and use her body to his heart's content as he feasted upon the passion that blazed between them.

He turned the music louder and drove. The setting sun created a dazzling backdrop of reds, oranges, and purples for the tall, modern buildings of downtown Memoree, but those dense city blocks soon gave way to uniform suburban streets. He passed schools, strip malls, and supermarkets, passed quiet parks and residences that all looked the same after a few minutes.

For an instant, he longed for the uniqueness of the fae realm, where no two things were quite the same. Where everything was bristling with magic...

And danger.

Always danger.

As though I need a fucking reminder of that place.

Kian hadn't forgotten why he, like so many incubi and succubae before him, had fled to the mortal realm. He didn't want to think about the treatment he'd received in his earliest years. He didn't want to think about the scorn, mistrust, and ridicule he'd faced, didn't want to think about the constant attempts to control him. To dominate him.

And he certainly didn't want to reflect upon the fact that all that cruelty had been directed at him because of what he was.

No. There was only one thing worthy of his focus tonight, only one thing worthy of his time—Willow.

I will have what is mine, he thought as he parked in front of Willow's house. He turned his head to look at the building, and his usual smirk settled easily into place.

For all his nervousness and distress, he was eager to see her. He tucked his hair behind his ear and exited the car to walk to her front door. All he had to do was behave in his typical manner —calm, seductive, confident—and everything would fall into place.

She would fall into place—right into his lap.

And yet he couldn't pretend his heart wasn't racing as he mounted the porch, couldn't ignore the panic skittering through his mind. What if she denied him? What if he failed to win her?

No. She will *be mine.*

Loosely balling his fist, he raised it and rapped on her door. He waited, and when no answer came, he knocked again.

"I'm sorry, but Willow isn't home right now," someone said from the other side of the door in a muffled voice that sounded suspiciously like Willow's.

"How unfortunate," Kian replied, leaning closer to the door. "But it's fine. I'll wait until she's back. I've nothing if not time."

The deadbolt clicked, and the door swung open to reveal Willow on the other side, one corner of her mouth quirked. "You really don't give up, do you?"

He chuckled and shook his head. "These little games only encourage me, Violet. You're the one who's going to give up."

Movement at her feet caught his attention. Her cats had gathered behind her, silent guardians sitting with their intent, wary eyes locked on Kian. At least they weren't growling or hissing anymore.

He dragged his gaze up to Willow, taking in her appearance slowly. She'd changed into snug jeans and a dark green off-the-shoulder top with a matching belt around her waist. Her hair hung about her shoulders in soft curls. Even her makeup was a little more elaborate than it had been earlier. Despite her insistence that they were not going on a date, it seemed she'd been anticipating him.

Kian grinned. "This your usual evening attire, or did you dress up just for me?"

She rolled her eyes. "Don't let this get to your head. I just happen to be hungry."

"Well, you seem to be in luck. I happen to be here to take you to dinner."

Fuck. Where *am I taking her? Didn't forget that tiny detail, did I?*

"Great." She slipped outside, closed and locked the door, and dropped her keys into her purse. She smiled as she shouldered the bag. "Let's go eat."

As delighted as he was by her enthusiasm, Kian couldn't help his suspicion. "You seem oddly excited considering you've been adamant about not dating me, Willow."

Willow pressed two fingers to his chest and walked them up to the base of his neck. "Because...this is not a date, Kian." She tapped his chin and stepped down from the porch, following the walkway toward his car. "This is you taking me to dinner. So we can eat."

He caught his bottom lip with his fangs as he stared at her ass. Was she aware of the sensuality she radiated? Was she aware of the power she had over him?

"Tonight is certainly about eating," he said as he hurried to catch up with her. He darted past Willow at the last second, reaching the car just before she could, and spun to face her again, drawing in her delectable scent. "And it is certainly a date."

She laughed. "You're incorrigible."

He opened the door and stood aside, waving her in. "And you're a temptress."

"Still not a date," she singsonged as she entered the car.

Kian offered her a charming smile. "So confident, and yet so wrong." He closed the door before she could respond.

Just wanted to remind you, Kian, that you have no fucking idea where you're going.

This suave seducer act is about to crumble if you don't think of something.

Anything.

Clenching his jaw, he walked around the hood of the car, mind racing but oddly...empty.

He'd watched humans for centuries. How could he have no solution to this dilemma? It should have been so easy. He spent most nights around the very bars and restaurants mortals always frequented! How had he learned nothing, retained nothing? How had he missed all the details that should've been of aid now?

Because my goal was always to fuck and feed.

The places he'd prowled were hunting grounds selected only because they'd be filled with humans in the right mental state to easily fall under his spell. It didn't matter what kind of food they were eating, what alcohol they were drinking, or the décor of the fucking restaurant. None of that was important.

All that mattered was the pleasure. The power.

That wasn't the case with Willow. He couldn't feed from anyone but her, and she had no intention of making it easy for him. She gave him samples. Sips. Each was more potent than anything he'd received from anyone before, and each was more maddening than the last. He'd always received whispers from mortal happiness—drops of energy, barely noticeable. It had always taken sexual gratification to feed him.

Yet her happiness, her joy, was sustaining him, even after he'd been starving for weeks. That shouldn't have been possible. Why her? Why now?

He knew only that he needed more of it.

He needed all of it. All of her.

Willing the tension out of his expression, he opened the driver's side door and entered the vehicle. Willow chuckled.

Kian arched a brow. "Something amusing?"

"After finding out what you are, it's strange knowing that you drive a car like a normal person."

"How else would I get around?"

"I don't know. You said you were fae, so I just...imagined you flying with fairy wings."

"Only occasionally. That's hardly practical most of the time."

Her eyes widened. "Wait... You *do* have wings?"

Kian smirked. "Oh, have I not shown you? I suppose it will have to wait for another time. You're quite hungry, and I'd hate to keep you waiting."

He started the engine, shifted into drive, and settled his hands on the wheel. His foot remained on the brake, firm and unmoving. The engine thrummed, eager to burn fuel, to eat the miles, and Kian simply stared ahead.

Fuck.

Performance anxiety? Really? Incubus and performance anxiety were meant to be mutually exclusive concepts!

"Is something wrong?" Willow asked.

"I..." Kian's mind twisted, searching for a way to turn this situation into a boon, to play it off smoothly. But wooing this female was going to be exponentially more difficult if he had to weave a tapestry of lies in order to do so. He turned his face toward her. "I have no idea where to take you, Willow."

She briefly searched his face before smiling softly. "I know where we can go."

Something about that smile sparked warmth in Kian's chest. He had the odd sense that it was a private smile, one just for him. And he knew it had stemmed directly from the kindness and compassion in her heart.

He'd never concerned himself with such things. But with her, they meant more than he could comprehend.

Kian drove, following Willow's directions, and he could not

deny his intrigue when she refused to tell him where they were going. When they finally reached their destination, he wasn't sure what to think.

A drive-in eatery—Big Dave's Burgers, according to the sign. Home of the thickest shakes in the northwest.

The place was old. He vaguely recalled seeing many restaurants of its sort decades ago, when the human world had felt so different from what it was today. There were abundant parking places in the lot, a sheltered, outdoor eating area with tables and benches, and the small restaurant itself, where humans waited in line to order food, separated from the busy kitchen by the cashier counter. With the sun having fully set, the restaurant was lit up bright with floodlights and colorful neon lights accenting the structures.

Kian arched a brow. "This...is not what I expected."

"You expected me to pick some fancy place?"

"No. But what little I understand about human courtship is that it involves some degree of"—he waved a hand in the air— "showing off one's wealth, let's say."

"Maybe for some people. But it's not always about money. And sometimes when a girl's hungry, she just wants a burger." She opened her door and planted one foot on the ground before she paused to point a finger at him. "Also, this isn't a date. Now come on."

Laughing, Kian climbed out of the car. Humans sat in their vehicles and at some of the tables, chatting and sharing food in an atmosphere of ease, comfort, and happiness. This wasn't at all like the places he frequented.

And he couldn't deny that the change was welcome.

He fell into place beside Willow as they walked toward the building, barely noticing the people that glanced his way. There was only her. Her energy, her vibrancy, her everything.

When they reached the ordering window, a burly man leaned

an elbow on the counter, beaming a wide smile at Willow. His nametag marked him as Dave. "Evening. What can I get started for you folks?"

Willow returned the smile. "Hi! Can I get a cheeseburger combo with a chocolate shake?"

"You got it." The man jotted her order on a pad, using abbreviations that were all but meaningless to Kian. "And for you?"

"Ah..." Brow furrowing, Kian looked over the menu. How many variations of hamburger did humans have? How could there really be that much of a difference between them? "I think... I'll let my date order for me." He met Willow's gaze and offered her a grin as he looped an arm around her shoulders and drew her against him. "She knows what I like to eat."

He didn't miss the blush staining her cheeks.

"Um, he'll have the same as me," she said.

Dave chuckled. "All right. Two number ones with two chocolate shakes." He tore the paper from the tab and handed it to someone behind him before giving them their total.

Kian slipped his wallet out of his pocket and paid. "That makes it official, doesn't it, Violet?"

She peeked up at him. "You're impossible."

Yet she didn't shrug off his arm as they stepped away from the window to await their food. If anything, he could've sworn she moved just a tiny bit closer. And she fit so perfectly there, so naturally, like their bodies were made to be together no matter the position.

Gods, there were *so* many positions he longed to try with her... So many ways he longed to coax every drop of pleasure from his human.

The absurdity of the situation struck Kian anew in that moment. An incubus on a date with a mortal, getting cheeseburgers and milkshakes. Standing together. Smiling. Happy.

Though there were people everywhere, surrounding Kian

with a storm of desires of varying power and insistence, he didn't notice any of them. The unrelenting tide of emotions that always assaulted him could be tuned out with adequate concentration, but he didn't have to concentrate when he was with Willow. She held his focus so wholly that everything else just faded away.

As much as he wanted more from her, this was...pleasant.

Then their order number was called, and the spell shattered. Willow deftly slipped out of his loose hold and returned to the counter to pick up their tray of food. After asking for some sauces and extra napkins, she met Kian's gaze, beckoned him with a nod, and walked to an empty table, where she sat down.

Kian seated himself across from her, bending a bit awkwardly to get his long legs over the bench and under the table.

"Here," she said, placing a wrapped burger, a cardboard tray of fries, and a tall foam cup in front of him. She unwrapped the straws and poked them into both the drink lids.

He stared down at the food. "What am I meant to do with this?"

"Um, you eat it. You just pick it up and put it in your mouth."

Resting his elbows on the table, Kian leaned toward Willow and grinned. "How about I put my mouth on you instead?"

She blushed, and he felt a rush of desire from her. He drew it into himself, relishing the taste, the thrill. He couldn't wait until he got her really excited. Gods, that was going to be sweet.

Ducking her head slightly, she glanced at the nearby tables, some of which were occupied by families. "Does everything have to be sexual with you? Wait, don't answer that. You're an incubus. Of course it does." She plucked up one of her fries and held it to his lips. "Try it."

"This isn't the sort of nourishment I require, Willow."

"But you can eat it, right?"

He frowned. "Yes, fae can eat mortal food."

129

"Then eat with me. You brought me out to dinner, but I'm supposed to just eat alone? Meals are better when shared."

There was no point in him eating any of this food. It would do nothing for him, offer no sustenance. Still, he'd planned to eat with her tonight, if only for the sake of appearances. His resolve to do so was bolstered by a strangely hopeful glint in her eyes, by a new desire from Willow that he'd not felt before, one that he had trouble defining.

She wants to share this with me, he realized suddenly.

Keeping his eyes locked with hers, Kian lowered his head and opened his mouth. He extended his tongue, ensuring the first thing it touched was her finger, from which he licked the salty sweetness of her skin before taking the fry between his teeth and stealing it from her hold. He delighted in her quick intake of breath and the sip of arousal that followed. He bit into the fry.

"Mmm." He nodded as he chewed, smirking at her. "I can't be sure if it's the flavor you added to it or not, but that is good."

Willow laughed. "You just confirmed my prior statement." She picked up another fry and ate it. "So you've really lived all this time without eating? Like, actual food?"

Kian plucked a fry from his own basket and took a bite. The sensation of chewing food was strange, but the taste was pleasant. He could see why humans enjoyed this. "I've tried a few things over the years. Sampled alcohol and substances your kind considers somewhat more illicit. But food...well, I've never had any reason to eat it."

His enjoyment had rarely come from his own experiences, anyway. It was all stolen. Taken from others, from elsewhere.

"What does...pleasure taste like?" Willow asked.

"That varies from person to person, and it depends very much on its cause. When it's pleasure taken in the misery of others, it tends to have a bitter tang. But when it's pure, when it's liberated from everything else so it exists only for its own sake..." He ran his eyes over her again, and he nearly shuddered at the memory of what they'd shared—and what they would share in the future. "It's ambrosial."

She unwrapped her burger, eyes downcast. "And how often do you...do you have to have sex? Do you have to feed?"

"Usually every few days. But after I had you, I went nearly a week without needing to feed. When my hunger finally returned, I found that I couldn't draw from anyone."

A crease formed between her brows. "Why?"

"Because you, Violet"—he reached out and placed a finger beneath her chin, tipping her face up so she met his gaze—"are my mate."

Thirteen

ornament

Willow withdrew from his touch. "What?"

He hadn't just said what she thought he had. No. That...that couldn't be right.

"You are my mate," Kian replied, his gaze unwavering. "The Fates have marked you as mine."

"You're lying."

He leaned to one side, propping his chin on his fist. "Things would be much easier for me if I was."

"But...but you're an"—she glanced from side to side, bent over the table, and lowered her voice—"*incubus*."

His eyes rounded, flashing brighter than usual. "I am?"

"No. No, you don't get to do that. You don't get to make fun of me after dropping a bomb on me like that."

"I'm sorry, Willow. That wasn't my intention. But what should I do?" Kian's brows angled down toward the bridge of his nose, and a crease formed between them as he sat up straight. "Everything I've ever known was altered in an instant. You unmade my world, mortal."

"You can't put the blame on me." Willow picked up her burger and took a disgruntled bite. She barely tasted it.

"Fuck," he rasped, "you're even sexy when you're irritated."

"Can you stop trying to get in my pants for even one minute? Anyway, I'm stuffing my face. There's nothing sexy about that."

Kian smirked. "Ah, Violet. I can think of something to put in your mouth we might both find arousing."

Willow released a heavy breath through her nostrils. "Can you feel my desire right now?"

His lips stretched into a grin. "Always."

She snatched up a fry and threw it at him. It bounced off his cheek and fell onto the table with grains of salt scattered around it. He blinked and stared down at the fallen fry, lips parting as though he meant to speak.

Only a confused huff emerged from his mouth.

"What, you didn't sense my desire to throw something at your smug face?" she asked.

He laughed and brushed the salt from his cheek. "I've never met anyone like you, Willow."

"Maybe that's because you never actually took the time to get to know anyone."

The humor faded from his expression quickly, smile falling. "No, I suppose I haven't. I've never needed to know anyone." A shadow passed over his face, and for an instant, the long years he must've lived were apparent in his eyes. "I've never needed anyone. Not until you."

Willow glanced at the family seated at a neighboring table. The two children were making goofy faces at one another, using their fries as fake moustaches, eyebrows, and fangs, while their parents laughed. An ache formed in Willow's chest. That was what she'd wanted, what she'd longed for. A family of her own. A *loving* family. It had always seemed so far out of reach, and she was beginning to lose hope of ever having it.

"What exactly is a mate?" she asked. "Do you mean like, soulmates?"

"It's..." He sighed and shook his head. "Soulmates, yes, but on a level mortals can scarce imagine. I can't even imagine it, and part of me doesn't want to. Because it's...everything. And as you've already surmised, I've tended to be somewhat noncommittal in my past relationships."

"All the more reason this won't work, Kian." Willow set her burger down and wiped her hands with a napkin. "I'm done dealing with men like that. It...it hurts too much to give everything you have to someone, only to realize they never intended to give anything back to you."

"I can promise you pleasure, Willow. Anything else...I can only try."

"You saw my bookcase. If I want pleasure, all I need to do is pick a book and break out my vibrator. Happy endings all around. That's all a girl needs."

Kian tilted his head, eyes narrowing as he studied her. "You say that, but you don't believe it. We both know that's not what you really want."

"I already told you what I really want, Kian. *Love*. I want the love of someone who will be there for me when I feel like the world is breaking apart around me. Someone who will share not just joy and laughter, but sorrow and pain. Someone who will fight with me but love me all the more for it." Tears stung her eyes. "I want someone who will still want me when I'm wrinkled and old, who will love me until my final breath."

His features softened, and his lips fell into a faint, contemplative frown. Willow's heart thumped as he silently stared at her. She felt like her heart and soul lay bare to him, and she wasn't sure why that vulnerability didn't frighten her more.

As much as she wanted him to say something, anything, she was glad he didn't. She didn't want empty promises, couldn't have stomached any lies. However difficult it could be to swallow, she only wanted the truth from now on.

If only she'd been able to determine the truth of her own heart when it came to Kian.

Finally, he pushed himself to his feet, rounded the table, and held a hand to her. "Come with me, Willow."

"Where?"

"There's a place I'd like to show you."

She glanced at their food—her burger partially eaten, his untouched in its wrapper. "But we haven't finished dinner."

"Bring it with you."

"What about yours?"

He huffed, rolling his eyes, and turned to the table. He snatched up his burger, tore off the wrapper, and in several quick, huge bites that had lettuce and globs of ketchup raining on the tray, devoured almost all of it.

"There," he said through the food he was still chewing.

Willow blinked. "Ooooookay." She shook her head and chuckled. "Was it good at least?"

"Great." He furiously wiped his mouth and hands with a napkin, his silvery rings gleaming under the overhead lights as his fingers moved. "Ready to go now?"

She took another bite of her burger, unable to suppress a smile as she chewed. "You seemed very human for a moment there, messy eating and all."

"Just wait, Violet. You'll see some messy eating soon enough."

"Well, I think you lasted longer than a minute that time."

"There is a very obvious, innuendo-laced reply to what you just said, Willow, but I'll refrain."

Willow rolled her eyes. Standing, she gathered their trash and brought it to a nearby garbage can, keeping only her chocolate shake. "We can go."

Kian took her free hand and led her back to his car.

They hopped in, he turned it on, and then they were on the road. The indecision and uncertainty he'd demonstrated at the start of the evening was gone. As he drove out of the suburbs and onto darker backroads, Willow found herself glancing at him more and more frequently. Without so many streetlights around, the gentle glow of the instrument panel gave an otherworldly cast to Kian's face.

It was almost like seeing him without his glamour.

I should be alert. He's taking me away from the city, away from help...

Stop it.

If Kian wanted to hurt her, he could have done it any time. He didn't need to drive her somewhere secluded, where there'd be no witnesses. He could literally make them both invisible.

Willow forced herself to sip her shake.

Soon enough, they were winding along heavily wooded roads that climbed steadily higher, the car's headlights serving as the only source of light. Any sense of direction she might've maintained was destroyed. But it was nice. It was peaceful. She'd always found something soothing about driving at night with no other cars on the road, secure in her own little bubble of warmth and safety.

He turned down a narrow side road and followed it deeper into the woods. It ended in a small parking lot, where he stopped the car. The headlights shone directly on a footpath ahead.

"Almost there," he said as he killed the engine and opened his door.

Willow stepped out of the vehicle and closed the door. Cool wind blew around her, lifting her hair and sending a chill through her. She crossed her arms and looked around. With the headlights off, everything so was dark, and it felt like civilization was hundreds of miles away.

She heard the rear door on the driver's side of the car open and close, and then Kian was there beside her. He swept something over her shoulders, something with comforting weight and warmth, something that smelled wholly of him.

His coat.

It was...incredibly thoughtful of him.

She grasped the coat and pulled it tighter around herself. "Thank you."

"Of course." He slipped his arm around Willow, tucking her against his body, and walked her along the footpath. His guidance was welcome, as she couldn't see a thing in the darkness.

The path was short, but it led to an astounding change in scenery, ending at a hilltop overlook with a low stone wall. The sky stretched out overhead, all shimmering stars and dark patches of cloud, and beneath it sprawled the shallow river valley. Memoree lay at the valley's heart, its buildings defined more by the countless lights shining from them than their true shapes. A warm, inviting glow blanketed the city, one which wasn't so apparent from down on the streets.

It all seemed so small from up here. So quiet. So lovely.

Willow took a step forward, away from the security of Kian's body, and placed her hands atop the stone wall. "This is beautiful."

He moved to stand beside her. "I hoped you'd like it. I come up here from time to time when I need to...I don't know, to escape from it all? When I need perspective."

"Perspective on what?"

Kian glanced at her. Blue light sparked in his eyes before he faced away, looking down at the city. "My place. I live down there, amongst your kind. Spend my days surrounded by mortals. But I've always been...apart. I've seen this world change, Willow. I've watched towns grow and collapse, I've seen cities blossom from wilderness, I've seen wars ravage once beautiful lands. And yet what did all that mean to me?"

137

Bending forward, he leaned his arms on the wall and shook his head. "Whenever I felt as though those problems, those worries, were my own, I came to this place—or places like it in other towns. To remind myself that I *am* apart from it all. That mortals are my prey. My source of food, nothing more. Their wants and needs matter to me only so far as the sustenance I can draw from them.

"And yet I stand here tonight...and I cannot find that detachment."

Willow stared at him, uncertain of her feelings. His words reminded her anew of just how inhuman he was, not only in appearance, but deep down in his heart. She was prey. She was one of the people that lived beneath him, one of the mortals he would never have thought twice about had fate not intervened.

"Why?" she asked softly.

"I already told you, Willow. You unmade my world. I don't know how the pieces fit back together, only that they don't without you."

"Oh." Something in her belly fluttered, and she pressed her hands to her middle as though that could stem the sensation.

His fingers, firm but gentle, took hold of her chin, and he guided her to face him. "Whether I asked for it or not, I have that connection now. You are that connection. I didn't bring you here to make you feel insignificant. I brought you here to share this place with you. To talk. The things I read mentioned that dating is supposed to be about getting to know someone... And I find I very much want to get to know you, Willow."

Warmth suffused her body. She reached up, grasped his wrist, and pulled his hand down, dropping her gaze as she brushed her fingers over his knuckles and rings. "I...would like to get to know you too."

"What would you like to know?"

"Well, for starters... How old are you?"

138

He, too, watched the play of her fingers, a tiny smile curling on his lips. "Let's say four hundred, give or take a few decades. The beginning of my life was spent in places where time doesn't flow quite the same as you're used to, which complicates the calculation."

Willow snapped her head up and gaped at him. "Wait. You said four *hundred*?"

Kian narrowed his eyes. "Yes."

She released his hand and stepped away. "Holy shit, you are old. I mean, I figured you were older, but...but not that old."

He scoffed and raised his hand, sweeping back his hair. "I'll have you know that four hundred years is nothing to my kind. Many fae would still dismiss me as a child at my age."

"I'm only twenty-seven. That's a blip compared to your life-time. How does that even work? It's like...you're robbing the cradle."

Kian folded his arms across his chest and leaned his hip against the stone wall. "As far as I'm aware, most fae don't rob cradles anymore. So unless you mean twenty-seven months instead of years, I hardly see the issue. You're a mature, consenting adult, aren't you?"

She wrinkled her nose at him. "It's still so strange."

Talk about an age gap.

Bracing a hand on the wall, Willow lifted her legs over it one at a time and sat atop it. She folded her hands in her lap and looked out at Memoree. It had been her home for the past nine years, a third of her life. But how brief had that life been in comparison to Kian's?

He'd been around long before there was a city here, long before any of this land became part of the United States, before the country even existed. It was hard to imagine what this area had been like when Kian was young. Untamed forests, primal, dangerous, and beautiful. Unsullied by human ambitions...

She couldn't fathom how much the world had changed in his time.

"You're speaking to an incubus, Willow," he said gently. "My age is hardly the strangest thing about this, wouldn't you say?"

"Yeah, you're right." She smiled at him. "Where were you born? Here or..."

"Beyond the Veil, in a realm called Tulthiras. The Evergarden. Where the fae hold dominion and everything is brimming with magic." He stepped over the wall with eerie grace and sat beside her, letting out a sigh. "All it really means is that everything is dangerous and deceptive, words hold true power, and those with the most potent magic rule unopposed."

"It doesn't sound like you like it there."

"I find it isn't a very friendly place, especially for incubi and succubae. But it has its beauty."

"Do you have any family?"

"I'm sure I have blood kin scattered across a myriad of realms, but no. There's no one who would really fit the word family." He brushed a finger along her arm, and even through the coat, it sent a thrill through her. "And you? Where were you born, Willow? What of your family?"

"I was born in Florida."

"You're quite far from home."

"It never felt like home there." She swung her legs and stared down at the city lights. "I was what you'd call an accident. I wasn't planned, wasn't wanted, but my parents had me regardless. And they regretted every moment of it. They thought the right thing to do was to get married, but they were miserable. They fought constantly. I think growing up around it just desensitized me to their screaming matches. The only times I was happy were when I visited my grandparents on my dad's side. They were the only ones who made me feel loved as a child. My mom's parents disowned her for marrying my dad, so they were never in the picture."

Willow rubbed her hands to warm them and drew the sides of the coat more snugly around herself. "I was picked on a lot in school. Because of life at home, I had turned to food as a comfort, so I was on the chubby side growing up. Kids are cruel, and sometimes they'd call me names and oink or bark at me. It hurt, but I didn't always let them get away with it." She chuckled. "I got into a fight with one of the more popular girls once and bloodied her nose. She stopped picking on me after that, but there were other bullies over the years. I just learned to ignore it. I had a couple close friends that I spent time with, and that was all I needed."

"Things got worse when my grandparents died in a car accident." She released a shuddering breath as that old pang of loss struck her. "My dad took it really hard and closed himself off from everyone. He'd just sit there at the kitchen table some nights, chewing his food with this blank expression while my mother screamed at him. And I... I just felt lost and alone. I mean, what does a nine-year-old really understand about death? All I knew was that the only people that ever truly loved me were gone.

"When I was eleven, my parents got divorced. It didn't make life any easier. I was forced to live with my mom on weekdays, and my dad most weekends. He had no idea how to take care of me, and always acted like I was an inconvenience. My mom liked to go out constantly, and I swear she had a new boyfriend every month, one of whom...got a little handsy with me when I was fifteen." Willow clenched her teeth as she recalled the shame she'd felt. "My mom accused me of flirting with him and blamed me for ruining their relationship. It didn't bother her that her boyfriend had assaulted her underage daughter."

She glanced at Kian.

His expression was hard set, jaw muscles ticking, and his eyes were dark. Though his glamour was still in place, his features looked sharper. Deadlier. For the first time, he wasn't oozing sensuality; he radiated menace.

"Sorry," she said. "Guess I'm just kind of vomiting my crappy childhood at you."

His gaze eased, and some of the stiffness bled from his posture. "Don't be sorry. I want to hear it all. I want to feel what you felt...what you still feel." He reached up and brushed her hair back from her face, his nails trailing across her cheek as he tucked the strands behind her ear. His hand remained there, tracing the curve of her ear. "I cannot pretend to relate your experiences, but my early years were rife with unpleasantness of their own. I know the feeling of...being unwanted."

Trying to ignore the tingles his touch produced, Willow arched a brow. She couldn't quite wrap her mind around this seductive, sensual, gorgeous man having ever been shunned or left out. "You do?"

He nodded, and his hand dipped, the pads of his fingers stroking the side of her neck while his thumb lightly touched her cheekbone. "I told you there are many sorts of fae. Mine is not well-loved by the rest. We're considered parasites. Leeches. Beneath the others, mockeries of what fae are meant to be. But we're also feared, because our magic can influence even other fae, though they are much more resistant than mortals. And because we can feed from them, from their power, and grow powerful ourselves.

"So, I found scant welcome in Tulthiras. The only ones who wanted me there sought to possess me, control me. Just as Florida never felt like home to you, the Evergarden was never a home to me. I am but one of many of my kind who have found solace here amongst mortals, though..." Something shifted in his eyes, a glimmer of vulnerability that made his gaze impossibly more entrancing. "I did not feel any less alone in this realm."

"It's like you're adrift between two worlds, not feeling like you belong in either."

"Yes. Exactly that." The smile he gave her was small, but it was warm, gentle, and genuine, and it pierced straight to Willow's heart.

To have lived for so long, never feeling like you belonged anywhere... To have interacted with so many people but never making a connection with any of them...

"I'm sorry you've gone through life feeling that way," she said.

"I have learned to take what little pleasures the Fates have delivered unto me." He grinned and lowered his face, burying his nose in her hair and breathing in deep. "Like purple-haired temptresses..."

Willow laughed and gave him a gentle push away. "I'm not even trying. You just won't take no for an answer."

He leaned back with a chuckle, but caught her hand on his chest, holding it there with his fingers curled around it. "Whereas I am trying harder than I ever have, Violet. You've turned the tables on me, but I'll emerge victorious in the end."

"We'll see."

"We shall." He squeezed her hand, and his expression sobered. "Now, I don't believe you finished your tale."

Willow stared at his hand. It was big and warm, covering hers so perfectly, and his chest was solid beneath her palm. She could feel the steady thump of his heart. "I guess not. You sure you want to hear more?"

"Are you warning me of what's to come or assuming I'll be bored, mortal?"

"I guess I figured you'd be bored. I mean, you've lived for so, so, so, so—"

"Yes, so, so long, I get it," he said with a laugh.

Willow grinned, but it faded. "So yeah. I hated living with my parents. I found places to go if I wasn't locked in my bedroom reading to escape my life. I spent a lot of time at the library, or went to friends' houses, but those friendships faded as we got older. They all had lives of their own, boyfriends and girlfriends, after-school activities and sports practices. And they were always going out to do stuff. I never had the money to join them and felt bad when they offered to pay all the time. At sixteen, I also landed my first job, and I worked as many hours as I could get. Besides spending some money on a junker car and gas, I saved every penny for the day when I could move out and be on my own."

She fiddled with the zipper on Kian's jacket. "When I turned eighteen, I found an ad online for an apartment here in Washington. It was tiny, but it was affordable, and I jumped at it. I was so happy to leave Florida behind. To be out on my own, to never have to deal with my parents and their resentment again. It was like this huge, crushing weight had been lifted off me. It was...freedom.

"I hardly had any belongings, so it wasn't hard to fit it all in my little car for the cross-country drive. I knew I needed to find a job as soon as possible when I got here because my savings would only last so long. I ended up taking a position in Verity's, a department store down the block from my apartment. It was supposed to be temporary, but I guess they liked me, because they kept me on. I worked there for a couple years, training in pretty much every department. And then one day I saw a posting for a position in the portrait studio.

"I thought it'd be a nice change of pace. It was one of the few things I hadn't done in the store, and the pay was supposed to be better, so I applied. I got the job, and...I loved it. I discovered my passion there, found what I wanted to do for a living. I took classes, took a lot of photos for practice, and eventually started my own business. I made a profession out of it. Throw in several failed relationships during that whole time"—She spread her hands in front of her—"and here I am now."

"Yes, here you are. With an incubus of all things."

Willow smirked. "Who would've thought?"

"Reality is even stranger than your books, isn't it?"

"Not unless half-spider, half-humanoid creatures exist too."

Kian laughed and shook his head. "No one can claim you humans lack imagination. Though I wouldn't be surprised if there are such beings somewhere beyond the Veil. Gods know what exists in the wilds of the other realms."

"So there's a chance..."

He caught her chin and leaned close, eyes boring into hers. "Mortal, you are *mine*."

Willow chuckled. "I haven't agreed to that."

"That doesn't change anything."

That strange fluttering returned in her belly. She examined his face—his perfect, sensual, deceptively human face. Now that she knew what lay beneath it, she could discern things even his glamour didn't quite hide, like the subtle glow in his eyes, or the specks of glittering blue in their depths.

"Does it get tiring, using magic to disguise yourself all the time?" she asked.

Again, his expression softened, and he stroked his thumb along her jaw. "No. It's natural. I rarely think about it at all. But when I do let my glamour drop... Well, I feel something akin to the freedom you described when you left Florida."

"You can drop it now. You don't have to hide from me."

He smirked. "Oh, I have your permission, do I?"

Willow snorted and withdrew from him. Swinging her legs back over the stone wall, she hopped down. "Just figured that since there's no one else around, you'd want to...be yourself." Brushing off her backside, she faced him.

"I understand." He turned away from the city as well, but instead of coming down, he climbed up to stand atop the wall, casually unbuttoning the cuffs of his shirt. "You want to bask in my glory, don't you, Violet?"

"On second thought, keep your glamour. I don't need to—" Willow narrowed her eyes when he began to unfasten the front clasps of his corset. "What are you doing?"

"Giving you exactly what you want." Kian slipped off the vest, dropping it to hang over the wall, and then those long, dexterous fingers went to work on his shirt. He tugged it free of his pants and undid each button from top to bottom, revealing his chest slowly. Tantalizingly.

"I didn't tell you to undress!"

"You want to see me, Willow." He slipped the shirt down one shoulder, then the other, and peeled it off. It fell atop the vest, already forgotten. "The real me."

His glamour melted away. Before her eyes, his pale skin took on a slight grayish hue, his features sharpened, his ears lengthened and tapered to points, and horns materialized on his head. His nails grew into black claws, and his canines became more pronounced. The blue of his eyes spread to take over their whites and ignited with an ethereal glow that reflected on his silver piercings.

"Here I am." Kian spread his arms, and something new appeared that made Willow's breath hitch.

Iridescent gossamer wings.

They unfurled behind him, emitting their own dim luminescence. Four of them, like dragonfly wings, shimmering a faint blue that shifted toward purples and greens as they moved. They looked delicate, run through with flowing, swirling patterns that couldn't have been natural, and yet they radiated an air of power and majesty.

Willow was glad it was just the two of them here beneath the expansive, starry night sky. Because this moment...was for her. Kian had revealed himself fully to her.

And he was achingly beautiful.

He could be mine.

No. No, Willow. Don't let your thoughts go down that path. He's an incubus, remember?

Unbidden, her tongue slipped out to run across her lips. Her mouth was dry, her heart was thumping, and she felt very, very warm. "What...what's it like having wings?"

Kian's diaphanous wings flapped lazily, shimmering even more vibrantly as he glanced at them over his shoulder. "It's... normal. As normal for me as it is for you to not have them. Not that they see much use in this modern era."

Willow's fingers flexed. "Can I touch them?"

Fourteen

K ian stared down at his little mortal. Silence had enfolded him, leaving only the rapid beating of his heart to mark the passage of time. Everything else was frozen. A moment in stasis, plucked out of the stream and dangled by the invisible threads of the Fates.

He'd already shown Willow more than he ever should have, more than he'd shown anyone. Why? Why was he standing here, exposed, displaying himself to her? Preening for her? Why had he not immediately denied her request? There shouldn't have been anything to think about.

A fae's wings were...sacred. Powerful. Vulnerable. A source of immense strength and simultaneously a great weakness.

To permit a touch required the utmost trust. It was the deepest intimacy in which a fae could partake, second only to the sharing of one's true name—both actions usually being reserved for mates.

Willow hadn't accepted that she was his mate, and Kian hadn't accepted what their connection meant. He needed her for his survival, yes, and she genuinely intrigued him... But this seemed a great leap.

Yet he found himself stepping down from the wall despite his reservations. He landed lightly on the grass, eyes locked with hers, and drew in a deep breath. The air was redolent with her sweet fragrance, which fit so perfectly out here, away from the city stench.

How can I be doing this?

How can I not do it?

His heart quickened as he turned to offer her his back. Bending slightly forward, he flattened his palms on the top of the stone wall. Tension rippled through the muscles of his back, but he willed it away, focusing on the distant city lights. Focusing on her scent.

The muted crunch of dirt and rustling of grass underfoot signaled Willow's approach.

"They're so beautiful," she said softly.

His skin prickled in awareness. He could almost feel her hand hovering over his upper right wing, could almost feel her warmth, but she didn't touch him. Not yet. His wing twitched.

"Go ahead, Violet," he rasped. "But be gentle with me."

She chuckled. "Says a man who embodies everything but gentleness."

He hummed, and fire sparked low in his belly, spiraling outward. "Remember, Willow... I feel your desires. I'll be gentle when that's what you truly want."

The flare of lust from Willow forced him to press his lips together and grasp the stone beneath his hands. He drank it in, desperate for more, as his cock hardened. Her desire had never fully faded, but she'd done well holding it in check. A slip like this was something he was loath to waste.

Her fingers came down on his wing. It was a delicate brush, so light that he wondered if he'd only imagined it, but when she trailed those fingers down, a thrill raced along his spine. Kian couldn't stop the tremor that swept through his body. He drew in a shaky breath. His shaft pulsed, straining against the confines of his pants.

Willow traced the intricate patterns on his wing with that same tender touch. Pleasure coursed through the limb, racing to coalesce at his core. His claws scraped the stone as his grip tightened. No one had ever touched his wings, no one had ever gifted him with such sensations, no one had ever made him yearn so deeply for more.

Every moment of it was bliss and agony, fire and ice, overwhelming pleasure and hopelessly vast need.

Her touch was exquisite torture, and he never wanted it to end.

Kian wanted her hands on him—not just on his wings, but on his body. He wanted to feel her touch again, wanted to feel her cunt wrapped around his cock, wanted to taste her lips and hear her cries.

He wanted her.

When her fingers met the sensitive skin around the base of his wing, Kian bared his teeth, unable to stop a growl from escaping his throat as his wings fluttered.

Willow hastily withdrew her touch. "Sorry. I didn't mean to make you uncomfort—"

There was no conscious thought involved as Kian spun toward her, only driving, instinctual need. He captured her face between his hands, angled it toward him, and slanted his mouth over hers. Fire danced across his lips, spiced by her irresistible flavor. Her surprise quickly gave way to pleasure. He devoured it, dropping his arm to her waist to tug her body against his. Kian groaned when her belly pressed on his cock, and his eyes fell shut.

Willow's arms looped around his neck, and the coat hanging from her shoulders fell to the ground. Her fingers delved into his hair, clutching the strands, and she stood on her toes, leaning her body against his. Her lips parted, and her tongue flicked his piercing before she sucked it into her mouth to tease it.

"Fuck, Willow."

In answer to her teasing, he nipped her lip with a fang, coaxing a satisfying shudder of delight from his little mortal. He deepened the kiss, his tongue stroking and coaxing hers, each move a whisper of promise for delights to come. Thrilling heat raced just beneath his skin, and a red haze tinted the darkness behind his eyelids.

The energy she emitted was so pure, so potent, so unique. If he'd harbored any lingering doubts, they were shattered in that moment—he would *never* be able to feed from anyone else again.

And that didn't matter. She was all he wanted, all he needed. All he craved.

He dropped his other hand, palming both her ass cheeks, and ground his pelvis against her. Ecstasy hammered him in waves, each of which was colored, flavored, and enhanced by Willow. Her spirit, her desire, her essence, her warmth, softness, and feel, her breath, her voice, her scent.

She was everything, she was all.

An ache so fierce that it nearly wrung a cry from his throat thrummed in his cock. The friction was too much and not remotely enough. But it wasn't what he wanted. He needed to be buried in her heat, needed to feel her inner walls clamping around him. Needed her essence coating his cock. He needed to look into her eyes as their bodies joined and know that she wanted it too, that she needed it just as much as him.

Willow moaned. Her hands shifted to his shoulders, fingers clenching, nails biting. Gods, he wanted those hands to slide lower, to stroke every inch of flesh on their way to his pants.

Kian growled a curse and slid a hand to her front, wedging it between their bodies. It curled between her thighs to cup her sex.

Even through her jeans, he felt the flame of her desire. He applied pressure, pushing his fingers down on her clit.

She gasped. Her desire surged along with her pleasure. He could smell her arousal, and within moments, he would have it on his tongue as it thrust deep inside her, slaking his thirst.

Kian moved his hand up to the button of her jeans.

Willow stiffened in his hold. Her hands flattened on his shoulders, and she shoved against them as she tore her face away, abruptly breaking the kiss. She stumbled back, chest heaving, lips kiss-swollen, and eyes bright.

Trembling, she pressed a hand to her chest and shook her head. "No. No, we can't do that again. I'm...I'm not ready for that, Kian."

Despite the chill that had overcome his skin the instant their bodies were separated, Kian burned. He'd never known such need before her. Had never felt such desire...not from himself. It would've been so easy to step forward and kiss her again. He knew her resolve wouldn't last, knew she wanted the very thing she was struggling to resist. He knew she wanted him.

All she needed was a little push.

But as he looked into her eyes, he saw something more.

Fear.

Was she afraid of Kian, of what he was? Or was she afraid of what he made her feel? Whatever the cause, it was enough to douse those fires and clear the red haze from his mind. He did not like seeing fear in her eyes. It bothered him just as much as the sadness she'd borne on the night they'd first met.

Despite this pull toward Willow, despite his wants, Kian didn't need to have her now. She'd been feeding him every moment they were together, had been sustaining him with every laugh, every smile, every heated look. As much as he hungered for her, he wasn't *hungry*.

He didn't yearn for what she could give him...he yearned for her.

Kian raised his hands, displaying his palms. "You don't need to fear me, Willow. I told you, I'm not going to harm you."

"I don't... I'm not..." She sighed heavily, ran her hand through her hair, and looked down at the ground. "I am scared."

Though her words only confirmed his suspicions, they were no easier to hear. Each was like a vise being clamped around his chest, making it harder to breathe, making his heartbeat falter and slow.

Fear. He'd spent his entire existence focused on desire and pleasure. Never once had he considered inflicting fear, never once had he wanted to *be* feared, not even in those bygone days when Lachlan had tried to persuade him toward it.

Yet it might not have bothered him so much were she anyone else.

With a slow exhalation, he willed his glamour back into place and dissipated his wings. The area around him dimmed. Only in its absence did he recognize the amount of light he emitted in his true form. Willow must have noticed too, because she looked up at him then, flicking her gaze over his face.

"I'm not scared of you," she hurriedly said, "or your appearance. I'm not scared of what you are, either, not exactly. But I am scared of what that means, and of...of how intense things are with you. I'm scared of...what I feel when I'm with you."

"Ah, Willow." Something shifted deep within him, something warm and strangely soothing.

She dropped her gaze again, brow furrowed. "It's like I'm drowning, and every time I reach the surface, I can't draw in enough air. But when I go back under, I...I want to fight it a little less. I want to succumb, to just let go and let that water close in around me. What I feel with you is deeper and more powerful than anything I've ever felt before. It's frightening. Because I know the more I feel...the more it's going to hurt."

Willow's turmoil, her tumultuous, conflicting emotions, suffused him, and the cold won out over his inner heat. This wasn't how he was supposed to make anyone feel, especially not his mate. But what could he do to comfort her? What could he say to put her at ease?

This isn't all just because of me. The scars she carries... Eli, and the others before him. They left those there.

The anger that soured his gut at that realization would do neither Kian nor Willow any good. It was useless, impotent, the perfect emotion to encompass how he felt just then.

He turned away from her to gather his clothing, pulling on his shirt and vest without bothering to button them. Having his back toward her didn't shield him from her feelings. When he was done, he faced Willow again, crouched to collect the fallen coat, and closed the distance between them in a few slow, deliberate steps.

Gently, he swept the coat over her shoulders before curling a finger beneath her chin to tilt her face up. He searched her gaze, unsure of what he sought, wishing he had the right words to say. None came.

So he spoke in a different way, leaning down to brush his lips against her forehead. She shivered.

Lowering his hand, he grasped the lapels of the coat and drew them together, pulling the garment more snugly around her. "Let's get you home, Violet."

They returned to the car in silence, and that silence continued as Kian drove along the winding, wooded roads that led back into the city. So many times, his lips parted, and words danced on the tip of his tongue, but no sound emerged. How could he assuage her fears when he was just as uncertain? All this was new to him as well.

His world was irrevocably changed, and he didn't know how to navigate these feelings. He didn't know anything about relationships. For him, everything had been about instant gratification, about bursts of pleasure. Making someone feel good physically was a simple matter, one in which he was well-versed. Of course, it had helped that his survival was linked to his ability to give pleasure.

But making someone *happy*? Making them feel content, whole, fulfilled, making them feel secure...

He didn't know how the fuck to do all that.

Too soon, they arrived at Willow's house. As he pulled up to the curb, a pang of sadness seized his chest. He squeezed the steering wheel.

For the first time in his existence, he was distraught at the thought of parting with a mortal. How many had he left behind? But he didn't want Willow to go, didn't want her to leave him.

Not that I'll allow it. She's fucking mine.

"I'm sorry if I ruined the night," she said.

"You didn't ruin anything," he replied. "I enjoyed your company. And the cheeseburger."

A little laugh escaped her as she looked at him. "I doubt you tasted it with how fast you shoved it in your mouth."

He smiled, thrilling in the bit of joy she emanated. "I'll take it slow next time."

"Thank you for the not-date, Kian." She leaned toward him and pressed her lips to his cheek.

The kiss was chaste, sweet, and over before he'd had time to process its meaning. Her eyes met his as she drew back with a smile. After unbuckling her seatbelt, Willow opened the door and stepped out of the car with her purse in hand. She shrugged off his coat, folded it over her arm, and laid it on the seat. "Good night."

"Good night, Willow." His cheek tingled with the memory of

the kiss as she closed the door and walked toward her house. He watched her, transfixed, his mind racing but oddly quiet.

Every one of her steps amplified his urge to follow her. He clutched the steering wheel, forcing himself to remain in place, to puzzle out what that kiss had meant. It had been so tender, so affectionate, so warm, unlike any kiss he'd ever received.

She opened her front door and slipped inside. Just before she shut it, she peeked out at him, and their eyes met again.

He understood then. It was there in her gaze, in her small, shy smile, in her slight hesitation before closing the door.

She'd kissed him like she cared about him—not about what he could do for her, not what he could provide, but *him*. More than ever, he longed to go to her, to take her in his arms, to kiss her, to hold her. But he couldn't do any of that.

Kian shifted the car into drive. Pulling away was the most difficult thing he'd ever done, and he succeeded only because one thought, strong and certain, repeated in his mind.

She is mine.

Fifteen

The man grasped the top of the wrapper in both hands and tugged. When the plastic didn't tear, he scowled.

Kian watched from his seat on the low wall of the plaza's central fountain. The human male's desire had caught Kian's attention. This mortal harbored great anticipation for the packaged snack cake, more than Kian might've thought possible.

The man pulled on the wrapper again, arms trembling and face reddening with the exertion. A flare of frustration leapt up alongside his want, the two emotions blending to strengthen one another. He huffed and relaxed, shifting his hold to the wrapper's corner.

The plastic tore effortlessly.

With a grunt, the man removed the snack from the wrapper. His anticipation again swelled to the forefront. It was, in its way, a sort of pleasure—or rather, a whisper of pleasure to come. Holding the cake almost reverently in one hand, he used the other to drop the wrapper in the trash can beside him.

But the plastic clung to him. He flicked his hand, managing

only to shift the wrapper enough for it to stick to the backs of his fingers.

Muttering to himself, the man shook his hand with increasing force, each failed attempt to dislodge the offending wrapper further fueling his annoyance.

Kian leaned forward and braced his elbows on his thighs. The whole display was oddly fascinating.

The man let out an angry growl and swung his arm down hard. His fingers struck the metal rim of the can with a heavy clang. He reeled, swearing in surprise and pain, and hooked one arm over the other to clutch his hand to his chest.

The plastic wrapper fell. It floated and twirled on the gentle breeze, drifting close enough to the trash can opening to brush the rim before continuing to the ground.

Undoubtedly fueled by pain, the man's frustration soared to new heights. He bent down, snatched the wrapper up, and crumpled it in his hand with excessive aggression before throwing it into the can. It didn't stick to him this time.

Shoulders heaving, he glared down at the trash, shaking his wounded hand and stretching his fingers, which sported angry red welts across their knuckles. When he finally looked up, he started. Several other humans were standing nearby, staring at him questioningly. His face reddened again, this time with embarrassment.

"Yes," Kian whispered to himself, "you are in the middle of a busy plaza."

After offering a hesitant, awkward wave to the bystanders, the man turned and hurried away. His embarrassment endured, wavering only when he lifted the cake and took a big, hurried bite.

Despite his other, stronger emotions, a little burst of pleasure flowed from the man.

To have experienced such powerful feelings because of a snack, something so minor, so insignificant...

The more Kian watched these mortals, the less he understood

them. He sat back, bracing his hands on the stone to either side, and swept his gaze slowly across the plaza.

This place, Silverpine Plaza, was one of many outdoor shopping areas that had become so popular in Memoree in recent years. Most such places were almost indistinguishable from one another. Nice shops and restaurants, neatly manicured landscaping, walkways paved with stylized cobbles. People always flocked to spots like this, but clear skies and warm sunshine had brought them out in droves today.

It was the perfect sort of place for Kian to linger while he waited for Willow to finish her work.

So many humans, so many emotions, and all of them so different from what he saw and sensed at his usual hunting grounds. There had to be a lesson in this. There had to be some insight to draw, some key to greater understanding that he was missing.

Such extreme emotions over a snack cake... Why? It shouldn't have been important. What did a few seconds of time matter? The snack would've tasted no less sweet because of the brief delay.

Perhaps...

Kian frowned as his eyes settled on a woman pushing a stroller with a baby strapped inside. For a being who could outlast time itself, a single moment was irrelevant. Days passed in the blink of an eye, years in the space between breaths. But humans were born, lived, and died in a matter of decades.

Was that the lesson? These mortals burned bright and fast. Every moment, every concern, every sorrow and joy, was amplified for them. They viewed the world differently because they would be in it for only a short while.

Or, rather than some profound wisdom regarding the human condition, I simply witnessed a man having an embarrassing but ultimately trivial experience.

Mortals milled past him, each preoccupied with their own

wants, their own worries, their own lives. Thanks to his glamour, none looked his way. He was in no mood to be approached by anyone. Only one mortal held his interest. Only one mortal was worth his time.

Kian ran his tongue across his lips. Willow's taste lingered there, and he groaned at the reminder. He'd brought her breakfast again earlier today, and he had taken his own meal in the form of another kiss, as he had the last few mornings. Leaving her house, especially after that, had been hard. Really fucking hard.

He wanted more. Another taste, another touch. The essence of her, of her desire, of her arousal, was fresh in his memory, teasing him constantly. His every instinct demanded he remain at her side, and they grew stronger with each day. Before long he wouldn't be able to stay away. Before long he wouldn't be able to deny his needs.

Gods, he craved her.

His roving eyes settled on a pair of human females walking hand-in-hand. They met each other's gazes and smiled, their eyes practically aglow with desire and something much, much deeper. With something much more potent and meaningful.

Kian craved Willow, but he was only beginning to understand what that truly meant.

Yes, he wanted her delectable body, wanted to fuck her over and over again in every way conceivable, wanted to explore every avenue of carnal pleasure with her. But more than that, he simply wanted to be in her presence. He wanted to have that simple, casual intimacy with her, to hold her hand as they walked, to look into her eyes and have the world fade away. He wanted to talk with her, to hear her laugh. He wanted to be gifted with the brilliance of her smile, because when she was happy, all the universe brightened.

He wanted to learn everything about her, body, mind, and

soul. Wanted to hear every story she had to tell, wanted to know everything she found amusing, scary, exciting, disgusting, infuriating, and saddening. He wanted to know her completely—and wanted her to know him in return. To see him like no one, including Kian himself, ever had.

The two women leaned toward each other, shoulders and heads touching gently, all without missing a step.

Two hearts beating in time. Two minds, two souls, intertwined...

And it wasn't just those females. Everywhere he looked, he saw another couple enjoying each other's company. Sharing conversations, food, and laughter. Kian had spent his existence hunting desire, seeking raw, unbridled pleasure, but how much had he missed?

What would it be like to eat food with Willow that neither of them had ever tried? What would it be like to visit a place together that neither had ever visited, to do something neither had ever done? What would it be like to, after four hundred years of detachment, finally explore everything this world had to offer, all with his Violet at his side?

He longed to experience every moment of joy, sorrow, and pain, every triumph and every struggle, every miracle and every tragedy, with her. Longed to be strengthened by her and be her strength. To face it all, the good and the bad, with her hand in his.

Who the fuck have I become? When did I get so contemplative and sappy?

"Gods, Willow," he rasped. She'd changed him more than should've been possible.

But Kian still needed to learn. He still needed to decipher the way humans thought, the way they felt and shared their emotions, the way they earned each other's trust. He would've thought it a simple task, as he'd always believed humans were simple creatures.

But if nothing else, his time with Willow had taught him that mortals were unnecessarily complicated beings who often couldn't sort out their own feelings, much less those of their fellows.

Sighing, he ran his gaze over the storefronts around the plaza. So much information to absorb, so much of which lay right in front of him, yet it was all maddeningly cryptic. Other fae would laugh in Kian's face were he to suggest that humans were so difficult to puzzle out.

And more than a few of those fae would attempt to flay him alive were he to suggest that their estimation of mortals was, in fact, completely wrong.

His attention halted on a male human who'd just emerged from a flower shop called In Bloom Floral with a bouquet of pink roses in hand.

Gifts. Humans enjoyed receiving gifts, and it was customary for a man to lavish his woman with them. According to the internet, mortal females especially enjoyed receiving flowers from their lovers. It was considered a thoughtful, romantic gesture.

Kian wasn't entirely sure why. Flowers were things of great beauty, yes, but they were also so ephemeral, especially when cut. Wouldn't they simply serve as reminders of the limited human lifespan? As reminders that all mortals would eventually wither and die?

Seriously, Kian? Do you really think they spend every moment obsessed with their own inevitable deaths?

A chill formed in his chest, spreading outward like frost creeping across a windowpane. Even Willow would eventu—

"Not pursuing that line of thinking," he growled. She was his mate. All she had to do was accept him, and he could seal their mating bond. Then his lifeforce would be hers.

And regardless of his doubts, mortals liked flowers. As much as she clearly appreciated his breakfast deliveries every morning, he wanted to give his mate something more than food.

Kian pushed himself onto his feet and strode toward the florist's. He allowed his invisibility to fade, trusting that most humans were too oblivious to notice him appearing out of thin air.

His steps brimmed with subtle excitement. He couldn't help but anticipate Willow's reaction to receiving fresh flowers. Would she offer him one of those smiles, or perhaps a kiss? Would she throw her arms around him?

Would she feed him without either of them trying, as she'd done so many times lately?

A little bell jingled over the door when Kian entered the shop. The woman behind the counter, who wore a green apron and was wielding a pair of scissors as she worked on a flower arrangement, smiled at him. "Welcome in! If you need help with anything, just let me know."

"Thank you," he replied. Though he was already browsing the items for sale, he didn't miss the way the woman's eyes widened when she saw him, didn't miss them darkening with lust—and nor did he miss the flare of desire she emitted.

Before, her lust would've presented a welcome opportunity for what mortals might've called an afternoon delight, though he'd preferred the term afternoon snack. But he had no interest in that, no interest in her. All he could muster was mild irritation.

The Kian of a few weeks ago wouldn't have recognized his present self.

He walked slowly around the shop, lingering near each arrangement, studying petals and colors, drawing in scents. All so pretty, so vibrant. Like his Willow. But which would she appreciate most?

There were roses of many shades on display, both alone and

mixed with other flowers. What was it his research had said? Each color represented something different. The red ones were love and passion, but what of the rest? If he chose the wrong color—one that signified friendship or condolences, perhaps—it could ruin everything.

Kian glanced around again. There were more varieties of flowers here than he could name. Did each type have its own meaning, and did those meanings vary by color?

He stopped at a woven basket filled with violets, folding his arms across his chest and lifting a hand to stroke his chin. Their fragrance reminded him of Willow, and their color would complement her hair perfectly. But would they send the right message? Would they properly convey his feelings?

"How can anyone choose correctly?" he muttered.

"Did you need some help?" the shopkeeper asked, her voice a little huskier than before.

Help. The very notion of asking a human for aid, of being in a situation where he needed the help of one of the creatures he fed upon, was insulting.

Willow is human too.

A twinge of guilt struck him. She wasn't a creature, wasn't his prey. She was his mate.

And if Kian was going to give her a gift, it would be a gift he chose.

"Yes, actually," he said, walking to the counter.

The florist's eyes roamed over him as he approached, and her fingers curled on the countertop.

Kian planted a hand on the edge of the counter and leaned toward her. "I need to purchase flowers for my mate."

The florist's brow furrowed. "Your...mate?"

Humans don't fucking use that word that way, Kian. They barely use it at all in this country.

"Yes. My *soul*mate." He glanced over his shoulder, toward the entrance, and lowered his voice. "And as she's very special to me, I'm going to need only your finest flowers."

The gleam in the woman's eyes grew wistful, but she didn't let her disappointment into her voice when she spoke. "Well, you're in luck. Everything we sell is the best."

He smiled. "Good."

"So, what is it you'd like? We can do custom arrangements if nothing is quite right."

"Ah, there's my problem. I'm not sure what she likes."

"Oh. Well, uh... Roses are the traditional choice for romance, and we can—"

"Yes, we'll do roses. But I also want everything else."

"I-I don't think understand."

Kian straightened and looked around the shop, waving vaguely. "All of it. One of every arrangement. Just the way you have them is fine."

Her eyes widened. "Sir, that's..."

"What I want." He leaned an elbow on the counter and nodded toward the cash register. "Go ahead. I'll settle the bill now, to demonstrate my sincerity."

As though in a daze, she worked the register, occasionally glancing up at him as she tallied items. After what seemed an eternity, she produced a total.

Kian withdrew his wallet from his pocket and counted out the cash in hundreds, sliding the stack to her. "This should cover it."

Her face paled as she accepted the money. "When would you like to pick these up? Or would you prefer delivery?"

"Delivery." Kian plucked up a pen from the little jar on the counter and jotted down Willow's address on the back of one of the In Bloom business cards on display, sliding the card to the florist. "They need to be delivered here this evening."

"This evening?" The florist shook her head. "Sir, I just...that's not possible. It'll take a full day just to get everything prepared, and then to transport it all..."

"Ah. Well." He opened his wallet again and took out the same amount of money he'd paid for the flowers. "This should cover any associated difficulties, shouldn't it?"

Though he couldn't sense the details, he felt the woman's inner struggle, felt her conflict. But after staring at the money for a time, she nodded slowly.

"Good." Kian returned his wallet to his pocket. "Thank you so much for your help." Turning, he walked toward the door.

He heard the woman move, heard the quiet tone of an outgoing call come from her phone.

"Hey, Dana," she said, voice flat. "Sorry to call on your day off, but I'm... I need you to come in for the afternoon. No, I understand. Yes, there's a big order, but this one, um... Well, there's a bonus involved."

The bell jingled as Kian opened the door and stepped outside. His excitement had only grown. A new gift for his mate, a new offering. A new reaction to enjoy. His beautiful mortal would be surrounded by beautiful flowers tonight, and he knew that none of those flowers would compare to her radiance.

But why stop with flowers? Humans loved gifts, and he was finding his own indirect joy in purchasing things for Willow. There were shops all over. Surely, he could find something more for her...

He'd only managed a few steps when his gaze fell upon a store across the plaza. Pandora's Toybox—an adult store specializing in adult toys.

He chuckled. "Oh, this is perfect."

What better gift than something to enhance her pleasure? In a way, it would be a gift for them both, as whenever Willow felt good, so did Kian. Perhaps it was a little selfish, but when had he ever claimed to be altruistic? He could admit his greed, especially when it came to his lush mortal. He wanted as much of her as he could get.

He wanted all of her.

Grinning, he strolled toward the Toybox.

Sixteen

❦

Willow lifted her camera and zoomed in on the couple sitting on the bed—Kimani and Darren. It was their tenth wedding anniversary, and they had wanted to do something special, so they'd reached out to Willow to arrange a couple's boudoir shoot. Willow loved it when she got to work with couples. It wasn't often that men were willing to participate with their partners, but Darren had been absolutely supportive and amazing with Kimani.

He sat with his back against the headboard and his wife between his legs, her head on his shoulder. He wore only a pair of black satin boxers, while Kimani was in a low-cut, lacey red bra and matching underwear that beautifully complemented her dark skin.

"Darren," Willow said, "could you rest a hand on Kimani's chest? Yes, just like that."

"Tempting, isn't it?" Kimani teased with a chuckle.

"Baby, you have no idea how hard this has been," Darren said. "Literally."

"Darren!"

"Oh, you can't tell me you don't feel it."

With rounded eyes, Kimani looked at Willow. "I am so sorry."

Willow laughed. "It's fine. Honestly, I love how openly affectionate you guys are. I'm glad you both feel comfortable here."

Kimani turned her face and looked up at Darren, cupping his cheek in her hand. She smiled, and the love that shone from her eyes made Willow's heart squeeze. "He does love me."

"Love every single bit of you." Darren pressed his lips against hers.

Willow was quick to take a few pictures, wanting to capture this moment of pure, undisguised love between the couple. It was times like these that she was especially aware of that dark, yawning cavern of loneliness inside herself, of her yearning to be loved just like this.

Her thoughts turned to Kian.

For the last few mornings, he'd shown up at Willow's house with breakfast for her. A bagel and coffee yesterday, a croissant and a hot cocoa today. They'd spend time talking as she got ready for the day, and before leaving, he always stole a kiss.

His breakfast.

And oh, God, that man could kiss. The way his lips moved against hers, that teasing tongue, and his taste... He made her toes curl and her panties wet every single time.

Willow shook off those thoughts and forced herself to focus on the here and now. She was working, and Kian had already occupied her mind far too much. "Kimani, could you turn your face toward the window and tilt your chin down?"

The woman did as instructed. "Like this?"

"Perfect. Close your eyes and smile softly. Darren, keep your hand on her chest, and move your mouth close to her ear, like you're about to tell her a secret."

Darren grinned. "Oh, there's plenty I want to whisper in her ear."

Kimani chuckled and playfully swatted his hand. "Behave."

Willow took several pictures before having them lie down in another position. She climbed onto the bed so she could take some shots from a higher angle.

When the session was over, Willow hooked her camera up to the computer to transfer the pictures while the couple dressed. She'd touch up the images tomorrow, but she never changed anything about the clients themselves—she only made alterations to the colors, balance, and occasionally the focus. Her goal was to capture the natural beauty of the people she photographed.

"I can't tell you how much I appreciate this, Willow," Kimani said as she approached. "This experience has been wonderful and so much fun."

"I'm so glad you loved it. And the pictures are amazing. I can't wait for you to see them."

"I can't wait either." Kimani spread her arms. "Can I hug you? I'd really love to."

"Aw, of course!"

Kimani embraced Willow tightly. "Thank you. I know these pictures are going to be special."

Willow smiled, and the women separated.

Darren walked up behind his wife and wrapped his arms around her. "Thanks, Willow."

"Anytime. I'll call you guys when they're ready to pick up."

"Sounds good." Darren dropped his mouth to his wife's ear. "Now, I can't wait to get you alone..."

Kimani laughed. "Guess we better get going. Have a great night, Willow!"

Willow grinned. "You too!"

The couple left hand-in-hand. Willow waited until the pictures had finished transferring before she shut down the computer, took the top comforter off the bed, and locked up the studio. She followed the short path to the back door. The sun was setting, and splashes of orange, violet, and pink painted the darkening sky. Crickets were already chirping in the long shadows cast by the sunset, filling the evening air with soft music.

Once inside, she dropped the comforter into the washing machine and started it. She smiled. It'd been a long, busy day, starting with a newborn baby photo session—which always required time, patience, and a bit of luck—and ending with back-to-back boudoir shoots. But it had been a good day. She loved spending time with her clients, loved helping them capture those special moments.

Bebe, Remy, and Loki ran into the laundry room and rubbed against her legs, meowing.

Willow chuckled. "I know, I know. Dinner time."

She walked into the kitchen with the cats running ahead of her. Their meows became louder and more demanding as they reached their dishes.

"You guys act like you don't get fed three times a day." She poured food into their bowls, and they dove in, quieting immediately. Willow ran her hands over their backs.

Not feeling up to cooking, she heated up a can of soup and ate at the kitchen island counter, scrolling through social media on her phone. After cleaning up, she paused to eye her cats. "Don't cause any trouble while I'm in the shower."

Bebe stared back, licking her chops.

In the bathroom, Willow undressed and hopped into the shower, doing her hardest *not* to think of Kian as she washed her hair and cleaned her body.

Of course, she failed...but she didn't fight it.

As hot water cascaded down her body, Willow closed her eyes and cupped her breasts, pinching her nipples and gently rolling them. She imagined Kian's hands were caressing her; large, confident, tipped with claws. She pinched harder. The sensation zipped right to her clit. Her nipples hardened between her fingers.

Releasing one breast, she smoothed her hand down her belly toward her pussy. As her fingers slipped between her folds to softly circle her clit, she thought of that night in the hotel with Kian, thought of the way his tongue had delved into her depths, how it had licked and stroked her. She thought of his hands grasping her firmly, holding her still as he ravaged her with his mouth, tongue, and teeth, all while he stared up at her with scorching hunger.

Yet this was no memory. In her imagination, she saw his inhuman, glowing blue eyes. There weren't pointed fingernails digging into her flesh but black claws. Horns rose from his head, begging for her to grab hold of them, and those glorious, diaphanous wings spread from his back.

Her heart pounded erratically, and her core ached to be filled. She quivered with want; she wanted him there with her, touching her, kissing her, fucking her.

Willow increased the pressure and speed of her finger. Her hips undulated, and she panted, squeezing her breast as the pleasure sharpened. She released it an instant later, thrusting out her hand to brace her palm against the shower wall. Tingles broke out over her skin as her thighs trembled.

"Kian," she whispered.

Pleasure burst through her in an electric shock. It stole her breath and made her body strain, each wave more powerful than the last. Willow cried out and clamped her thighs together around her hand, but she didn't stop strumming her clit, even when it became too much. She wanted this.

She wanted him.

Finally, when she could take no more, she relented, pressing firmly on her throbbing clit. She rested her head against the wall as she caught her breath, her body weak and heavy. Her sex clenched.

As good as the release had felt...it couldn't compare to what she truly craved.

Kian.

Willow groaned, withdrew her hand from between her thighs, and washed herself.

She hadn't lied to him that night at the overlook. What she felt for him, even after such a short time, was powerful. It was difficult to maintain distance with Kian when everything about him felt so right. She could so easily fall in love with him.

No. Can't let that happen, Willow.

God, the pain she'd suffer if he ever betrayed her...

Nope. Don't think about it.

Exiting the shower, she swiftly dried off. Her flushed skin prickled in the cool air. She wrung her hair out with the towel to shed as much of the excess water as she could.

Willow pulled on her underwear, a pair of gray pajama shorts, and a loose, long-sleeved top. A pair of cozy fluffy socks added the final touch of comfort to her loungewear. Grabbing the blow dryer off the hanger on the wall, she dried her hair.

Once she was done, she turned off the light and padded to the kitchen. She was ready to wind down, which meant snuggling on the couch with her favorite blanket, a movie, and a glass of wine.

She'd just poured the wine when the doorbell rang.

Willow frowned, set the wine bottle down, and glanced at the clock. It was almost eight. No one usually visited her at this time of night, and she wasn't expecting any packages. Kimani and Darren might have forgotten something, though Willow was sure they would've texted her if that was the case.

She walked to the door and peeked through its window. The frosted glass only granted her a distorted view of someone standing on her porch. "Who is it?"

"Delivery from In Bloom Floral for a Miss Crowley," a man replied.

Willow's brow furrowed, and she glanced at her cats, who had gathered nearby. "Huh?"

They just blinked at her.

She unlocked the deadbolt and cracked the door open far enough for the chain to catch. A man wearing a green t-shirt with *In Bloom Floral* printed on it in flourishing script stood on her porch, holding two flower arrangements in vases.

Willow arched a brow. "Um, that's me, but..."

"These are all are for you, then," the man said.

All for me?

Unlocking the chain, Willow opened the door wider and peered past the man. Three other people stood behind him, each with their own armful of flowers—some in vases, some in baskets, all in varying colors and sizes.

"Wait, all of these?" Willow asked.

The man smiled sheepishly. "Yeah. But, uh, this is just some of them."

"Some of them? What do you mean?"

"There's more in the van. Oh, and...in the cars."

"What? I...I didn't order any of these."

"They're from him," said one of the women behind the delivery man, turning her head and nodding toward someone outside Willow's view.

Willow stepped out onto the porch. Her eyes widened when they landed on Kian.

He stood at his car, which was parked along the curb in front of two other cars and the florist's van. He leaned back on his vehicle, hands in his coat pockets and a sultry smirk upon his lips. Even from that distance, even in the deepening darkness, she could make out the smug gleam in his eyes.

"Evening, Violet," he called.

"You... I..." Willow blinked.

"Should we bring these inside?" the delivery man asked, drawing her attention back to him.

"Um, sure? Just...put them wherever there's room, I guess."

He nodded and stepped into her home.

Willow crossed her arms over her chest as she watched the other delivery people file in. They soon emerged, hurried back to their vehicles, and retrieved another load of flower arrangements. In her shock, she quickly lost count of the number of trips they made—and the number of bouquets and vases they carried inside.

She looked away from them only when Kian approached her. "Kian, what is this?"

He stopped beside her, leaning a shoulder against the house. "I bought you flowers, obviously."

"When you buy someone flowers, it usually means a single bouquet. This looks like you bought the whole shop!"

"I did."

"But...but... This must've cost a fortune!"

"Ah, Willow, what value does money hold compared to your happiness?"

Willow opened her mouth to say something only to snap it shut. The whole shop? What was she supposed to say?

"That's all of them," a woman said as she and her companions exited the house. She smiled at Willow. "We hope you love them."

Willow returned the smile. "Thank you." As the delivery people walked to the curb, Willow looked back at Kian and swept a hand toward the parked vehicles. "This is ridiculous."

He grinned, and damn him if it wasn't stunning. "If by ridiculous you mean amazingly thoughtful, you are correct."

Shaking her head, she stepped back into her home and stopped abruptly. Floral arrangements covered every flat surface that had been available—the windowsills, the tables, the bookcases. "My house looks like a botanical garden vomited into it."

Kian chuckled behind her. "You've quite a way with words."

She pressed her fingers to her temples and closed her eyes. This was unbelievable. Exhaling slowly, she lowered her hands, opened her eyes, and turned toward Kian. He had followed her inside and closed the door, and now was standing not a foot away from her. She took a step back.

"Kian, there is such a thing as overdoing it." She gestured to her living room. "As thoughtful and as sweet as this is, it's all too much."

His brow knitted, his smile fell, and his shoulders slumped ever so slightly. "You're displeased?"

The way he deflated sent a guilty pang to Willow's heart that made her feel like the worst person in the world. "No. No, I'm not," she hurried to say. "It's just... You don't need to buy me."

Sighing, Kian moved closer and brushed the backs of his fingers over her cheek. "I'm well aware that I cannot buy you, little mortal. I just didn't know which ones you'd like."

"You could have asked me."

"That would've spoiled the surprise." He took hold of her hand and lifted it, pressing a kiss to her knuckles. He froze. Nostrils flaring, he inhaled deeply, and his chest rumbled. "Oh, Willow, Willow, Willow."

She tried to ignore the way his growl made her clit twitch. Brow creasing, she asked, "What?"

"You've been having fun without me." He breathed in again and chuckled, the sound filled with wicked promise. Using his thumb, he raised her finger, and, gaze locked with hers, slid it into his mouth.

Her breath hitched, her eyes flared, and heat pooled between her thighs as he sucked. The desire she'd felt in the shower was nothing compared to what she felt now. Her breasts grew heavy, and her nipples tightened into hard, aching points. He twirled his tongue around her finger, and slowly, oh so slowly, pulled it out.

"You're more delicious with every taste," he purred.

Oh fuck.

Willow yanked her hand from his grasp and wiped it on her shirt. "Okay, um... No more of that."

"You're adorable when you're flustered." He leaned forward until his mouth was beside her ear. "And remember, I know when your words and your wants don't align, Violet."

She pointed her finger at him, but when she realized it was *that* finger, she snatched it back. "There is still such a thing as consent. My body reacts naturally, but that doesn't mean I'm in agreement."

Kian hummed and brushed her hair back, tucking it behind her ear. "You'll get there in time." He retreated a step and spread his arms wide. "Now tell me, my sweet, which flower is your favorite?"

With her skin still tingling where he'd touched her, Willow looked around the room until her eye caught on a bright yellow sunflower. She walked to it, plucked it from the vase, and held it up to Kian, who'd already dropped his arms. "This."

"Why that one?"

She turned the flower toward herself and gently stroked the petals with her fingertips. "Because looking at it makes me happy."

He smiled. The expression was subtle, warm, and intimate in a way he'd rarely displayed. And though it did not blaze with his usual passion and lust, it held a different sort of charm—one that could eventually prove even harder to resist. "Then I will be sure to shower you with sunflowers."

Willow chuckled. "Let's hold off on the flowers for a little while."

"Fortunately, I bought you another gift." Kian's lips took on that devilish slant. "One wholly unrelated to flowers."

She slipped the sunflower back into its vase. "Kian, you really, really don't need to buy me things."

"And if I were to say that it pleases me to make these offerings to you?"

Willow rubbed her arm and smiled sheepishly. "I guess it's okay?"

"Hmm. I'll...moderate my impulses from now on. The last thing I want to do is make you uncomfortable." His eyes swept over her, very slowly, their hunger having returned. "Quite the opposite, in fact."

He reached inside his coat and withdrew a small black box from an interior pocket. Holding the box on his palm, he offered it to her. *Pandora's* was emblazoned on the lid in golden script, and the box was too large for Willow to assume it was jewelry.

She accepted it. The box had some weight to it, only further ruling out the possibility of jewelry. Taking hold of the lid, she slid it off and peered inside.

Willow blinked.

No. Is that...? It couldn't be, could it?

A purple silicone butt plug with a heart-shaped, amethyst gem at the end rested upon a bed of black velvet inside.

"Oh." It was all she could really say at that moment. Of all the things she might've guessed he would give her, this would never have crossed her mind.

"Do you like it?" he asked.

"Ummm..."

"What is it, Willow?"

She looked up at him. His brows were slanted down, and there was uncertainty in his eyes.

"It's pretty, but... Kian, you know what this is, right?"

He gave her a dry look. "Willow, I'm an incubus. Of course I know what a butt plug is." He smiled. "And that one will be a beautiful adornment for your luscious ass."

Warmth filled her cheeks. "It's just, well, these aren't usually given as gifts. At least, not when people first meet."

"We met weeks ago, Violet." He grinned and dipped his chin toward the box. "Would you like to try it?"

"What? Now? No!" She smacked the lid back onto the box.

Kian shrugged, waving nonchalantly. "Now, later, whenever."

Willow set the box on the console table next to one of the many vases. "I've...never..."

"Never had someone fuck your ass?"

Blushing profusely, Willow shook her head. She couldn't believe she was having this conversation. Well, maybe she could, considering what he was. And it wasn't like they hadn't been intimate before.

When she turned back toward him, Kian grabbed her by her hips and tugged her against him. She gasped, flattened her hands on his chest, and met his gaze.

His lips were spread in a salacious grin that revealed his fangs. "Then I will be the first to claim yours."

Willow's core clenched. Lewd thoughts filled her mind; Kian behind her, his hands on her hips, his claws digging into her skin, his cock pushing into her ass. What would it feel like? Would it hurt? Would it be pleasurable?

"You're thinking about it, aren't you Willow?" Kian asked, voice husky. When she pulled away, he released her.

"I'm not," she said over her shoulder as she walked into the kitchen.

Kian's boots thudded softly on the floor as he followed. "How naughty of you to lie to me. Shall we include a spanking when I inevitably claim that delectable backside?"

Did she want him to spank her?

...*Yes.*

"No." She picked up her glass of wine—which had been buried amidst another cluster of flower arrangements on the counter—and took a hearty drink.

"Ah, alcohol. Eager to lower your inhibitions?"

She refilled the glass. "I am eager to *relax*."

Kian leaned on the island counter, his blue eyes nearly glowing. "So, let's relax. Perhaps a massage? As you're well aware, I'm rather good with my hands."

Willow rolled her eyes. "I'm going to watch a movie. You can stay if you promise to behave, otherwise you can walk your fairy behind right out that door."

"I bet you enjoy watching me walk away."

"Your ass is quite nice, but that's beside the point."

He laughed and turned his palms up. "You win. A movie it is."

Seventeen

༄

"I knew you'd see it my way." Willow tried to hide her smile as she took another drink of wine before making her way into the living room. "You know, you could relax yourself and maybe...drop your glamour? I've already seen you."

"You could also take off your clothes. I've already seen you."

"Not the same thing." After shifting a couple flower-filled vases around, she set her glass atop a coaster on the end table, lifted her blanket, and sat on the couch with her legs curled to the side. She usually had to fight her cats for a spot, but they were likely hiding after the delivery had caused such a commotion.

Picking up the remote, she turned on the television.

Kian removed his coat, draped it on the arm of the recliner chair, and kicked off his boots. As he approached the couch, he unbuttoned the sleeves of his dress shirt and rolled them up. The first change happened subtly, but Willow's heart quickened when she noticed it—his skin was paling to that soft, ashy gray.

Her eyes jumped to his face. She watched as his features sharpened, his ears lengthened to points, and horns sprouted from his temples. His irises lit up, the blue light spreading to cover the whites of his eyes and cast a gentle glow on his cheeks. When he grinned down at her, his canines were even longer.

Willow swallowed and forced her attention to the television. He sat beside her, reclining with an ease that might've suggested he'd already worn his own butt-groove into the couch.

Trying to ignore him, Willow scrolled through lists of movies on various streaming services, seeking something that sounded interesting. What kind of movies did Kian enjoy? Did he even watch movies at all?

One of his hands slipped beneath the blanket and cupped her calf. She blinked as he drew her leg across his lap, peeled off her sock, and began massaging her foot.

"Remember, you agreed to behave," she said.

"You've had a long day, Violet," he said with a saccharine smile. "Just helping you unwind."

Willow narrowed her eyes, though she couldn't prevent the smile tugging at her own lips. She quickly turned back to the screen so her hair would hide her expression.

His hands did feel good. Like, really, really good. He knew exactly where every bit of tension hid, no matter how deep, and always used exactly the right amount of pressure to massage it away.

She clamped her lips together before she could release a contented sigh.

You need to do something here, Willow. Spoil the mood.

The next movie on the list popped up, and her smile widened. A gory horror movie.

Perfect.

She made the selection, set the remote down, and picked up her wine.

The rating screen appeared, listing the reasons the movie was R-rated. Blood, strong violence and gore, language, sexual content.

Wait, sexual content? Crap.

"Hmm. Are these the sorts of films you usually watch?" Kian asked, hands continuing their work.

"Yep," she said, adding a pop to the *p*.

Kian chuckled. "Intriguing." He ran the tip of a nail down her sole, making her squeak and jerk her foot away. "I can't wait to explore your dark side, Willow."

She scrunched her nose at him. "Soooo, you want me to go on a killing spree and chop people up with an axe?"

Taking hold of her foot again, he guided it back onto his thighs. "You know that's not what I mean. Everyone has those secret desires they keep buried deep. Those wants they are too ashamed or afraid to admit. On some level, everyone wants a little...wickedness from time to time."

"Mmhmm. Now, shh, moving is starting." She took another sip of wine.

He laughed again and resumed the massage, though she swore there was something different in the way his fingers moved now. Something more...suggestive, more sensual. Something that sparked a quiver of anticipation in her belly.

The movie played, and Willow tried hard to focus on it, to keep her eyes on the screen and not on the man beside her. But that proved difficult as he removed her other sock and continued to rub her feet, his hands occasionally traveling up to her calves. It didn't help that the alcohol was taking effect, warming her from within, making her body grow lax. Her skin tingled, and there was an insistent pulse in her core.

Willow set her glass on the coaster, sighed, and wiggled down until she was lying on her side.

"Comfortable?" Kian asked.

"Mmhmm..."

The couch creaked as Kian shifted. Willow wasn't immediately aware of what he was doing, but it became apparent when he braced a hand on the cushion behind her and lowered himself onto his side, gently wedging his body between hers and the backrest. One of his arms slipped under her head, offering support, while he hooked the other around her middle. A firm tug nestled her back against his front.

She drew in a sharp breath, but she couldn't bring herself to pull away. He was solid, warm, real, and the way they fit together was just so right, so perfect. She practically melted against him.

"How about now?" he whispered, his breath tickling her ear and making her shiver.

"What are you doing?"

"Just getting comfortable too, Violet." As he spoke, the rumbling of his chest against her back made Willow's nipples harden.

His spicy, alluring scent thickened, and Willow breathed it in, growing even more intoxicated. "You're supposed to be behaving."

Kian's palm settled over her soft belly. "I am."

For an instant, Willow experienced a flare of self-consciousness, and she hated it. She'd worked hard over the years to love her body, to not feel ashamed of it, but those insecurities still crept up on her sometimes. They'd never fully go away. But with the way Kian so lovingly caressed her, with the way he looked upon her...

He hadn't shown any disgust or displeasure when it came to Willow's body. With him, it was the complete opposite.

He'd worshipped her.

She thrust those insecurities from her mind.

The movie continued, but Willow had no idea what was happening. All she was aware of was Kian. His heat, his scent, his body, which molded to hers...and the hard length of his cock against her ass.

Why am I fighting this? Why am I fighting what he makes me feel?

That could be the alcohol talking, Willow. It makes you horny, remember?

And yet, she couldn't bring herself to care.

Willow brushed her fingers back and forth over Kian's forearm. "Are you hungry, Kian?"

"For you? Always."

"But are you *hungry*?"

"You give me enough to take the edge off, whether you mean to or not."

Which meant he was never truly fulfilled, never satisfied. Which meant he still hungered. She recalled the glimpse she'd caught of him when he'd found her after her meeting with Amanda. His eyes had been dull, cradled by dark circles, and his cheeks had been sunken in. Though he was beautiful, he still wasn't nearly as vibrant as the first time they'd met.

He needed to feed.

And he depended upon Willow for nourishment.

Reaching over her head, she carefully felt around the end table until she found the remote, pointed it at the television, and pressed the power button. The screen went black.

He chuckled. "Movie not to your liking?"

"Wasn't really paying much attention to it." She tossed the remote onto the floor.

"Oh? Is something distracting you, little mortal?"

"You know exactly what you're doing, Kian." Willow clasped his hand and guided it down. It slid over her belly, under the blanket, and beneath the waistbands of her shorts and underwear, until his fingertips came to rest just above her pussy. She withdrew her hand, leaving his in place. "Feed."

Kian was silent, and had grown very, very still.

"You're giving into me?" he asked, voice low, husky, and just a little hesitant.

"You need to feed."

185

He skimmed the tips of his nails over her pubic hair, sending fresh tingles through her. "Are you drunk?"

"No. Maybe just a little tipsy. But I'm aware, and I want this."

"You're sure?"

"I mean, if you don't want to..." Willow settled her hand on his forearm to pull it away.

Kian's arm tensed, and he cupped her sex. His grip on her was firm and possessive. "Far be it from me to refuse what is freely given." He brushed his nose over her hair, beside her ear. "Spread your thighs for me, Violet."

Heart quickening, Willow shifted her hips to spread her legs. She was thankful for how large her sofa was. Her breath caught when Kian's fingers parted her sex and glided through her slick.

"Gods, you're so fucking wet," he growled. He continued to lazily stroke up and down, spreading her essence, leisurely caressing her labia. "Is this what you thought about when you touched yourself earlier, Willow? Was it my fingers you imagined?"

He hadn't even touched her clit yet, but he was eliciting such strong responses from her body already.

Willow's grip on his arm tightened. "Yes."

His tongue flicked just beneath her ear as he dipped two fingers into her pussy, pumping them slow and deep. "Did you think of my tongue on your cunt?"

Willow shivered as whispers of pleasure coursed through her. She spread her legs wider and arched her hips into his touch. "Yes."

Kian chuckled, the sound dark and sultry, as he kicked away the blanket and braced his leg over one of hers to lock it in place. Pulling his fingers out, he dragged them through her slit up to her clit and circled it, his movements gentle and unhurried. "And did you think of my cock, Willow? Did you fantasize about me fucking you?"

That pleasure coiled at her center, sending spiraling echoes through her limbs that made her squeeze his arm and grasp the cushion beneath her. "Yes," she whispered. "I did."

A restlessness filled her, an urgent need for more. Unbidden, her hips undulated in time with his strokes. As much as she wanted him to press harder, to bring her to that delicious peak, she loved this slow, tantalizing buildup. The sensation pulsing through her heightened with every sweep of his fingers around her clit, promising ecstasy to come. Heat spread through her.

Panting softly, Willow reached up and cupped the side of his head, brushing her fingers over his pointed ear and the base of a horn. She turned her face toward his. Kian's brightly glowing eyes met her gaze.

"Fuck, you are so beautiful, Willow." He slid his fingers back down and thrust them inside her.

Her pussy clenched around them, and she moaned.

"See how you cling to me?" He pumped them in and out, again and again. "How hot and wet you are? You were made for pleasure, Willow." He lowered his face. "You were made for me."

Kian pressed his mouth to Willow's. The kiss began slow, at odds with the rapid pace of his fingers, but he soon sucked her bottom lip into his mouth and nipped it with a fang. She shuddered in his hold. He chuckled, and his tongue soothed the sting before coaxing her lips open and slipping through, seizing control. It swirled and stroked in time with the movements of his hand.

The sensations built upon each other, creating a swell of heat and pressure inside Willow.

He shifted, curling his arm beneath her until his hand slipped under the collar of her shirt to capture her breast. Willow arched into his touch. He kneaded her tender flesh and pinched and twisted her nipple, every tug making her clit twitch.

Willow gasped against his mouth and gripped his horn, pulling him closer. She craved more. Her tongue stroked his, traced his fangs, and teased the piercings on his bottom lip. His mouth was sublime, tasting wholly *other*. And his kisses? She could lose herself in them forever.

When he slid his fingers free of her pussy, a gush of slick followed. Then his fingertips were back on her clit, and this time, he was merciless. He strummed that swollen bud hard and fast, assaulting her with a torrent of overwhelming sensation.

She tore her mouth from his with a cry and tipped her head back, but her eyes remained locked with his. "Kian..."

He stared down at her fervently. There was no humor in his glowing eyes, just unbridled lust and feral possessiveness. "Feed me, Willow," he growled. "Give it all to me. Let me hear you. Let me see you. Let me *feel* you."

She'd never believed it when women in romance novels climaxed upon command, had thought it pure fantasy, but Kian proved her wrong. His deep, sensual voice, combined with his touch, his scent, and his consuming gaze, took dominion over her. Her thoughts shattered, and a cry of sweet agony tore from her throat. Willow's body tensed, and her eyes snapped shut as white-hot pleasure blazed through her.

She surrendered to the flames, to the heat, to the searing ecstasy. She surrendered to the fact that Kian's touch was the only thing keeping her bound to reality.

The sound of her harsh, uneven breathing filled the room, and she clung to him, writhing as wave after wave of pleasure swept over her. This was nothing like what she'd felt in the shower, nothing like she'd ever felt with her own hand.

It was all him. It was all Kian. Whether it was due to his natural talent or his magic, Willow didn't care. She just wanted more.

And he gave it to her, stroking her clit relentlessly.

She bit her lip, silencing a strained cry. Kian's head swooped down, and he captured her mouth in another kiss, taking her wild gasps into himself as his lips ravished hers.

"Oh God! Kian, please," she begged. "Stop. No more."

"Give me another, Willow," he growled against her mouth.

"I can't..."

"You can." He pinched her clit.

Willow came again with a hitched, broken cry. Her back bowed as her sex contracted and spasmed, spilling her essence. Kian slipped his hand down and thrust his fingers hard inside her, again and again, and her pussy clenched around them, eager to pull them deeper. He crushed his mouth to hers and held her close. Willow was helpless but to ride out the storm, desperately seeking shelter against his hard body.

His kiss gentled as the maelstrom inside her calmed. It was drugging, enticing, lulling. His fingers continued to pump, slow and soothing. Her sex quivered, and her body trembled.

She felt his lips stretch into a smile, felt his piercings against her mouth, just before he lifted his head. His dangling hair tickled her shoulder. Willow opened her eyes. Kian's gaze burned, hot and bright.

Sliding his fingers from her pussy, he withdrew his hand from her shorts and lifted it. The slick clinging to his skin shimmered in the light. Kian slipped those fingers into his mouth. He groaned as he slowly dragged them out, sucking them clean.

"Fuck, Willow." Kian's tongue emerged to run across his lips. "When you finally accept me, I will feast upon that delicious cunt until my insatiable thirst is quenched."

Willow's sex clenched. She was tempted to say yes. Oh God, was she tempted. Tempted to strip off her clothes and let him lick her to his heart's content and beyond, to lose herself on an endless sea of bliss.

But no. Not yet. She was not ready to take this any further. She...needed time. This had been about feeding him, and by the light of his eyes and the luster of his skin, he'd received ample nourishment.

Softly panting, Willow turned her body more fully toward him, rested her head on his biceps, and pressed her forehead against his chest. She tucked her arms between their bodies and let his scent enfold her. "You're so sure I'll accept you?"

Kian lifted his leg and stretched it out alongside Willow's as he wrapped his arm around her. "No reason to pretend, my Violet. We both know it's inevitable."

Willow hummed softly, but she didn't respond. She knew he was right. It wasn't a matter of if, but when. She felt it in her heart —Kian was the one she'd been waiting for. And yet...her fear of being hurt still lurked deep within, its tendrils having spread like overgrown vines that wouldn't hesitate to constrict her chest whenever she made the mistake of hoping. She wanted him, wanted whatever life she could have with him. But what he was...

You can take it slow, Willow. There is time.

She closed her eyes, content to remain here in his arms. A heaviness settled over her, brought on by the wine and the pleasure Kian had wrung from her. She felt relaxed, sated, and safe. He combed his fingers through her hair, his steady, unhurried touches coaxing her toward sleep.

Willow didn't fight it.

Eighteen

A slow smirk spread across Kian's lips. Willow's silence told him everything—she wasn't ready, not yet, but she knew this could only end one way.

She would be utterly, irrevocably his.

That knowledge amplified the arousal buzzing through him and deepened the ache in his cock. That ravenous haze had suffused his vision, staining his world a delirious crimson. He wanted more from her, wanted everything, and he wanted it now. But he could only bring himself to hold her a little closer, a little tighter.

Why not take more?

Because she'd accomplished exactly what she'd intended. Kian had been fed, and gods, had it been good. Her contentment washed over him in tender waves, each instilling him with a flicker of energy that would ensure he'd not need sustenance for a long while.

But that alone wouldn't have been enough to stop him. The fulfillment of his needs did not dampen the fires of his longing, not even slightly.

The rules for mortal-incubus interactions didn't apply to her. He couldn't charm her with magic, couldn't heighten her desires until they were too powerful for her to resist. And his pursuit of her had broken all the personal rules he'd adopted. Kian had pushed beyond his understanding, beyond his experience. He still wasn't sure what he was doing, but it was clear that he could only push so far, so hard, before he'd drive her away.

Which meant he had to restrain himself.

Willow would give him only what she wanted to give, and only when she was ready.

But more than anything, he resisted his urge for more because the way they were lying together felt so right. Because she fit against him so snugly, because her body was so languid, so warm, so soft. Because right now, he couldn't imagine himself anywhere across all the realms but right here, with Willow tucked securely in his arms.

This was new. Intimate, tender, almost...profound.

She shifted her leg, and her thigh brushed his shaft.

Kian hissed. His cock twitched, straining so hard against his pants that he was certain it would explode. He clenched his jaw against the discomfort, against the thrill.

"Not fair," he rasped, glancing down at her. "You're not—"

The words died on his tongue as he beheld her face. Willow's eyes were closed, her dark lashes creating delicate shadows on her flushed cheeks. Her full, kiss swollen lips were parted, allowing her slow, deep breaths to flow freely. Serenity had smoothed her features. In that moment, Willow had no cares, no struggles, no pain.

She was at peace.

His smile eased.

Kian wanted more of her body. He longed to run his tongue over every inch of her skin, to learn every contour with the tips of his fingers, to feel her shudder and convulse around him. He longed to discover every single way to pleasure his mortal, and then he would strive to create new ways.

Bending his neck, he placed a tender kiss atop her head and inhaled, drawing in her sweet, flowery scent, which was tinged with that of her arousal.

He wanted more of this too. This shared quiet, this stillness. More of the simple yet powerful satisfaction of holding her in his arms and just...existing together.

She fed me.

Something warm and gentle unfurled in Kian's chest, and the lust haze gradually receded from his view.

Willow enjoyed his touch, had reveled in the pleasure he'd given her, had craved more. Even now he sensed her want. Yet her desires hadn't been her primary motivation. She'd acted not because she wanted, but because he needed.

She hadn't shed her reservations, hadn't overcome her hesitancy. Her inner conflict remained. Her heart was immense, and she felt very, very deeply—and she was aware of it. Aware enough to fear the power of what Kian made her feel.

Tonight, she'd briefly set those reservations aside. She'd set them aside for Kian.

She knew he hadn't been able to feed from anyone but her. She knew she was his only source of sustenance. And despite her misgivings, despite her concerns, she'd put his needs before her own tonight. That was no small thing.

Hell, it was bigger and more important than Kian could rightly comprehend.

He'd only revealed himself to one mortal in all his life—Willow. None of the countless others had known his nature, had understood how he fed, had realized that he lived off their gratification. Had they known what he was, would any of them have freely offered what he required to survive? Would any of them have ever considered Kian and his needs?

Would any have fed him voluntarily?

He couldn't answer those questions, not with any certainty. But he guessed that most of those people would've fled upon learning he was incubus. In their ignorance, so many humans had relished his company. They'd lost themselves to passion and pleasure, they'd acted with wild abandon, had said and done things they would never have considered saying or doing on their own.

But even under the belief that Kian was a normal, attractive human, had any of them ever taken his wants and needs into account? He'd given, and they'd taken, unaware that he was the one who'd gained in the end.

Kian combed his fingers through her soft hair. Willow, this precious little mortal, his Violet, had thought of his wellbeing. She'd benefitted from it, of course. But that she'd brought it up at all, that she'd considered his needs...

And what if she just used that to justify her selfishness, Kian? What if she said she wanted to feed you just so she wouldn't feel the guilt of having you pleasure her without reciprocation?

He frowned, brow furrowing.

Living for so long amongst mortals had certainly strengthened the cynicism he'd first learned in the Evergarden, which had proven a necessary survival skill in the mortal realm. Yet that cynicism was wrong here. It was inappropriate, perverse, sickening.

He hated that he'd doubted her intentions for even an instant. Though he couldn't pretend to know Willow's inner workings, he felt her emotions as clearly and fiercely as he felt his own, and he knew she wasn't that kind of person.

His Willow wasn't manipulative. She didn't twist people to her own ends, didn't take advantage of the vulnerable, didn't see opportunity in the misfortune of others. She wasn't the sort who'd use him for pleasure.

She's nothing like me.

A cold, rough tendril slithered around his heart and squeezed.

He quickly cast those thoughts aside; dwelling on them would do him no good.

It was best not to worry. Best to take things as they were, to avoid looking too deeply. Whatever her motivations, Willow had fed him, and though that feeding hadn't been nearly as potent as when they'd fucked in the hotel room, it had filled Kian more than anything since that night. That was all that mattered.

It was also the biggest shadow looming over him.

He was satiated, but he craved more. Full, but painfully aroused. Relaxed, but taut with desire. He was aware of Willow's body, of every tiny point of contact between them, aware of her soft breath on his shirt, of the subtle rise and fall of her chest, of the gentle, barely perceptible beating of her heart.

And he was aware that her thigh was still against his cock, its heat baking into him through their clothing. His shaft throbbed. Agony pulsed through his groin, keeping his balls tight and overly sensitive, making his lower belly simultaneously hollow and heavy.

Willow was right there. He could still taste her on his tongue, could still smell her arousal in the air, and he knew that if he reached into her panties again, he'd find her soaking wet. A single touch would rekindle her passion. He doubted she would protest being woken that way.

Yet he knew that he would not be able to stop, that fingers would not suffice. His need grew by the moment, expanding into a ravenous, boundless void that could only be satisfied by Willow in her entirety.

He needed to fuck her. Hard, fast, relentlessly. Then slow and sensually. He needed his cock deep inside her cunt, so deep that he would feel the vibrations of her moans and cries, so deep that they would be one. He needed her soft, thick thighs around his hips, squeezing. Needed her hands on his chest, her nails raking his flesh. He needed to see lust gleaming in her half-lidded eyes, needed to see her hair tousled, needed to see her chest heaving with her panting breaths, her nipples erect, her—

Kian stiffened. One of his hands had crept down her back, coming to rest on her ass. Another heartbeat, and he would've grasped her thigh. Another breath, and he would've thrown her legs wide and sliced through her clothes with his claws.

His pulse thundered in his ears, and his fingers twitched with indecision.

Kian wanted her, needed her. And she wanted him. She couldn't hide it, even if she denied it outwardly.

And still, Willow had repeatedly demonstrated immense self-control. She'd refused to give in to her desires, refused to become a slave to them, even at their strongest. Because this meant more to her. Sex meant more to her.

She means more to me.

That was why he hungered for her so deeply, even now. That was why he yearned to have her. Why he couldn't just...take her. If he succumbed to his desires, if he violated her trust and ignored her boundaries, he chanced rousing the shadowy beast lurking in his heart and unleashing its dark, dangerous, unending appetites.

For all fae, there existed a fine line between order and chaos. A fine line between light and dark. For incubi in particular...

Once those bestial desires were let loose, they would demand far more than pleasure. Beings like Lachlan knew that all too well —they reveled in it.

That primal part of Kian, which whispered to him through his instincts, demanded he rut his mate. It demanded he claim her, demanded he put his mark on her, demanded he dominate her and show this world and all others that he was her master in every way, that she *belonged* to him.

But the rational part of Kian knew there was a distinct difference between Willow being his and Willow belonging to him.

Was it possible for his desire for her to become twisted? To become something damning? If he crossed that line and gave in to his basest instincts, he risked falling. Risked turning into a thing that he despised, a thing that violated the way he'd tried to live and went against his morals, however limited in scope they were.

If he took from Willow now without her consent, if he cast aside his own resistance, he would only be opening a path for everything deeper and darker. He would be welcoming chaos into himself—or rather awakening the chaos that had always dwelt within. And he would devour her in every way possible. There'd be nothing left. All the things he was coming to adore about her would be gone, and only only raw, primal hunger would remain. There'd be only sensation, unadulterated pleasure without substance.

And he'd lose Willow.

He'd lose his mate.

The thought of Willow no longer being in his life was like a shard of ice piercing his chest, freezing cold and agonizing. A sour tang of fear spread with that ice, pooling in his gut, unlike any emotion he'd ever felt on his own.

He needed to leave.

He needed to leave *now*.

Kian let out a slow, harsh breath through his nose and shifted his hips back just enough to break the contact between his crotch and her leg. The pressure in his cock flared. He bit his lip to keep himself from groaning, and he didn't allow his body to move as he waited out the ache.

When the discomfort had subsided enough for him to think somewhat clearly, he set about the next step of his increasingly difficult task—extracting himself from his current position. Carefully as he could, he slipped his arm out from beneath Willow, settling her head on the cushion.

She stirred as he pushed himself up. Kian stilled.

"Kian," she mumbled.

He stroked her cheek. "Sleep, Willow."

Kian stared at her, unmoving, until she settled again. Then, with continued care, he lifted a leg, swung it over her, and planted his foot on the floor. Bracing a hand on the backrest, he climbed off the couch, somehow managing not to disturb her further.

He paused with his back toward her, closed his eyes, and bowed his head. For a while he simply breathed, willing the heat and tension out of his blood, seeking calm.

Need to leave. For her. I need to leave for her sake.

Forcing himself to move, he stepped into his boots, snatched up his coat, and swept it on as he walked around the couch. The front door was only a few steps away. Once he was outside, with the closed door serving as a barrier between him and Willow, he'd be all right. He'd be able to go.

By light and dark, he wanted to believe that.

But as he curled his fingers around the door handle, he stopped. He knew the last thing he should've done was look at her again, but his head turned, and his eyes fell upon Willow.

The sight caught him off guard. Her blanket was on the floor, forgotten, and she lay on her side, purple hair splayed across the cushion beneath her. She'd curled up a little, her limbs drawn in closer to her body. She seemed so small, so...alone and out of place. The flowers filling the room only strengthened that perception.

Kian's throat constricted as he thought of all the times he'd slipped out while the human who'd just provided him with nourishment was recovering from overwhelming pleasure, unaware of his departure. As he thought of all the mortals he'd abandoned while they were at their most vulnerable, all the people he'd left bereft after using them for his needs.

He couldn't do that to Willow. Would never do that to her.

Fuuuuuck.

He built tall, thick walls in his mind, hoping they would be enough to keep the beast contained for a little longer, and walked back around to the front of the couch. Crouching, he slipped his arms under his mate. She stirred again, but only to turn toward him and nestle her cheek against his arm.

Perfect. She's fucking perfect.

Kian stood, lifting her off the couch and holding her limp form against his chest. He ignored the heat of her body, ignored her enticing scent, ignored the still burning fires within him, and carried Willow to her bedroom.

The room was soft and feminine, its colors and décor suiting her perfectly. Purple and white bedding, a canopy draped with lacy white cloth as lovely as it was delicate, and tiny strings of lights, currently dark, running up the posts and across the canopy. What was it he'd seen humans call those? Fairy lights?

Unless she'd been inspired to redecorate upon learning Kian was fae, he couldn't help but wonder if those lights were another little detail woven in by the Fates.

He laid her gently atop the bed. She shifted toward him as he withdrew, but settled quickly, curling an arm under her head and letting out a contented sigh that was followed by the slow, even breathing of slumber. Kian loosened the bedding and drew the blanket over her. Delicately, he brushed her hair out of her face, tucking it behind her ear. His fingertips stroked her soft, smooth skin.

This female was more dangerous than anyone he'd encountered, whether fae or human. The spell she'd cast over him was the most potent magic in existence. Nothing made him feel as powerless as she did.

Something compelled him to switch on the fairy lights. Their warm glow bathed her skin, lending her more vibrancy. Perhaps when she awoke, she'd look up at those lights and think of him.

His feet refused to move when he tried to go. Standing at her bedside, staring at her, he wanted nothing more than to lie beside her, put his arms around her, and sleep. But he couldn't trust himself to sleep. Couldn't trust himself to behave. Not when every instinct inside him raged to claim his mate in every way possible.

Movement drew his attention to the foot of the bed. All three of Willow's cats had leapt onto it, and now sat in a row, staring at him with huge pupils.

"I'll entrust her to you, then," he whispered, as though the choice had been his.

The only response he received was an impatient flick of Bebe's tail.

Temptation urged him to kiss Willow before he left, but he knew better than that. Even a chaste kiss would lead to memories of the taste of her lips, of the breathy sounds she'd made in the heights of passion, of the way her slick cunt had contracted around his fingers...

Kian spun away and stalked out of the room. His frantic stride carried him to the kitchen, where he stopped to write a quick note.

Had a wonderful time, Violet. Hope you rested well. You'll need all your strength when I come back for breakfast.

He hung it on her refrigerator before rushing out of her house and locking the door behind him.

Nineteen

"**B**rian's been such an asshole since his promotion," Jamie said as she piled steak, peppers, and onions on her tortilla. "He's cutting hours for his department, which just means he's riding everyone to get the same amount of work done in way less time, and he acts like anyone who doesn't like it must be lazy or bad at their job. And what is he doing while his teams bust their asses? Standing around flirting with the young, pretty girls he hired. But he still has the nerve to brag like he's personally getting all that work done and he's God's gift to freaking Verity's."

Willow shook her head and took a sip of her margarita. When she'd been hired at Verity's after moving to Memoree, Brian had already been working there for a year. He was a good-looking guy with a serious superiority complex. Even when he'd been on the same level as Willow and Jamie, he'd acted as though he was in charge, getting away with it mainly because he'd kissed the managers' asses.

It was no wonder he'd been promoted a couple times in the years since.

"I am so glad I don't have to deal with that anymore." Willow picked up a chip from the basket at the center of the table, broke it in half, and scooped up some salsa. She popped it in her mouth and chewed. Salty sweetness swept over her tastebuds, followed by a hit of spiciness.

She loved Casa Roja. She and Jamie had been coming to the restaurant for as long as they'd known each other, meeting here at least twice a month during their lunch breaks. Well, during Jamie's lunch breaks, since Willow's schedule was quite flexible.

"I've got my own team in a separate department, and he still pisses me off to no end." Jamie folded her fajita and took a big bite. She used a finger to wipe a drop of sauce from the corner of her mouth. "You're so lucky you don't have to deal with this crap anymore."

"I ran off and never looked back."

"I should take a page out of your book. Find a hobby, make a career of it, and work for myself. Maybe I could even sell pictures of my feet." Jamie grinned. "I heard that makes some nice money, and I think I have pretty hot feet."

Willow laughed. "Yeah, your feet are pretty cute."

"Oh! That reminds me. We should get pedicures soon."

"We should," Willow replied as she stirred her sour cream into her chicken taco salad. "That'd be the perfect time for me to take some pictures of your sexy feet."

Jamie snickered. "I'll hold you to that." She took another bite of her fajita and made a sour face. "You want to know something else?"

"What?"

"I slept with Brian."

Willow gaped at her friend, nearly dropping her fork. "No, you didn't."

"I sure did."

"You never told me this! When?"

202

"Last December. It was the day of the company Christmas party, while he was still a lowly team lead like me. We both had a little too much to drink, one thing led to another, and we went back to my place. Didn't make it to the bedroom. Hell, we didn't even make it to the couch. Fucked right on my living room floor."

"I can't believe you had sex with Brain. And he's still been a jerk?"

"He's worse. Probably didn't help that I kicked his ass out when it was over."

"Wow." Willow leaned forward and raised her brows, lowering her voice. "How was it?"

"It was absolutely shitty. I mean, I was drunk, but not drunk enough to enjoy *that*. He might as well have been humping my thigh for how fast he came. And he was about to fall asleep on top of me until I shoved him off and told him to leave."

"Still can't believe you never told me this."

"Believe me, I wish I could forget it. Thought maybe if I didn't say anything, it'd be like it never happened."

Willow chuckled. "Doesn't work that way."

"Don't I know it."

They ate their food, basking in the ambiance created by surrounding conversations and the upbeat music from overhead speakers. For a while, Willow debated whether she should tell Jamie about Kian. Was it too soon? It wasn't like she could be entirely truthful, regardless—not just because Jamie wouldn't believe that he was an incubus, but because it wasn't Willow's secret to tell.

How could she really define her relationship with him, anyway? If she admitted to her friend that she was dating Kian, how could she keep insisting to him that they weren't?

Aren't we, though?

While she'd seen Kian every day, they hadn't done more than kiss after she'd fed him on her couch five nights ago. At first, she had wondered if that night had been an especially vivid dream, brought on by the wine and her potent fantasies, but it certainly hadn't been. If the sensation in her clit the next morning hadn't been proof enough, the note Kian had left on her fridge confirmed that it had all been very real.

She almost snorted as she recalled what he'd written.

Had a wonderful time, Violet.

Willow couldn't deny the twinge of hurt and disappointment she'd felt that morning. Part of her wished he had stayed the night, that he'd lain beside her, slept beside her. Wished she had awoken in his arms. But he'd left her alone, having taken only what she'd offered and no more.

You can't be upset about that, Willow.

She wasn't. She was just...conflicted.

But she had to admit, waking beneath the soft glow of the fairy lights on her bed's canopy had been...sweet.

Now, she'd come to anticipate the doorbell ringing every morning, when Kian would bring her breakfast and take his own from her lips. She could still feel the warmth of his mouth on hers, could still taste him on her tongue, could still feel his arms wrapped around her, his hands clutching her as though he couldn't get close enough.

Willow smiled, and something bloomed in her chest.

"What's that smile for?" Jamie asked.

Startled, Willow looked at Jamie. "Huh?"

"You're smiling like you just had a night of great sex."

Picking up her margarita, Willow brought it to her lips and took a deeper drink.

Here it goes.

"Do you remember Kian?" she asked.

"The hot goth who banged your brains out?" Jamie wiggled her eyebrows.

Willow laughed. "Well, that's one way of putting it." She set her glass down. "We...ran into each other again a little over a week ago."

Jamie's eyes widened. "You did? And you're just now telling me?" She bounced on the cushioned booth seat. "Please, please tell me you got his number. You're not letting him get away again, right?"

"He didn't quite give me a choice." Because, apparently, he didn't really have one himself when it came to Willow. Feed from her or die. And he'd also happened to follow her home, not that she could tell Jamie those little details. "He's adamant about us dating."

"And?"

"Jamie, it's only been a month since Eli."

"So?"

"Sooo...don't you think that's a little fast to be jumping into another serious relationship?"

"There's not a rulebook for this kind of thing, Willow. You don't have to go through some government-mandated mourning period for a failed relationship before you're allowed to hook up with someone else."

"We're not having sex."

Wait, does fingering count as sex?

Jamie rolled her eyes. "I don't see why not. You already fucked, so why hold out now?"

"Because that was only supposed to be a one-time thing. I was never supposed to have seen him again."

"Seems like fate had something else in store for you. Okay, let me ask you this—he's hot, right?"

Willow leaned back in her seat. "I already told you he was. But appearances should have no bearing on being in a relationship with someone."

"You still have to have physical attraction. And you guys

apparently have it. He's also good in bed, so that's another plus for him. Is he a decent guy?"

Willow caught her bottom lip between her teeth and looked through the window beside their booth. She didn't really know Kian, except that he was an incubus who'd lived a promiscuous life. He acted as though humans were beneath him, as though they were his prey, his food. But...he'd been sweet to her, in his own cocky way.

"I think so," she said.

"And he wants to date you."

Willow looked back at her friend. "He does."

"So what's the issue?" Jamie plucked up a tortilla chip, dipped it in the salsa, and bit into it. She waved the remainder around nonchalantly. "No one says you gotta get married. Date the man for a while, have a little fun while you're at it, and see where it goes."

You are my mate. The Fates have marked you as mine.

"I feel like it's different with Kian." *Understatement, Willow.* "I barely know him, but I just feel so much when I'm with him. I'm scared that if I open myself up, I'm just going to end up hurt. Again. And this time... This time I feel like it would gut me."

Jamie folded her arms on the table and held Willow's gaze. "I know. But if you don't take the chance, you could miss out on something truly amazing. Love doesn't come without pain. Sometimes, they really are one in the same. But you have to take that leap, Willow. And you know that I'm a phone call away, any time."

Willow smiled. "I know you are."

Who was Willow trying to kid? She and Kian *were* dating, no matter how often she tried to deny it. And she...wasn't mad about it. But she was anxious. Everything could go so, so wrong, and her heart was already far too invested.

It had been from the beginning.

"Also"—Jamie sipped from her soda—"you can tell him that if he hurts you, I'll be coming after his ass."

Willow almost snorted. Considering what he was, she highly doubted Kian would be scared of Jamie. But it sure would've been funny to see her friend try to intimidate him.

Jamie picked her phone up off the table and turned it over. "Shit! I'm gonna be late." She took another big bite out of what remained of her fajita. "Sorry, didn't realize how much time had passed."

"Don't worry about it. I got the bill this time."

"Thank you." Sliding out of the booth, Jamie embraced Willow. She pulled back, slipped her handbag onto her arm, and stuffed her phone inside. "I'll call you to get those pedicures set up, okay?"

"Sounds good. I'll talk to you then."

"Great. See you later!"

Willow waved and grinned. "Don't be making sexy eyes at Brian."

Jamie playfully gagged before she turned and hurried toward the exit, weaving between the tables.

As Willow waited for the waiter, she munched on her salad and chips. She was in no rush. She didn't have any clients scheduled today, didn't have any other plans. It was a day off for her. Maybe she'd do a little window shopping while she was in the city, or even stop by her favorite antique store.

"Anything else I can get for you?" the waiter asked as he stopped at the table.

Willow looked up at him and smiled. "No, I'm good."

He nodded, returned the smile, and set the bill on the table. "Take your time, amiga."

"Thank you."

She twisted toward her purse, which lay on the seat beside her, opened it, and searched for her wallet. When she saw a notification on her phone, she pulled it out, and her heart quickened. A text from Kian. She unlocked the screen.

Attached to the text was a selfie of Kian, lying on a bed with black and red sheets. His head was tilted back, his lips were parted, his smoldering eyes stared into the camera, and every inch of his delicious chest was bare. One hand rested on his abdomen, as though it were sliding toward his...

Willow's eyes rounded as she quickly clutched her phone to her chest to hide the screen.

"Oh my God," she breathed, cheeks burning. Something wicked stirred inside her, filling her core with heat. Feeling as though all eyes were on her, as though everyone knew what she'd just seen and how her body was reacting, she swiftly glanced around the dining room.

No one was paying attention to her.

Discreetly turning away from the other diners, she glanced down and lifted her phone away from her chest. Kian's fingers, with those sharp, black nails, pointed straight at his cock. Its base was just visible above the edge of the black sheet draped over his pelvis, which offered a tantalizing outline of the rest of his shaft. But she didn't need to see it in it's entirely to recall what it looked like—or what it had felt like inside her.

Willow squeezed her thighs together and looked at the text above the image.

I know you're always thinking of me, Violet, but I want you to know that I'm also thinking of you. Thinking about those luscious thighs draped over my shoulders, thinking about your sweet cunt spread and soaking wet for me, about fucking you with my tongue.

The hollow, needy ache in her core grew, and her clit twitched. If Kian's goal was to arouse her, he'd definitely succeeded. The image alone would have turned her on, but combined with his words? She couldn't stop her memory from leaping back to their first night together, when he'd pinned her writhing body to the bed while he brought her to climax with his mouth.

Skin feeling much too warm, she pulled enough cash out of her wallet to cover the check and leave the waiter a good tip, set it on the table, and stood up. She tugged her skirt down as she stepped away from the table. She needed to get out of the restaurant, needed to get away from the noise, the cooking odors, and all the potential prying eyes.

When she got outside, she drew in a deep breath. The air was cooler out here than in Casa Roja, which felt wonderful upon her heated skin, but it didn't temper the inferno in her core.

A surprising realization struck her as she walked away from the restaurant.

Kian sent me a picture of himself.

Hadn't he told her it was in his best interest to avoid having his picture taken? And yet, he'd sent one to her. He trusted her.

She stopped and raised her phone, greedily taking in the image once more.

It is so unfair for a man to be so damn gorgeous.

She saved the image to her phone and sent a reply. *It's too late to take that picture back. It's mine now.*

Those little dots appeared, and Willow's belly fluttered. Kian's response only intensified her inner heat.

Look at it whenever you feel the need to touch yourself. Though, the real thing is available if you'd like a more interactive experience.

Her mind instantly went back to what they'd done on her couch, and her lips spread into a grin even as she blushed. *You're impossible. And a tease.*

You know I'm willing to do much more than tease, Willow. You need only ask.

Glancing up, she slowly proceeded along the sidewalk. She knew she should've refrained, but she wanted to be cheeky, wanted to tease him back. She couldn't stop her fingers from sending a response. *What if I were to ask right now?*

Well, little mortal, you'd find out just how fast I can fly.

She chuckled, but a thrill swept through her. She'd tasted his passion, had received traces of it with every kiss he'd bestowed upon her, and she knew that once he unleashed it fully, he'd be seared into her very soul.

Though she knew she was playing with fire, her fingers moved over the letters on the screen. *Just how fast can you f—*

Someone collided with her, knocking the wind from her lungs. Willow's phone tumbled to the ground, and she stumbled back, nearly tripping over her own feet before large hands grasped her upper arms to steady her.

"Oh! I am so, so sorry," Willow said in a rush once she'd righted herself. She looked up at the stranger. "I wasn't looking... I, uh..."

The stranger, who stood at least a foot taller than her, was dressed in a dark gray suit. He had short, tousled black hair, sharp, angular features, and a square jaw. A shadow of facial hair framed his full lips. But it was his steel gray eyes that held her spellbound.

He chuckled. "Not what I envisioned when I imagined your body against mine."

Willow laughed. "Do those pickup lines actually work?"

The man leaned closer, his smooth, deep voice falling lower. "Every time I need them to."

Twenty

A tingle crept down Willow's spine. The sensation wasn't unpleasant, but neither was it comforting. "Oh, well, um... They don't work with me." She took a step back. "I'm...also kind of with someone."

He allowed her that little distance but didn't release his grip on her arms. "So not committed?"

"It's complicated."

"It always is, isn't it?" He slowly trailed his hands down her arms as he crouched, keeping his intense gaze fixed upon her.

Willow shivered, conflicted by the sensations this man caused in her. His touch felt good, better than it should have, but it only added to the unease she harbored deep down. She clung to her discomfort—that was what she should've been feeling. That was the only reaction she should've had to this. But why wouldn't her feet move any further? Why couldn't she pull away from him?

Her phone vibrated. The man plucked it up off the ground. "But you'll find that with me, things are very, very simple."

Simple. That sounds...so nice. So easy.

He rose slowly and drew closer to Willow until there was barely any space between them.

A spicy musk with a touch of expensive leather overtook her senses. The tingling within her spread, making her skin prickle and her nipples harden. Her pussy, already wet due to her thoughts of Kian, grew slicker with heat.

What was wrong with her? Why was she reacting like this?

"Yours?" he asked, holding the phone out to her.

Willow reached for it, desperate to escape. "Yes. Thank you."

He lifted it, dangling it just out of her reach, before he dropped it into her purse. The fingers of his other hand grasped her chin, keeping her gaze locked with his. "Such pretty eyes you have." He brushed his thumb along her jaw. "Let's make use of all this desire. You want that, don't you?"

Her phone buzzed inside her purse. "No, no, I..."

"I can feel your desire, your need. I can give you that release."

The stranger's voice flowed into Willow. It was so strong, so confident, so alluring, so...insidious. She felt his words worming deeper, forcing their way between her thoughts, strangling her willpower.

This was all wrong. Willow...didn't want this. It was Kian she wanted, not this stranger. She needed to run, to scream, to find help.

But all she could do was stare into this man's eyes and nod as something heavier pressed into her soul, instilling her with want, igniting a lust that had Willow reaching for him. Her hands slid up his chest to clutch at the vest beneath his suit jacket.

"That's it," he whispered, dropping his hands to her hips and pulling her against him. "Give in to me. Give in to your desire."

Alarms blared in the back of Willow's mind, but she couldn't heed them. Her head was fuzzy. Hazy. And her body... it didn't seem to belong to her anymore. Like a master puppeteer, the man guided her to the alley behind the restaurant, and she was only distantly aware of how dangerous this was, how wrong this was, those misgivings drowned out by a consuming need.

Her fingers worked at the buttons of his vest, tearing them open to reach the shirt beneath. Skin. She wanted to touch his flesh, to feel his heat, wanted his body against hers.

He chuckled, the dark sound rolling over her as he pressed her back against the building. It was colder in the shade, and the smell of rotten garbage drifted to her nose, but it was swiftly obliterated by his leather and musk aroma. His scent clouded her thoughts further and fanned the flames of her lust. The stranger took her purse and dropped it to the ground. With it out of the way, he grasped his shirt and tore it open.

Willow immediately flattened her hands on his bare chest. Heat radiated from him, so much delicious heat.

He hooked the collar of her dress, along with the bra strap beneath it, and tugged them aside to expose her shoulder before dropping his mouth to her neck. Willow gasped when he latched on and sucked hard. She arched against him. Something in the back of her mind continued to scream and cry, but it was muffled, becoming quieter with every moment.

The man slipped a leg between her thighs and raised it until his knee pressed to the apex of her sex. Willow's internal scream fell silent. She moaned, grinding herself against his leg, driven by raw, carnal need.

"Ah, your lust. It's so potent, so delicious," he said against her throat. Raising his head, he placed a fingertip beneath her chin and lifted her face to his. "I need more." His gaze dipped to her mouth, and he leaned forward.

His lips drew close enough to hers for his warm breath to tickle and tease her skin. She needed his kiss, was desperate for him to slant his mouth over hers, to take everything from her.

A growl reverberated off the surrounding concrete. Though

familiar, the sound was startlingly primal, and it cut through the thick haze in Willow's mind.

The stranger grunted. His head snapped back, and then he was torn away from her, his nails scraping her skin as his hold broke. She staggered forward, eyes widening as the man slammed into the wall of the opposite building.

The entire alley shuddered, and bricks cracked behind his back. A tall figure dressed in black was there, his hand around the man's throat, with a shock of white hair hanging over one shoulder.

Kian?

It was like a bucket of ice water had been poured over Willow's head, suffusing her with cold. She released a harsh exhalation as her rapid, pounding pulse permeated her being. Her body trembled with equal amounts of lust, dread, and fear.

What had she done?

The dark-haired stranger grabbed Kian's arm, his lips peeling back in a fanged snarl. His eyes, a steely gray before, now glowed crimson. "What is this, Pale One?"

Willow's heart skipped a beat as a wave of something powerful swept into her. It twisted everything inside her, weighed down her limbs, and intensified that inner chill. She stumbled back until she hit the wall.

He's not human. He's... Oh God, he's like Kian!

"You touched what was mine!" Kian snarled as he hammered his fist into the stranger's face. The man's head snapped aside, but turned back toward Kian immediately, and that power, that oppressive force, strengthened.

Willow's knees nearly buckled. She pressed her hands against the wall, clutching for purchase and finding none.

"Release me," the stranger said through his teeth. His voice echoed unnaturally in the alley, seeming to build on itself.

Eyes blazing blue-white, Kian let out another growl. His fist was clenched so tight that his knuckles had gone completely white, and tremors coursed along his arm, clearly the result of immense tension. After a moment's hesitation, he threw a wild flurry of blows at the stranger. The dark-haired man struggled to defend himself. Their movements were almost too fast for Willow's eyes to follow—they were a whirlwind of savagery, clawing, striking, and wrestling, but Kian seemed to have the advantage.

She could only hope the glimpses of blood she caught amidst the chaos weren't his.

"Enough!" the stranger roared.

Another blast of power struck Willow, pressing her backward harder. Her nails scraped the rough wall.

Kian sprang away from the man, halting directly in front of Willow with his shoulders heaving, his hair a tangled mess, and his hands raised, ready to strike.

The stranger stared at Kian as he lifted a hand to dab the blood from his split lip. Other cuts oozed blood on his cheeks and jaw. Strands of hair hung in his face, his suit jacket was torn at the sleeve, and there were a few more scratches on his bared chest.

He straightened and swept his hair back with a harsh gesture before tugging his disheveled clothing into place. "Explain yourself, Kian."

Kian maintained his agitated stance. "I do not answer to you, Lachlan."

"Perhaps not. But we all adhere to the accord." Lachlan looked past Kian, fixing his gaze on Willow. "You interfered with my feeding. You know the rules."

That oppressive force faded, and desire stirred in Willow's core again. She drew in a sharp breath, squeezed her thighs together, and shook her head. "No. No, stop it!"

"Leave her alone," Kian growled, adjusting his position to shield Willow with his body.

That unwanted, alien desire diminished, but it didn't go away. Willow pressed a fist to her belly. She struggled to steady her breathing, to slow her heart, to retake control of herself, but she still felt Lachlan's influence inside her. Still felt the stain left by his magic.

Lachlan chuckled. "This one is ripe with desire. I felt it from quite far away, and it lured me right to her. If you wanted a taste that badly, you should have asked. I would've shared."

"She is mine," Kian said firmly.

"She does not bear your mark."

"Yet she belongs to me all the same."

"Hmm." Lachlan's footsteps echoed along the alleyway, but Kian's body kept the dark-haired fae out of sight. Finally, Lachlan halted, and chuckled again. "You're young, Pale One, but youth grants you no right to claim ignorance of our ways. I should know. I taught you myself, didn't I? If this mortal is yours, mark her. But while she bears no sigil, she is fair game."

"I have declared my claim on her, Lachlan. Walk away."

"Oh? Is it that simple now? Then who is to say I did not already declare my own claim upon her?" He laughed. "After all, she does bear my mark...of a sort."

Eyes widening, Willow pressed a hand over the spot on her neck where he'd sucked. Her skin crawled beneath her palm. She swallowed the bile rising from her gut, digging her nails into her flesh as though she could tear off that taint.

Kian growled again and clenched his fists. A drop of blood trickled from his hand, hanging on his thumb claw briefly before falling to the ground. "Touch her again, and I will—"

"You'll what, Kian? Please, tell me exactly what you think you'll do. I look forward to the amusement." Lachlan's steps drew nearer, and he lowered his voice. "By the accord, you are the transgressor here. You have wronged me. And it is well within my rights to demand this mortal as compensation."

"Leave," Kian gritted. "Before I tear out your fucking throat."

Silence gripped the alleyway, and the stifling tension in the air made it seem like a breathless eternity before Lachlan spoke again.

"This dispute might easily have been resolved. In fact, were it not for your stubbornness, we could've avoided it entirely. Haven't I shown you my capacity for mercy and forgiveness? For generosity? All these years, all these wrongs you've done me... You've worn my patience quite thin, Pale One. But you'll learn respect in time."

Kian's fists trembled. "We could outlive the cosmos, Lachlan, and you still wouldn't earn my respect."

"Another challenge. It always is, from you." Lachlan sighed. "If I happen across this mortal again and she remains unmarked, I will take her. She will be mine in every way. And I will use her until she has nothing left to give."

"You so much as gaze upon her again, Hollow Prince, and I'll demonstrate exactly how little your fucking accord can protect you."

Lachlan's chuckle was unconcerned. "Take care, mortal. I'm sure we'll see each other again soon."

Then his footsteps were moving away at a nonchalant pace. Willow held her breath as she listened to them gradually fade, until her thumping heartbeat became the louder sound.

Kian lowered his hands, though he kept them balled, and let out a heavy exhalation. Tension still radiated from him, and his movements were uncharacteristically stiff as he looked at her over his shoulder. "You all right, Violet?"

Something inside her broke in that instant. All the emotions that had been held back by fear and adrenaline poured out. Her face crumpled, and a sob burst from her throat as tears spilled down her cheeks. "I'm sorry. I'm so sorry. I didn't want that. I couldn't... Oh God, I couldn't stop. I'm sorry."

"Ah, Willow." He turned toward her, and when he put his

arms around her, she clung to him, burying her face against his chest. Gently, he kissed her hair. "Don't be sorry. It wasn't your fault."

"It was wrong. I couldn't fight him. And I almost... If you hadn't come..." A shudder wracked her, and she couldn't stop the trembling that overtook her as she turned her face and pressed her cheek to his chest. "I can still feel him inside me, Kian."

Kian cupped the back of her head, stroking her hair. "He's gone now. You're in control. Only you."

Willow shoved away from him. "But I wasn't! I knew it was wrong, everything about it felt wrong, but I couldn't stop. I still let him. I was even..." She shook her head as more tears fell. Her next words made her ill. "Is this what you do?"

Those beautiful, sculpted lips of his fell into a deep frown, and some of the light fled from his gaze. He lifted his hands, showing his blood-streaked palms to her. The wounds he'd inflicted on himself had already healed. "Easy, Willow. I'm not your enemy."

"But you're like him. That...that's how you feed."

His eyes flashed. "I'm *nothing* like him. I only charm people who are already interested. Already willing. I've never warped anyone's desires like he does, I've never bent anyone to my will."

But how could she believe him after what she'd seen, after what she'd experienced? Was what she felt for Kain even real?

Or was he manipulating her?

Willow looked away from him, lower lip quivering. "How do I know you haven't done it to me? That you haven't charmed me?"

"Gods, Willow. I haven't. I swear it, beneath sun and sky."

She wanted to believe him, wanted those words to be true so badly it hurt. "How can I be sure?"

He closed the distance between them and cupped her jaw with both hands. When he guided her face up toward his, it was clear that there'd be no refusal, no resistance. Kian stared down into her eyes, jaw muscles ticking. "Because if I had, I would've already fucked you, over and over again." He pressed his forehead to hers. "I told you. My magic doesn't work with you."

Willow clutched his shirt. "But you tried. That first night we met. You tried to use it on me, didn't you?"

"I thought I had. You wanted me, I felt it, and I thought *I* had given you the final nudge toward taking what you desired." He laughed humorlessly. "And then you fucking left me. For all your want, you walked away, Willow." Lifting his head, he once more met her eyes, and gently wiped away her tears with his thumbs. "What you felt then, and what you feel now, is real. No amount of my magic can change it."

Willow sniffled and searched his gaze, searched that beautiful, glittering blue. And she knew. She knew he was telling the truth. It was there, open and raw, in his eyes, in his voice. "What did he mean about marking me?"

Kian pressed his lips together and glanced down the alley in both directions. "There is a means by which a fae can mark a mortal with a magical sigil. It declares ownership to all other fae. Marks the mortal as property, which is considered off-limits to others. And it serves as a bond between the fae and their mortal. One through which the fae can exert further control."

"You mean...like a slave?"

"Yes, like a slave. Not always...but often. Sometimes worse."

"And you intend to put your mark on me?"

"*Never*," he growled vehemently, the light in his eyes flaring. "I've not done it once in all my years, Willow, and I'm certainly not going to start with you."

Her tension eased upon hearing those words, but only slightly. Though Lachlan was gone, his presence lingered within her, its icy roots having sunk deep. No matter how much she willed it, her body refused to cease its trembling. "I'm scared, Kian."

Kian wrapped his arms around her and held her against him. "I won't let him hurt you."

"Down this way," someone called from the alley entrance, making Willow start.

"What the hell was it?" another person asked from the same area.

Willow turned her head in that direction to see a group of people funneling into the alleyway, all of them wary as they scanned the area.

"Felt like an earthquake or something," one of the men said.

Kian reached down and picked up Willow's purse. "We need to go."

Her brow furrowed as he looped the strap over her shoulder. "But...but won't that look suspicious?"

He gave her a lopsided smile. "It won't look like anything. They can't see us."

Oh. Right.

Curling an arm around Willow, Kian led her away from the approaching people, who had reached the damaged brick wall and now stood speculating about what had caused it. Their voices barely registered for her anymore.

She focused on Kian, on his solidness, his warmth, his scent, and she wished his presence could blast away the memory of what had happened. She wished she could forget. The rest of the world was a blur as they walked.

And then he drew to a stop. Kian's voice, so deep and soothing, stirred her back to awareness.

"Let's get you home, Violet."

Willow blinked. They were standing in front of her car.

He opened the passenger side door. "Get in, Willow."

Still in a daze, she climbed into the car. Before she could even reach for the seatbelt, Kian pulled it across her body and buckled it, checking to make sure it was secure.

He smiled and brushed the back of a finger across her cheek. Tingling warmth spread outward from his touch. "Good girl."

Despite everything that had happened, her core pulsed with his praise. Why did those words affect her so strongly even now?

Kian stood, shut her door, and rounded the car, getting in on the driver's side. After adjusting the seat and fastening on his own seat belt, he pressed the ignition to start the engine.

"Kian?" she asked as he pulled onto the road.

"Hmm?"

"How did you know where I was parked?" She frowned. That wasn't the right question, wasn't the important question. "How did you know where I was at all? Not that I'm not thankful you showed up when you did, I just...don't understand."

That slanted smile returned to his face, and he glanced at her from the corner of his eye. "I happened to be in the neighborhood." He lifted a hand from the wheel and turned it palm up. "Because I followed you."

"You followed me?"

"Yes, Violet. I followed you."

"So...you *are* stalking me."

"The way you say that word makes me think it's the wrong one." He came to a smooth stop at a red light and turned his face toward her. "I'm...*protecting* you. I'm not pulling up a hood, throwing on sunglasses, and shadowing your every step. Today, I followed you the area, watched you go into the restaurant, and occupied myself nearby. When you suddenly stopped responding to my texts, I decided to make sure you were okay."

His hands clenched the steering wheel, making it creak. "I was on my way to the restaurant when I saw you in the alley."

Willow was torn. Kian following her was wrong. And yet...

had he not done so, had he not been there, Lachlan would have...
He would have...

Oh God, and *she* would have...

She curled her fingers on her thighs, gathering the fabric of her skirt, as another tremor swept through her. Her stomach twisted. The wrongness of what had happened, of what she had felt, of her loss of control, was already so immense and overwhelming.

Letting herself think about what might've happened had Kian not shown up in time would be crushing. It would break her.

"You're my mate, Willow," Kian said gently, pulling her thoughts back to now, back to him. "I have this...instinctual need to be near you. It drives me to keep you safe. Even when there's no apparent threat."

Her eyes dipped. Though any wounds he might've suffered in his fight with Lachlan had healed, his fingers and silver rings were smeared with dried blood. He'd fought for her. In one of the most terrifying moments of her life, he'd come and fought for her. Had anyone ever done that for Willow? Had anyone cared enough?

"Thank you," she said quietly.

Twenty-One

Fire coursed through Kian's veins in time with the pounding of his heart, each wave hotter and fiercer than the last. Time and distance were only feeding the flames. He knew his outward calm would crack if this continued, that his rage would burst to the surface like lava during an eruption. The only thing allowing him to maintain his tenuous control was the understanding that Willow needed him.

He glanced at her. She'd gone quiet after thanking him, and now sat with her arms wrapped around her purse and her legs tight together, like she was trying to make herself as small as possible.

A deep ache ran through his chest. Fury and vengeance wouldn't help her now. All his drive to protect her, to seek justice for what Lachlan had done, was useless. It wouldn't change what he was seeing now. It couldn't change what she was feeling.

Even the night they'd met, when her long-term relationship had come to an abrupt, unhappy end, Willow hadn't been this distraught. Three years of Eli hadn't done even a fraction of the damage Lachlan had inflicted in a few short minutes.

Clenching his teeth, he turned onto her street. They'd be at her house in moments. And then what? What could he do for her, how could he help her? He didn't know how to comfort mortals, didn't know what words would ease their anguish. He was an immortal fae, an incubus. He knew how to fuck. These feelings... They were new. The torrent of emotions swirling in the car, overwhelmingly potent despite being unspoken, would be impossible to sort. He wasn't even sure where her feelings ended and his own began.

He knew only that he would not quit. He would find a way. He had to find a way.

Once the car was parked in her driveway, he exited the vehicle and hurried to her side. She was already climbing out when he reached her. Tears welled in her eyes as she looked up at him.

Blood—his blood—stained her cheeks where he had touched her earlier, standing out starkly against her pale skin despite having been diluted by her tears. She wiped her eyes with the heel of her hand before hugging her purse to her chest again.

Kian put his arm around her shoulders, drawing her against him, and walked her to the front door. She dug her keys out of her purse. They jingled in her shaking hand as she unlocked the door and pushed it open. Kian stepped inside with her.

Security. She needs to feel safe.

His mind raced, and a flood of thoughts that would be of no help threatened to claw their way to the surface, but he somehow held them down. Pausing, he turned and locked the door behind them, including the deadbolt and the chain.

It wouldn't stop a determined fae, but short of finding someone capable of casting warding spells throughout the house, it was the best he could do.

Willow dropped her purse on the arm of the sofa. She stood there, shoulders curled in, rubbing a hand along her bare arm.

The bright, carefree woman he'd come to know was nowhere to be seen now.

She looked up at him. "I...I need to take a shower."

Though reluctant to let her out of his sight, Kian forced himself to nod. "Go ahead. I'll be here, Violet."

He watched as she disappeared into her bedroom. With a frustrated groan, he ran his hand through his hair. When he lowered it, he noticed the blood dried upon his fingers.

"Fuck."

Kian took a step forward only to falter when he noticed something else. All three of Willow's cats had gathered outside her bedroom, where they sat side-by-side, staring at him. Not just staring, but doing so in the only way of which cats seemed capable —judgmentally.

"I haven't forgotten our agreement," he said. "I did not harm her."

The orange cat, Loki, swept his tail to the side and blinked. None of the felines moved otherwise.

With a huff, Kian strode to the guest bathroom. He turned on the hot water and examined himself in the mirror.

His shirt had been pulled loose and sported a few tears. Subtle darker spots on the black fabric stood out to his keen eyes. Blood. Mostly Lachlan's, but that didn't ease Kian's resurging anger.

He hastily tugged off his rings and scrubbed the blood off them beneath the hot water. After setting them aside, he removed his shirt, wadded it up, and tossed it onto the counter. He washed his hands, face, and chest, using a potentially excessive amount of hand soap in the process. As the bubbly, red-tinged water swirled down the drain, he couldn't stop his thoughts from tumbling along paths he'd been struggling to avoid.

But you're like him. That...that's how you feed.

Grasping the edge of the counter, he leaned over it. Tension locked his muscles.

I'm not like him. I'm not...a monster.

Yet hadn't Kian used his charm on countless humans? Hadn't he preyed upon their desires, manipulated them with magic, and pushed them to do things they wouldn't likely have chosen to do with clear minds? Hadn't he used his power to influence their thoughts just enough to suit his needs?

Before Willow, he'd never had to face the repercussions of what his kind did to mortals. He'd never had to witness what that magic could do to them. He'd never considered the violation, the disgust, they endured. He'd never imagined the trauma of having one's control stripped away. Of becoming slave to desire.

That's not exactly honest, is it?

Because he had seen some of those repercussions. He had witnessed the violation, the degradation, the cruelty. He'd seen humans have their free will stripped away. And gods, he'd felt it down in his soul. It had thrown his memories right back to Tulthiras, back to the very fae overlords from whom he'd fled to begin with. Back to the beings who'd sought to take Kian's free will.

But he'd chosen to look away. He'd chosen to pretend it didn't matter, because *he* wasn't the one doing it.

Why should he have wasted time sympathizing with humans, worrying about their wellbeing, anyway? Mortals had been prey. Willow had been prey.

And today, she had been Lachlan's prey.

Kian bared his teeth in a snarl.

Oh, he'd fucking known all along. That was why his rules existed—so he never had to face those consequences, never had to consider them, never had to feel even an inkling of guilt. So he could convince himself that he was better.

Incubi like Lachlan took whatever they wanted. They used their potent charm to overpower any protest, to *insert* desires into a mortal's mind. To control. That Kian's techniques weren't quite so invasive didn't make a difference. Whatever consent he'd convinced himself his mortal victims had given was just as invalid as any consent Lachlan took.

For all his efforts to curtail the dark, animalistic desires at his core, for all his struggles to keep the beast chained, what distinction could really be made between Kian and Lachlan? Perhaps other fae were right in how they viewed Kian's kind.

Incubi were parasites. Leeches. Never to be trusted, never to be believed. Their very nature was to lie, exploit, and steal. To prey upon everyone. In the end, it was all the same. Technique didn't make a difference, and Kian's flimsy moral code couldn't change the outcome.

Through the eyes of anyone else, Kian and Lachlan were the same thing.

"No," he growled, claws scraping the counter. "I don't instill fear in them. Don't feed off their pain. Don't break them, drain them, and discard them like refuse."

Was that enough?

His glamour crumbled. He studied his reflection, stared into his own glowing blue eyes, and he couldn't decide what he saw. A void, eternally hungry, devouring everything that came close? A well of passion, of potential, of...caring? A thinking, feeling being...

Or a beast?

But what choice did he have? How else was he to feed, to survive?

"This won't help her," he rasped. "You won't help her. Not like this."

He inhaled, filling his chest until it hurt, and held it in as he counted the beats of his heart.

Willow needed someone grounded. Someone solid, dependable. Someone to show her that even though her world had been shaken, it was still intact. Someone who could support her until she regained her balance. She needed to know she wasn't alone.

Was that someone Kian? Was he capable of it?

His brows slanted down, and his nostrils flared as he bared his teeth. "Doesn't fucking matter. I will be whatever she needs. Anything."

He picked up his shirt and dropped it into the trash can beside the counter before leaving the room.

Bebe, Remy, and Loki retained their positions outside Willow's bedroom, just as alert as before. Kian paused, but he did not allow himself to delay for long. He gingerly stepped over the cats to enter the bedroom, turned toward them, and took hold of the door.

They twisted their necks to continue staring.

"I'll see to her," he said gently. He shut the door.

Two muffled sounds chased away the silence of the room, both coming from behind the closed door of her bathroom—that of the running shower and Willow's sobs. Kian's insides twisted into knots and sank, pulling everything taut. He clenched his fists, making his claws bite into his palms, but nothing could relieve the devastation her anguish caused him.

There were a great many sounds he longed to hear from her lips. This was not one of them, and it never would be.

"Not fucking leaving," he growled as he kicked off his boots. Breath ragged, he paced back and forth in the space between her bed and the bathroom door, heart skipping every time she made another pained sound, every time he heard her draw in a shuddering breath.

He needed to burst through that door and take her in his arms. Needed to hold her, kiss her, tell her he was here, that he would keep her safe.

"Calm. She needs calm. And a little fucking space, you damned fool."

Gritting his teeth, he halted and forced himself to sit on the edge of her bed. He hunched forward, wings twitching, and clasped his hands together. Even with his elbows on his thighs, he couldn't stop his leg from bouncing. His thumbs moved with their own restlessness, claws absently scratching his skin.

An eternity passed, each moment of it a new pinnacle of agony.

The water turned off. Kian sucked in a breath and stilled, listening as Willow moved within the bathroom.

His muscles tensed, eager to spring into action, to rush to her side. He clamped his teeth down on his lower lip and strained to remain in place.

Finally, the door opened to reveal Willow, with her long, damp hair uncombed and her body wrapped in a large blue towel. One of her hands was clasped over the side of her neck. She took two steps into the bedroom before she came to a stop, her red-brimmed eyes meeting his. Her bottom lip quivered.

"I can still feel him, Kian," she said, her voice soft, thin, broken. Powerful emotions flowed from her, crushing in their weight and intensity. This was sorrow from the deepest parts of her soul. "No matter how many times I tried scrubbing away his touch, it's still there. It's like he's embedded inside me."

Kian shoved himself up and closed the distance between them. He searched her face, resisting the urge to reach for her, until his gaze dipped to her neck. Taking a gentle hold of her wrist, he lifted her hand away.

Anger swirled in his gut. The mark Lachlan had left was still there, dark and purple, but now the skin all around it was an irritated red.

No matter how many times I tried scrubbing away his touch, it's still there.

229

The realization that she'd been speaking literally—that she'd stood in the shower, rubbing at her skin desperately, hurting herself further—nearly broke him.

Releasing her arm, he cradled her face in his hands. Fresh tears flowed from her eyes, which were so big, filled with suffering and fear.

"You're safe, Willow." Kian wiped the moisture from her cheeks. "It's just us now. Only us."

"But why is my skin still crawling like he's here? He...He violated me, body and mind. He made me do things, Kian, things I would never have done. I would never have..." Her voice broke with a sob as more tears fell. "I would never have betrayed you."

Those words pierced straight through his heart, nearly stealing his breath. If she felt like she'd betrayed Kian, that meant... That meant she saw him as more than a bothersome incubus who'd attached himself to her life.

Could he dare to hope that she'd accepted him? That she'd accepted they were mates?

He wrapped his arms around Willow and drew her against him, smoothing a hand over her hair. "Hush, Violet. You didn't betray me, and you didn't betray yourself. You feel this way because he was making you do things you didn't want. Because he was manipulating you, overriding your will." He turned his head and brushed his lips over her temple. "You once told me that just because your body reacts, it doesn't mean you're in agreement. He forced your body to react. He forced you to agree. You were never given a choice, Willow."

She clutched at his back and sniffled. "I don't ever want to feel that again."

"I won't let him hurt you again. Won't let anyone hurt you."

Willow rubbed her cheek against his chest, and Kian continued holding her, offering all the silent comfort she needed in that moment. He felt her tears on his skin, felt the subtle trembling of her lips, felt her soft hiccups, and they all added to the rage blazing inside him. Despite that anger, he gentled his touch as he combed his fingers through her hair and stroked a hand down her back.

He would not hurt his Violet. He'd never hurt her.

Gradually, she calmed. Her breathing became soft and even, and she no longer shook in his arms. She loosened her grip and, tentatively, explored his back with her hands, sliding them lightly up and down. When her fingers brushed the bases of his upper wings, Kian's breath caught.

He didn't stop her as she ran her fingers along the sensitive limbs.

Pleasure pulsed in the wake of her touch, tingling down his spine and continuing lower still to gather in his belly. Heat skittered just beneath the surface of his skin. His every nerve was awakening, becoming hypersensitive, lighting up in anticipation.

No. Not the time, Kian. Shouldn't be feeling pleasure now. Shouldn't be feeling desire.

Clenching his jaw, he tried to ignore the sensations, but his defenses weren't holding. The walls he'd constructed in his mind had already cracked, and they were falling. He tightened his hold on her.

"Willow," he rasped, pleading. There was so much more he wanted to say, but no other words would emerge.

Her hands glided back down to the roots of his wings and caressed them. "Will you stay with me tonight, Kian?"

With the effect her touch was having upon him, she might as well have been stroking his cock.

He hissed through his teeth, barely holding back a shudder. "Was going to whether you asked or not."

Willow turned her face and pressed her lips to his chest before she tipped her head back. Kian looked down at her.

"I know what I feel with you is real," she said. "It was real that first night we were together, and it has been real every day since. I don't want to fight it anymore." Her eyes glistened with gathering tears. "I want you. And I...I want you to replace his touch with yours. I want to feel *you*, not him. I want your mark on me, heart, body, and soul."

Twenty-Two

Kian's heart constricted in response to those words.

I want your mark on me, heart, body, and soul.

The emotions radiating from Willow intensified. Her pain was still there, her fear, but they were overpowered now by something stronger. Kian had often detected it from mortals, but he'd never felt anything like it directed toward him.

And he'd never encountered anything nearly as potent as what he felt from Willow in that moment. It was warm, vast, and full.

It was staggering.

He knew what it was, and he sensed all the complexities that came with it, all the hopes, doubts, and fears. But he could not bring himself to admit it, to name it.

It was not for incubi to experience. At least, he'd never believed it was, much less that anyone would feel it for him.

Or that *he* might feel it.

Yet here he was—and there it was. His chest was brimming with that emotion.

"Ah, Willow." He pulled back and brushed his knuckles down her cheek. Her eyes shone, the lingering moisture from her tears making the green even more vibrant. As his hand continued down, he stroked her mouth with his thumb, coaxing her lips to part. "I could spend a hundred thousand years walking every realm and never find another soul as beautiful as yours."

She clutched the top of the towel and let out a shuddering breath.

My mate. She's my mate.

Mine.

The beast at Kian's core roused in response to that thought. He needed to mark her. To make it clear to this universe and all others that she belonged to him. To rut her until she could take no more, and then rut her again, and again.

To take everything from her.

No.

This was not about feeding. This was not about lust. This was more.

Tonight, he would cherish the gift that had been given to him, that had been fated to him. The gift that was his and his alone, that was more precious than any Kian or anyone else had ever received.

Tonight, he would give back. He would give to her.

Kian tipped her head back farther and leaned down. He touched his lips to her cheek, trailing light kisses across her damp skin. The saltiness of her tears blended with her usual sweetness, creating a new taste that was uniquely Willow, and though he hated how it had come to be, he loved that he was experiencing her in a new way.

When she closed her eyes, he kissed her eyelids, and then his mouth followed the bridge of her nose down to its tip. Each kiss altered the fires that burned within him, making their heat warmer and more tender but no less intense.

He leaned his forehead against Willow's. Her soft, hesitant exhalation teased his lips before he slanted his mouth over hers.

She yielded to him, and Kian led her in a slow, sensual dance of lips and tongues, of mixed breaths, of twining souls.

Willow smoothed her hands up his chest to settle them on his shoulders. The desire radiating from her suffused Kian and made every sensation sharper, stronger. Her soft, sweet mouth grew more pliant with each beat of their hearts.

Kian slid his hand up along her jaw and into her hair to cup the back of her head. He broke the kiss, smiling when she leaned toward him, seeking more. Her eyes slowly opened.

"My lovely mortal." Kian pressed another kiss to her lips before tilting her head to the side. "Do you know how hard it has been to resist you?"

He dipped his head, kissing her jaw. "Do you know how utterly you have consumed me?" His mouth moved to her neck, trailing down, caressing her smooth flesh. "Do you understand how fiercely I have yearned for you?"

When he reached the purple mark Lachlan had left, Kian had to swallow back another surge of rage. He brushed his lips over the bruise. "I would kill for you."

Willow shivered, and her fingers curled against his shoulders. "Kian..."

He kissed that spot again, dabbing it with his tongue. "Anyone who hurts you will learn the meaning of pain. I will rend the flesh from their bones with claws and fangs."

He moved his mouth down and kissed the hollow at the base of her throat. Then he did the same to each of her shoulders. "And then I will tend to your every need, my Violet. Fulfill your every desire."

She released a shuddering breath. "What about your desires?"

A low growl rumbled from his chest. He lifted his head, locking his gaze with hers. "You are my desire, Willow."

He dropped his hands to the front of her towel and tugged the corner loose. The towel fell away, baring her curvy, luscious body. His balls tightened, and his throbbing cock strained against his pants. That deep, needful ache pulsed low in his belly, making his breath ragged and his heart beat faster.

"Gods. You are perfection," he rasped.

Kian touched the tip of a claw to her chin, grazing it down her throat and between her breasts before he ran the back of a finger over her nipple. It puckered beneath his touch.

Willow shivered and caught her bottom lip between her teeth. Somehow, he resisted the urge to suck that lip into his mouth, to nip it with his fangs, to reclaim her with a searing kiss. Hands framing her waist, he slowly lowered himself onto one knee, his lips following the path traced by his claw.

He stared up at her as he opened his mouth and extended his tongue, running its tip around the delicate flesh of her nipple. Her breath quickened. Then he pulled that hard bud into his mouth and sucked.

Willow released a shaky sigh. Her desire heightened, and he greedily drew it into himself. He wanted more, craved more.

More of her.

He cupped her heavy breasts in his hands, caressing them with firm, worshipful strokes as he lavished her nipple with his tongue. A soft moan escaped Willow, and her fingers delved into his hair.

Releasing the hard bud, Kian shifted his attention to the other, licking and sucking until it was as red as the first. Her body swayed toward him, and her head fell back.

Kian captured her nipple between his fangs.

Willow gasped, body jolting, and looked down at him with wide eyes.

"Eyes on me, Willow," he purred. "I don't want to just feel your desire. I want to see it in your gaze."

He took her nipple into his mouth again and soothed her pain with his lips and tongue. She skimmed her fingernails over his scalp with her fingernails, eyes half-lidded and gleaming with lust as she watched him.

"Good girl." Kian sank lower, leisurely exploring the soft flesh of her belly with his mouth as his hands descended along her sides, following her waist to her flaring hips. Her stomach quivered with her shuddering breaths, reacting to the tender attentions of his lips.

Her every response intensified his need. Her embrace of this pleasure—of him —was more potent an aphrodisiac than had ever existed, but he was determined to take his time and enjoy her.

He was determined to show her exactly how she deserved to be treated. To show her that she would always be first for him, she would always be his priority.

He lowered his other knee to the floor and spread his legs. His lips dipped below her belly button, drawing closer and closer to the source of her heat, and his breath shook in anticipation. He slid his hands back as they reached her thighs, palming her ass. Kian's mouth brushed over the small patch of hair on her pelvis. The tip of his nose touched it next.

There he paused, catching his tongue between his teeth to stop himself as he inhaled deeply. The perfume of her arousal filled his lungs. All his other senses failed in that moment, leaving only that scent, that heady, delicious, maddening scent, which was redolent of all her desire, all her need, all of her.

He couldn't suppress another growl as that primal, shadowy part of him stirred again. Willow's scent was imprinted upon him. It was part of him, and he would never have enough of it.

Thirst like he'd never known made his throat raw. His fingers flexed, pressing the tips of his claws into her skin. It shouldn't have been possible to need anyone as much as he needed her.

But he wasn't about to fight it.

Her desire surged when he hooked the back of her leg, lifted it, and draped it over his shoulder.

She swayed, making a startled sound, and Kian steadied her by returning his hands to her ass. He didn't allow her time to recover before he pulled her pelvis against his mouth.

His tongue delved between her silken folds, finding her already slick. He groaned and lapped at her cunt, running his tongue from bottom to top.

Willow tightened her grip on his hair and whimpered. "Oh God, Kian."

She was so sweet, so wet, and so hot. Closing his eyes, he thrust his tongue deeper into her center, eager for more of her essence. He drank greedily, squeezing her ass to clutch her closer. Seed seeped from his throbbing cock. Fuck, he needed her.

With his tongue coated in her flavor, he dragged it through her folds to her clit, swirling its tip around the little nub. Willow's breath hitched, and her hips gently undulated. She grasped and petted Kian's hair, hands moving sensuously, until they encountered his horns. Her fingers wrapped around them, squeezing tight, and she tugged him closer, increasing the pressure of his tongue on her cunt. Willow's hold only fueled his desire.

"Kian, please," she begged. "It feels... Oh God, it feels so good. Don't stop. Please don't stop."

"Not a fucking chance," he rasped against her. He pulled his right hand back and slipped it between her thighs, using his glamour to dissipate his claws as he thrust two fingers inside her. Her sex clenched around them. His wings twitched, rising from his back, and he groaned, nearly undone by his anticipation of the moment when it would be his cock enveloped by her body instead.

He pumped his fingers inside her, rubbing the spot that brought her so much pleasure as he continued teasing her thrumming clit with his tongue.

Breathy, needy moans escaped her, and she rocked her hips in time with his fingers, which gradually gained speed. Her slick ran over his hand and down her thighs.

His mate was so passionate, so sensual, so attuned to her desires despite how hard she'd resisted them. During moments like this, when she gave in and allowed herself to feel, she was white-hot, as bright and brilliant as a star.

Kian pressed his lips around her clit and sucked, lashing the swollen bud with his tongue. Willow let out a strained cry, her body tensing with a wave of pressure so powerful that even he felt it. That tension exploded in a blinding flash of ecstasy. Liquid heat burst from her, flowing into his mouth, and she spasmed, squeezing his horns as she curled over him.

She called his name, desperate, pleading, lost, and hungry, her every emotion now completely eclipsed by pleasure. He drank her essence eagerly, coaxing out more and more with his tongue and lips, keeping her bucking hips locked in place with his hands.

The nectar of the gods could not have compared to her taste. Nothing could have.

A ragged growl clawed its way out of Kian. Willow's pleasure flooded him, making his skin tingle, overcharging every nerve, buzzing through every shred of his being. And that now too-familiar ache deepened. His need for her was stronger than it had ever been, exceeding even the hunger he'd felt in those frantic weeks after their first night together. The universe was pulling him in every direction at once, and he would come apart if he didn't have her now.

It'd been too long—much too long—since he'd been inside her.

He rose, sweeping Willow off her feet as he spun around. A single stride carried them to the bed. Even as he laid her atop it, Kian dropped a hand to his waist and tore apart the leather and fabric of his belt and pants to open them.

Willow stared up at him, eyes aglow with need of her own.

Her cheeks were flushed, her full lips were parted, her damp hair was wild, and her thighs were spread. She'd never looked so beautiful.

Kian shoved his pants down. His cock sprang free, twitching in the cool air, but it didn't suffer the chill for long. He grasped her thighs, spread them wider, and thrust into her waiting, welcoming heat.

Pricking her skin with his claws, he threw his head back and snarled. Bliss rippled through him, shaking Kian to his bones. Willow's hot, slick cunt was paradise, contracting around him with echoes of her climax. It was nearly too much to bear.

"Fuck, Violet," he rasped.

Willow slipped her hands around his waist and pulled him even closer as she ground her sex against him, moaning.

He gritted his teeth and dropped his gaze to her. "I remember this. I remember the feel of you." Kian drew his hips back and pushed in again, plunging deep. "I've dreamt of this, craved this, yearned for this."

He caught her chin, forcing her eyes to remain locked with this. "I've yearned for you."

Willow took his hand, slipped his finger into her mouth—the same finger that had been inside her—and closed her lips around it. Lust surged through Kian as he stared at those lips, imagining them around his cock.

Her tongue twirled around his finger, and she sucked as she slowly slid it out. She settled his hand over her throat. "I dreamed of you too."

Kian curled his fingers firmly around her neck but didn't squeeze. He pumped his hips in a slow, steady rhythm, each forward motion punctuated by a burst of speed that seated him deep inside her. The contrast between those powerful strokes and the deliberate, gradual slide of flesh against flesh sharpened the pleasure infinitely. She matched his pace perfectly, meeting each thrust and drawing him in a little farther.

Soon, her pulse matched his, and their rapid, ragged breaths came in unison. Kian watched the passion in her eyes deepen, watched the tiny crease form between her eyebrows, watched her lashes fall. And he felt her body's responses—the quivering of her thighs, the tightening of her sex, the desperate press of her fingers against his flesh, the erratic shudders disrupting her rhythm.

This felt so good. *She* felt so good, so fucking good.

He needed more of her. He needed to reach that pinnacle, that moment when their mutual pleasure reached a crescendo and their souls succumbed to sweet, torturous bliss together. That moment when they became one.

Releasing her throat, Kian hitched one of her legs over his arm, braced a hand on the mattress, and leaned over her. He moved his hips harder, faster, grunting with each thrust, pushing all those sensations well beyond what should've been their limits.

Willow's breasts bounced against his chest, her breath was hot against his skin, and her soft cries filled the room. She wrapped her arms around Kian, and her hands found the bases of his lower wings.

A spark jolted through him, and he gasped, rhythm faltering, but he didn't stop. "Fuck!"

Then her body tensed, and her sex contracted around his cock. He sensed the storm that was about to consume her. A hot deluge of pleasure burst from Willow. An ecstasy he had never known rushed through Kian, enveloped him, and swept him away on its powerful currents.

Willow arched her back as she cried out. The tight suction of her pussy was his undoing. Rapture tore his mind apart, shredded his soul, and cast the pieces out into the universe.

Kian bared his fangs and growled. He slammed his hips forward, burying his cock as deep inside his mate as he could as seed erupted from him in great, shuddering spurts. His wings snapped out behind him, vibrating, and his claws sank into the bedding as he ground his pelvis against her.

He was weightless, untethered, adrift on the red ocean of pleasure she'd unleashed upon him.

Willow released his wings and moved her hands to his face, cupping his cheeks. She dragged his head down—dragging him back to reality—and crushed her lips against his.

The breath fled Kian's lungs, and Willow took it into herself as they were both battered by another climax. Their bodies trembled and their muscles tensed, but that kiss, *gods*, that kiss!

Before Willow, he would never have believed that a simple meeting of lips could say so many words without making a sound, could convey so many emotions in the space of a heartbeat, could mean so much.

His wings slowly flapped, and he leaned atop her, sinking deeper into the kiss, deeper into her, as he released the comforter to grasp a fistful of her hair. Willow softened the kiss, caressing his lips with hers, and he groaned when her tongue ran over his piercings. He released her leg to pull her closer, and she curled it around his hip. Their panting breaths mingled as they came down from the heights of their pleasure, but that pleasure did not ebb.

And Kian was in no rush to move. That warm, soothing afterglow was settling over him, enfolding him in crimson, lulling him to rest, to relaxation.

He was exactly where he wanted to be. Inside his mate with their limbs intertwined, sharing this moment, this intimacy. He'd felt this only once before, and only briefly—that first night with her, right before he'd fallen asleep. When he'd awoken to find her gone, he hadn't yet realized just what he'd tasted with her, just what they'd created when they'd come together. He hadn't understood what the strange hole inside him had been, or why it was so massive.

But he knew now.

Willow broke the kiss and pressed her forehead to his. "Kian."

"My sweet mortal, my lovely Violet, my Willow." Kian lifted his head to look down at her.

She smiled and stroked her thumbs over his cheeks.

Whatever words he'd been about to speak vanished when he looked into her eyes. Their emerald depths, now tinged purple by his red haze, brimmed with emotion—with potent, warm emotion even stronger than the lust he and Willow had just shared. That emotion flowed directly into his soul to fill him with energy like he'd never felt.

The heat that spread through Kian now began in his chest, intensifying with every moment he spent looking into her eyes. He knew what this was, even if he couldn't say it, and it was so far beyond anything he could've imagined.

For the first time in his long life, Kian hadn't fucked. What they'd shared hadn't been about lust, hadn't been about feeding, hadn't been about him. It had been so, so much more than that.

They'd made love.

"You undo me," Kian said in a thick, deep voice. He tenderly swept the damp strands of hair off her forehead and cheeks and lowered his face again, capturing her mouth in a lingering kiss. She reciprocated, and whispers of her pleasure drifted through him.

He reveled in the feel of her soft, smooth curves, reveled in her heat, in her taste. Never in his life had he enjoyed a mortal after he'd fed from them. But with Willow, he would savor every possible moment.

Yet he knew they could not stay like this forever, however much he longed to. He knew he could not yet allow himself to succumb to the afterglow.

He willed that haze to fade and withdrew from her body, groaning as her sex clenched around his cock. Willow moaned, and Kian was all too tempted to thrust back into her, to return to that tight, wet heat.

He resisted the urge.

Barely.

Standing on the floor between her legs, he gripped her knees and held them open, staring down at her cunt. His seed, an iridescent blue-white, seeped from the plump, red petals of her sex. That primal, instinctual part of him longed to push it back inside her, to complete their unforged mating bond—and to allow his seed to take root inside her. To breed with her.

He glanced at Willow's belly. In that instant, he knew, someday, she would carry his child. Not now, not yet, but it was inevitable.

"What are you doing?" she asked.

Kian dragged his gaze up her lush body to meet her eyes. "Admiring what is mine."

Though Willow's cheeks were already flushed, he knew his words brought a fresh blush to her skin. For as passionate as his little mortal mate could be, she had her moments of bashfulness.

His lips stretched into a grin. "Stay here, Violet."

"Okay." She stretched her arms over her head and arched her back. "Not that I feel like I could move far anyway."

Kian laughed, his gaze lingering on her full breasts. "Oh, you tempting morsel..."

He left her to enter the bathroom, where he retrieved a washcloth from the linen closet and turned on the water. Once the water was warm, he soaked the cloth and cleaned himself, mourning the loss of his mate's essence. His only comfort was the fact that her scent would remain on his skin for a while longer, even if its potency was diluted.

When he returned to Willow with the washcloth, she had indeed moved, having scooted up toward the head of the bed, where she now reclined. She silently watched him approach. He climbed atop the mattress and pushed her thighs open.

Her brow furrowed as her knees fell outward. "What are you doing?"

"I am caring for my mate," he announced.

"That's actually really sweet."

"Hmm. Perhaps that's you leaving your mark upon me." Kian stared down at her sex. Temptation won over. He swiped his finger up along her folds, gathering his seed, and pushed it into her. Willow's breath caught, and her sex tightened. He withdrew his finger.

"What do you mean?" she asked a little breathlessly.

Let that be enough, Kian.

His seed would not take. He wouldn't let it. But there was a primal satisfaction in having it all inside her, a bestial pride he could not deny.

Kian ran the washcloth over her inner thighs. "I've spent so much time with you, Willow. It's only natural your sweetness would influence me."

Willow snorted.

He glanced up at her. "You don't believe me?"

"Not really."

"Call me a liar, mortal. Call me a fool," he said, moving the cloth over her sex. He gently pressed down on her clit. Her breath hitched, and he held her gaze. "So long as you call me yours, I don't care."

Her expression softened, though her eyes were solemn as they stared into his.

Wadding the washcloth up, he tossed it onto the floor. When he grasped the covers and tugged, Willow lifted her backside, allowing him to peel the bedding down. She slipped her feet beneath the blanket and scooted down to rest her head on her pillow.

Kian crawled up beside her. With wings folded down along his spine, he lay on his side behind her, wrapped an arm around her middle, and pulled her body flush to his, tucking her ass against his groin. He drew the covers over them. Brushing his nose through her hair, he inhaled deeply, drawing in her scent.

Willow smoothed her palm along his forearm until her hand rested atop his. She yawned, and with a little wiggle, nestled more snugly against him. His cock twitched.

"Ignore that," he muttered.

She chuckled. The movement of her ass against his shaft certainly didn't make it any easier to control himself.

"We didn't use protection," she said.

"You're safe. Fae don't carry disease, and my ilk can only conceive babes when we will it. You'll not carry my child until I allow it."

"Okay. Wow. That's...handy."

He slid his hand up between her breasts to settle his palm over her heart. "Mmhmm."

They lay like that for a time, Kian soothed by the steady, easy rhythm of her heart, until she asked in quiet voice, "Did you mean what you said, Kian? Are you mine?"

Kian drew her a little tighter against him and lifted his head, placing his lips close to her ear. "I am, Willow. Eternally."

Twenty-Three

Willow opened her eyes to the dim, grayish light of dawn filtering through the sheer curtains of her bedroom window. Had she really slept that long? She blinked slowly as her awareness expanded and her memories returned. Lunch with Jamie; Lachlan, the compulsion, the assault; Kian.

Kian.

Are you mine?

I am, Willow. Eternally.

Her pulse quickened as those words echoed in her mind and wrapped around her heart, filling her with such hope. Did she dare believe them? Did she dare believe that this man, this other-worldly, fae being, was hers and hers alone? It seemed too fantastical to be true.

Kian's warm breath stirred her hair. He lay against Willow's back, one arm securely wrapped around her middle, legs intertwined with hers. His scent was thick in the air, fragrant, spicy, rousing.

And there was something hard and prominent pressed along the curve of her ass.

Her nipples tightened, and Willow bit the inside of her lip. She'd had his cock inside her, but it had been more than that.

They'd...made love.

And Kian stayed with her afterward. He'd spent the night with her.

Her eyes stung as warmth blossomed in her chest.

Every time she'd been hurt, spurned, or betrayed in a past relationship, another crack had formed in her heart. Maybe she allowed herself to care too swiftly, too deeply, but she couldn't change who she was. She enjoyed connecting with people. She loved learning about them, loved seeing them smile, loved getting little glimpses into their lives and their happiness. But when it came to romantic relationships, that drive to connect, to care, had only ever opened her to more hurt.

Willow had never found someone who treated her with the same respect and love she'd given them.

Please, Kian. Please don't hurt me.

She remained quiet and still, savoring this moment, savoring his closeness, his warmth, and the gentle possessiveness of his hold.

Until the call of nature became too insistent and ruined it.

Taking great care not to wake him, she shifted her legs forward and wrapped her fingers around Kian's wrist. She lifted his arm high enough to ease out from beneath it before she turned and lowered it to the bed. Sitting on the edge of the mattress, Willow looked at Kian. Her breath caught.

He was captivating.

The blanket rested low over his waist, leaving his upper body on display. His pale gray skin was radiant, the silken white strands of his hair shimmered in the light, and the glow of his eyes was so strong that it was just visible through his eyelids.

And his wings... They gave off their own gentle luminescence that made them look like delicate works of crystal lit from within.

Though she'd seen him sleeping on the night they'd met, she hadn't known what he was then. Now, it was surreal to witness. Something about sleep seemed so mundane, so weak, so...human. And his features in repose were so different than they were while he was awake.

With his brow smoothed and the corners of his mouth curled up in the merest hint of a smile, he looked almost innocent. The darkness that sometimes lurked in his eyes was nowhere to be seen now. The mask he wore for the world was gone.

She saw vulnerability on his face, but also peace. She saw the subtle but profound relief of a person who'd finally found someone after so many years alone, and it made her chest constrict, because God, she recognized it. She felt it herself.

How could he be hers? How could *this* be hers?

Mechanically, she brought her fingers to her forearm and pinched herself. She winced at the pain.

Nope, not a dream.

Willow wanted him again. But as much as she longed to touch him, she didn't dare. She didn't want to wake him.

Because she really, really had to pee.

She padded to the bathroom and gently closed the door before turning on the light. When she turned, she caught sight of herself in the mirror. Her hair was tousled, her nipples were red from Kian's attentions, and there were dark stripes of bruising on her hips, some accompanied by thin red scabs.

Willow twisted slightly and laid a hand over the bruises. She chuckled when she spread her fingers, making them line up with the marks. They'd been left by Kian's fingers, the scratches by his claws. She looked up.

Her elation fled as her gaze fell upon the mark on her neck.

Her skin began to crawl, but she swiftly pushed her revulsion aside.

Not going to let that monster ruin this. Not going to let him ruin what Kian and I shared.

She used the toilet, cleaned up, brushed her hair and teeth, and washed her face. Turning off the light, she took hold of the doorknob and paused to take a deep breath.

Yesterday, she and Kian had been as intimate as anyone could be. So why was she so nervous about returning to her bedroom? Why was she so nervous about returning to him?

Because I'm scared that something is going to happen, that I'm going to lose him.

Because... I might already love him.

Her heart raced, and her lungs felt restricted, as though they couldn't hold enough air.

Willow shook her head and drew in several deep, calming breaths.

No, it couldn't be. It was too soon. She felt affection for him, but...it couldn't be love. Not yet.

Exhaling slowly, Willow opened the door and stepped out. She came to an abrupt halt.

Kian was no longer asleep.

He lay propped up on an elbow, hair hanging over one shoulder. His lips spread into a sultry grin as his half-lidded eyes, which shone brighter than ever, met hers. "Morning, Violet."

His gaze devoured her inch by inch, and when his tongue slipped out to wet his lips, Willow shivered.

"You look well rested," she said.

"And you look well loved."

Willow's skin flushed as she approached him. She stopped beside the bed and lightly ran her fingers over the blanket covering him. "I was."

Kian reached out and traced one of the bruises he'd left on her hip. His smile faltered. "Did I hurt you?"

"No. You didn't. You made me feel good, Kian."

He gently covered the bruises with his palm. "You wear my marks well, mortal."

She grinned. "Should I walk around naked in public to show them off?"

His fingers flexed, and the prick of his claws sent a thrill across her skin. He growled, "Fuck no." Slipping his arm around her, he tugged her closer and pressed his lips to the bruises. "You're mine, Willow."

Kian trailed kisses across her hip and over her lower belly, each one soft and soothing, like the fluttering of butterfly wings against her skin. Yet each also poured heat into her veins. His lips could be so delicate and precise, but they were also capable of such savagery, such force. Whatever he did with them was always right. Always perfect.

She fought that blossoming ache in her core as his mouth moved lower. The tickle of his warm breath was almost more than she could bear, and it amplified her inner fires tenfold. Her heart beat faster, harder, and she caught her lip with her teeth, fraught with anticipation, with want. Just before his lips would've brushed the top of her pussy, Willow braced her hands on his shoulders and pushed him away.

Kian fell on his back with a grin, tucking his hands behind his head. "Ah, Willow, am I to go without breakfast?"

Damn it, even his playfulness was a turn on.

Willow pressed a finger to the center of his chest. "Maybe you just need to be a little patient." She slowly ran her finger down his abdomen toward the blanket, which was doing a poor job of hiding the evidence of Kian's desire.

His mouth slanted to the side. "When it comes to you,

waiting is the cruelest torture. But I'll gladly endure every second of it."

She grinned. "Good boy."

He chuckled, the sound low and sensual. "Until you want me to be bad."

"Be good a bit longer, and you'll be rewarded." Willow climbed onto the foot of the bed, between his legs. She gathered the blanket in her hands and slowly drew it down, uncovering Kian's body inch by delicious inch. His cock sprang free. It was hard and thick, and the piercing at its tip gleamed.

Releasing the blanket, she crawled closer to him, her eyes locked with his. "I decided to have my breakfast first."

Kian lifted his head and propped himself up on his elbows, the playfulness having vanished from his expression. A tiny crease formed between his eyebrows as he searched her face, and his lips twitched down ever so slightly. "What are you doing?"

Willow arched a brow as she planted a hand beside his hip. She trailed a finger from her other hand down the underside of his cock from piercing to base, making it twitch. "You're an incubus, Kian. Shouldn't it be obvious?"

His lips parted as he took in a soft, shaky breath. "It should be."

She wrapped her fingers around the base of his shaft. "Then let me make it a little clearer." Bending down, she ran the flat of her tongue up the length of his cock and flicked his piercing.

A tremor coursed through Kian, and his fingers curled, puncturing the sheet with his claws. He hissed her name. Impossibly, his shaft thickened in her grasp, and seed gathered at its tip.

It was the same shimmery blue-white she'd seen that first night. She hadn't questioned it then, had thought it must've been due to lubricant from the condom, but no. It was him.

Because of course he'd have magical cum.

Willow smiled and toyed with his piercing, teasing him,

enjoying every hitch of his breath, every twitch of his body, every quiver of his eyelids. She swirled her tongue around the head of his cock before taking it into her mouth and sucking.

And oh God, he tasted sublime. She moaned. His seed was sweet and heady, an erotic drug that she craved more of.

His wings snapped out, brushing across the bed as they shuddered.

"Fuck!" Kian growled through bared fangs.

The ache in Willow's core expanded, permeating her with heat. She felt her slick trickling down to wet her inner thighs. His taste, his reactions, and the raw desire in his eyes fanned the flames of her arousal, making them hot enough to consume her.

Keeping her lips tight around his throbbing shaft, Willow took him in deeper. She worked his length, steadily gliding her mouth up and down, pumping her fist at his base to ensure she pleasured every part of his cock.

Kian lifted a hand and delved his fingers into her hair. His breaths grew ragged, and the glow of his glittering blue eyes brightened. His head had dipped back a few times, dark lashes fluttering, but he fought to keep his eyes open, seemingly unwilling to take them off her.

Willow quickened her rhythm, dragging her tongue along his cock with every upward pull of her mouth, flicking his piercing when she reached the head. Her clit throbbed, but she didn't succumb to the temptation to touch herself. This was about Kian. This was about his pleasure.

Raising his knee, he undulated his hips. "Gods, Willow. Your mouth. Fuck, don't stop."

Stretching her lips farther, she took him deeper still, uncaring of the discomfort in her jaw. Willow wanted this. She wanted to give him this. And she wanted to taste more of him, wanted all of him. Her teeth nicked him, and he hissed, but he guided her head to keep going.

Finally, she pulled back to focus on the top of his cock, sucking with fast, shallow motions.

The scrape of his claws against her scalp was a thrill that only urged her on faster. Muscles trembling with tension, he lifted his hips off the mattress, bucking them erratically while holding her head firmly in place. And she took every bit of him.

He drew in a stuttering breath. His abs rippled as a larger tremor rocked him from head to toe, and he drove his pelvis forward.

Kian growled her name as his hot seed burst into her mouth and spilled down her throat. His wings stretched beyond the edges of the bed, quivering, their flecks of blue and green sparkling in the early morning light to make the room just a little brighter.

Willow pulled back slightly and rapidly stroked the base of his shaft, milking him for all he had, greedily drinking his otherworldly sweetness. She needed more of it, more of him. She would never get enough.

Every slight change of pressure from her lips, tongue, and fingers triggered a new spasm in him, a new explosion, and stole his breath. Her slick ran freely between her thighs. Knowing that she could give this inhuman being such immense pleasure that he was left completely at her mercy was more arousing than anything she'd experienced.

When his climax eased, Kian collapsed atop the bed. Willow slowly slid her mouth up. He shuddered at the movement, eyelids again fluttering, and muttered, "Fuck."

Once his cock was out of her mouth, she glanced down at it. His glistening shaft throbbed in the air, a steel rod wrapped in the smooth velvet of his skin. She slipped her tongue out and ran its tip from his balls all the way up to the piercing again.

Another drop of cum seeped from his slit. She caught it on

her tongue and moaned as she swallowed it. She couldn't get enough of his taste.

He laughed shakily, chest heaving as he panted. Smiling, Willow licked her lips and glanced up at his face.

Kian's eyes met hers. The ravenousness of his stare sent a jolt straight to her pussy.

Before she could act, he released her hair, sat up, and grasped her under her arms. She let out a delighted laugh as he dragged her over him, the sound cut short by his lips slamming against hers in a kiss that immediately forced her eyes shut.

She leaned atop him, melting against his hard body, and lost herself in the kiss as his lips and tongue caressed hers, taking her taste—and his—into his mouth.

Cupping her jaw in his hand, he broke the kiss. Willow opened her eyes to look down at him. Though his usual gleam of sensual mischief remained absent, his gaze retained that scorching heat, now tempered by something deeper.

"No one has ever put my pleasure before theirs," he rasped, stroking her cheek with the pad of his thumb. "No one has ever tended to my wants, my needs. No one but you, Willow."

Willow frowned, combing her fingers through his hair. "How is that possible?"

A wistful gleam entered his eyes. "Because no one cared, myself included. Until you."

It was only then that she realized just how lonely his existence had been, and her heart broke for him. To have lived for so many years and been involved with so many people without anyone caring enough to consider anything other than what he could give them...

Yes, he'd seen them as his prey, as his food. But how different might his life have been if even one person had cared just a little bit?

Would he have met Willow if someone had?

Maybe it was selfish of her, selfish and cruel, but she was glad there'd been no one else. She was glad she got to be the one to connect with him, to get to know him, to care for him. To see him as more than the one-night stand as which he'd originally presented himself. To see *him*.

And to...be his mate.

Are you mine?

I am, Willow. Eternally.

Her chest constricted.

Kian brushed his mouth over hers again, and playfully nipped her bottom lip with his fang. "I love the taste of you." He flicked the tip of his tongue over hers. "I love it even better when you taste of me."

Arousal coiled low in her belly, chasing away her lingering anxiety. He grinned and smoothed his hands down her back until he gathered her ass in his palms. "I sense that you have a few unfulfilled desires of your own, Violet."

Kian lifted his hips, and the hard length of his cock glided between the wet folds of her pussy.

Willow's breath hitched. "You're... Already?"

He laughed. "Oh, Willow. I'm an incubus, remember? I'm always ready. I can make you come as many times as you wish." His cock pulsed between their bodies. "Or as many times as I wish. And right now..."

Faster than Willow could comprehend, Kian slipped out from beneath her, leaving her on hands and knees as he positioned himself behind her. His hands caressed her hips and massaged the globes of her ass, pulling them apart. Willow blushed and tried to shy away, but his grip was firm.

"I want to fuck you. I want my cock buried deep in your cunt, I want to feel your heat, hear your screams." He slapped her ass.

Willow cried out and started at the sharp sting, which made her pussy clench in response.

Kian rubbed the spot he'd struck. "I want everything, Willow."

She turned to look at him over her shoulder. He was on his knees behind her, his eyes ablaze with lust, possessiveness, and wicked promise. His hair rested over one shoulder with a few stray strands caught on his horns to hang along his cheek. Those beautiful gossamer wings were spread wide.

He was a gorgeous fae god.

Her god.

"Then fuck me," she said.

Kian grinned, flashing his fangs. "Ah, Willow. I was going to anyway, but hearing you demand it...that calls for something special."

He reached toward her nightstand and tugged open the drawer. His hand dipped inside.

Willow's eyes widened. She knew exactly what was in there. "Kian!"

He chuckled as he held up her pink rose vibrator. "You have quite a delightful little stash of toys. Lucky for you, I love to play." He tossed it back into the drawer and took out the butt plug he'd given her, along with a bottle of lube.

Oh fuck.

"How did you—"

"Find this? Come now, Willow. It's not as though you've gone through much effort to hide it."

"This is my bedroom. My nightstand."

"So it is." He snapped open the bottle's lid with his thumb. "And I've explored every inch of it while you were working."

"Kian!"

His head swooped down, and he bit her ass cheek, making her yelp. Even that made her clit twitch in anticipation.

"I love it when you say my name." He settled his claws lightly

257

over her spine and skimmed them down toward her ass. "But I want to hear you scream it."

Upturning the bottle of lube, he drizzled a generous amount down her crack and slid his finger to her rosette, circling it, gently pressing against it. Willow curled her fingers into the bedding and clenched her anus against the intrusion.

"Ah, ah, Willow. You need to relax." Setting the bottle aside, Kian reached around her with his other hand and cupped her pussy, dragging his fingers through her slit. He growled. "Fuck, you're dripping."

He found her clit and stroked it. Pleasure unfurled inside her, and her breaths came in soft pants as she rocked against his hand. The heat in her core flared, spreading through her veins, gathering under her skin to make every part of her ache for more.

Willow closed her eyes and moaned, giving herself over to the building sensations, to his masterful ministrations.

Kian continued circling her clit. "The way you move..." He pressed tender kisses along her back. "I never knew I could need someone as badly as I need you, Violet."

"Mmm." Her thighs quaked, and her skin tingled. She rasped his name as she edged closer and closer to her peak.

All too soon, he stopped, withdrawing his hand.

Her eyes flashed open. "No!"

Kian chuckled and flattened his palm on her upper back, urging her down onto the bed with her ass in the air. "Not yet, my passionate little mortal."

A low buzzing noise filled her ears.

Oh God, this is really happening.

More lube dribbled onto her, dripping down her ass and to her sex. And then she felt it—the blunt tip of the vibrator against her anus. She gasped, eyes flaring, and squeezed the bedding in her fists as Kian pressed the toy in. The vibrations pulsed through her, pleasurable and intense, making her clit throb. They were also a welcome distraction, redirecting her focus from the pressure and burn as the plug stretched her.

"That's a good girl," Kian said, one hand massaging her ass as he continued to slowly work the butt plug into her. "A little more."

Willow panted and pressed her forehead onto the bed, trying her best to keep her body relaxed. Her pussy contracted as the vibrations buzzed through her pelvis. It was such an odd yet exhilarating sensation, and she never would've imagined it would feel so good.

When Kian inserted the rest of the plug, Willow moaned. The pressure, the stretch, the vibrations—her every nerve was alight. She was close to coming again. So, so close.

Kian settled his hands on her hips and stroked her backside with his thumbs. "Your ass is beautiful, Willow."

"Kian, please," she breathed. "I need you inside me."

"You beg so sweetly."

One of his hands fell away, and he soon dragged the broad head of his cock along her sex, stroking her clit with his piercing.

Then he pressed the head against her opening. With torturous, deliberate slowness, he pushed into her, making her feel every glorious inch of his shaft until she'd taken all of him.

She moaned, she whimpered, she took quick, shallow breaths and clutched the bedding, overcome by the sensation of utter fullness.

"Fuck, your cunt feels so good. I could stay inside you forever." Kian flexed his fingers, pricking her skin. The pain only heightened the pleasure enveloping her. He growled deep and low. "But I need to fuck you."

"Yes. Please. I can't..." Willow pushed back against him, taking his cock deeper. "Kian, I can't take it anymore."

He groaned.

"You're mine, Willow. All fucking mine." Kian drew back.

The slide of his shaft, coupled with the merciless pulsing of the vibrator, made Willow's legs too weak to support her, but his strong hands allowed her no escape. With a deft yank on her hips, he drove deeper into her than ever. Willow's body rocked, and a breathless, soundless cry escaped her throat.

Before she could recover, he pounded into her again and again, setting a brutal pace that hardly gave her a chance to breathe. He did all the work—he held her up, he pulled her to meet his every thrust, he kept her body in motion. She was at his mercy, and God, was it bliss.

Pleasure coiled in her core, winding tighter and tighter and yet expanding to permeate her entire body, her mind, her soul. She couldn't think, couldn't see. All she could do was feel. And Kian's expert movements ensured she felt *everything*.

It was so much, too much. Blistering pleasure burst through her, shattering Willow, shattering reality, leaving her to be devoured by brilliant, blinding rapture.

Twenty-Four

K ian's pace faltered as Willow came undone. The sensations were overwhelming. Her hot, wet heat contracting around his shaft; the merciless vibrations from the toy; the tremors coursing through her body; the powerful flow of energy. It was all so much. It was all so fucking sweet.

Baring his teeth, he snarled and pumped into her faster, harder. Her slick eased his motions, but she was still so tight. Gods, her cunt could fucking crush his cock right now and he'd beg her for more.

More. More. More.

The word echoed in his head, resonated in his soul. It grew louder with every one of his ragged breaths. He needed more of her, all of her.

He needed to seal their mating bond. To claim her in all ways.

Torrents of pleasure built in his groin, creating agonizing pressure. His instinctual drive to claim her built deeper inside him, but it was no less painful. That dark, buried part of him needed to perform the ritual. It needed them bound fully.

He strengthened his grip on her hips and fucked her harder still. She'd melted in his hold already, her body pliant to his every whim. He relished the control. Relished what she offered him.

The energy she'd given him yesterday still coursed through him, crackling with power. He'd never been so full, had never felt so strong, so invigorated. How was it possible for him to still hunger so much for her? How was it possible for his yearning to remain so deep and consuming?

Because this isn't about feeding.

With her, it never was.

Not even in the beginning, before he understood what she was. Before he understood what she would mean to him.

He didn't need her pleasure, he needed her. All of her, in every way. And the longer he denied that bond, the longer he fought those primal urges, the harder it would be to control them. The harder it would be to control himself.

"You are fucking mine," he growled, smacking her ass.

Willow cried out, her pussy squeezing his shaft.

Kian slapped her ass again. "Say it!"

"Yes! Yes, I'm yours."

He knew it was true, felt it down to the core of his being, but words weren't enough. That covetous part of him needed the bond, and it would settle for nothing less.

Soon.

He would make his eternal claim upon her soon. He would hear his true name from her lips. But he would not sink to the depths of fae like Lachlan, would not rob Willow of her choice. He would not make a slave of the female who was meant to be his equal, who was meant to join with him, soul-to-soul.

His chest rumbled with a groan as the growing pleasure crackled through him. Her cunt clung to his shaft every time he drew back, and it clamped down to draw him farther in with every forward thrust, intensifying the pressure inside him, intensifying the ache.

Kian clenched his jaw and exhaled harshly through his nose as he fought the inevitable tidal wave. He wasn't ready for this to end, not yet. He would enjoy every moment of it, every moment of her, until he couldn't hold on any longer and his climax carried him to oblivion.

Willow lay with her head turned aside, her cheek upon the bed. Her purple hair was in disarray, spread across her back and shoulders, with stray strands on her face. Her eyes were shut, her brow was pinched in pleasure, and her lips were parted.

Kian's eyes dipped. Bright red handprints on her ass and new marks on her hips accompanied yesterday's bruises and scratches, bold against her pale flesh. The flare of her hips was even more pronounced in her current position, granting a full, luscious view of her rounded, bouncing ass.

Each time he drew his hips back, the purple gem on the plug shimmered. It coaxed his gaze lower still.

His heartbeat became thunderous as he stared at the spot where their bodies connected. He watched his shaft, glistening with her essence, slide back, watched her tender, pinkened flesh yield to his thrust, watched her legs tremble.

He'd never seen anything so fucking erotic. And it was all his.

She was all his.

His arm darted out, and he gathered a fistful of her hair. Her eyes opened to meet his, their green darkened and gleaming with lust, clouded with pleasure. Kian tugged on her hair, forcing her to rise onto her hands and arch her back, forcing her lush, willing body to take every single one of his ruthless poundings.

Her breathy moans escalated in volume and pitch, joining the clapping of thighs and Kian's bestial grunts to create a primitive, lascivious song.

Willow whimpered, and her cunt quivered around his cock. "Kian! I...I can't! It's too much!"

"It will never be enough," he snarled as he let go of her hair to wrap his arm around her middle. His hand found her sex, which was stretched taut around his shaft, dripping with her essence, radiating heat. He pressed on her clit hard and stroked it.

Willow tensed, every part of her body locking up. And then she released a choked cry, dropping her head and shoving her hips back to seat Kian even deeper as her cunt gripped his shaft. She shuddered, and her inner muscles contracted so strongly that they nearly pushed Kian out. Her liquid heat flowed around his cock and soaked his hand.

He slammed into her, banding his other arm around her to keep her pinned against him. Her convulsions were more than he could withstand. Kian's wings spread and fluttered. His lips peeled back, and his growl grew into a roar as ecstasy cleaved through him, shredding every fiber of his being with its sinful, sensual claws. She screamed his name, pleading, but there was no respite from the pleasure.

His hips bucked involuntarily. Still, he held her captive against him, unwilling to relinquish her. His seed flooded her, each wave pulling something taut in his belly and balls, each wave a new bout of delicious torment.

Though he was no longer pumping his hips, that vibrator did not relent its assault. Willow's pussy pulsed around him, and her body shook as she cried, moaned, and begged between desperate, heaving breaths. Kian groaned, his cock twitching as another spurt of seed was wrung from him.

Loosening his grip on her, he slipped a hand between their bodies and pressed the button to turn off the butt plug. The vibrations stopped, but Willow's trembling did not. Her sex continued convulsing around his shaft as aftershocks from their orgasms swept through them.

They collapsed, and Kian caught himself on an arm, careful not to crush her.

He lay over her for a time, forehead resting on her back as he caught his breath. His free hand trailed over her soft skin, following her curves, and slowly, he kissed along her spine and shoulders. The hint of saltiness from her sweat complimented her sweetness perfectly.

Willow hummed. "Kian..."

His heart constricted at the tenderness with which she'd said his name, and he couldn't help wondering how his true name would sound when she said it the same way. He couldn't help but anticipate the thrill it would spark in him and the warmth it would spread through his chest.

"Thank the Fates I found you that night, my Violet," he whispered. Those weeks that he'd suffered, that he'd starved, had been a small price to pay for this. For his Willow.

She ran her hand over his thigh. "I'm glad I said yes."

"Ah, Willow." He pressed another kiss to her back, letting this one linger, and breathed her in. Her alluring scent mingled with the smell of sex—and of him.

He could've lain there forever, lost in her fragrance, soothed by her heat, basking in the afterglow of what they'd shared, but he knew that wasn't possible. Despite his reluctance, Kian withdrew his cock from her. They both moaned at the loss. The chill of the air against his shaft was a necessary agony, taking the edge off his continued arousal.

Kian's limbs were heavy as he pushed himself upright. He placed a hand on her back, smoothing it down her spine until it reached her ass. "Relax and breathe, Willow."

Her body eased. Kian grasped the base of the toy and gently pulled, coaxing a low groan from Willow.

Once the vibrator was free, he smoothed his palm over the bruises on her hip. "You all right?"

She chuckled and turned her face toward him. "I don't know if I'll ever walk again, but I feel amazing."

A smirk lifted the corner of his mouth. "Don't worry, mortal. I'll carry you anywhere you need to go." He climbed off the bed, retrieved the washcloth he'd dropped on the floor yesterday, and wrapped the toy in it, setting it aside to clean later. His wings flicked and relaxed against his back.

When he returned to the bed, his mate had pushed herself up onto her hip. Her hair hung over her shoulder in disarray, and she looked up at him with half-lidded eyes that were so trustful, so serene, so...affectionate. Again, his heart squeezed.

"And right now"—he slipped his arms under Willow and lifted her off the bed, cradling her against his chest—"it's to the shower we go."

She looped her arms around his neck and smiled. "It's so strange how effortlessly you can pick me up."

He carried her toward the bathroom. "Why is it strange?"

Willow gave him a droll look. "I'm not exactly small, Kian. No matter how many times you call me little."

"All a matter of perspective, Willow." Turning sideways, he stepped through the doorway. "You're as light as a feather to me. And this delectable body fits so perfectly against mine."

He captured her mouth with his as he stopped. His tongue traced the fullness of her lips until she opened to him, and then he deepened the kiss, keeping it slow and tender.

Kian didn't break the kiss until he'd lowered Willow onto her feet. Her arms remained around his neck, and she held on as he pulled away, standing on her toes to seek more.

Chuckling, he pecked another kiss on her lips, ducked out of her hold, and stepped back. He couldn't stop his eyes from raking over her. "You're more beautiful every time I look at you, Violet."

She blushed, but her smile was wide. "I feel beautiful when you look at me."

He hooked a finger under her chin. "You should feel it all the time. Your radiance has nothing to do with me."

Before he could succumb to the urge to kiss her again, he strode to the shower and turned it on. Once the water was steaming, he pulled Willow inside and closed the sliding glass door. Hot water cascaded over them.

Kian swept his hair behind his shoulder, plucked a bottle of bodywash off the shelf, and opened it. He drizzled the soap into his palm. Setting the bottle down, he guided Willow to turn her back toward him.

Starting at her neck, he ran his hands over her, massaging her flesh as he cleaned her. Her muscles relaxed under his touch, and she swayed in silent contentment, which tasted just as sweet as her most intense pleasure.

His cock throbbed. The mere act of touching her, of making her feel good, nearly drove him wild with desire.

No. I am tending to my mate. She needs time to recover. Time to rest.

He cleaned her shoulders, her arms, her back, and then slid his hands around her sides. She shivered as his fingers brushed over her ribs. Then his fingers reached the undersides of her breasts. Drawing in a quiet, unsteady breath, he cupped that soft, ample flesh, lifting and squeezing. Her nipples hardened beneath his palms as he kneaded her breasts.

Willow hummed, her head falling back. She leaned toward him, and the head of his cock bumped her back.

That instant of contact sent a jolt of pleasure through Kian. He hissed through his teeth, pivoting his hips backward.

She glanced at him over her shoulder, a sultry grin on her tantalizing lips. "I think you poked me."

Tending to her. Caring for her.

But gods, that ache was so pervasive, so persistent.

"Just ignore it, Willow," he said.

"Kind of hard to ignore that thing."

His balls tightened, and his cock twitched as though seeking her of its own accord. He caught his bottom lip with a fang, biting down, but the pain didn't curtail his desire. "You're telling me. I have to live with the fucker."

Willow laughed and turned toward Kian, flattening her palms on his chest. She peered up at him through wet lashes. "Guess I have to live with it too."

He'd been impressed by her ability to resist her wants, but when Willow took charge of them, when she owned them, there wasn't anything sexier in the world.

"Fuck," he rasped. "Willow... I don't want to hurt you."

"You won't." She dropped her right hand to his cock and wrapped her fingers around it. "I won't break, Kian."

He grunted as she stroked him, and his wings snapped out, only to be blocked by the walls of the shower. The coldness of those walls sent a shiver down his spine that only intensified his pleasure.

Kian tried to restrain himself. He truly did. But with the fire in her eyes as she stared at him, with the way she stroked his cock so boldly, so confidently, with her standing before him, so wet and willing, so fucking sweet and tempting...

How the fuck was he supposed to resist her?

A snarl tore from his chest. It might've been a curse or a primal, wordless sound, but it didn't matter. He was beyond caring.

He hooked his hands under her ass and lifted her. She threw her arms around him, fingers clutching his hair. Pressing her back to the wall, he spread her thighs.

Their eyes met again; their souls stared into each other with ravenousness, passion, and something infinitely deeper and more potent. Something that filled Kian with fire and fury, that

cemented his knowledge of the only cosmic truth that mattered—
Willow was his.

He drove into her waiting cunt with a growl and surrendered
to their mutual desire.

Twenty-Five

Willow stood in her kitchen, bent over the island counter, with the late morning sunlight shining through the open window. A gentle breeze swept inside, carrying the musical sounds of the chimes hanging on the patio.

Absently, she dunked a tea bag into her mug, studying one of the sunflowers in the vase in front of her. She smiled. The flowers Kian had bought her still dominated the kitchen and living room, many of them looking as fresh as they had nearly a week ago. They perfumed her home and added so much color and life to it. They were also a constant reminder of the fae who'd given them to her.

Not that she could ever forget him, even for a moment.

Willow's smile stretched into a grin.

Kian had given her another gift along with the flowers, a surprising gift that had finally been put to use today.

She rubbed her thighs together. Her body was still weak from what they'd done this morning—weak but so well loved. Her breasts and pussy were sensitive, and her ass was tender. Her skin sported bruises, scratches, and even a bite on her shoulder, which had been a result of Kian being overcome with pleasure in the shower.

What else could she have expected from sex with an incubus? Willow had never been taken so savagely, so vigorously, so passionately. Though despite how bestial Kian could be, Willow didn't miss the tender longing in the depths of his eyes when he looked upon her. When she was with him, it wasn't just sex. There was something more, something powerful, something compelling.

It was evident in the way he'd held her afterward. In the way he'd gently cleaned her, the way he'd soothed every scratch and bruise, no matter how tiny. It was in the way he brightened whenever she laughed or smiled.

She felt cared for. She felt cherished.

She felt...loved.

Willow pressed a hand over her heart as though she could slow it.

Kian had left about an hour ago to get a change of clothes from his place, since his clothing had been ruined in his fight with Lachlan yesterday. Willow already missed him. They hadn't known each other for long, but it was like Kian had said. This thing between them...

It was inevitable.

Willow sighed and lifted the mug to her lips, taking a careful sip of the steaming tea. "I am in deep."

Loki jumped onto the stool beside her. She looked at him, and he stared up at her with big green eyes.

"Have you guys accepted Kian yet?"

He meowed.

Willow smiled and scratched behind his ear. "I'll take that as a yes. You've all mellowed out around him."

Loki purred and arched his back as she ran her palm along it.

"Which is a good thing, because we'll be seeing a lot more of him from now on."

Would he consider moving in with her? After sleeping in his arms, feeling so safe, so content, and so right... How could she go back to sleeping alone?

But would Kian even want to stay in her plain little house? Where did he live, anyway? What was his place like? Would he ever take her to it? There was still so much she didn't know about him, so much to discover and learn.

The chime of the doorbell broke the peaceful silence, startling Loki, who leapt down from the stool and darted into the bedroom.

Willow's heart jumped with elation.

Kian's back!

Setting down the mug, Willow hurried to the front door, thrumming with excitement. She had a client coming later, and she wanted to spend as much time with Kian as she could before then. Unlocking the door, she flung it open.

Her heart dropped.

Eli stood on her porch, dressed in dark blue jeans and a red and black button-down flannel, with his brown hair slicked back but for an errant strand dangling over his forehead. His smile was wide, displaying his straight white teeth.

He held up a bouquet of red roses. "Hi Willow."

She didn't even look at the flowers. "What are you doing here, Eli?"

"I came to apologize."

"You already did that. I didn't accept it. And I'm pretty sure me telling you to go away and blocking your number was a sign that I didn't want to see you again."

He lowered the flowers with a sigh. "Come on, Will. Don't be like that."

"I don't want to see you, Eli. Go." She stepped back and closed the door.

Eli slapped a hand on the door before it was fully shut, halting its progress, and pushed it back open. "Just hear me out, okay?"

"There is nothing more for you to say, and nothing I want to hear from you. It's over between us."

"But I don't want it to be." He stepped across the threshold, standing directly in front of her. "I've had time to think. I know I fucked up. But Will, I miss you. What we had was special. I want you back."

"But I don't want you."

"Aw, come on, Willow." He reached out to touch her cheek, but she backed out of his reach. He frowned. "We were good together."

"No, we weren't. It just took me too long to realize it. I want you to leave."

Eli scowled and moved forward, forcing Willow to retreat farther. He closed the door behind him.

An alarm blared inside her, and she backpedaled to get more space between them. While they'd been together, he'd never hit her, never threatened her, but there was something unsettling in his eyes now, something disconcerting about the way he moved.

"This is bullshit," Eli said. "Are you seriously going to throw away a three-year relationship?"

"Are *you* serious right now? You threw that away when you cheated on me. But I'm glad it happened, I'm glad I found out who you really are before I wasted more of my life on you."

"Wasted your life on me? What the fuck? You were never like this before. You never talked like this."

"My eyes were opened, Eli. I deserve better."

He thrust his hand into his hair and dragged it through the strands. Glancing around the living room, he frowned. "Where'd all these flowers come from?"

"From someone who values me."

"You're with someone?"

"I am."

He clenched his jaw. "Wow. Didn't take you long to start fucking someone else, did it?"

Rage sparked within her chest. "Don't you fucking dare throw that shit at me. You were screwing someone else while you were with me. I was faithful to you the entire time we were together, and what I do now is none of your fucking business." She thrust her finger toward the door. "You need to leave. Now. Before I call the cops."

"Look, I'm sorry, okay? I shouldn't have said that. Like I said, I fucked up." He set the roses on the back of the sofa and approached her. She tried to move away, but he thrust his hand out, catching her wrist and pulling her toward him.

She gritted her teeth. "Eli, let me go."

"Just give me another chance, Will. I won't touch another woman again. I want us to start over. I really miss you."

Willow tugged on her arm. "Let. Me. Go."

"I know what will soften you up." He banded an arm around her waist and yanked her body against his.

She struggled, but he didn't let go. Releasing her wrist, he cupped the back of her head, preventing her escape as his head dipped.

"Eli, no!" She tried to turn her head away, but he only tightened his grip on her hair.

He pressed his mouth against hers.

That same sense of helplessness she'd felt with Lachlan overcame her. It was paralyzing, nauseating, humiliating. She hadn't wanted what Lachlan was doing to her yesterday, and she didn't want this now.

But Eli wasn't Lachlan. He wasn't a fae, wasn't using magic. He was human. Bigger than her, stronger than her, but human all the same.

A human with weaknesses.

The front door crashed open.

Eli started, and Willow took that moment to bite down hard on his bottom lip. His pained cry was cut short by a choked grunt when she rammed her knee up into his crotch. Her fist struck his jaw next, whipping his head to the side.

Flattening her hands on his chest, she shoved him away.

Eli stumbled backward and fell to the floor. Blood oozed from his lip as he doubled over, cupping his groin. "Fuck!"

With limbs trembling and chest heaving, Willow looked up to see Kian framed in her doorway.

Kian stared down at Eli, eyes blazing. With the morning light behind him, he seemed swathed in shadow—not an ethereal fae seducer, but a monster that had clawed its way out of darkness.

Her monster.

His gaze swung to her, not losing a shred of that intensity. Eli scrambled aside with another curse as Kian strode to Willow, nearly stepping on the fallen man. Despite the tension pulsing from him in withering waves, Kian's fingers were gentle when he took hold of Willow's chin and tilted her face toward his.

He brushed his thumb across her bottom lip. It came away smeared with blood. One corner of his mouth curled up as he said quietly, just for her, "My vicious little mortal..."

"Who the hell is this, Will?" Eli demanded, his voice strained as he got to his knees. "Is this him? You left me for *him*? This emo goth freak?"

Dipping his head, Kian pressed his lips to Willow's, lingering briefly. That time was all she needed to eradicate the feel and taste of Eli's unwanted attentions. Of his assault.

Kian withdrew slowly, running his tongue across his lips to wipe away a smudge of crimson. The light in his eyes had shifted, had narrowed and focused into that dangerous glint she'd seen only once before—when he'd fought Lachlan.

"Excuse me for a moment, Violet." Kian turned his head

aside, glanced at the bouquet Eli had set atop the couch backrest, and plucked a single rose from the bunch.

"You're not in your right mind, Will." Eli let out a heavy breath, moving with clear discomfort as he grabbed onto the couch and began to rise. "I get it. You're hurt, I fucked up, and this...this is your way of getting back at me. Lesson learned, okay?"

Kian offered Willow one more smile. As he spun toward Eli, she saw that smile twist into a snarl.

Eli continued, "Maybe the emo guy should step out so we can ta—"

Kian's boot struck Eli in the chest. The man fell back, hitting the floor so hard that he would've bounced were it not for Kian following through to plant that same boot on Eli's throat.

Eyes bulging, Eli grasped Kian's boot, clawed at his leg, and thrashed on the floor, but the incubus didn't budge.

"You've nothing more to say," Kian growled. "You had your chance. And after what you did to her, I should tear your fucking heart out of your chest and shove it down your throat."

Eli's struggles intensified, and his face turned red, but still, he couldn't move Kian.

Willow gathered the hem of her blouse in her hands and clenched it, remaining silent.

Kian leaned forward, his shifting weight forcing a choked sound out of Eli. "You've no idea how tempted I am, *Eli*. You cannot fathom the humiliations you would endure, the suffering. To take your pathetic mind apart one thread at a time would be a delight to me. You have no idea what fucked up truly means. But I could show you, Eli.

"You deserve no less. You came here, to her home, and tried to force yourself upon her? Tried to claim what was never yours to begin with? She is *mine*. You were never even worthy of licking the shit off her heel. And it is only because of her compassion, because of her kindness, that I'm going to give you a last fucking chance to walk away. It's only because she is too good to witness what I would do to you, and I'll not have her waste a single fucking moment pitying the wretched husk you'd become before I was through."

Kian bent closer to Eli. "You're not going to come here again. You're not going to try to contact her again. You're going to forget she ever existed, because if you so much as think of Willow, I will find you and finish this for good. Understand?"

Eli nodded shallowly, unable to move his head any farther due to Kian's boot.

When Kian lifted his foot, Eli sucked in a desperate, ragged breath and arched his back off the floor, clasping his throat. His respite was short lived.

Kian sank down, bracing his knee on Eli's chest. He batted away Eli's attempted blows with the same amount of effort one would've used to shoo a fly before grasping the man's cheeks in one hand and squeezing.

"Also"—Kian twirled the rose between his fingers, turning the petals into a red blur—"sunflowers are her favorite."

He shoved the bud into Eli's mouth. Eli choked and fought, but his struggles were for nothing as the incubus twisted the flower and pressed it in more firmly. Tattered pieces of rose petal flew out with Eli's harsh exhalation.

Kian forced Eli's jaw shut, snapped off the rose's stem, and threw it aside before rising.

Eli rolled onto his side, coughing and spitting out the ruined flower. Kian grabbed him by the back of his shirt and dragged him out through the open front door. Halting at the edge of the porch, he tossed the man down onto the walkway.

Willow hurried to the door, heart racing as she stopped behind Kian to look past him.

Eli groaned, lying where he'd landed on the cement with his

features contorted in pain. Crimson stained his lips, a mix of his blood and the crushed rose petals, and the rest of his face was nearly as dark.

"Get the fuck out of here," Kian growled.

Dazed and sluggish, Eli unsteadily got to his feet and stumbled toward his car, which was parked in Willow's driveway, blocking her vehicle. He got in, slammed his door closed, and started the engine. The car peeled out, nearly hitting her mailbox as he drove away.

"Say the word, my Violet, and I'll kill him," Kian said, voice low and lethal.

Willow settled her hands on his back. Tension radiated from him. As much as she disliked Eli, as horrible as he'd been, he didn't deserve to die. But... Willow couldn't deny that Kian's ruthlessness in defending her had turned her on. And she only felt a little bad about what had happened.

Just a teeny, tiny bit.

"No. He's not worth it," she said.

Kian's shoulders rose and fell with his harsh, heavy breaths, and he kept his head turned in the direction Eli had fled. "But you are, Willow."

He spun toward her suddenly, bent down, and hooked an arm around her ass, lifting her over his shoulder as he straightened. Willow's world turned upside down.

She squeaked and braced her hands on his back as her hair fell around her head. "Kian!"

He strode into the house and kicked the door shut, snatching up the bouquet of roses as he passed the couch. He slammed them into the trash in the kitchen and continued toward her bedroom without missing a beat.

"Sorry, Violet," he said. "Still have some aggression I need to get out." He slapped her ass, sending a rush of desire through her before he soothed the sting. "And I have a willing mate with a soft, hot body who'll help."

Willow captured her bottom lip with her teeth in a grin. She made her answer as clear and concise as possible by slapping his ass in return.

He laughed as he carried her into the bedroom.

Twenty-Six

W illow was struck with a sense of déjà vu. Over a month ago, she'd walked along this same sidewalk beneath the same dark sky, had swept her gaze across the same fancy storefronts, had felt the same sense of mystery in not knowing where she was being taken. She was even wearing the same purple dress.

But the man beside her couldn't have been more different.

This man didn't dismiss her feelings, ignore her desires, or make her feel embarrassed for the things she enjoyed. This man didn't force her to adhere to his schedule, didn't make her beg for his time.

Kian *wanted* to spend time with her.

His hunger for Willow went so far beyond making love. He was ravenous when it came to learning about her, devouring every drop of information she offered, always seeking clues while he was in her home. Though he often presented himself as arrogant and self-absorbed, the truth of Kian was much deeper. He'd devoted himself to discovering every aspect of Willow one tiny piece at a time.

He'd lie with her just to simply talk, would cuddle and watch movies with her, and had even listened to her read romance books out loud beneath the fairy lights on her bed's canopy.

Though she'd been embarrassed when he'd first asked her to read those stories to him, it had proven well worth it every time they'd reached a spicy scene. He always interrupted before she finished, but she was never upset, because his reenactments were always infinitely better than the words on the page.

Of the scenes they'd reenacted thus far, her favorite had come up yesterday afternoon. In the book, the heroine had been bound by silk webbing so the spider monster could claim her as his mate. Kian's clever hands had demonstrated a talent for shibari that'd had Willow weak in the knees before he'd even finished tying her up.

Willow's core clenched, and her skin tingled with the memory of his hands moving over her as he'd conquered her body.

"Ah, Willow," Kian purred, casting his heated gaze down toward her. "Seems your thoughts have taken a wicked turn."

She grinned as she laced her fingers with his. His metal rings were cool against her skin. "I was just thinking about your... talented hands."

"I've the hands of a musician, considering the songs they coax from you."

Willow blushed. Oh, Kian had certainly wrung a variety of sounds from her as he'd played her body.

Her heels clicked on the sidewalk as they continued onward. She brushed her fingers over the purple satin and black lace of her skirt. "So why did you want me to wear this dress tonight?"

"You were wearing it the night we met. I just wanted to see you in it again, wearing it just for me." He leaned closer and whispered, "And this time, I'll be the one taking it off you."

Her desire flared, spreading warmth through Willow that chased the night chill from her bare skin.

He chuckled. "I see the idea appeals to you."

Anything that had to do with Kian touching her appealed to Willow.

I'm turning into a freaking sex fiend.

So what if I am? There's nothing wrong with having a healthy sexual appetite.

She felt the bass pulsing through the ground as they approached Reverb. Like the last time she'd passed by here, there were people lined up along the front of the brick building, awaiting entrance, and colorful lights spilled through the upper windows. A little farther ahead was the spot where she'd first seen Kian, the spot where they'd first looked into each other's eyes. Willow smiled.

That night had changed her life in ways she never could've imagined, in ways she still didn't fully understand.

And seeing that alley again, recalling the way Kian had stood there with his back against the brick wall and his knee bent, the way his eyes had widened when they met hers, that feeling of immediate, powerful connection...

She wished she could recapture that moment on camera.

But they never made it to the alley. Once they'd passed the line, Kian brought Willow to a stop and turned to face the entrance of Reverb.

Willow's eyes widened as she looked from the nightclub to Kian and back again. "You're taking me dancing?"

"The night we met, I felt a flicker of longing that was so different from all the lust and gluttony that clouds the air in these places." He brushed the back of a ringed finger over her cheek. "That's when I looked over and first saw you. When I first craved you."

She smiled and traced a finger down the front of Kian's black button-down shirt until it hooked on his vest. "I wanted to go dancing."

"I know. I saw that desire as clearly as I felt it." Covering her hand with his, he leaned down until his forehead touched hers. "My sweet, sweet mortal... You've gone far too long without someone caring about what you want."

If any walls had remained around Willow's heart, Kian would've obliterated them in that moment. But he had long since torn down her defenses. Tears stung her eyes, and Willow softly laughed. "You're going to make me cry if you keep talking like that."

Kian pressed a gentle kiss to her forehead. "No crying, my Violet," he said, his voice deep and low, his lips caressing her skin as he spoke. "Your tears would bring me to my knees right here, right now."

He drew back, and his mouth stretched into the most mischievous grin. "And you know how much I love being on my knees before you."

Willow pulled her hand out of his with a laugh and playfully slapped his chest. "Do you always think of sex?"

Kian arched a brow. "No, I *often* think of sex. I always think of you." He placed a hand on her lower back and steered her toward the club's entrance. "Now, let's go have some fun, shall we?"

She smiled at him, nearly vibrating with excitement. "Yes."

When the bouncer working the door noticed their approach, he opened the velvet rope and stood aside, using his body to block the front of the line.

Kian didn't miss a step as he guided Willow past the bouncer. The man didn't ask for their IDs, didn't question their bypassing of the line, didn't check any list or call anyone with his earpiece. He didn't exchange a single word or gesture with either of them. Once they were clear, he simply returned to his previous position, closing the rope again.

However brief it had been, the experience struck Willow as surreal. It was the kind of thing she'd only seen in movies.

Had Kian used his magic on the bouncer?

No, she didn't want to think about that. It would bring up memories she had no desire to recall. Maybe they just knew each other, or maybe Kian was...on the list?

How many times had Kian come here?

Kian pushed the door open, and a wave of sound blasted away Willow's questions, planting her excitement firmly at the forefront.

The industrial flare from outside carried on within the club, where brick, black metal, and distressed wood were the predominant materials. But the lighting, ever-changing with the thumping dance music, gave the place a warm, modern feel. A mezzanine with numerous tables wrapped around part of the space, overlooking the dance floor. The high ceiling enhanced the sense of size, making the place feel much larger than it really was.

Kian leaned down, putting his mouth close to her ear. Despite all the noise, his seductive voice was perfectly audible when he said, "Would you care for a drink first?"

Willow nodded, giving him a flirtatious smile. "I have been pretty thirsty lately."

He laughed and ran the tip of one of his long nails down the middle of her chest, toward her cleavage. "That you have."

With his arm around her waist, he led her through the throng to the long, curving bar that stretched across the side of the nightclub. Colorful alcohol bottles of all shapes and sizes stood upon glass shelves behind the bar, lit by many-colored lights. Crystal clear glasses were stacked on the counter beneath.

Kian and Willow squeezed into an open spot at the bar, with him standing just behind her. Desire flared within her as he pressed against her, and she couldn't stop herself from wiggling her ass against his groin.

Kian growled and dropped his hands to her hips, locking her in place. "Supposed to save that for the dance floor, my wicked mortal."

She settled a hand over one of his and looked up at him. "It was just too hard to resist."

"For you, it's always hard. But you must behave."

"An incubus telling *me* to behave?"

He leaned over her shoulder, brushing his lips over her ear. "Or don't. The night will end with me inside you either way."

Heat pooled between her thighs. It didn't matter how many times they'd had sex, Willow craved more of him. She longed to have his hands on her skin, to taste him on her lips, to feel his cock thrusting inside her, to hear his primal growls and groans and lose herself in the savagery of his release.

And then do it again and again and again.

Yep. I'm definitely a sex fiend.

Grinning, Willow folded her arms over the edge of the bar.

Kian raised a hand, catching the attention of one of the bartenders.

The bartender's features brightened with interest as he walked over to them, but he didn't so much as glance at Willow. His eyes were focused solely on Kian. He leaned an elbow on the counter. "Well, hello."

Kian handed the man a twenty. "Get her whatever she wants."

"Oh." The man blinked, and his smile faltered as his gaze dropped to Willow. "What can I get for you?"

His behavior wasn't anything new for her. Sometimes, it felt impossible to get bartenders' attention in places like this, especially when surrounded by bodies that were more in line with beauty standards.

But she couldn't blame the man for staring at Kian. She certainly stared at every opportunity.

"Can I get a daiquiri, please?" Willow asked.

"Sure thing." The bartender straightened and set about making her drink. His bare arms flexed as he poured ingredients and shook the cocktail in a metal shaker. Once he'd finished mixing, he poured the drink into a hurricane glass, topped it off with a slice of lime on the rim, and slid it toward her.

"Thank you." Willow smiled and picked up the glass, taking a sip. The citrusy lime mixed with sugar and rum was sweet, tart, and delicious.

The bartender looked at Kian and grinned. "How about you? Anything...special?"

"No," Kian replied.

The man's eyebrows fell as he glanced between Kian and Willow. "All right. Well, if you need anything else, just let me know."

Willow watched the bartender move on to the next patron before she turned toward Kian. "You're not going to have anything?"

Kian grinned and stroked a hand up her arm. "I've been drinking the whole time, Willow."

"Can you actually get drunk?"

"Not from anything humans make."

"So you have your own fairy drinks?" She took another sip of her daiquiri.

He twirled a lock of her hair around his finger. "We do. Fae wines are finer, sweeter, more complex, and more nuanced than anything mortals can dream."

"Can humans drink it?"

"It's not a question of can, Violet, but should. And I wouldn't advise it. They can be...unpredictable."

"How so?"

"They might intoxicate you. They might also drive you mad with desire, or lull you into a years-long sleep. They might compel you to share your darkest secrets or obey every command you are given. They might make you forget...everything."

Willow's eyes rounded. "Wow. Okay. Don't drink alcohol in fairy land. Got it."

Kian chuckled. "I think it's best you never find yourself in fairy land to begin with. You can only trust the drinks as much as you can trust the fae offering them—which is not at all."

She leaned closer to him, tipping her head back. "Can I trust you, Kian?"

His gaze softened, and the corners of his mouth rose in a subtle, tender smile. He cupped her jaw and gently stroked her cheek with his thumb. "Yes."

Willow's heart flipped, and she turned her face to kiss the pad of his thumb. She lifted her glass to his lips. "Here. Try it. It won't steal your soul."

He halted the glass by curling his hand around hers. "It couldn't possibly. That's already yours."

She didn't resist when he guided the daiquiri to her mouth, making her drink. As soon as the glass was lowered, Kian dipped his face, pressing his lips to hers. His tongue trailed across the seam of her mouth before he sucked on her lower lip. The drink was all the sweeter this way.

His chest rumbled with an appreciative growl. "Maybe it won't steal my soul, but I am feeling another effect." He released her hand, dropping it to her ass, and tugged her firmly against him.

Willow gasped, feeling the hard evidence of his arousal through her dress.

Kian skimmed his lips along her jaw and brushed them over her neck, just beneath her ear. "Shall we dance, little mortal?"

His breath was warm on her skin, which tingled everywhere he touched. Her nipples tightened, and that heat in her core intensified. She knew he felt her desire. She knew he understood it was just for him.

Pulling back, she downed the rest of her daiquiri in one big gulp and set the glass atop the bar a little harder than she'd intended. That didn't stop her from grabbing the front of Kian's vest and dragging him toward the dance floor.

He stumbled behind her and let out a deep, devilish laugh. "I'll take that as a yes."

Twenty-Seven

The dance floor was chaotic and hazy, dominated by gyrating bodies and blurred faces. Flashing overhead lights cast neon glows on the dancers and created deep shadows between them. Everything was perpetually moving, perpetually changing, but there was one constant—Kian. He was there the whole time, always with Willow, always touching her. And he was all she focused on. However big the crowd around them, she only really saw him.

The music had long ago become something she felt more than heard. It pulsed over her skin, through her veins, in her bones, in her soul. She moved to it without inhibition, knowing that Kian was moving with her. Knowing they were in sync.

Their bodies fit together, flowed together, every sensual motion answered by another. It was a perfect balance—an intimate push and pull that felt tantalizingly close to sex.

Kian grasped her hips and tugged her ass against him, banding an arm around her middle to keep her in place as their hips swayed to the beat. He brought his other hand up to her throat, tipping her head back against his chest and forcing her eyes to meet his.

In that moment, there was only Willow and Kian. Everything else, the whole world, faded away. It was just the two of them, their bodies, their passion. The fires blazing in his eyes mirrored those at her core. But there was so much more than hunger in his gaze, so much more than the lust consuming them both.

He looked at her like she was the only star in the sky on the darkest of nights.

Like she was all that existed in his universe.

The intensity of it stole her breath. A surge of overwhelming emotion flooded her, constricting her chest and making her heart stutter. It was too much. It was frightening.

It was...love.

Willow turned and slipped out of his arms, pressing a palm to her chest. Her heart wouldn't stop pounding.

"Willow?" His voice sounded far away, muffled, barely audible over the music. "What's wrong?"

Running a hand through her hair to sweep it back, she looked up at Kian and offered a timid smile. "I think I just need some water."

Kian grasped her shoulders and frowned down at her. The concern in his eyes only intensified the feeling in her chest. "Come. We'll find you a place to sit, and I'll fetch some water."

Her legs moved automatically as he guided her off the crowded dance floor. Many of the dancers seemed lost in the rhythm, blissfully unaware of their surroundings, and Kian used his body to shield her from their abandon.

All she could do was try to breathe.

He can feel my emotions.

Oh, God, what is he feeling from me now?

Does he know?

Impossibly, her heart quickened, and her breaths came short and shallow.

Please, please don't have a panic attack.

"Easy, Violet." Kian's grip on her shoulders tightened slightly. "I have you. You're all right."

The rest of Reverb was almost as crowded as the dance floor. Kian paused, sweeping his gaze across the nightclub. He growled. "Every fucking table taken?"

"I'm okay," Willow said, but her voice was so thin that even she couldn't hear it.

"Excuse me," Kian said, touching the arm of a passing waitress.

She shied away from his touch, lip curling in disgust, until she turned her head to look at him. Willow had never seen anyone's demeanor thaw so fast.

"Hey," the woman said, pressing her lips together as she looked Kian up and down. "What can I do for—"

"We need a pitcher of water."

There was something in his voice, something subtle but powerful. It was like another layer beneath his words, and it made them carry farther than they should have, considering the easy tone with which he'd spoken.

The waitress's expression again changed, the lust and interest that had brightened it fading. Her eyes would've been almost vacant were it not for the hint of confusion in them. "Sure. I'll be right back."

She turned and walked away.

Kian led Willow to a nearby table, where a couple sat across from each other with several empty glasses and open beer bottles standing between them. Both the man and the woman were staring down at their phones, him with his elbows on the table, her turned on her chair so her shoulder was toward him.

"Move," Kian said. Again, there was that ripple of power in his voice.

The couple sat up straighter, their expressions going blank as they looked up at him.

A low growl rumbled in Kian's chest. "Leave. Now."

Without a word, the couple put their phones away, stood up, and walked toward the exit.

Kian guided Willow to a now vacant chair. As she sat, her gaze lingered on the departing couple.

Taking her face between his palms, Kian forced her to look at him. "Are you all right?"

Her brow creased. "Did...did you compel them?"

His jaw muscles ticked. "It doesn't matter. You need to tell me what's wrong, Willow."

"It does matter, Kian. It isn't right."

He dropped onto a knee, bringing his eye level closer to hers. "They'll be fine. Confused but fine. My only concern is for you right now. There's...so much. I can't make any of it out, Willow. What's happened?"

Willow swallowed thickly as she searched his eyes—his deceptively human eyes. She wanted him to drop the glamour. She wanted to see the real him, not the false face he presented to the world. But she knew that wasn't possible. Not here.

She drew in a deep breath and released it, willing her heart to slow. "I'm...I'm okay. I think I just got overheated, and it made me feel a little dizzy."

And I had a bit of a panic attack because I'm in love with you.

Shakily, she reached up and clasped his wrist. "But please, don't do that again. I've felt that helplessness, Kian. Even if it's only a minor thing, it's not right to take away their choice."

"Gods, Willow," he rasped, shaking his head. His thumbs caressed her cheeks. "Even now, so much compassion. I will try. For you, I will try. But I cannot promise more than that." Kian's expression hardened around the fire in his gaze. "Because if I had to choose between you and anyone else, the world could fucking burn for all I care."

There were so many emotions swirling within her—panic,

fear, elation—but the most prominent of all was love. Her heart sang with delight. Yet that other part of her, the one that had been hurt so many times, warned that this was all too good to be true, that it was happening too fast. That...that this was her mistaking lust for love.

But if it was just lust, why would she be feeling so much, so deeply? Why would the thought of losing him be making her chest tight, why would it suffocate her?

"Here you go." The waitress placed two empty glasses on the table and filled them with water from a plastic pitcher, which she set on the table before leaving.

Kian lowered his hands from Willow and plucked the closest glass off the table. He held it up to her. "Drink."

"Thank you." Taking the glass, she drank swiftly and deeply, glancing at Kian over the rim. She didn't stop until she'd swallowed every drop. She drew in a shaky breath and wiped her upper lip with the back of her hand.

"Now"—Kian took the glass from her and returned it to the table—"tell me what is bothering you, Willow."

"I need to use the restroom."

His eyebrows fell. "I can't help but feel like you're trying to avoid me."

Willow winced and scrunched her skirt in her hands. Somehow, she managed to give him a small smile. "I know. I...think I am. And I'm sorry. I just need a moment to myself, away from the noise and heat."

Away from you.

She might not have said the words, but the hurt that flashed in Kian's eyes suggested he'd heard them all the same. And that made her feel ten times shittier.

He let out a long, heavy breath. "If that's what you need. I will escort you."

Willow shook her head. "No. Please, just stay here and wait

for me. I'll be fine. Tonight has been fun, it really, really has been, but... I promise we'll talk about it soon, okay? I just need a moment."

Staring at her silently, he searched her eyes, his own filled with uncertainty. Finally, he lifted a hand and brushed his thumb across her bottom lip. "All right." He rose and sat in the other chair, not taking his gaze off her for an instant. "Hurry back to me, Violet."

Willow stood and hesitated, wanting to reach for him, to touch him. Instead, she kept her arms at her sides and walked away, weaving through the crowd to get to the restrooms.

Thankfully, there wasn't a line. She entered an empty stall and used the toilet, taking that time to simply breathe, to gather herself. The music was muted, blaring briefly every time the restroom door opened. Multiple people came and went, their voices echoing off the room's tiles as they spoke near the sinks, and toilets flushed as loud as jet engines.

What was she doing?

I'm hiding in the freaking restroom.

Willow groaned, propped her elbows on her legs, and buried her face in her hands.

She'd never thought it was possible to fall in love with someone so hard, so fast. Love at first sight was a fantasy, something that only happened in books and movies, in fairy tales. It just...it didn't happen in real life. It couldn't. Lust at first sight, though? That happened all the time. And that was what she and Kian shared. It was about companionship, fun, sex.

Really, really good sex.

You know that's not all it is, Willow. Stop lying to yourself.

She *was* lying to herself. She was running from her feelings, because everything she felt for Kian was just so immense. So...right.

What did the length of time they'd known each other matter?

She'd been with Eli for three years, and it hadn't resulted in love, faithfulness, or respect. What Willow had come to feel for Kian in the short time they'd known each other, what she'd felt from him, was so much more genuine and meaningful than anything she could've found with Eli or anyone else in a lifetime.

The Fates have marked you as mine.

Maybe it had just been a matter of time, of overcoming trials, before Willow and Kian could meet that day. Maybe soulmates were real...and Kian was hers.

I love Kian.

Her earlier panic didn't return.

Willow lowered her hands. "I love Kian."

"You go girl!" some said in a slurred voice from the stall beside Willow's.

Willow's cheeks warmed, but she laughed.

She cleaned herself, pulled her underwear back up, and smoothed her dress. After flushing the toilet, she stepped out of the stall to wash her hands. When she looked up at herself in the mirror, she was smiling.

I love Kian.

And maybe...maybe he loves me too.

He was also out there, waiting for her. Worried for her.

No more hiding. No more running.

Anxious to get back to Kian, Willow dried her hands and hurried out of the restroom, plunging back into the dark nightclub with its flashing lights and thumping music. Turning her body, she slipped between a couple large groups that stood about conversing and drinking and looked up toward the table where Kian was sitting.

She froze.

There were three women gathered around Kian. One was sitting atop the table, skirt drawn up high and legs crossed, enticingly running her fingers up and down her bare thighs. Another was seated in the chair Willow had vacated. The last stood behind Kian with her hands braced on the back of his chair as she leaned over him, speaking with her mouth near his ear. Her long, blonde hair fell over his shoulder.

Kian's lips moved. Willow couldn't make out anything he said, but that didn't matter, because the woman grinned, cupped his face, turned it toward her, and pressed her mouth to his.

Everything inside Willow turned cold, so cold that it was difficult to draw a breath. All the hurt and betrayal she'd felt from Eli and the others before him roared to the surface, and all of it combined still couldn't compare to the pain she felt in that moment.

No. No, please, no.

Tears blurred her eyes.

Not him. Not Kian.

But what Willow was seeing didn't disappear. Kian was still there, and so was that woman kissing him.

And Willow couldn't stay there and watch. She turned and fled, pushing through the crowd, her vision obscured by tears that would not stop falling. A sob caught in her throat, and she clamped her lips together to hold it in as best she could.

Finally, she reached the exit and burst out into the cool night air. She sucked in one breath after another, clutching her hand to her chest as though it could hold together the pieces of her breaking heart.

She should have known. Should have known that what she had with Kian wasn't real. But she'd convinced herself, had let herself hope, had believed she—

No. She did love him. Because if she didn't, why would it hurt this badly?

Was she truly that unlovable? Was it really so easy for people to use her and cast her aside? And Kian...

If she wasn't even good enough for the humans she'd dated,

how could she ever have been good enough for an incubus? It had only been a matter of time before Kian grew bored and moved on.

A new anguish seared her heart as a worse thought flitted through her mind.

What if it had all been a ruse because Willow was the only one Kian could feed from? What if all the sweet, passionate words he'd spoken had stemmed from his survival instinct and not anything he truly felt for her? What if everything they'd shared had been built on lies and deception?

You can only trust the drinks as much as you can trust the fae offering them—which is not at all.

A soft whine rose from her chest, and this time, she couldn't stop a cry from escaping. Tears streamed down her cheeks. She hugged herself and strode away from the nightclub, ignoring the stares from bystanders, ignoring their pitying looks. She didn't care where she was going, so long as it was away.

Twenty-Eight

Kian's soul cried out in a banshee's wail of pain, disgust, and betrayal that was amplified from somewhere outside of himself. His stomach cramped and sank, and fiery, crushing pressure seized his chest. It was so overwhelming that it prevented him from moving, from thinking. He was frozen, paralyzed by shock.

Wrong. This was horribly, sickeningly wrong.

The woman leaned her weight into the kiss, pressing her body against his as she slipped her tongue into his mouth. She tasted of overly sweet cherry lip gloss and sour alcohol.

No.

Kian slammed a hand on the table, rattling the glasses and bottles atop it. The music raced, its frantic beat a mockery of his pounding heart. He shoved himself up from the chair, tearing his head out of the woman's hold and severing the unwanted contact between them.

She gasped and stumbled backward, bumping into the neighboring table.

Kian barely heard the ensuing commotion. As the people at

the other table voiced their surprise and irritation, Kian dragged his forearm across his mouth, desperate to erase the woman's taste, to end the heated sting pulsing across his lips. His skin itched, and he fought back a wild urge to tear at it with his claws.

"What the hell?" demanded the woman who'd taken Willow's seat as she rose.

Gods, he could still taste that fucking kiss.

He spat on the floor, making the woman who'd kissed him cry out and pull her foot away. But spitting made no difference. Spinning toward the table, he grabbed the pitcher and raised it, pouring water into his mouth.

Freezing water and chunks of ice ran down his cheeks, chin, and throat, barely assuaging the lingering discomfort. He rinsed out his mouth and spat into an empty glass, immediately repeating the process.

Though the taste faded, that sense of wrongness remained unwavering.

"What is wrong with you?" the woman who'd kissed him asked with a huff.

"Fuck off," he growled.

"You weren't like this last time."

Only then did he look at her. Blonde hair, hazel eyes, a slight tan. Her lips were tinted pink, and gold eyeshadow adorned her eyelids. Anger and hurt warred on her face. He tried to recall a time, a place, but nothing came to him.

"Don't fucking touch me again," he said.

"What the fuck? You didn't have a problem with it when we hooked up before!"

He wanted to deny her insinuation, wanted to charm her to get her to shut up and get the fuck away from him, but he couldn't bring himself to do so. Her face was one of thousands. After a while, they'd all looked the same, male or female. Whether he'd fed from her a month ago or years ago, he didn't recall this woman.

Recent experiences had taught him to sympathize with the mortals he'd used, and perhaps, at another time, he might have been gentler. But all he could think about was his mate. All he could consider was the distress she'd clearly been in, and this...this betrayal.

Because it didn't matter that he hadn't initiated the kiss, didn't matter that he hadn't wanted it. In his distraction, he'd failed to sense the signs that were always there. He'd failed to anticipate what had happened so often in the past.

He was an incubus. People were naturally drawn to him, and they tended to throw themselves at him, seeking the pleasure he could provide. This woman and her companions had made no effort to hide their desire as they'd approached Kian's table, especially once they'd started talking to him.

His disinterested responses hadn't been firm enough. Yes, his thoughts had been consumed by Willow, but that was no excuse. He should've done more.

Kian spoke through gritted teeth. "Fuck. Off."

"You're a fucking asshole." The woman tugged the strap of her purse higher on her shoulder.

"Yeah, I hope your dick rots off," one of her friends added.

They had caused this trouble for him. He wasn't the villain here.

But if they wanted to treat him like one...

All the power he'd built lately—all the power Willow had fed him—roiled within Kian, just as volatile as his emotions. He knew in that moment that his magic had the strength to bend these mortals completely to his will. To break them. They wouldn't have been able to resist *any* command he gave them, no matter their desires.

A ragged breath escaped his lungs as he forced his magic

down. If he used it like that now, if he resorted to employing his charm in anger, for revenge...

He knew exactly what he'd become. *Who* he'd become.

And he'd just told Willow he'd try not to use his magic on other humans.

The woman and her friends stormed off, leaving only the people at the next table, who glared at Kian until he met their gazes. They all swiftly turned away from him after looking into his eyes.

"That's right, it *is* none of your fucking business," he muttered. Plucking a napkin from the holder on the table, he wiped off his face, pressing hard enough to make the paper tear.

It was time to go. His tolerance for this place had evaporated. Without Willow, he couldn't stand being here, and her enjoyment of the club had already ceased. The thought of staying here much longer only made his nausea resurge.

Need to tell her about this.

He tossed the wet, wadded napkin onto the table and scanned the club. The colorful flashing lights and dense crowd made it difficult for even his keen fae eyes to identify any individual human, but he knew Willow instinctively. He would've spotted her if she were out there.

Kian tugged his phone out of his pocket as he strode to the edge of the dance floor. He sent a text message to Willow.

Ready to get out of this place? We can drive the backroads, roll down the windows. Better air than you'll find in the restroom.

He pressed send and returned his attention to his surroundings. He hadn't wanted to let her out of his sight to begin with, not when her emotions had been so tangled and intense that even she seemed unsure of what they were. All the same, he didn't want to dismiss her wishes.

She'd said she needed some time, and he would give it to her. But his heart quickened with each passing second, and that uncomfortable itch under his skin only worsened. The knots in his gut pulled tighter every time he checked his phone to see if she'd replied to his message.

She hadn't.

Kian and Willow had been so passionate while they'd been dancing, so in tune with one another. He'd felt her excitement, had felt her joy. What the fuck had happened? What could've so suddenly and thoroughly altered the course their night had been taking?

"Fuck." He stalked forward, cutting directly across the dance floor on his way to the restrooms.

Two minutes wasn't a long time to wait for a response, but all things considered…

A small line had formed outside the women's restroom when he arrived. Perhaps that was all—she'd had to wait, and had only just made it in. He wanted to believe that, but he couldn't shake his worry. Couldn't shake what he'd felt upon realizing that woman was kissing him.

Anguish. Betrayal. A cry from the depths of his heart…

And from the depths of another heart?

Shaking his head, he paced along the hallway. The women waiting to get into the restroom stared at him. A few whispered to each other, one bit her lip as her gaze roamed over him, and another called out to him suggestively.

Kian didn't acknowledge them, and he didn't slow. He checked his phone again, and again, and again. His message remained unread, unanswered.

Something was wrong. Something more serious than she'd let on, more serious than he'd guessed. And the instincts she'd awoken in Kian drove him to find her because he needed to know she was okay. He needed to see her, feel her, hold her.

Fuck this.

He strode to the door of the women's restroom, threw it open, and stormed across the threshold. "Willow?"

The two women at the sinks stared at him wide-eyed through the mirror. One of them said, "I don't think you're supposed to be in here."

The other woman nudged her companion with an elbow. "Who cares?" She turned toward Kian. "Hi."

Kian continued past the women, moving to the stalls. "Willow, are you in here?"

"That was kind of rude," the first woman muttered.

"Kind of hot, too," the second replied.

He knocked on one of the closed doors, prompting a startled cry from within. Not Willow. Not his mate. As he moved on to the next stall, ice formed in his veins, spreading a slow, sinister cold through him.

He knew she wasn't in here. She would've said something. She would've emerged to usher him out, cheeks burning red with embarrassment.

"Fuck," he growled.

"Yes, please?" the woman at the mirror said.

"Maybe go get security instead of trying to climb on his dick?" called someone from within a stall.

"You'd be trying to climb on his dick too if you were seeing what I'm seeing."

Kian didn't give any of them a backward glance as he exited the restroom. He unlocked his phone and called Willow, eyes raking across the club as the line rang.

New, terrifying possibilities invaded his mind with each ring. What if she'd had an accident? What if she'd been taken? What if—

Not fucking helping yourself!

After five rings, he heard her voice.

"Hi, you've reached Willow Crowley at With Love Photography. I can't take your call right now, so please leave me a message with your name and number so I can get back to you as soon as possible. Have a wonderful day!"

"Damn it, Willow, where are you?" he demanded before he ended the call.

As he made his way to the front of the club, he found only more faceless mortals, whose existence he was aware of only because of the emotions they pumped into the air. He shoved past them, neither hearing their protests nor seeing the looks they cast at him.

The front door slammed against the wall when he pulled it open. He strode out onto the sidewalk, turning his head from side to side to look along Central Boulevard. Even when the door swung closed, the music continued pulsing around him, a reminder that escaping into the cool night air had not resolved his situation. His glamour threatened to drop, and his wings itched to be free, to give him flight, to hasten his search.

Kian looked at the bouncer working the door. "The woman I came with—purple hair, purple and black dress. Did you see her leave?"

The bouncer lifted a hand to halt the line of people waiting to enter before turning his head toward Kian. "Yeah." He jabbed a thumb to the left. "She went that way."

"Was she alone?"

The man nodded.

Kian didn't waste another breath. He ran in the direction the bouncer had indicated, weaving around and between the groups of mortals strolling along the sidewalk.

She'd walked out of the club alone. Not a word to him. She hadn't answered his text, hadn't answered his call, she'd just...left.

It felt like a blade had been plunged into his chest. He could barely breathe, could barely think, and now his worry was battling new emotions—anger and hurt. Willow had just walked away. She'd done that to him once before, on the night they'd met.

Kian wouldn't let her do it again.

He passed at least a dozen shops and restaurants, only looking through their windows to check for a glimpse of purple hair. Finally, he spotted her up ahead, walking alone.

Jaw clenched, he closed the distance between them rapidly, reached out, and grasped her elbow, bringing her to a halt and spinning her to face him. "Willow, why the fu—"

His heart stopped, and the words died in his throat. Her eyes were red and shimmered with tears, making their green irises brighter in contrast, and there were faint black smudges beneath them from her makeup. More tears streaked down her cheeks.

The pain in her gaze, the pain radiating from her, grasped that blade in his chest and twisted it.

She furrowed her brow and yanked her arm free. "Leave me alone, Kian."

Everything within him set back into motion all at once. That hurt remained, as did his concern, but his anger had been replaced by confusion. And that confusion was likely the only reason her words didn't shatter him.

"What's wrong, Willow? What happened?"

"What happened?" she asked, almost incredulously. "What *happened*? You..." Anger flared from her, striking him hard. She wiped her cheeks and shook her head as a humorless laugh escaped her. "I can't believe this."

"Can't believe what?" He reached for her, meaning to cup her face between his hands, but she recoiled from him. Curling his fingers, he let his arms drop. "I can feel your emotions, but I can't read your mind. You haven't told me a fucking thing."

"Who is she?"

He understood then. Not what she'd been feeling before she left for the restroom, but what she felt now. She'd seen. A single fucking moment of Kian's guard being down, a single case of him reacting too slowly, and she'd seen it.

"She's no one, Willow."

"Sure as hell didn't look like no one to me. She looked awfully familiar with you."

Kian ground his teeth together. He could almost feel the other woman's lips against his, could almost taste the alcohol and lip gloss, and it made his stomach churn anew. "I fed from her in the past. She seems to have mistaken that for an open invitation."

Someone walked by, giving Kian a look.

"The fuck you looking at?" he growled at them.

The person started, eyes rounding, and hurried away. Kian returned his gaze to his mate.

"You fed from her," she said quietly.

"Fucked her. Is that what you'd prefer me to say? Is that what you want to hear?"

She looked away from him, bottom lip quivering as her eyes filled with fresh tears.

Fuck!

"How many other people have you fucked there?" she asked.

"I don't know, Willow. I don't even remember most of them."

"So you brought me to a club where you've probably fucked what, just about half the people inside?"

He let out a slow, strained breath, and battled to stop himself from reaching for her again. "I brought you to a club where you wanted to dance. I didn't think about who else would be there, because none of them matter to me."

"And when will I cease to matter? When I'm no longer useful to you? When you're finally able to feed from someone else?"

Kian couldn't hold himself back any longer. He surged forward and caught her face between his hands, forcing her to look at him, not allowing her to escape, even when she grasped his wrists and tried to pull away.

"Never, Willow," he rasped. "You will never cease to be the most important thing in my universe. Even after the last spark of my soul fizzles out and there's nothing left of me, you will be my everything."

A soft cry spilled past her lips, and her tears trickled onto his hands. "You said I could trust you!"

"And I did not lie. I was watching for you when she kissed me, Willow. I was worried about you. And even though I didn't ask for it, what she did... I feel like I betrayed you. My whole fucking soul is screaming in protest of it." He brushed his thumbs over her wet cheeks. "I can't change what I am, can't change the past. I have fed from countless humans. I cannot feel shame for that. I will not apologize for surviving.

"But I am sorry for the pain my past has caused you tonight. Sorry that my negligence, my failure, put you through this. I should have driven them away sooner. Should have rebuked their advances immediately and harshly, but I was distracted. All I could think of was you."

Her grip on his wrists tightened, but she no longer fought his hold as she searched his eyes. "You didn't kiss her?"

"No." Kian wiped away more of her tears. "Everything I've said to you has been the truth. I've spent four hundred years experiencing everyone else's joy like a...a fucking voyeur. Despite how many people I've been with, I have never once felt like I was part of anything. I've always been on the outside. I've always been...alone.

"But you have awoken something in me, Violet. All the emotions I've felt from humans, all the connections I've seen them make around me, I finally understand. I finally feel it myself. I can finally say these emotions are mine, and they are all because of you."

Willow's features strained, as though she were struggling not to cry again. But now it wasn't sadness or hurt at the forefront of her emotions. It was something warm, something uplifting. "Kian…"

He smiled and lowered his face, brushing his lips over her forehead. "I'd be hollow without you, Willow. Just like I was for all those years before I found you. You gave me what I wanted." Kian drew back and met her eyes once more. "You taught me to love, my little mortal. And I love you."

Willow leapt at Kian and threw her arms around his neck, catching him off-guard. She clung to him tightly, desperately. The soft sounds of her weeping caught the attention of several passersby. Kian wrapped his arms around Willow and held her close, glaring at anyone who dared cast a judgmental glance their way.

He wished he could have spoken those words somewhere private, away from prying eyes. Wished that his confession had been preceded by happiness rather than pain and anxiety. But he would never regret telling her that he loved her.

And now that it was out, he would say it again and again, no matter the time, the place, the audience.

"I'm sorry," she said, voice thick with emotion. "I'm not trying to change you. I don't want to change you."

"Ah, my Violet." Kian smoothed a hand over her hair, holding her a little tighter. "I'll always be an incubus. That will never change. The only difference is that now, I'm *your* incubus. I chose this. I chose you."

She sniffled and gripped fistfuls his shirt. "When I saw you, when I saw her kissing you… All I could think was the worst. That's all it's ever been for me, one hurt after another. I couldn't breathe, Kian. I didn't want it to be you too. But you were there with her and…and… It hurt so much."

Her words wrapped around his heart and squeezed, and Kian felt every bit of her anguish, every bit of her pain. He pressed a kiss to her hair. "I will *never* betray you, Willow."

Willow drew in a shaky breath. "I love you."

Kian forced himself to hold still lest he crush her in his embrace, lest he cast off his glamour right here, in front of all these mortals, and take flight with his mate in his arms, lest he kiss her with passion enough to melt them both where they stood. The sound of those three words from her lips eclipsed all the pleasure he'd experienced throughout his entire life.

"I realized it in the club," she continued, "while we were dancing. And it... God, it scared me, Kian. I fought it all this time, tried to convince myself it wasn't love. I...I didn't want to fall for you because I knew if I ever lost you...it'd shatter me." She shook her head and pulled back to look up at him, her eyes bright. "But it didn't matter how much I fought it, because I knew I was already in love with you long before tonight."

He let her emotion flow into him, let it fill him, and even when it overflowed, he took in more. Nothing had ever felt so good. Good and...familiar. He'd felt it from her before, and though he'd not understood what it was at the time, some part of him had been aware.

Astonishingly, despite the power of her love, despite its fullness, Kian's love for her remained just as strong. His own elation endured, bright as ever. He didn't know how there was room for him to feel so much, but he would not question it. He would cherish it forever.

"Willow..." Kian withdrew his arms from around her and smoothed her hair back, clearing loose strands from her face. His thumbs wiped away the last of her tears. "There's a place I want to bring you. A place I've never brought anyone else."

Twenty-Nine

Though the car ride was quiet, Willow found comfort in it. She welcomed the respite from the noise and crowds of the nightclub and the bustling boulevard. She was tired, both physically and emotionally, and it was nice to be away from all that, to sit and rest while being able to hear her own thoughts.

But it was so much more than that.

The silence between her and Kian as he drove was warm, natural, and anything but empty. All the words they'd spoken, all the emotions they'd shared, echoed in the air without being voiced. For this little while, their language was one of touch and sight—his hand on her thigh, firm and possessive yet gentle; glances as meaningful as they were brief; the slight upturn of lips in easy contentment.

Those small gestures communicated everything she and Kian might've said to each other.

A soft smile settled on her lips. Willow was in love with a man who loved her back with the same depth and intensity, if not more so.

Her eyes wandered as they drove deeper into Memoree's heart, drawn by all the lights and increasingly tall buildings. She didn't come downtown often, especially at night, and couldn't begin to guess where they were going.

Finally, Kian turned into a parking garage at the base of a towering building. He followed the arrows up, level by level, until they reached an area with larger, reserved parking spaces. He pulled into one directly in front of a bank of elevators.

They exited the car, and he wrapped an arm around Willow's shoulder, leading her to the lone elevator at the end of the short hall. It was marked *Private*. He inserted a key beneath the keypad on the wall, turned it, and then punched in a pin. The elevator doors slid open silently, and he and Willow stepped through.

There were only two choices on the interior control panel —*Garage* and *Penthouse*. Kian pressed the latter.

The fluttering in Willow's belly wasn't just because of the elevator's upward motion. Was he...was he taking her to his home? Was this really happening?

Her restless fingers toyed with the fabric of her skirt. She pressed her lips together, barely stopping herself from bouncing on her feet.

Kian chuckled. The rich, sultry sound flowed straight to her center. "Excited?"

She looked up at him. "Nervous."

His expression softened, and the tiniest, most tantalizing frown tugged down his lips. "Why are you nervous?"

"This is your home."

He hummed thoughtfully. "My residence. A place I spend time. But home...that doesn't quite fit."

Willow's brow furrowed. "Why's that?"

"*Home*. Doesn't that word imply more? A sense of comfort, of belonging? Of living?" He scoffed. "I've existed here. But only in the last month have I lived at all."

I've spent four hundred years experiencing everyone else's joy like a...a fucking voyeur. Despite how many people I've been with, I have never once felt like I was part of anything. I've always been on the outside. I've always been...alone.

Her heart constricted for him. To have been alive so long, merely existing?

The elevator announced its halt with a gentle ding. Willow faced forward and drew in a steadying breath.

A penthouse apartment. A freaking penthouse apartment. She had no idea what to expect, especially not from a place owned by a four-hundred-year-old incubus.

The doors glided open.

The space before her was sprawling and open, though the colors made it feel smaller. Tiny, dim lights in the ceiling cast a glow more suited to a show room than a home. The gray wooden floor had slanted slats that formed alternating arrow patterns, and the walls were a combination of modern gray brickwork and black wainscotting with a vaguely Victorian flair.

Kian led her out of the elevator. Ahead were long black couches over a black rug, matching end tables and a coffee table in black, silver, and clear, polished glass, and a long, glass-enclosed fireplace with more of the intricate brickwork at the base. A huge TV was mounted on the wall across from the larger couch. Every pillow looked perfectly arranged, every remote control was exactly in its place. Even the coasters were neatly stacked, as though they'd never been used.

There was a huge black bookshelf against one wall, filled to the brim with books, a black piano in another corner, and a violin propped on a stand beside it.

She understood perfectly what he meant now. While this place was stylishly furnished, it was dark and cold. Unlived in. There were no photos, no knick-knacks, no collectibles, souvenirs, or pieces of art that spoke of Kian, his character, or his experiences.

"One moment." Kian reached aside and touched a control on the wall.

The fireplace blazed to life, immediately adding warmth to the room, and the curtains along two of the walls slid open.

Her breath caught in her throat. Floor-to-ceiling window-panes looked out over the city.

"Welcome to the place I sometimes sleep, Willow."

Willow walked to the windows. A spacious terrace wrapped around the outside of the apartment. Beyond that were the city lights, night sky, and stars. The view from the overlook he'd taken her to had been stunning, but seeing it from right here, in the middle of it all...it was a different sort of magical.

"This is beautiful," she said.

She felt him approach behind her, and his reflection appeared on the glass, his pale face just over her shoulder. His blue eyes gleamed like the most brilliant stars against the backdrop of the night sky. Her gaze ran over his sharpened features, from his chin to his sculpted, pierced lips, up to those dark, expressive eyebrows, and higher still to the tips of his horns.

Really beautiful.

"With you here, it is," he said. "You make it a view worth taking in."

Blushing, Willow turned to face him. "Don't you normally appreciate the view here? Otherwise, why bother having a place like this?"

His smile was uncharacteristically wistful. "Perhaps because I already felt apart, and this place allowed me to also feel...above. From here, I could always look down upon my prey."

She stepped closer to him, reached up, and flattened her palms against his chest.

Kian covered one of her hands with his, hooking a finger from the other beneath her chin to tilt her face up. "Is this sorrow for me, little mortal?"

"I know what it feels like to live in two separate places and feel unwanted in both."

"Ah, Violet," he rasped, releasing her hand to wrap an arm around her.

She smiled, running her palms up to his shoulders and threading the fingers of one hand through his long white hair. "I'll always want you."

He tipped his forehead against hers and closed his eyes. He held her for a time, somehow gentle and possessive at once, before he said in a low voice, "There's something I want to show you."

Opening his eyes, he stepped back and took her hand. Willow followed him across the living room and past the spotless kitchen, where she glimpsed not a single utensil, pot, pan, or appliance apart from the microwave and huge fridge. They continued into a hallway with several closed doors on either side—all, unsurprisingly, black. The dim lights made those doors seem almost imposing, amplifying the mystery of what was behind them.

He stopped at the last door on the right. It looked like all the others, but as he reached for the handle, Willow swore she spied a smudge of purple on the metal fixture.

The door opened into a dark room. The curtains only allowed a bit of light through, turning everything in the room into looming, indistinct shadows. She entered behind Kian. The glow of his eyes fell upon nearby objects, but it wasn't strong enough to reveal what they were. It almost seemed like a room filled with furniture covered by sheets.

Then he switched on the lights. Willow's eyes widened as she looked around the room, stunned.

The rest of his apartment was all blacks and grays, but here, there was color. So much color. Paintings covered nearly every inch of the walls, and easels, some with cloth-shrouded canvases, stood all around the room. The tarp spread across the floor was spattered with paint of every color imaginable, and the big table that held dozens of jars and tubes of paint, paint brushes, and palettes had fared little better.

But as Willow studied the paintings and absorbed what she was seeing, her surprise only deepened.

Many of the works were moody, dark, favoring shades of red, black, and gray whether they were abstract or contained figures. A few were lighter, with greens, blues, and yellows. There were landscapes scattered here and there. The familiar Memoree skyline under a night sky, viewed from the overlook he'd taken her to. A rugged coastline during a storm. A river flowing through a canyon. And several more of places that were too lovely, too alien, to be real. Places with colors too pure, with white trees and flowers unlike anything she'd ever seen, with a sky that seemed to bleed into the crystal-clear surface of the lake beneath it.

Willow lightly traced her fingers over one of those paintings. "Are these...?"

"Memories from beyond the Veil," he replied. "Hollow attempts to recreate the hollow beauty of that realm."

"They're wonderful. Magical."

He laughed gently. "They're also as close as I ever want to get to Tulthiras again."

She looked back at him to find that he'd not moved any farther into the room. "You really never want to go back?"

"I have everything I need right here, Willow." His eyes were fixed on her, leaving no question as to what he meant.

Her heart quickened, and a whisper of pleasure coursed through her. She looked away from the scorching intensity of his gaze, inhaled deeply, and forced her attention back to the artwork. The paintings of the Evergarden were so surreal. Like vivid, impossible dreams.

As she wandered farther into the room, the color purple

became prominent in more and more of the paintings.

She swept her eyes around the walls, following the apparent progression. First, abstract purples with splashes of green. More colors gradually crept in, and a figure began to take form—a figure that was startlingly familiar to her. A woman with lavender hair and green eyes.

Willow's lips parted in wonder.

She saw herself in a variety of poses, under a variety of lighting, against a variety of backdrops. Saw herself captured in breathtaking realism and passionate stylization. But in every painting, she was vibrant, even when there was clearly sadness in her eyes.

Each stroke had been made with such care, with such thoughtfulness. With such purpose. Several of the paintings depicted her in the very dress she wore now. Others showed her in lingerie—some of the same lingerie she'd worn in her boudoir photos years ago—or with cloth tastefully draped over her private parts, while a few more had her erotically baring everything. She recognized moments she'd shared with Kian in some of the paintings, though he wasn't in any of them. Moments when she'd been laughing, smiling, or staring into the distance contemplatively.

In every painting, in every pose, she was...beautiful.

She was seeing herself through Kian's eyes.

Willow stared at the final painting. It was the largest canvas in the room, resting upon an easel next to a glass door that let out onto the terrace. In it, she stood on the bridge near Central Boulevard, the wind tugging at her skirt and hair, all the reflected lights making the dark river below look like a road paved with stars. There was a hint of sorrow and pain in her eyes. And yet, somehow, the image instilled in her a sense of hopefulness. A sense of possibility.

It was like the Willow in the painting could hop onto that starry path and follow it to happiness, to her destiny. To anywhere she wanted to go.

That bridge was where she and Kian had first spoken. It was where she'd made an impulsive decision that wasn't supposed to have meant anything, but which had changed everything. A decision that had brought them to this moment.

"Kian..." She turned toward him. "These are all of me."

He nodded, and finally walked deeper into the room. His gaze settled on the earlier paintings in the sequence, the more abstract ones in shades of purple. "After I first had you, these colors tormented me. I could not put brush to canvas without using them. Violet and emerald..."

Kian stopped in front of a portrait of Willow and lovingly ran his fingertips over the face on the canvas. "Before long, I realized it wasn't the colors at all. It was *you*. You were haunting me. Your voice, your face, your body, your taste, your essence. I prowled the streets, desperate to feed, but not once could I find even a spark that would enable me to take what I needed. Only when I let you dominate my mind again could I feel any arousal, any excitement, anything beyond the bitterness, frustration, and desperation that was swallowing me."

Slowly, he continued forward, shrinking the distance between them. "I didn't understand then. Even when I found you again, even when I realized you were my mate, I didn't truly understand. But I do now. My soul itself yearned for you, Willow, because you were meant to be mine. Because you *are* mine."

Willow remained still, unable to look away from him, hardly able to breathe. She'd known of his need for her. He'd told her that she was his mate. But she'd never realized the gravity of it, not until now, not until his confession. Not until seeing all this.

"You haunted me then, and you haunt me now." Finally, he reached her, and caught her chin with his fingers. "How could I ever do you justice on a canvas? A dozen paintings, a hundred, a thousand... I will never be able to encompass all of who you are.

"I cannot even choose which of your features is my favorite. Is it these eyes, that sparkle when you laugh?" The light of his gaze warmed as he stroked her bottom lip with his thumb. "These soft lips, that can disarm me with a single smile or crush me with the slightest frown? Your hair, as vibrant as your soul, or your hands, so gentle but sure? It is an impossible choice. But if I had to choose, Willow... I would choose your heart. With all its joy, all its compassion, all its love. Your heart, which leads you to put others before yourself. Your mortal heart, which has claimed mine completely."

He slid his hand up along her jaw, guiding his fingers beneath her ear and into her hair as he leaned his face closer to hers. "I have met many beautiful creatures, Willow. But you are the only one I've known who is utterly captivating both inside and out. You shine brighter than all the rest, be they mortal or fae."

Tears stung her eyes. She touched her fingers to his brow, tracing it, before caressing his cheek. "I don't know what to say to all that."

"Say you are mine."

She laughed softly. "That seems so simple compared to what you've confessed. But yes. I'm yours, Kian."

His expression was serious, his gaze so focused, so controlled. "I need you to understand what that means, Willow. If you are mine, if we seal our bond, there is no going back. Our souls will be tied forever, and not in the figurative way in which you mortals always speak."

"It doesn't change my answer, Kian. So long as you are mine, then I am yours."

Kian smiled, wide and brilliant, and his blue eyes sparkled with pure, radiant love.

He wrapped his arms around her and dipped his head, capturing her lips in a hungry kiss that kindled a fire in her core. His hot tongue traced the seam of her mouth, and Willow opened to him. He teased and coaxed, tasted and seduced, and shivers of desire raced through her, stirring that smoldering heat into a blaze.

And she returned the ravishing kiss with equal passion. Slick gathered between her thighs, and her sex pulsed with a heavy ache.

He crushed her against him. Willow felt his want for her through their clothing, felt the hardness that she longed to have inside her.

She dropped her fingers to the buttons of his shirt, eager to rid him of it so she could feel his bare skin under her palms. But the damned buttons wouldn't slip through the holes fast enough.

Kian pulled away with a laugh, leaving her lips tingling with want. She squeezed her thighs together as his hands moved toward those buttons. Willow was desperate to touch him again, to kiss him again, to feel every bit of him.

He didn't waste time. He grasped his shirt and vest in both hands and ripped them open. Several buttons fell onto the tarp underfoot, quickly joined by the torn clothes as he swept them off. Awe briefly overcame her need when his wings materialized behind him, glittering with their own light of. They fanned out.

Instead of returning to her, he stepped to the terrace door and opened it. The breeze swept in, lifting the shimmering white strands of his long hair and making Willow's dress whip around her thighs. A shiver coursed through her.

Kian held his hand to her. "Fly with me, Violet."

Willow's eyes widened as she flicked her gaze past him, to the night sky. "*Fly?*"

"I won't let you fall."

Her heart sped. She wasn't afraid of heights, but she wasn't exactly fond of not having the ground beneath her feet either. Except... Willow trusted Kian. She knew he'd never let anything happen to her. Knew she'd be safe.

She smiled and took his hand.

Thirty

Kian's fingers curled around her hand, and he led her through the doorway. As soon as she was outside, he tugged her body against his, guiding her arms up around his neck before locking her in a firm embrace. He bared his fangs in a mischievous grin.

Willow furrowed her brow. "What's that look f—"

He leapt into the air.

Willow's stomach sank. No, sank wasn't the right word—her stomach plummeted right out of her body. She screamed as air rushed by and her hair whipped into her face. Hooking her thighs around his waist, she clung to Kian with every ounce of strength she could summon.

"Not that I mind when you're vocal, Violet, but do you want the whole city to hear you?" Kian asked, that smooth, deep voice rumbling into her.

"Not funny, Kian! Oh, my God... Don't you freaking dare let go!"

His hold on her strengthened. "*Never.*"

And then their ascent gained even more speed. Willow caught his hair in a desperate attempt to find better purchase, scraping his scalp with her nails, before she shut her eyes and pressed her face against his neck. She whimpered, repeatedly said his name, begged him, cursed him, the words and sounds tumbling out unbidden. It was such a strange sensation—she felt weightless and impossibly heavy all at once, like gravity was dragging her down hard but she was still rising higher and higher.

Apart from the wind and the noises she'd made, it was silent. All the city sounds she would've expected were absent. There was just the air, cool against her skin but not cold, and a sense of vastness around her. A sense of the world being so big, so limitless.

"I have you, Willow. You can open your eyes," Kian said.

Taking in a shaky, fortifying breath, Willow opened her eyes and tentatively peeked over Kian's shoulder.

She'd flown in planes before, had once looked down on this very city while it glowed beneath the night sky, but the view from that little window was nothing compared to this. Memoree sprawled out far, far below, all of it made tiny by distance. She could see everything for miles around—the towering downtown buildings, the stadiums and parks, the traffic flowing along the streets, the river winding through it all. She could see where the city eased into the suburbs, and the forested hills beyond the city limits.

Above it all, the sky stretched into infinity. Soft gray clouds drifted amongst the glimmering stars, but nothing was so bright as the full moon, which hung round and huge over the city.

Her gaze shifted to Kian. His wings were shimmering blurs, moving faster than her eyes could perceive, and his skin was pure alabaster under the moonlight. With that silver glow cast upon him, and his silken hair flowing in the wind, he looked more ethereal than ever before.

He looked more beautiful than ever before.

And his eyes were upon her with all his intensity, all his love, as if the marvelous view didn't exist. As if the world didn't exist.

"I never realized it, but I wished for you long, long ago," he said. "When I first crossed into this realm, I felt that hollowness inside myself. Felt that missing piece. I saw mortals living, feeling, loving, and I wished to feel it for myself. To have a mate who could fill that emptiness, who could make me feel all the things I sensed around me every day. I wished for you, hundreds of years before you ever existed. And even if I'd had to wait ten thousand years, it would have been worth it."

Warmth unfurled in her chest and spread through her limbs, chasing away the night chill. She tightened her hold on him. Her eyes burned again, threatening new tears—as if she hadn't shed enough already tonight. "I wished for you too, before I ever knew you were possible. And I'd suffer through all the pain, rejection, and heartache again and again, just to have a single night with you." She brushed her lips across his. "I love you, Kian."

"Arythion." His voice rippled with power, and that word flowed into Willow, warming her further and making her skin tingle.

Willow raised her head. "What?"

"My true name is Arythion Shyrik. I freely offer it to you now, Willow Ava Crowley. Keep it in your heart forever, and let it serve as the thread that binds our souls together as we forge our bond with blood, seed, and lifeforce."

That power increased, thrumming through her. Something compelled her to repeat those words, but it wasn't his magic—it was from within herself. It was that sense of rightness, of...destiny. She'd always been meant to speak those words to him at this moment.

"I, Willow Ava Crowley, give my name to you, Arythion Shyrik, to keep in your heart forever. Let it serve as the thread that binds our souls together as we forge our bond with blood, seed, and lifeforce."

"Ah, Violet." He leaned farther back, allowing more of her weight to settle upon his body. "Give me your hand."

Willow pointedly glanced down. Far, far below, the city streets lazily rolled by as Kian flew backward.

Kian chuckled. "Trust me. I will never let you go."

Pressing her lips together, she slowly withdrew an arm from around his neck. Even when he released his hold with his own arm, she felt solid, secure, safe. He gently grasped her hand, his thumb sweeping across her palm until the tip of his claw touched the pad of her thumb.

He stared into her eyes. "Blood."

She felt his unspoken question—*are you ready?*

Willow nodded.

He flicked his claw across her skin. She started at the flash of pain. Before any blood had flowed from the wound, he partly released her hand to slice his forefinger claw over his own thumb. Crimson welled on their skin, glistening in the moonlight. The sting of Willow's cut flared just before he pressed his thumb over it.

The pain vanished instantly.

Kian smiled. "As for the rest..."

Seed and lifeforce.

Willow's eyes widened even as her sex clenched in response to his tantalizing implication. "Out here?"

"By light of moon and stars, Willow, I will make you mine." Kian drew her thumb to his mouth, slipped it between his lips, and soothed it with his tongue before slowly pulling it out and releasing her hand. He smoothed his palm down her body, stroking every curve, until it reached her thigh. "Now be a good girl and free my cock."

He gathered her skirt in his hand, tugging it up. Those clever fingers hooked her panties and forced them aside, baring her sex, before delving into her slick folds.

Willow's breath hitched, and she clenched his shoulder as sensation rippled through her. This couldn't be real, couldn't be anything but a dream, and she didn't care. If it was a dream, she didn't want to wake up. She never wanted this to end.

Staring into his blazing eyes, she glided her hand down his chest, following the familiar muscles of his abs down to his waistband. Her thighs quivered as his fingers teased her pussy, but she held them tight around his hips as she unfastened his pants. Once the garment was open, she dipped her hand in, grasped his hot, throbbing cock, and pulled it out.

Kian growled, increasing the pressure on her clit. Willow whimpered. Pleasure coiled in her belly, and her core cramped with need.

"Not yet, my love," he rasped, stilling his fingers. "You don't get to cum until I say so. Not until your cunt is filled with my seed."

Her pussy clenched, eager for that promised seed. Eager for him. She looped her arms back around his neck, pressing her breasts to his chest. "Kian, please. I need you."

"My sweet mortal. My mate." He shifted both hands to her ass. Lifting Willow's hips as much as her locked legs allowed, he lined up the tip of his cock to her entrance and slammed her against him. His cock plunged deep inside her.

Willow's lips parted with a silent cry. Pleasure unfolded within her. Her nails bit into his back, and she dug her heels into the backs of his thighs. He was thick and hard, and she could feel his quick, steady pulse, could feel the cool metal of his piercing. But she wanted more. She wanted him deeper.

Kian's hands flexed, and his claws bit into her skin. His features were strained, with brows pinched and fangs bared. "Fuck, you feel like paradise." He pumped his hips, grinding against her clit and pushing deeper, further stretching her around him.

Willow moaned. Her slick dripped down her inner thighs, cold against the wind.

"So fucking hot." He growled, and the sound flowed into her, stimulating her hardened nipples through her dress. "Hold on to me."

His lips collided with hers. Willow's thoughts scattered in the wake of that kiss as her and Kian rolled in the air, and he thrust hard into her again. The universe spun around her, but she felt no fear now. All she could focus on was Kian. Every ascent, every dip, and every fierce snap of his hips drove his cock deeper inside her, assailing Willow with surges of ecstasy.

Kian's mouth ravished hers, bruising and hungry. His lips demanded her submission, his fangs nipped and teased, and his tongue led hers in a dance as passionate as it was punishing.

Everything about this moment was consuming. Everything about it edged her closer and closer to release.

"Kian," she moaned, breaking the kiss. Her breaths came short and fast.

He pressed his forehead to hers and met her gaze. "Do you feel how well we fit together?" He drove into her with a grunt. "Do you feel how perfect this is?"

Willow whimpered, twitching from the drag of his cock along her clit, from the feel of his piercing stroking her inner walls. "Yes."

"Fuck, you're perfect. And all fucking mine."

Kian shifted the angle of her pelvis and quickened his pace. Each stroke sent a burst of euphoria through her, each stroke made his eyes flare brighter, each stroke made the heavens tremble. The boundless sky could not contain the overwhelming pleasure engulfing her.

"Cum for me." Kian flicked his tongue across her lips. "Give me your essence. Open to me. Share with me your lifeforce as I give you mine."

Yes, her soul whispered.

The pressure inside her erupted. Her body tensed, her pussy clenched, and Willow's eyes squeezed shut as she threw her head back and cried out into the starry night.

Kian's glowing blue eyes lingered in her vision, filling the darkness behind her eyelids.

"Willow," he growled. His hold on her strengthened, his claws pricked her flesh, and his shaft swelled an instant before his heat flooded her.

His roar joined her cry, and for an instant, they were no longer flying. Their bodies were suspended in the air, suspended in the universe, truly weightless, truly free.

Then they were falling. The fluttering in Willow's stomach only amplified her pleasure.

Shuddering, Kian banded his arms around her and cupped the back of her head with one hand, locking Willow in place while his seed spilled into her.

A powerful rush swept through her. That thrilling sensation permeated her body right down to the tips of her fingers and toes, infusing her entire being with utter, inescapable bliss. Though her eyelids remained closed, the afterimages of his eyes only intensified, and she felt something indescribable—a powerful force wrapped around her heart, a force both fierce and gentle, soothing and passionate, possessive and protective.

She felt Kian. Not just his seed, not just his body, but all of him. His heartbeat pulsed through her, his pleasure washed over her, his love encompassed her. Her every nerve tingled with awareness of him. Willow was completely, soulfully lost in her mate.

Her awareness of the world crept back, her every sense gradually recovering. She felt the air speeding past them, felt her dress flapping against her skin. She felt his heat, and his pulsing cock, which was still firmly inside her. She heard their breathing despite the roar of wind, and she was keenly aware of every tiny bit of contact between them.

Somehow, Willow convinced her eyes to open.

She looked up...

Or rather, she looked *down*.

Her muscles flexed, and her sex clenched for an entirely different reason.

"Kian," she said, voice high with alarm.

He clutched her tighter and groaned, lips stretching in a dreamy grin.

Still, the ground continued its approach, which was much faster than she cared for.

"Kian!"

"Fuck, I love it when you cry out my name." He gripped her hair, crushed his lips to hers, and swallowed her fear with a kiss. His wings flared, sparkling in the moonlight.

Gravity tore at Willow as his wings caught the air, countering their freefall. Kian twirled her around as he kissed her, until, finally, they were upright and hovering.

When he lifted his head, any words Willow might have said died in her throat.

His half-lidded eyes were fixed on her. Though the passion and hunger they always bore were still present, something different defined their glow now, something that made her almost feel his gaze like a physical caress—reverence.

How was it possible for one look to make her feel so much? For one look to communicate the unfathomable depths of his love for her, to make her feel like the most beautiful, most cherished, most precious thing in all existence?

No words needed to be said.

Willow pressed her lips to his in a tender kiss and nestled her head against his neck. He rested his cheek on her hair, lazily massaging her scalp with his fingers, and held her more firmly. With their bodies and souls connected, they soared beneath a sea of stars.

Thirty-One

Moonlight streamed in through the window and fell across the bed. Though he could see well enough in the dark, Kian appreciated that silvery luminescence. It made Willow's pale skin and purple hair ethereally radiant against the black and crimson of his bedding. And with her features relaxed in the serenity of sleep...

She looked like a moon goddess. His moon goddess.

He smiled. He'd smiled so much tonight that his cheeks hurt, but it was the sweetest discomfort.

Kian sat atop his bed with his back against the headboard and his legs stretched out. Willow lay beside him, her head resting on his abs and her hand on his stomach. She'd curled up against him, one leg bent over both of his, with all but her head and one arm snug under the blanket.

He smoothed a hand over her damp hair, gently catching a strand and winding it around his finger. Her warm breath flowed over his skin, feeding directly into the warmth in his heart.

"My sweet mate," he whispered. "All mine."

His awareness of her had been amplified beyond his imaginings. Her emotions—her contentment and love—flowed into him unimpeded, combining with his to become wider, deeper, and impossibly more potent. He felt the steady beating of her heart as clearly as he felt his own. He and Willow were all but one.

Kian brushed his other hand back and forth along her forearm. She didn't stir. Her sleep was deep, restful, and well deserved. Tonight, she'd gone from carefree joy to heartache, from heartache to the bliss of love and the awe of a completed bond. She'd been exhausted even before he'd carried her into the heavens and sealed his claim.

Barely holding in a chuckle, he swept a loose lock of hair off her cheek, tucking it behind her rounded ear.

When they'd landed on the balcony, Willow had told Kian that while their flight had been the most amazing, memorable, and powerful experience of her life, she was glad to have her feet on solid ground again.

After Kian had let her go, she hadn't managed to walk a single step before her knees buckled, and she would've fallen had he not been there to catch her. Yet Willow had laughed in his arms. She might've been blushing, but her skin had been so delightfully flushed from their lovemaking that he couldn't tell.

She'd joked that her body just needed a minute to readjust to the existence of gravity, but Kian hadn't waited. He didn't need an excuse to gather her in his arms, but he was unwilling to forgo an opportunity. He'd cradled her against his chest and carried her across the threshold.

That first step into his apartment after bonding with her had been profound. The place had suddenly felt more welcoming, less hollow. And the fullness of what they'd shared, of what they'd done, had washed over him.

Their lives would never be the same, and he never wanted to go back.

Willow stirred, hugging him tighter, sliding her leg a little higher, and nuzzling her cheek against him. He curled his fingers around her arm and drew in a deep breath. The feel of her soft, smooth skin against his was a thrill without equal.

Somehow, he'd restrained himself in the shower. She'd needed rest more than anything, so Kian had tenderly washed her delectable body and massaged away the tension and aches from her muscles. He'd dried her with the biggest, fluffiest towel he owned afterward. Her soft, pleased moans throughout certainly hadn't made his resistance easier, but he'd persevered.

Kian was...complete. For the first time in his life, there was no hole to fill, no void to feed. For the first time, he was wholly at peace. The joy he felt, the love, the sense of belonging, it wasn't secondhand. It was his.

It was *theirs*.

He traced the shell of her ear with the back of a claw and caught his lip with a fang. Heat swirled at his core, and he felt its mirror inside his mate. Even in her slumber, her desire for him had not diminished.

And though he was nearly full to bursting, his yearning for her had only grown.

For centuries, he'd experienced the world through the wants of everyone around him. He'd never had the luxury of being able to want—feeding had been a need that could not be ignored. Incubi and succubae were beings of desire and lust, but what had Kian truly understood about either, apart from how to manipulate them, how to take advantage of them?

Despite all the emotions he'd felt from mortals, despite all their desires and dreams pulsing in the air around him every day, he'd never truly understood because he'd never wanted anything himself.

Or at least, he'd never realized what he wanted. He'd buried his true desires deep in his heart when he'd crossed into the mortal world. So deep that he'd all but forgotten them until her.

Never would he have guessed that anyone, especially a mortal, could make him feel so much, so intensely. Never would he have guessed that he could feel so protective and possessive of someone, that he'd be willing to do anything for her.

Before he met his mate, Kian never would've believed he could be so consumed by anyone or anything.

His life had been defined by fleeting encounters, by shallow connections formed and severed with equal swiftness. And he would have laughed at anyone who suggested he would *want* to form any sort of lasting attachment. Why would he want to fall for another person, to lose himself in them? Why would he want to give all of himself to one person when he could sample from anyone, anywhere, as he pleased?

The very notion had been unfathomable. Impossible.

Yet here he sat, happy. Fulfilled. In love. He couldn't imagine things being different, and he didn't even want to try.

He hadn't lied to Willow. Everything he needed was right here.

She stirred again, stretching her arm around him and shifting closer. The hard buds of her nipples brushed his side, and heat radiated from her sex, warming his thigh. When he inhaled, the air was perfumed with her arousal.

A low, strained groan sounded in his throat, and his cock twitched, hardening with each beat of his heart.

My mate needs to sleep.

Though she still did not wake, her leg inched higher, moving closer to his aching cock.

He glanced at the alarm clock on the nightstand. She'd had a few hours of sleep, and there'd be time for her to get a few more in before sunrise. That'd be more than worth it to remind her that she was his...

And that he felt her every desire, whether from her conscious thoughts or her dreams.

Slowly, he slid down, flattening his back on the mattress. Willow whimpered as his movement disturbed her, but her eyes remained closed. Sliding an arm under her head to support it, he scooted lower and turned onto his side, facing her. His eyes cast a soft blue glow on her face.

His hand glided between their bodies, grazing her smooth, warm skin, until he found her cunt. He slipped a finger between her folds and groaned again.

She was already wet.

He stroked her gently, teasing every bit of flesh around her clit with his fingertips, and watched as the tiniest creasing of her brow broke the serenity on her face.

Her fingers curled, raking her nails on his back, as her expression tightened further. Her lips parted. Still he caressed her sensitive flesh, drinking in the growing scent of her essence. Soon, her hips were rolling with his movements.

Her eyelids fluttered open. The light from his eyes only intensified the gleam of lust in hers.

Willow smiled and let out a breathless chuckle that was cut short by a moan. "Mmm. Not a bad way to be woken up."

Grinning, Kian lifted her leg over his hip and pressed the head of his cock to her entrance. He slowly pushed into her. "Ah, my sweet mate, it's about to get much, much better."

Thirty-Two

Willow woke with a sense of heavy contentment, but she didn't open her eyes. Not yet. She wanted to bask in Kian's heat, to relish the feel of his body against hers, the feel of his arm wrapped around her, his palm on her breast, his breath tickling her hair. She wanted to fill her lungs with his alluring scent.

She also wanted to contemplate this feeling in her heart. It was strange, too large for the space it filled, but it was also...comforting. It was right. Gentle and caressing but firm and supportive, solid, dependable. And that feeling assured her that there was someone to catch her if she fell. That there was someone she could turn to when she was afraid or uncertain, someone who would shield her from the darkness and pain.

It was love. A love that had been fully expressed, fully accepted, fully reciprocated.

Willow smiled. Her body was languid and sore, but it was a good kind of soreness. A really good kind of soreness.

I think I've had more sex in the last week than I have in my entire life.

It had also been the best sex she'd ever had in her life. She'd even had sex while flying. Flying!

Never thought I'd join the mile-high club...especially not while I wasn't even on a plane.

Lips stretching into a grin, she opened her eyes. Morning sunlight streamed through the gaps in the curtains, casting bright rays through which sparkling dust motes drifted.

She inhaled deeply, once more taking in Kian's spicy sandalwood and jasmine scent. If only she could spend the whole day with him, just like this. If only it were possible to capture these moments with him forever.

Her stomach grumbled. Willow pursed her lips and scrunched her nose against the involuntary declaration of hunger.

But of course, these moments were always fleeting. Life called —or more accurately, bodily functions called.

She glanced at the clock on the nightstand. It was a quarter to eleven.

Willow stared at the digital numbers as something scratched in the back of her mind. Something was supposed to happen today, she'd had something scheduled...

Her eyes widened. "Oh shit!"

Grabbing the covers, she flung them aside, tore out of Kian's arms, and scrambled off the bed.

Kian awoke with a snarl, whipping the blanket off the bed so hard and fast that it snapped in the air. That sound was immediately followed by that of his feet hitting the floor.

Willow turned toward him and froze in place.

He stood on the opposite side of the bed, reminiscent of a beast facing down a pack of challengers. Kian's wings were fanned out, his hands were raised, brandishing his black claws, and his muscles rippled with tension. His white hair hung wild about his shoulders, which heaved with his ragged breaths. Kian swept his gaze around the room.

"What's wrong?" he growled. "What happened?"

"Oh. Uh..." Her eyes dropped to his cock. It was standing stiffly at attention, the piercing at its tip glinting in the morning light. He was fierce, primal, and her body responded with a flare of heat between her thighs.

His stance deflated, and he tilted his head, looking at her. His eyes blazed, but their ferocity was dulled by confusion.

Willow's skin flushed. "Umm..."

Kian furrowed his brow and dropped his hands. "I..." He let out a huff, shook his head, and smiled. "Can't say I don't appreciate the view, but what's going on?"

It was the fire in his gaze that urged Willow to action. Her eyes rounded, and she hurried toward the bathroom. "I'm late!"

"Late?"

"I have a client I'm supposed to meet for lunch at twelve-thirty." Willow skidded to a halt in the bathroom, snatched up her clothing, which he'd peeled off her before their shower last night, and raced back out, heading straight for the bedroom door. "She's having me do a bridal boudoir shoot, so there's a lot to go over, and—"

Her eyes landed upon Kian, who was leaning against the bedpost with his arms folded across his chest. His expression was a mix of mild confusion and amusement. Based on his posture, he was quite unbothered by his nakedness.

She ran her eyes over him. "You're okay, right?"

He quirked a dark eyebrow. "Me? I thought you were in trouble."

"Nope, just late." Willow grinned, opened the door, and paused to peek back at him. "By the way, that was really, really hot." She took off into the hallway, disentangling her panties from her dress and flicking them out to straighten them.

"What was?"

"The whole ready to kill for me thing you did there," she said over her shoulder as she strode down the hall.

She reached the living room, tucked the dress under her arm, and stumbled into her panties without stopping. Her strapless bra was a little trickier, but she managed to draw it on backwards, clasping it herself before twisting it around and tugging it up over her breasts. She raked her gaze across the room. "Shoes, shoes... Where did I leave my shoes?"

Kian chuckled, drawing her attention to him. He'd moved to the entrance of the living room, where he stood with his hands on his hips, still naked. Still hotter than sin.

"If you give me a moment to get some pants on, Willow, I'll drive you home," he said. "Hell, maybe I'll help you dress first."

Willow snorted. "I can handle getting dressed on my own. But I'll take the ride."

His lower lip stuck out in an exaggerated pout. "Why not both?"

"Because we both know my clothes would end up back on the floor and I'll definitely miss this appointment." She slipped her dress on, wiggling her hips to get it into place.

"That's no fun, Violet."

"Be a good boy, and I'll reward you later."

He grinned and stepped back into the hallway, vanishing from sight. Willow let out a steadying breath and continued her search while reaching back to try to zip her dress the rest of the way.

Where had she put her shoes? She couldn't recall if she'd taken them off in here, or if she'd had them on while Kian had taken her flying.

No, I definitely had them on.

She remembered stumbling in her high heels after Kian had set her down on the terrace last night. So they were either in the bathroom, and she'd simply not noticed them in her rush, or they were somewhere in his bedroom.

Or had she taken them off in the art room?

Willow combed her fingers through her hair, frowning as they caught on a few tangles. She'd have to race home so she could get cleaned up and changed, grab her tablet with her portfolio, and get to the restaurant to meet her client in time. She didn't have time to hunt down her damn shoes!

"Allow me," Kian purred behind her. Willow straightened, gasping at his sudden presence, but he slid up her dress's zipper before she could turn around. She shivered.

God, she wished he were pulling it down instead. Wished she could—

"Here you go, little mortal." His hand appeared over Willow's shoulder, dangling her shoes in front of her.

"Oh. Thank you." She reached for the shoes, but he lifted them away.

"Sit down, Willow."

She looked back at him. He'd put on a pair of jeans and a black t-shirt. His wings were gone, and his features were masked by his glamour.

"I've never seen you dressed so casually before," Willow said.

Mischief danced in his eyes as his free hand crept toward the hem of his shirt. "I could go more casual, if you prefer."

Willow leveled a finger at him. "Clothes on."

Kian chuckled. "For now. Sit down."

"I love it when you're bossy." Willow plopped down on the sofa.

He knelt before her, took hold of one of her ankles, and raised it onto his knee, slipping her shoe onto her foot. Kian hummed. "And I love it when you heed my every command."

Cum for me.

Willow caught her lower lip between her teeth.

Damn it, Willow! You have an appointment. A time sensitive *appointment.*

With dexterous fingers, Kian fastened the strap. Every little touch sent a tingle through her that traveled all the way to her clit. She clutched the edge of the sofa. Since they'd bonded last night, she was far more sensitive to his every touch, which made it all the harder for Willow to keep her ass planted on the cushion while he put her other shoe on.

"Difficult, isn't it?" he asked, looking up at her from beneath those long, dark lashes.

Willow exhaled in a rush. "I want you to fuck me so badly right now."

Kian settled his hands on her knees and smoothed them up her thighs and under her dress as he rose, leaning over her until their lips were a hair's breadth apart. "And I want nothing more than to slide into your dripping cunt and fuck you until the universe collapses."

Willow's pussy clenched. Her eyelids fluttered, and she eased forward, needing his lips on hers.

He pulled away and held out his hand. "Come, my love. Your chariot awaits. I'll even pick up your favorite coffee on the way."

She blinked, then playfully glared at him as she slipped her hand into his. "Oh, you dirty fairy."

He laughed as he drew her against him. Though his eyes appeared human, they blazed down at her with that otherworldly intensity. "We'll play dirty later."

They took the elevator down to the garage, hopped into his car, and drove. Willow's eyes repeatedly flicked to the dashboard clock, which kept ticking away the minutes, but she didn't feel the stress she should've been feeling.

Being with Kian, who kept his hand on her thigh as he drove, and feeling this fullness, this love...it had a way of making her problems seem insignificant. She'd get to the meeting on time. Everything would be okay.

As promised, he stopped at her favorite coffee shop, where he parked and ran inside. She might've asked why he hadn't just gone through the drive-thru, but when he emerged from the shop with a steaming cup in hand before even a single car had made it through the line, she understood.

Lines were optional for Kian.

Willow rolled her eyes and shook her head.

She sipped her coffee as they finished the trip, drinking the last few drops just as he pulled up in front of her house.

"Don't be concerned if your cats look at you differently," Kian said. "They'll get over it."

"What do you mean?"

"Blood, seed, and lifeforce." He pressed a hand over her chest. "You're still human, but you're also more. And, well, you aren't exactly mortal anymore, Willow. My eternal life is yours to share."

Wait, what? Eternal life...

She hadn't thought about that at all when they'd made their bond. Immortality wasn't anything she'd ever wanted, wasn't anything she'd ever thought about. It was just so big. So incomprehensible.

"That's, um..."

"A lot, I know. But you don't have to face any of it alone."

She smiled at him. "Yeah, you're right. We'll figure it out, won't we? Not like we don't have time to."

His fingers flexed over her chest, pressing the tips of his claws to her skin ever so lightly. "We will, Violet. We will. But For now, just understand that the spirit of a fae exists within you, and your cats...they might need a little time to adjust."

Her eyes rounded in horror. "Are they going to hate me now?"

Kian laughed, returning his hand to her thigh and giving it a squeeze. "Hate you? No. Cats think too highly of themselves to bother hating anyone. But they might judge you just a tiny bit."

"But they're my babies!"

"They'll still love you, Willow." His expression sobered as he stared into her eyes. "It's impossible not to."

Her heart thumped. She simply couldn't handle how loved he made her feel.

Removing her seatbelt, she leaned across the center console and pressed a kiss to his mouth, letting it linger. He caught her chin and returned the kiss, his lips caressing hers.

"When will you be done?" Kian asked, voice husky.

"Around three."

"I'll be back at three, then."

She pulled away, and he released his gentle hold. Willow hesitated as she reached for the door handle.

Why was it so hard to go? Why was it so hard to leave him when she knew she'd see him again in a few hours? Everything inside her was screaming for her to stay.

"Willow?"

She turned, took his face between her hands, and kissed him again, pouring every ounce of her love into it. He cradled the back of her head in his big hand, his nails grazing her scalp as he pulled her closer.

When she finally broke the kiss, she stared right into his entrancing eyes, and she saw everything she felt mirrored in them. "I love you."

"I love you too, Violet," he said, stroking her hair.

Willow smiled and pecked another kiss on his lips, causing him to chuckle before she forced herself to exit the car.

"I'll spend our time apart thinking of all the dirty things we're going to do this afternoon."

She cast him another teasing glare. "You're trying to make this difficult."

He grinned. "Just building anticipation. Think of me."

Willow stuck her tongue out at him.

"Oh, you'll be putting that to use later."

341

"Jerk." She shoved the car door closed and turned toward her house.

As she walked toward the front door, she could hear his muffled laughter. With a mischievous smile of her own, Willow reached back, grasped the hem of her skirt, and lifted it, giving him a quick flash of her ass.

The laughter cut out, replaced by a very distinct, very horny, "*Fuck!*"

Thirty-Three

Willow was so happy she was practically floating on air as she drove home. Despite the rush to make the appointment on time, lunch with her client had gone wonderfully. The bride-to-be was excited and couldn't wait for her photoshoot next week. She'd listened to all of Willow's ideas, had offered some great suggestions of her own, and had been overflowing with joy about her coming wedding.

Willow felt that same elation. In a way, she'd just been married herself, and she'd longed to get back to Kian throughout the meeting.

She loved waking up in Kian's arms, loved teasing him, loved being teased by him. She loved the fervent light in his eyes and his wicked yet charming smile. She loved how he made her feel safe, how he made her feel seen.

She simply loved being with him. Loved him.

I'm mated to a fae.

The reality of that was staggering. Part of Willow still couldn't believe it was true. Only a couple months ago, fae had been nothing more than a myth to her—a myth she'd never given much thought to beyond the fae romances she'd read. They appeared in books and movies, but they were never supposed to be real.

And Willow had somehow ended up fated to one of them.

But it's more than that, isn't it? I'm not just fated to Kian...his immortal lifeforce is part of me now.

Willow slowed the car as she neared her house, pulled into the driveway, and cut the engine. She grabbed her purse and checked her phone. Her meeting had ended sooner than she'd expected, so she had some time before Kian would arrive.

She was tempted to text him and tell him to come over now, but she wanted to take a shower first, since she hadn't had time in her hurry to meet her client. And the house needed some tidying, anyway. There were wilting flowers to throw away, and though the clean laundry was all neatly folded, she hadn't quite gotten around to moving it off the dryer and putting it away.

Climbing out of the car, she closed the door and locked it with the key fob. As she walked to the front door, she recalled flashing her ass at Kian when he'd dropped her off earlier, and she could stop herself from grinning. Willow knew she was going to pay for that.

And she certainly anticipated that punishment.

She never would've done something like that with anyone else, especially not Eli, but with Kian... Being with him was freeing. She could be herself, could be quirky, carefree, or inappropriate, could be playful, seductive, sensual. She could explore her desires, her fantasies, and know that he would never judge her. He would never mock her or make her feel inferior.

Willow entered her home, locking the door behind her. Bebe, who was lying on the sofa, lifted her head, while Loki and Remy eased toward Willow cautiously, their noses twitching. Their lingering uncertainty broke her heart a little. They'd kept their distance from Willow when Kian had dropped her off, and she'd taken some time before leaving to give them love and attention. They'd eventually warmed to her after realizing she was still herself, but it was like Kian had said—they just needed time to adjust.

"Hey babies," she said, smiling as she crouched and extended her hand.

Bebe jumped down to join the others. All three cats moved closer, sniffing Willow's hand. Finally, they butted their heads against her palm, eager for pets and scratches.

She obliged, chuckling. "I knew you'd still love me."

After filling their food dishes and giving them some extra treats, she went through the many, many floral arrangements, removing the wilted and dead flowers and filling the vases with fresh water before straightening up the living room and kitchen.

She'd do the laundry later.

Or...maybe tomorrow. She'd definitely get to it tomorrow.

She headed to her bathroom, started the water, and pinned her hair up before stepping into the steaming shower.

Since she had time to kill, she relished the hot water. Her breasts—and certain other parts of her—were extra sensitive, a welcome reminder of what she and Kian had done and what they would do again soon. But as she ran the soapy loofah over her body, she realized that the other reminders he usually left during their passionate lovemaking were gone. There were no bruises on her hips, no scratches, no bite marks.

Brow creasing, she lifted her thumb and examined it. Anytime she'd had a split on one of her fingers, it had hurt for days, and sometimes felt like the most painful thing in the world. Kian had sliced open her skin last night, yet there was no cut, scab, or scar of any kind there now. Only pale, unbroken flesh.

You're still human, but you're also more.

Willow rubbed her finger and thumb together. There was an echo of soreness there, but it was distant and diminished. "Is this what he meant?"

She finished her shower in a daze. Binding with Kian had changed her in some fundamental way, had made her more, but how much so? He said she'd live forever, but what else did it entail?

Turning off the water, she grabbed a towel and dried herself off before wrapping it around her body and exiting the bathroom.

Her cats were immediately underfoot, staring up at her with huge eyes, meowing loudly, and rearing back on their hind legs.

Willow laughed. "I guess you've warmed up to me plenty now?"

She was careful not to trip over them as she made her way to the dresser. Their meowing didn't quiet as she pulled on some underwear, tossed her towel into the hamper, and dressed in a pair of pajama pants and a tank top.

When Willow moved toward the doorway, Loki growled, startling her, while Bebe and Remy darted in front of her. She stopped and looked down at her cats. They were all gathered around her with their backs arched, fur standing on end, and faces turned toward the hall.

"What's going on?" she asked with a frown. She took another cautious step toward the doorway, and they all growled and hissed.

They'd never acted like this before. Was it because of the change she'd undergone? Or perhaps Kian was here, and they were holding some sort of feline grudge against him for bonding with her?

Willow found that thought a little funny.

She chuckled. "You guys are just going to have to get used to him."

A tall figure dressed in dark clothing stepped into the doorway, filling it.

Willow started, heart skipping a beat. "Kian, you sca—"

She gasped, eyes widening and skin crawling in alarm.

Not Kian. Not fucking Kian!

"Don't worry," Lachlan said in a deep, cold voice that slithered up her spine, "they won't have to put up with me for long."

Ice formed in Willow's veins, freezing her in place. Everything she'd felt in that alley, everything he'd done, rushed back to her in that instant. And this time, there was no pretense, no illusion. Lachlan had dismissed his glamour. His eyes were the color of dying embers, matched by hair that was now fiery red, and his skin bore a golden sheen. A single pair of curving horns rose from his temples, as black as his soul. The five o'clock shadow that'd darkened his cheeks and jaw was gone, having given way to sharp, elfin features that only enhanced the cruel glint in his stare.

He was beautiful, but it was a hollow, indifferent, sinister beauty, capable of inspiring nothing but unease.

Loki, Bebe, and Remy spat, hissed, and growled at her feet.

"You, on the other hand..." A malicious smile curled upon Lachlan's lips. "Come here."

Willow felt his power flow over her, felt its arcane fingers prodding, searching for something to latch onto, seeking control, and her stomach sank in revulsion. But her feet didn't move.

The fae's features darkened, eyes flaring crimson. "Now!"

She remained in place.

The cats swiped their claws at him as he entered the bedroom. Willow backed away a step, heart racing despite feeling like it was caught in a vise. Lachlan scattered the felines with a kick and thrust out his hand, catching Willow's wrist in an iron grip.

"No!" Willow pulled and twisted her arm, attempting to dislodge him, despite knowing her strength was nothing compared to his.

He tightened his hold, and she cried out in pain. If he exerted any more pressure, he'd crush her bones. "I command and you obey, mortal!"

Gritting her teeth against the waves of power battering her, Willow glared at him. "Fuck you."

Lachlan yanked her hard. She collided with his body, and it was no different than running into a concrete wall. Willow grunted and reeled from the impact.

His eyes bore down into hers, brightening. "Soon."

He dragged her out of the bedroom before she could regain her senses. The cats charged, yowling, but Lachlan slammed the bedroom door shut. There was a thump as one of the cats struck the door, followed by frenzied scratches and paws sliding underneath, their claws digging into the flooring.

"Fucking beasts nearly gave the game away." Lachlan strode into the kitchen, tugging Willow behind him.

"What do you want?" she asked, heart pounding frantically. Her only consolation in that moment was that he hadn't harmed the cats.

At least not yet.

"What do I want?" Lachlan laughed, drawing her to a halt.

Again, his magic surged. Willow was more aware of it than ever. Its immense force pressed down on her, pressed in around her.

He turned toward her. "It is not about what I want, mortal, but what I am owed. Respect. Reverence. *You*. Kneel."

That last word rippled in her mind, echoing and building upon itself in a twisted, amplified version of what Kian had done in the nightclub. But she'd experienced such magic before that night, hadn't she? When she'd first encountered Lachlan, he'd used his voice in the same way. It had been subtle, seductive, and persuasive. And she'd been unable to resist.

Never again.

Willow held his gaze. "No."

He bared his fangs, and the unnatural pressure in the air around Willow intensified. With a furious snarl, he shoved her onto one of the stools at the island counter. Her back struck the counter's edge. She grunted as she teetered, nearly falling off the stool, but she caught herself by slapping a hand down on the counter, inadvertently sending one of the flower-filled vases crashing to the floor.

Lachlan's merciless fingers clutched her jaw, and he forced her face up toward his as he leaned over her. His claws bit into her cheeks, pricking her flesh. Willow hissed against the pain. She reached up and grasped his arm to pull it away, but it didn't budge.

"I'm not surprised that he didn't mark you. He's never been one to obey, even when his rebelliousness might cost him everything. And he's always been soft. Weak. Too weak to embrace his potential." He strengthened his grip, making her eyes burn with tears. "But *this*..."

He lowered his face, brushing his nose across her cheek as he inhaled, and stopped when his lips were beside her ear. "I smell him on you, mortal, and I sense him *in* you. Not only has he disrespected me, but he's insulted our very species. Instilling his lifeforce in a human...it is an affront to everything our people are."

Lachlan lifted his head and shifted his thumb, dragging his claw along her cheek. Stinging heat trailed in its wake. Willow's breath hitched, and she felt blood trickle from the wound.

"Still"—he retraced the cut with the pad of his thumb, gathering her blood—"you are rather delicious." Lachlan slid his thumb between his lips, sucking the crimson off its tip.

He groaned as he pulled it free. "The taste of your fear is exquisite. I think—"

Lachlan's brows fell, and his eyes narrowed. He turned her head to examine her cheek. At the edge of her vision, she saw the sinister light in his eyes grow, saw his mouth stretch into a wide grin. When he trailed his thumb over the cut again, she felt only a whisper of the sting, the heat, the sensation barely more noticeable than the stickiness of her own blood and the roughness of his skin.

Lachlan hummed with delight that made her stomach churn. "Intriguing. I've never had the opportunity to play with a mortal who healed so quickly. Your kind usually break so easily. Perhaps this will be more entertaining than I'd anticipated... *Kian* will be put in his place, and I'll have a new toy for the foreseeable future.

"I'd planned to add you to my collection regardless, but this" —he dragged his tongue up her cheek, making Willow cringe— "will make you the most unique addition."

Chest heaving, Willow yanked her face away. The movement caused his claws to scratch her, triggering fresh agony, but she barely noticed. She clenched her jaw. Fear thrummed inside her, chilling her bones but making her skin hot. She understood what Lachlan was doing. He was feeding on her fear, on her pain, just like Kian had said.

So she reached inside herself, down past that fear, and latched onto the emotion smoldering at her core—anger. All the anger she'd never let herself embrace while she'd struggled, when she'd been put down and rejected, all the anger she'd bottled up from feeling unwanted and being cast aside, it all rose to the surface. It was bolstered by her anger at Lachlan's assault and his stealing of her choice, at him seeing her as an object to do with as he pleased.

But stronger than all that was her anger at having finally found happiness only for this asshole to barge in and try to take it away.

Lachlan chuckled and stepped away from her, approaching the knife block beside the sink. He drew the largest knife in the set. The sound of metal scraping against wood was thunderous in the otherwise silent room.

"Good, mortal. Hold on to that rage." He turned the knife, and the blade glinted. "That will make it all the more satisfying when I break you."

Oh fuck no.

Willow leapt off the stool, crying out as her bare feet came down on thick shards of glass from the broken vase. She slipped, but somehow remained upright and kept going, pushing through the stabbing pain as she raced for the front door. If she could get outside, into the open... If she could just get away from Lachlan for a little longer, long enough for Kian to get here, then...

Hope swelled in her chest as she thrust out her hand and her fingers closed around the door handle. Her muscles tensed, ready to turn the knob and tug the door open.

Lachlan rammed into her from behind, pinning her against the door. The breath burst from her lungs, and crushing pain flared through her.

Grasping her hair, he yanked her head backward, spun her around to face him, and shoved her against the door. He pressed his body over her. His laughter lashed at her heart, deepening the chill that had gripped her.

"Spirited little creature, aren't you? I'd intended to await our guest of honor, but I simply can't resist." He rubbed his cheek on her hair, drawing in another deep breath.

Willow struggled, bracing her hands against his chest and pushing, turning her head, kneeing and kicking him, but she couldn't overcome him, couldn't fight back.

The tip of the knife touched her belly. Willow froze. Everything was cold now—the rage she'd summoned was gone, swallowed up in the shadow of her terror.

"Your willpower doesn't matter," Lachlan purred. "Your

anger, your *love*. Meaningless. You and I are dancing, and the music isn't going to end for a long, long while."

He pushed, and the steel blade pierced her skin and sank into her body. Stunned, she looked down to see the knife protruding from belly, dark blood slowly running across the metal and soaking into her tank top. Then the hot agony struck her.

Willow screamed.

Thirty-Four

T hough Kian's hand held the brush, he could only watch it move. It was not guided by conscious thought, but by something much deeper, something nestled in his heart. This was inspiration like he'd never experienced. Stroke by stroke, this painting was emerging directly from his soul with frightening speed.

A night sky spattered with stars. A huge full moon. Two figures intertwined before it, suspended in the air, made radiant by the silvery light.

This was unlike anything he'd ever created, and not just because of that startling inspiration, not just because of the clarity and potency of his vision. This was the first time in hundreds of years that he was painting himself. It was also the first time he was painting for someone else.

Though Willow had driven him to reach new pinnacles of form and expression in his art, all his paintings of her over the last few weeks had been for himself. They'd been Kian's means of exploring his complex, evolving feelings for her, his way of satisfying his obsession when he couldn't be near her. Before her, he'd painted to purge the emotions he'd felt from the mortals around him. She'd helped him discover his own emotions to express.

But this painting, this attempt at capturing the moment when their bond had been sealed and their souls had come together fully, was for Willow. An offering. A gift. An expression of everything he felt for her.

He paused and tapped the screen of his phone, which lay on the table beside his easel.

Two-twenty-five. Only three minutes had passed since the last time he'd checked. He faced the longest thirty-five minutes in the history of existence.

How was it possible to be so swept up on a tide of artistic passion that the minutes blazed by while also being hopelessly adrift on a sea of longing that stretched every instant into an eternity? A few hours should've been nothing to him, especially with this project to pass the time, and yet the wait was agonizing.

He needed to be with her. Every part of him yearned for her touch, her warmth, her scent, for the brightness of her smile and the musicality of her voice. Without her...he felt off. It was a strange feeling, one that he couldn't entirely define, but it had settled deep inside him. The universe was just a bit off-kilter while they were apart.

Soon. I'll be back with her soon.

All his instincts had demanded he stay with her earlier. They'd demanded that he chauffeur her to her meeting, sit beside her through it, and bring her home afterward—probably following a bout of lovemaking in the car to take the edge off his appetite. The only thing that had stopped him was Willow.

She hadn't said anything about it, hadn't uttered a word, but he knew her. She loved her work, had dedicated herself to it. She loved helping people feel beautiful. The income was meaningless to her when compared to the sense of fulfillment the work provided her. He would never do anything to threaten that, would never do anything to disrupt her happiness.

So, he'd driven to his apartment, where he'd busied himself by packing a suitcase with clothing and toiletries to bring to her house. Having spare clothes on hand made more sense than having to travel across town every time he popped a button off a shirt or tore a seam—which had become a frequent occurrence while he was with her.

As he'd exited his bedroom, he'd happened to glance into the art room. The open curtains had provided an unhindered view of the terrace and the skyline beyond. The surge of memories that had struck him in that moment, all from the night before, had pushed him straight to a blank canvas.

His mate spent her days taking photos to capture the beauty of other people so they could see it for themselves. Kian wanted to spend his days showing Willow her beauty. He wanted her to know that she outshone the moon and stars—not just last night, but always.

Kian's hand stilled. A heavy lump coalesced in his chest and sank into his gut, leaving an unsettling hollowness in its wake. His skin crawled with a pulse of unease.

"Too long away from her," he muttered. A few hours had felt like too much time apart from Willow even before they'd sealed their bond. Now it was torture.

He checked the time again. Two-twenty-eight.

Kian set the brush back into motion, but the strokes came slower and with less certainty. His instincts had urged him to go to Willow ever since he'd dropped her off earlier, making their demands known in a ceaseless quaking from the depths of his soul, but their voices had changed now. Those instincts had grown into a roar that was clawing up his spine.

If he left now, he'd arrive at Willow's around two-fifty. Ten minutes early was fine, wasn't it? He doubted she'd complain.

Better to be early than to spend these last few minutes in agony, anxious and impatient, fostering a sense of doom that was nothing if not wildly overdramatic.

And if he were to arrive at her home before she returned, perhaps he could surprise her. A nice, hot bath sounded like the perfect thing to help his mate relax and unwind—at least until she realized that he intended to join her.

The size of her tub would necessitate a great deal of close contact between them...

He quickly picked up his phone, slipping it into his back pocket, and gathered his brushes, placing them in a container of water. He was about to bring them to the sink when his phone buzzed.

Willow.

His heart sped, and his hand darted back, snatching his phone free. The split-second glimpse he had of the screen was enough for him to see her name on the caller ID before he hit the accept icon. He brought the phone to his ear.

"I knew you couldn't wait that long to have your next taste of me, Violet," he said, grinning.

The reply came in a masculine voice that pierced Kian's heart like a shard of ice. "I'll have more than a taste this time, Pale One."

All the concern, panic, and terror Kian had felt when Willow had disappeared from the nightclub flared back to life inside him.

Lachlan chuckled. "I can almost taste it from here. Who knew you were capable of such potent emotions? Who knew you were capable of being caught speechless and afraid?"

A new fire arose within Kian to accompany those other emotions—rage, fraught with withering heat.

My mate. Mine. My Willow, my Violet...

"What have you done to her?" Kian demanded, forcing the words out through clenched teeth.

356

"Nothing irreversible. Not yet. We've just been testing the limits of the gift you've given your pet."

"Lachlan, I will—"

"You will listen," Lachlan growled, "because every order you disobey, every ounce of disrespect you show, will bring her more pain, and I will drink it greedily."

Heat roiled beneath Kian's skin, and every shred of his being protested as he tamped down his fury. "Then speak, Hollow Prince."

"That's already one mark against you, Pale One."

There was a pained, terrified whimper in the background.

"Willow!" Kian reached out as though he could grab hold of her, but his hand only closed on empty air.

"Come to me, Kian," Lachlan said. "Come and finally learn your place. Come and bow at my feet, and I may find mercy enough to let you continue your pitiful existence."

Kian's jaw was clenched so tightly that his fangs felt on the verge of breaking. "Where?"

"Your pet's house, Pale One. We'll be waiting."

The call ended, leaving only deafening silence.

Flames roared in Kian's chest, consuming him utterly. He tore off his shirt and threw it aside, summoning his wings as he threw open the terrace door. He leapt into the air, wings pumping in a frenzy to carry him toward Willow's house. The wind threw his hair back, and buildings shot past in a blur, but he only pushed himself faster.

Soon, Willow. Gods, hold on. I'll be with you soon.

357

Thirty-Five

Kian's feet slammed onto the concrete as he landed, sending a jolt through his bones. Leaning into the momentum leant by his flight, he raced across the last couple yards of the walkway and bounded onto the porch, barely slowing as he reached the front door.

Willow echoed through his mind, her name repeating with each thump of his heart, growing louder and louder. He could feel her now. He could feel her ahead, could feel her fear.

The door was unlocked. Kian shoved it open and burst across the threshold.

His mind assessed the scene before him in the space between his rapid heartbeats. A trail of crimson spatters and smeared, bloody footprints led to the kitchen. Glass shards, flowers, and scattered petals lay in a puddle of water on the kitchen floor. And there, upon a stool at the island counter, sat Willow, with Lachlan looming beside her.

Her clothing was torn and stained with blood, more of which stood out starkly against her too-pale skin.

A torrent of emotion crashed over Kian as his gaze met hers.

The fear and anguish radiating from her gleamed in her eyes, but something else briefly broke through—relief.

Kian charged toward her.

"No, no," Lachlan said, curling an arm around Willow to press a kitchen knife to her throat.

Her breath caught.

Kian froze, having only made it a few steps into the house. A sickening combination of fire and ice coursed through him, becoming more pervasive and intense with each moment. He couldn't bring himself to move, not while she was threatened, but everything within him railed against standing still.

"Release her," he growled.

Lachlan smirked beneath his burning red eyes. When he spoke, his words buzzed with charm, thickening the air. "Close the door."

The weight of Lachlan's voice pushed in on Kian from all directions. He felt its insidious tendrils caressing, scratching, and scraping as they sought a way in, but he gritted his teeth and remained in place. "Release her."

Lachlan's smirk faltered for an instant. "She's proven quite resilient thus far, Pale One, thanks to the lifeforce you gifted her. But do you truly wish to find out if she'll heal after I slice open her throat?"

Kian locked his gaze with Willow's again. Her eyes were so big, so full, brimming with so many emotions that he never wanted her to feel. Without looking away, he stepped backward and pushed the door shut.

The sounds of it striking its frame and the latch catching boomed with profound finality.

"So you are capable of obedience," Lachlan said.

Fear and fury continued their tumultuous dance within Kian, building so much pressure inside him that an explosion was inevitable. Every one of his muscles strained against the urge to go to her, and his soul itself clawed at his willpower, fighting to get to his mate.

Clenching his fists, Kian looked Willow over. Despite her fear, the state of her clothing, and all the blood, he didn't see any open wounds. That was miniscule comfort. "Are you all right, Violet?"

Willow pressed her lips together and drew in a breath before forcing them into a small, trembling smile. "Been better."

He'd thought it impossible for the ache in his heart to deepen, but her response proved him wrong.

"My brave, strong mate," he rasped.

Lachlan snarled and grabbed a fistful of Willow's hair, forcing her head back. Her hands rose, grasping his forearm, but she didn't struggle. A drop of blood welled on the edge of the knife at her throat. Tremors rocked Kian's limbs as he fought to remain in place, battling his own powerful drive to protect her, to avenge her pain, to fulfill his promise and keep her from harm.

"How dare you address this lowly beast with more respect than you've shown your better?" Lachlan's magic rippled in his every word, lashing out aimlessly. "You should be calling me your king, should be begging my forgiveness for your transgressions!"

Kian's lips peeled back, baring his fangs. His claws bit into his palms, and warm blood flowed from the wounds, but the pain was nothing compared to that caused by the sight before him. An inferno of rage spiraled through him, flooding his limbs with scorching, impotent strength. His magic, stronger than it had ever been, swirled within that maelstrom, crackling like lightning through the flames.

All that power, and for what? It couldn't help Willow now. It couldn't overcome Lachlan.

He could sense Willow's heartbeat, racing just as fast as his own. He could sense her anger, too, underlying her fear, and he knew that despite everything, she was far from broken.

His eyes lingered on Willow's for another heartbeat. In that moment, he hoped his gaze expressed everything he longed to say. *I love you, Willow. You are my everything. I am sorry for this. For all of this.*

Then he forced his attention to Lachlan. "What would you have of me?"

"Fealty. Loyalty. Submission." Lachlan's brows fell low, and he narrowed his eyes as he raked them over Kian. "You."

The darkness that had always lurked within Kian roared in response, awakening like a dragon crashing out of its den, spewing flame into the sky and spreading its shadowy wings wide.

Freedom was an illusion more dangerous and powerful than any glamour ever cast by a fae. It wasn't real, not in this realm or any other. There was no escape from those who desired power and control, no escape from those who sought to dominate and rule.

Kian's eyes returned to Willow's. He understood suddenly that her fear and concern was not only for herself—it was for him. With a fucking knife to her throat, she was still worried about Kian, about his life, about his safety.

Nostrils flaring, Kian filled his lungs with a burning breath, locked it inside, and forced himself down onto his knees.

Lachlan's eyebrows twitched up, and his expression slackened with surprise before he grinned. Laughter bubbled from him, slow and disbelieving at first but quickly becoming dark and heated, confident, triumphant. And his charm flowed out with that sound, striking Kian like waves battering the shore.

"A mortal..." Shaking his head, Lachlan forced Willow onto her feet. "Obstinate for centuries, and a mortal is what finally brings you to heel. You refuse my every offer, reject me, spurn me, only to bind yourself with *this*?"

Keeping his hold on Willow, Lachlan kicked the stool aside and walked forward. She clutched his arm, stumbling and straining to match his gait while keeping her head back to reduce the pressure on the blade against her skin.

"As I have told you time and again, we are as gods in this realm, Pale One." Lachlan advanced toward Kian, Willow firmly in his hold. "Even the lowliest of us stands as a prince amongst these humans. Together, we can be the masters of all. Imagine the feasts you might have shared in if only you'd taken my hand?"

Kian's wings shuddered as he held himself back from leaping to his feet, as he forced his arms to remain down at his sides, as he swallowed his pain and fury and let it coalesce in his gut. "I cannot say I've mourned the lost opportunity. You feed on obsession. On terror, pain, and sorrow. Is it any wonder that we're looked upon as leeches if you are considered our paragon?"

"Oh, Kian." Lachlan chuckled as he came to a stop before him. Keeping an arm around Willow's neck, he released her hair, lowered his hand, and brushed his fingers down Kian's cheek. "Pleasure is sweet, but I've more refined tastes. It would benefit you to broaden yours. All I've ever wanted is for you to be strong. To be proud. To accept what we are. It's long past time for you to shed these childish rules of yours.

"These mortals are as cattle to us. They are sustenance. What I take from them is no more consequential than what food they stuff into their faces. And they have such a plethora of flavors to offer." Lachlan glanced at Willow, grin widening. "So, so much..."

"You have me now," Kian said through his teeth. "Leave her be."

"Are you mine, Pale One?" Lachlan's features darkened, but his eyes grew brighter. The fullness of his magic bore down on Kian. "If you are mine, give me your name."

That power was so heavy, so thick, strong enough to steal the air from Kian's lungs and crush him...

"Your true name," Lachlan said, his voice hardening as layers of magic wove through it.

Kian clamped his jaw shut. He didn't collapse under that weight, didn't look away from Lachlan. And though he'd doubted his ability to resist Lachlan's magic in the past, he somehow knew he could resist it now. He was no longer afraid of it.

Lachlan scowled and caught Kian's jaw in hand, tipping his head back. "Defiant even now."

"Please, don't hurt him," Willow breathed. She let out a choked sound when Lachlan tightened his arm around her throat and glared at her.

"Without this mortal, I don't have you at all. That's why I'm going to keep her. Though I can't say I'm not excited by the prospect of a beautiful toy that doesn't break quite so easily. And her lust... I saw her appeal even before I knew you had claimed her. Did he give you his true name, mortal?"

Pressing her lips into a tight line, Willow averted her eyes from Lachlan's hungry gaze.

Lachlan bared his fangs. His magic swelled, making the air itself tremble. "Tell me his true name."

Willow's skin paled further, her brow creased with strain, and her nostrils flared with a heavy breath. But she didn't open her mouth, didn't speak a word.

"His name," Lachlan growled into her ear.

She met Lachlan's gaze again. Defiance shone in her emerald eyes, cutting through her fear, her stress, her suffering. "No."

Lachlan chuckled. "You haven't marked her, but you've made her yours all the same, haven't you, Pale One? Somehow your bond has made her resistant to my charm... Just another thing for me to test. I suspect that resistance has its limits. When it comes to mortals, there's always a limit, and it is usually so quickly found."

His red eyes returned to Kian. "But you haven't accepted that truth yet, have you? Not when it comes to her. Is it because you cannot see, or because you refuse to?

"These humans are like leaves. So numerous, so fragile. They sprout and grow in a matter of heartbeats, and they fall just as quickly, swept away on the autumn breeze before they crumble to dust. Granting immortal life to one of them will not change their nature. You should never have given them any more thought than you would to a leaf on the forest floor, Pale One."

Kian shifted his gaze to Willow. Every moment since he'd met her stood out in his memory with startling clarity, so much brighter and fuller than the countless moments that had preceded them. Even now, she was radiant. Lovely. Even now, she was *her*... She was *his*.

"And their brief lives hold more beauty and meaning than you will ever know, Hollow Prince," Kian said. "You are a parasite, stealing emotions from the very creatures you so loathe to fill the void inside yourself, but it will never be filled. It will consume you."

Lachlan's grip strengthened as his eyebrows angled down. His claws bit into Kian's flesh. "You are a pale imitation of me. A mockery, a faded echo. You should look upon me in awe. The blood that flows through my veins is power, it is authority!"

"It is a cruel joke played upon you by the Fates. Had your blood any true meaning, you would be in Tulthiras, sitting upon a throne. But you know they'll kill you if you return, because you are a reminder that they are not perfect. That the control they flaunt is an illusion. That they can't even master their own base urges. You are a reminder that they make mistakes, that their judgment is flawed. That they are not beings to be worshipped."

Willow cried out as Lachlan shifted her to the side and leaned forward, grabbing a fistful of Kian's hair. He stopped his face not an inch away from Kian's. "You should be grateful for the opportunity to call me your master. But you'll learn. Both of you will learn. Learn your place. Learn that you...are mine."

His claws scraped Kian's scalp as he tightened his hold on

Kian's hair. He smiled. "You have no idea how satisfying it is to finally see you on your knees for me, Pale One."

Lachlan slammed his mouth over Kian's, eyes falling shut.

That overwhelming sense of wrongness Kian had felt in the nightclub returned, a thousandfold stronger than before. His soul quaked with revulsion, thrashing as though to detach itself from his body, to escape from this affront to everything Kian held dear —this affront to his love, his fate. He looked past Lachlan, meeting Willow's gaze.

Anger sparked in her eyes. The same anger he'd felt from her before, which had been burning beneath her fear. Anger and...determination.

Something unspoken passed between them. An understanding, a promise made heart-to-heart, soul-to-soul.

Willow's life had been lonely and unhappy. She'd suffered, she'd struggled, she'd felt trapped. But she had chosen to leave that life behind. She'd chosen to claim a new life for herself, to run away from everything she'd ever known and find her happiness. And even when she'd been beaten down by the universe, even when she'd hit low points that might have broken other mortals, she'd held on. She'd kept going.

That look in her eyes told him she wasn't done fighting for her happiness—not remotely.

Kian and Willow would have their lives, their love. They would have each other. And even a fae like Lachlan could not stop them.

Lachlan groaned deep in his throat and leaned deeper into the kiss. His hold on Willow slackened.

She slid her hands to Lachlan's wrist and swiftly angled the knife away from her throat, ducking under his arm. Lachlan's groan turned into a growl, and he broke the kiss, pulling away from Kian, but he wasn't fast enough. Baring her teeth, Willow yanked down on Lachlan's arm and shoved hard. The knife struck him in the ribs, sinking deep. She scrambled away from him as he cried out in pain and startlement.

Kian grabbed the other fae's hair and locked him in place. "I wasn't kneeling for you."

Fear and pain twisted Lachlan's features, making the glow in his eyes waver.

Crimson descended over Kian's vision. The firestorm that was his rage surged and consumed him, and he welcomed it. Kian lunged at Lachlan, opening his mouth wide and yanking the other fae's head back. As Lachlan fell backward, Kian sank his teeth into Lachlan's throat.

Hot blood flowed into Kian's mouth. He slammed Lachlan's head against the floor and whipped his own away, tearing out a chunk of the other fae's throat.

Lachlan's cries became choked, gurgling, desperate, fists and claws striking and raking at Kian. Straddling his opponent to pin him on the floor, Kian hammered his fist into Lachlan's face, forcing the fae's head to the side and pressing it down. His other hand found the handle of the knife jutting from Lachlan's ribs and twisted it.

Lachlan thrashed. His claws shredded the flesh on Kian's arms, chest, and shoulders, and his magic blasted outward, an unrelenting current of power lashing wildly. Even without Lachlan speaking a word, his magic was oppressive and coercive— it demanded Kian cease his assault, demanded he submit, demanded he surrender.

"Have you learned, Hollow Prince?" Kian said. "The love from a single mortal heart has made me stronger than you ever could have become from their fear. You have no power over us."

Distant pain echoed across Kian's skin from the dozens of wounds Lachlan's struggles had opened, and his soul strained against the magical onslaught, but he didn't relent. No one would harm his mate and escape retribution. No one would threaten to seize her freedom, no one would make a claim upon her, without facing Arythion's wrath.

Kian would never stop fighting for her. Whether mortal or fae, lowborn or royalty, he would shy away from no foe. For her, anything. Everything.

"She's my mate," Kian growled, ripping the knife free. "My Willow, mine!"

One of Lachlan's flailing hands clamped over Kian's, squeezing around the knife handle. The potent magic that had been roiling within Kian flared in response. Power rumbled through his blood, his bones, his soul, and Kian didn't try to hold it back now. He let it all out, focusing it into a single command.

"Drive the blade into your throat."

Icy terror seized the light in Lachlan's gaze. His lips moved as though he was trying to speak, and blood bubbled from the gaping wound in his throat, which was already beginning to heal. Arm trembling, he pulled on Kian's hand and the knife grasped within it—pulled it toward himself.

Lachlan watched from the corner of his eye as the blade dipped, drawn lower and lower by his own hand. Desperate, choking breaths burst from his lips, forcing more frothy blood from his ruined throat. Nostrils flaring, his entire body tensed as the tip of the blade reached his neck. He didn't stop when the metal pierced his skin and crimson welled around the new wound. He only pulled harder.

"Now you know how it feels," Kian rasped. "Now you know what it's like to lose all your power, all your control. To be helpless. Now you know fear."

Lachlan's body shuddered as the blade sunk another inch, but the light of life remained in his eyes.

"Never again will anyone suffer the cruelty of your illegitimate reign, Hollow Prince." Kian pressed his other hand over Lachlan's and forced the knife down with all his strength, all his rage and fear, all his protectiveness and possessiveness.

The knife stopped only when its tip struck the floor beneath Lachlan. Kian grasped his foe's hair and tugged up hard, wrenching the knife downward to slice through flesh and bone. A pool of blood gathered beneath Lachlan. The crimson light in the incubus's eyes flashed, fizzled, and died.

Kian growled and dragged the blade across the last shreds of tissue holding Lachlan's neck together. Finally, chest heaving with ragged breaths, he released his hold on both the knife and Lachlan's hair.

The dead fae's head thumped onto the floor, coming to rest in a crimson sea, separated by several inches from the body it belonged to.

"Kian!"

Arms looped around his neck from behind, and a warm body pressed against his back between his wings.

Willow buried her face in his hair as she embraced him. "Is he...dead?"

Kian reached up and clasped her forearm. "He is."

"Like dead-dead? I've seen enough scary movies to know the bad guys always come back."

"Not this one," Kian said, bowing his head and letting his eyes shut as he caught his breath. The pain from his many wounds blended into one ceaseless thrumming. "Decapitation or removing the heart. The only ways to kill one of us."

"Are...you okay?"

"Me? Fuck, Willow!" He shoved himself to his feet and spun toward his mate, catching her in his arms and lifting her off the floor. Her legs immediately went around his hips. He cradled her tightly against him, cupping the back of her head with one hand as he pressed his forehead to hers. "I've never been so terrified in my life. Are *you* all right?"

A sob escaped her as she hugged him. "Being stabbed hurts. I one hundred percent don't recommend it."

Kian laughed, the sound made shaky by the collision of his lingering rage and fear with his love and relief. He held her tighter still and inhaled deeply. Even with the scent of blood filling the air, it was her sweet fragrance that rose above everything else, familiar, comforting, and alluring. "Never again, Willow. No one will ever fucking touch you again."

Epilogue

...ᕯ...

F *our Months Later*

The little speaker on the dresser filled the room with upbeat music. Willow hummed along, resisting the urge to sway her hips to the rhythm. Dancing wasn't really a good idea while she was standing on a ladder with a tray of wet purple paint atop it, paint roller in hand. Especially when she didn't want to drip anything on the dark wood of the wainscotting along the lower half of the wall.

She returned the roller to the tray, steadied herself by bracing a hand on the ladder, and glanced around the room. Her eyes roamed from the antique dresser and armoire she and Kian had refinished to the mirror standing in the corner, then past the door to the bathroom and on to the big four poster bed they'd brought from Kian's old apartment, the canopy of which was now adorned with ivy leaves, and tiny, starlike string lights. Opposite the bed stood the fireplace.

Her gaze settled on the painting above the mantle, and she smiled, thrilling in the heat it sparked in her core. It depicted Willow and Kian flying in front of the full moon, holding each other, loving each other. He'd captured that moment so beautifully, so perfectly, so magically, that her every glance at the painting stirred vivid memories of that night.

That hadn't been the only time he'd made love to her amidst the stars, but it had certainly been the most profound.

Everything had changed for them after they'd bonded.

Kian had moved into her house after the...*incident*. He'd refused to let her out of his sight, and she'd been grateful for it. She'd tried to put on a brave face for him, but Lachlan's attack had badly shaken her. If it hadn't been for Kian, if it hadn't been for the bond between their souls, which they'd only just cemented the night before the attack...

She shook her head and coated the roller in fresh paint, hoping to ward off those thoughts and the feelings they awakened. Lachlan was gone, and he'd never hurt her or Kian again. He'd never hurt anyone again. And the shadow he'd cast over Willow had faded a little more with each passing day, unable to withstand the happiness of the life she was building with her mate.

Touching the roller to the wall, she smiled again. Despite the events of that day, she would always remember her little house fondly. She'd worked hard to buy it, had worked hard to make it her own, and no one could take that sense of accomplishment away from her.

But she couldn't stay there. She couldn't walk through those rooms without being reminded of what had occurred.

Sad as she'd been to leave that house behind, she didn't regret the decision to move. She and Kian had looked at several properties around the city, but nothing had seemed right, nothing had quite met their needs.

Until they'd pulled up in front of this place—an old Victorian-style home, a bit rundown, a bit neglected, yet absolutely beautiful.

Yes, it needed work, and yes, it would've been well outside Willow's price range had she been buying the house by herself, but she and Kian had immediately known it was perfect. As they'd first walked the slightly creaky halls together, they'd seen the possibilities, the potential. The house had character. It had charm.

It had been fate.

And best of all, it was *theirs* now. Not Willow's, not Kian's, but theirs.

Not that she'd tell that to Loki, Bebe, and Remy, who already acted like the lords and lady of the household.

All the house needed was a little tender, loving care. They'd been giving it just that for the past month, working daily to fix everything in need of repair and bring out the personality hidden within these walls. Kian had proven himself quite the handyman, and he unsurprisingly looked sexy as sin with a toolbelt on. More than once, work had been put on hold because Willow simply couldn't keep her hands off him.

He'd taken to calling it *putting out fires*, though the flames never really died out. Not even a little.

Willow grinned. Even with those frequent interruptions, they'd accomplished so much. The major repairs were finished, leaving mostly cosmetic work to be done. She had her studio space downstairs, furnished and waiting for when she was ready to start seeing clients again, and Kian's painting studio was on the second floor, in the turret room overlooking the river.

And as a surprise, he'd set up a whole room just for her to keep books in. Her own private library. Kian had already unpacked her romance books when he'd revealed the room to her, but with every book she owned already upon them—and all the books from his apartment in their own neat section—there was still so much space on those shelves.

It was her goal to fill every inch of those shelves with books.

"I thought I was the painter," Kian said.

Startled from her thoughts, Willow twisted to look back at Kian as he sauntered across the room toward her. He was shirtless and glamourless, wings trailing behind him lazily. He rarely hid his true form while they were here. Willow wouldn't ever complain about that.

She smiled. "Seems I'm the artiste today."

"Hmm." Kian ran his gaze down her body, grin widening.

She knew what he saw—she was wearing old, paint-stained denim overalls and a white tank top, with her hair twisted up into a messy bun and smudges of purple paint on her arms and hands.

"Your work is certainly stirring a reaction in me, Violet," he purred, stopping behind her.

Heat always blazed in her core when he was near, but when he purred in that deep, seductive voice of his? God, there was no resisting him.

As if you'd ever want to, Willow.

Willow gestured to the surrounding room. "What do you think?"

"I think it's perfect."

She tapped her chin. "I don't know... I think I missed a spot."

He turned his head, scanning the walls. A crease appeared between his eyebrows when he looked back up at her. "Where?"

"Right here." Willow touched the roller to the tip of his nose and pulled it away, grinning. "*Now* it's perfect."

Kian pressed his lips together, letting out a heavy sigh. "So that's how you want to play, is it?"

Her heart quickened in anticipation. She nodded.

Grasping her hip, he reached an arm around her and lowered

his hand into the paint tray. "Perhaps you've forgotten, Willow. You're mine." He lifted his paint-coated hand and pressed it over her ass, giving it a firm squeeze. "Let my mark serve as a reminder, mortal."

That inner heat intensified, spreading through Willow. She turned toward him carefully, steadied by his hold. "I'm not sure that's enough. Once I take off these clothes, it'll be gone..."

Kian's glowing blue eyes smoldered. "Then *I'll* have to take your clothes off"—he hooked his arms around Willow's backside and lifted her over his shoulder, hand returning to her ass—"and ensure I leave something a little longer-lasting behind."

Willow shrieked with laughter as he turned and walked forward. She braced a hand on his back to support herself. When he talked like that, he made her melt. She loved it. Her free hand crept to his wings, and she lightly trailed her fingertips upward from the base of one, making him shiver. "You're probably covered in paint now, Kian."

"And?" He squeezed her ass again.

Willow's eyes widened as Kian neared the bed. "I'm covered in paint too."

"I know."

"Kian, the bedding!"

"I'll buy you new bedding, Willow." He tossed her onto the bed.

She bounced, and before she'd even hit the mattress again, Kian's hands had unbuckled the straps of her overalls. He hooked the garment with his fingers, peeled it off, and tossed it aside. Then he was over her, caging her in with his hands to either side of her head. The shadows cast on his features made his eyes even brighter, even hungrier. Her pussy clenched with a needful, deepening ache.

Kian dipped his head, brushing his lips along her cheek, her jaw, her chin and neck, as he wedged his hips between her parted thighs. A growl rumbled from him when he inhaled. "Fuck, you smell good."

He lifted a hand to grasp the collar of her tank top. His claws punctured the fabric, and he tore it down the middle, baring her chest. Her bra suffered the same treatment. "I'll buy you new clothes too."

She laughed.

With his hand still wet with paint, he cupped one of her breasts, leaving a handprint behind when he released the mound. "You look delectable in purple."

Those words had no right being as sexy as they were.

Willow's incubus swallowed whatever response she might have offered with a deep, passionate kiss that obliterated all her thoughts of bedsheets, painting, and renovations. She moaned, clutched his arms, and arched up against him.

A surge of lust swept through her. She wanted him, needed him, craved him. He was a drug she never wanted to give up.

Willow slipped her hands between their bodies to unfasten his pants. She couldn't wait any longer.

Kian's slow, sultry laugh made her nipples thrum. "Oh, my passionate, impatient mate."

"Damn right, I am," she said, opening his pants and grasping his cock. When she squeezed, stroked, and rubbed her thumb around the base of his piercing, he grunted and shuddered.

Rising on his knees, Kian caught her wrists, guided them over her head, and pinned them to the bed with one hand. He growled, "Well, you're going to have to be patient, my love. I plan to take my time enjoying you."

He settled the tip of a claw at the hollow of Willow's throat. She shivered, and her nipples hardened as he grazed her skin, trailing that claw down between her breasts and over her belly until it finally reached her underwear. His fingers brushed her inner thigh as they dipped between her legs.

"So wet for me." Kian grinned and hooked a finger under her panties, drawing the damp fabric away from her sex. A flick of his claw shredded the cloth.

Locking eyes with Willow, he angled his hips forward. She felt the cool metal of his piercing against her sex first, followed by the hot, broad head of his cock as he pushed inside her.

Her pelvis rose instinctually, reacting to her need for more of him.

Kian let out a low, ravenous hum and moved his hand to her belly, flattening his palm atop it and pressing down firmly, making her whimper. "Patience."

He pumped his hips shallowly, working himself a little deeper with each movement. "Ah, Willow. You feel so fucking good."

Willow's brow creased, and she moaned. The slow back and forth drag of his shaft sparked an electric current inside her that made her breath short, her skin tingle, and her toes curl. "Kian..."

His eyes, glittering with opalescent blues, held her prisoner, and she didn't want to escape. When he drew his hips back, nearly pulling out of her, Willow cried out and arched her back, desperate to chase him.

Kian snapped his hips forward, burying himself as deep as he could inside her. Willow gasped. Her lashes fluttered at the exquisite feel of him, but she refused to close her eyes, refused to look away. Her heart constricted at the love that shone within the depths of his gaze.

And this glorious fae was hers.

He released her wrists and lay over her, his hair falling to one side, lips parted and eyes half-lidded. A shudder coursed through him, and his cock throbbed inside her.

Willow wrapped her arms around him. "I love you."

"My sweet, beautiful Willow," he rumbled, caressing her cheek with his thumb. "Eternity is not nearly long enough a time to love you, but I will savor every fucking moment of it."

Author's Note

We hope you enjoyed Yearning For Her!

We had a lot of fun writing this book, especially Kian and Willow's interactions. Scenes like those allow Rob and I to really interact and make each other laugh. They let us reexperience the fun we had when we used to roleplay back and forth with one another.

Now I know many of you thought this: Is the heroine a self-insert of Tiffany?

The answer: Yes and no. While she does have purple hair, green eyes, and a few likes and interests that are similar to mine, she is Willow.

I just really, really had to write a purple-haired, plus size heroine who embraced and loved her body because it's what I wish I could do. I've fought with my self-image for so many years (and still do). It's a tough journey to learn to love yourself and the body you're in despite all its flaws. We know many people struggle with this, that many of you, our beloved readers, struggle with it. Know that we see you, and you are beautiful.

Which brings me to why Willow was a boudoir photographer. After the birth of our third child, I suffered through undiagnosed post-partum depression. I had lost so much weight before the pregnancy, but afterward, I just couldn't lose it again. I struggled. My sister and I saw an ad from a photographer who was doing boudoir sessions, and like I'm prone to do, I made an impulsive decision and jumped on the chance to do this new, exciting thing. Of course I was nervous and thought about backing out several times. Because...exposing my body on camera? My thick body with all its stretchmarks and imperfections? Why did I decide to do this?

But my sister and I went together (the photographer did back-to-back sessions for us) with our new lingerie that we purchased. The photographer had someone on site to do our make up and hair, and everyone was so friendly. When it finally came down to getting my pictures taken, the photographer was wonderful and made me feel so comfortable and sexy, and the environment felt so safe. She had me doing poses I never would have imagined myself doing—some with just my underwear and a strand of pearls!

When we were done, and she showed me the photos she'd taken...I bawled. It was me in those pictures. I couldn't believe it, but it was me. I was this sexy, confident woman. I was this seductress. And I knew for damn sure these pictures were going to blow Rob's mind. Haha! (Spoiler: He freaking loved them!)

Those pictures showed me that I was beautiful. That I am beautiful. Society's standards—and people in general—can be cruel and judgmental, but we don't have to define ourselves based on what others think. That is what I wanted to show with Willow. When she had her pictures taken, that was the moment she realized just how beautiful she was despite everyone else trying to put her down and tell her she wasn't good enough. She's not without the occasional doubts (who really is?), but she owns her body, and anyone who doesn't like that isn't worth her time.

Of course, Kian embraced and loved every delectable part of her.

So if you've ever thought about doing a boudoir session, I want to encourage you to do it. Please. Don't put it off because you want to lose weight first, don't dismiss the idea because you feel like you're too old. Just do it. Because you are beautiful right now, and you always will be. And you deserve to feel it. It was such an amazing experience, and I hope some of you can share in that.

As always, thank you for reading, and thank you for your support. It means the world to us.

Also by Tiffany Roberts

THE INFINITE CITY

Entwined Fates

Silent Lucidity

Shielded Heart

Vengeful Heart

Untamed Hunger

Savage Desire

Tethered Souls

THE KRAKEN

Treasure of the Abyss

Jewel of the Sea

Hunter of the Tide

Heart of the Deep

Rising from the Depths

Fallen from the Stars

Lover from the Waves

THE SPIDER'S MATE TRILOGY

Ensnared

Enthralled

Bound

THE VRIX

The Weaver

The Delver

The Hunter

ALIENS AMONG US

Taken by the Alien Next Door

Stalked by the Alien Assassin

Claimed by the Alien Bodyguard

STANDALONE TITLES

Claimed by an Alien Warrior

Dustwalker

Escaping Wonderland

His Darkest Craving

Yearning For Her

The Warlock's Kiss

Ice Bound: Short Story

ISLE OF THE FORGOTTEN

Make Me Burn

Make Me Hunger

Make Me Whole

Make Me Yours

VALOS OF SONHADRA COLLABORATION

Tiffany Roberts - Undying

Tiffany Roberts - Unleashed

VENYS NEEDS MEN COLLABORATION

Tiffany Roberts - To Tame a Dragon

Tiffany Roberts – To Love a Dragon

About the Author

Tiffany Roberts is the pseudonym for Tiffany and Robert Freund, a husband and wife writing duo. Tiffany was born and bred in Idaho, and Robert was a native of New York City before moving across the country to be with her. The two have always shared a passion for reading and writing, and it was their dream to combine their mighty powers to create the sorts of books they want to read. They write character driven sci-fi and fantasy romance, creating happily-ever-afters for the alien and unknown.

Sign up for our Newsletter!
Check out our social media sites and more!